Praise for the novels of

Laura Caldwell

Red, White & Dead

"A fresh, intelligent and emotional thriller. Laura Caldwell writes with an assured ease, showing a true sense of style and story, delivering a brilliant and complicated heroine."

—*New York Times* bestselling author Steve Berry

Red Blooded Murder

"Aims for the sweet spot between tough and tender, between thrills and thought—and hits the bull's-eye.... A terrific novel."

—#1 *New York Times* bestselling author Lee Child

"Take Izzy McNeil to bed tonight. You won't get much sleep, but you'll spend tomorrow smiling. *Red Blooded Murder* is smoking hot and impossible to put down."

—Marcus Saker [illegible] thor of *Good People* and *The Blade It* [illegible]

Red Hot Lies

"A legal lion [illegible] ping edge-of-the- [illegible] oint."

—*New York Ti* [illegible] Martini

The Good Liar

"A massive achievement, in one novel, launching a woman right up there with the top thriller writers around."

—International bestselling author Ken Bruen

The Rome Affair
"A fabulous, hypnotic psychological thriller. Laura Caldwell is a force we can't ignore."
—*New York Times* bestselling author Stella Cameron

Look Closely
"A haunting story of suspense and family secrets... you won't want to put it down."
—*New York Times* bestselling author Mary Jane Clark

The Night I Got Lucky
"Caldwell is one of the most talented and inventive...writers around."
—*Booklist*

The Year of Living Famously
"Snazzy, gripping...an exciting taste of life in the fast lane."
—*Booklist*

A Clean Slate
"A page-turner about a woman with a chance to reinvent herself."
—*Chicago Tribune*

Burning the Map
"A touching story of a young woman at a crossroads in her life."
—*Barnes & Noble.com* on *Burning the Map,* selected as one of "The Best of 2002"

RED, WHITE & DEAD

LAURA CALDWELL

ISBN-13: 978-0-7783-2666-3

Recycling programs
for this product may
not exist in your area.

RED, WHITE & DEAD

www.MIRABooks.com

Printed in U.S.A.

Also by Laura Caldwell

RED BLOODED MURDER
RED HOT LIES
THE GOOD LIAR
THE ROME AFFAIR
LOOK CLOSELY
THE NIGHT I GOT LUCKY
THE YEAR OF LIVING FAMOUSLY
A CLEAN SLATE
BURNING THE MAP

Dear Reader,

The Izzy McNeil series is fiction. But it's personal, too. Much of Izzy's world is my world. She's proud to be a lawyer (although she can't always find her exact footing in the legal world), and she's even more proud to be a Chicagoan. The Windy City has never been more alive for me than it was during the writing of these books—*Red Hot Lies, Red Blooded Murder* and *Red, White & Dead.* Nearly all the places I've written about are as true-blue-Chicago as Lake Michigan on a crisp October day. Occasionally I've taken license with a few locales, but I hope you'll enjoy visiting them. If you're not a Chicagoan, I hope you'll visit the city, too, particularly if you haven't recently. Chicago is humming right now—it's a city whose surging vibrancy is at once surprising and yet, to those of us who've lived here a while, inevitable.

The Izzy McNeil books can be read in any order, although Izzy does age throughout, just like the rest of us. Please e-mail me at info@lauracaldwell.com to let me know what you think about the books, especially what you think Izzy and her crew should be doing next. And thank you, *thank you,* for reading.

Laura Caldwell

ACKNOWLEDGMENTS

Thank you so very much to Margaret O'Neill Marbury, Amy Moore-Benson and Maureen Walters. Thanks also to everyone at MIRA Books, including Valerie Gray, Donna Hayes, Dianne Moggy, Loriana Sacilotto, Craig Swinwood, Pete McMahon, Stacy Widdrington, Andrew Wright, Pamela Laycock, Katherine Orr, Marleah Stout, Alex Osuszek, Erin Craig, Margie Miller, Adam Wilson, Don Lucey, Gordy Goihl, Dave Carley, Ken Foy, Erica Mohr, Darren Lizotte, Andi Richman, Reka Rubin, Margie Mullin, Sam Smith, Kathy Lodge, Carolyn Flear, Maureen Stead, Emily Ohanjanians, Michelle Renaud, Linda McFall, Stephen Miles, Jennifer Watters, Amy Jones, Malle Vallik, Tracey Langmuir, Anne Fontanesi, Scott Ingram, Deborah Brody, Marianna Ricciuto, Jim Robinson, John Jordan and Brent Lewis.

Grazie mille to Andrea Rossi in Rome for answering my many questions about the Camorra and the anti-mafia efforts in Italy, and *grazie* to Francesco Marinuzzi and Laura Roberts for their assistance with all things *Italia*.

Much gratitude to my experts—Chicago Police Officer Jeremy Schultz; criminal defense lawyers Catharine O'Daniel and Sarah Toney; pilot Jonathan Sandrolini, private investigator Paul Ciolino; journalist Maurice Possley and physicians Dr. Richard Feely and Dr. Roman Voytsekhovskiy.

Thanks also to everyone who read the book or offered advice or suggestions, especially Dustin O'Regan, Jason Billups, Liza Jaine, Rob Kovell, Katie Caldwell Kuhn, Margaret Caldwell, Christi Smith, William Caldwell, Matthew Caldwell, Meredith Caldwell, Liz Flock, Kris Verdeck and Les Klinger.

PART I

1

When it happened, it happened at night, the way bizarre things often do.

For a Sunday, and nearly midnight, the restaurant was buzzing. That's the way Sundays work in Chicago. Often the city is quiet—most people tucked under sheets by 10 p.m., newspapers sprawled on the floor below them. Other times, on a Sunday in June like that night, when the weather plays nice—the occasional puffed cloud skimming across a crystallized blue sky, a sky that gently settles into a soft black without losing the day's warmth—things can get a little raucous. And I'm the kind of girl who likes a raucous Sunday now and again.

So even though Rush Street wasn't my usual hangout, if I'd been surrounded by friends at that corner table at Gibsons Bar, the one by the windows that looked onto the street where people still strolled and lights still burned, I would have been very happy. But I wasn't with friends.

Dez Romano threw his arm over the back of my stool. Dez, short for Desmond, had dark black hair, even though he was surely a few years past forty, and it curled in pleasing twists, like ribbons of ink around his face. The somewhat thick bridge of his nose was the only coarse thing on Dez Romano's face, and he managed to make that look spectacularly handsome. He was so confident, so lit up with energy that you began to think every man should have such a face.

The story I'd been told by John Mayburn, the private investigator I moonlighted for, was that Dez had been named by his mother after a Catholic cardinal whom she admired. The religious connotation hadn't helped. Dez was now the head of his family business, as in *the* family business. Dez was, as Mayburn had said, "the new face of Chicago's organized crime."

Dez smiled at me now. I thought a smile by such a man would be flashy, a surface grin that easily revealed danger underneath. But it was genuine. Or at least it appeared so. I'd been told that, in some ways, Dez was the new kind of Mafia—the kind who had friends from all walks of life around the city, who opted, when possible, for courting rather than strong-arming, who made large donations to charities, not because he or his family business wanted something from them, but simply because every respectable business did so.

I returned Dez's smile, thinking that the problem with Dez wasn't his looks and it wasn't that he lacked generosity, whether toward a woman like me, whom he'd met at the bar, a woman supposedly stood up by a flaky friend or toward his associates. The problem was, at least according to the suspicions of the federal government, Dez ran an intricate business, an arm of the Italian Camorra, believed to be more ambitious and more ruthless than the *Cosa Nostra* faction made famous by *The Godfather* movies. In other words, Dez was also the old kind of Mafia. He wasn't afraid of strong-arming or something much more violent. No, not at all.

"So, Suzanne," Dez said, using the alias I'd given him, "where to from here?"

I laughed, looked at my watch. "It's almost midnight. I'd say home is where I'm going from here."

"And where is home?"

"Old Town," I answered vaguely.

I really did live in Old Town. When Mayburn first taught me to assume a cover name in order to conduct surveillance, he told me to always blend in some reality—some truth that couldn't be easily tied to your real life—or otherwise you'd forget or confuse yourself, and you could land in some very real trouble.

The blending of such truths hadn't exactly helped. My occasional moonlighting gig for Mayburn had gotten me into more than a little trouble, but I hadn't been able to turn him down this time.

I need a favor, Izzy, he'd said, earlier that night. *I want you to hang out at Gibsons. Act like you're meeting a friend at the bar, act like the friend canceled on you. Dez Romano is always there on Sunday. Throw that red hair over your shoulder and give him the famous Izzy McNeil smile. Talk to him. See if he says anything about Michael DeSanto.*

I didn't say that there was no "famous Izzy McNeil smile" that I knew of. I didn't point out all the things that could go wrong with this little "favor." Instead, I agreed rather quickly. Not because I needed the money, which I did, but because Mayburn was in love, the first time I'd witnessed such a thing. And yet it appeared he was about to lose his beloved to Michael DeSanto, a banker we'd helped put in jail for laundering money for the Mob. Correction: laundering money for Dez Romano.

"My car is outside," Dez said. "Let me give you a lift."

"That's all right. I'm a taxi kind of girl." I pointed out the window, where a few Yellow Cabs and Checkers floated by. "I won't have a problem. But thank you for dinner." I waved at the table toward the bottles of wine and grappa and the desserts in which we'd barely made a dent.

Dez answered that it had been wonderful, that he'd like to see me again. "I guess I should have asked before," he said, with a shy shrug that surprised me. "You're single, right?"

I answered honestly— "I am."

A few short months before, I'd juggled three men, and then suddenly there were none. Today, one was staging a comeback, and I wasn't sure what to do about that. In the meantime, although I was occasionally tortured about those who had left my life, I was free to date whomever I wanted. Even a ranking member of the Mafia, if only as a part-time job.

If I hadn't known who he was and what he did for a living, I wouldn't have blinked before agreeing to go out with Dez. I was about to turn thirty, and with my birthday fast approaching, it seemed the dating gods had flipped a switch in my head. I had never dated anyone much older than me, never really been interested, but now Dez's forty-some years compared to my twenty-nine seemed just fine.

Dez leaned his elbows on the green-and-white tablecloth and shot me a sexy kind of smile. "Would you go out with me sometime? Officially?"

Officially, I was about to say, *Sure,* This was what Mayburn had hoped would happen. I would listen for anything having to do with Michael DeSanto, and if nothing came up, I'd establish a contact with Dez so I could see him again, so I might learn something about Michael in the future.

I looked out the window once more, thought about how to phrase my answer. And then I saw him.

He was standing across the street at a stop sign, wearing a blue blazer and a scowl. He glanced at his watch, then up again, and as the cars slowed, he began to cross the street, right toward us.

I opened my mouth. I must have looked shocked because Dez followed my gaze.

"Hey, it's DeSanto," he said fondly. He looked back at me.

I clamped my mouth shut and met his eyes, trying to cover my panic with a bland expression.

His eyes narrowed. "You know DeSanto?"

"Um…" What to say here? *Actually, we met when I was pretending to be friends with his wife, Lucy, in order to sneak into his office and download files to incriminate him. Isn't that ironic?*

Mayburn and I had decided that if I was successful tonight and got to Dez Romano, and if I could somehow steer the conversation toward Michael DeSanto's name, I would ask about Michael, maybe volunteer that I'd once met Lucy—the woman Mayburn was now in love with—at my gym, or someplace similarly benign. But that plan had assumed I wouldn't actually *see* Michael; it assumed that Michael wouldn't pull open the door to Gibsons, and walk right in, and find me with his buddy, Dez.

I stood up. I leaned forward, hoping to distract Dez with a little cleavage. It worked. His narrowed stare relaxed. He glanced up at me and, to his credit, then kept his eyes there.

Meanwhile, my eyes shot toward the door. And there was Michael DeSanto, stopping to say hello to the maître d'.

Frig, I thought, attempting to stick with my stop-swearing campaign despite the circumstances. But I gave up quickly. *Fuck,* I thought. *What is he doing here?*

According to Lucy, her wayward husband was out of jail on bond, and although he was friendly with his compatriots of old, like Dez (all of whom had managed to avoid prosecution through one loophole or another), he wasn't doing business with them anymore. Rarely saw them much at all. As such, Lucy had felt it her duty, especially for her kids, to break up with Mayburn and give it a go with Michael, the father of her children, the man she was, or at least had been, in love with. And so their Lincoln Park home once again blazed bright, as did the lights on the security gates surrounding it. The whole thing had rendered John Mayburn bordering on positively vacant, which spooked me. Which was why I'd found myself agreeing to try and infiltrate the world of organized crime.

Yet now Michael was *here,* just out of jail, clearly stopping in to see Dez Romano. And about to come face-to-face with the person who was instrumental in putting him in jail. Me.

I took a step away from Dez, muttering, "Be right back."

I moved in the direction of the bathrooms, but when I realized it would put me in a collision course with DeSanto, I shifted, started to go the other way. I froze when I realized the exit and the bathrooms were both just beyond where Michael was standing.

He stopped then, completely still, looking at me with his eerily light brown eyes. He froze in exactly the same way an animal does when assessing a dire situation—with the knowledge that this might be the end, this might be the time to meet the maker, but with a sure clarity that there was going to be a fight before the end came.

I froze, too. I wished at that moment that I was better at this stuff, but no matter how much I'd learned from Mayburn, the whole undercover thing was simply not in my blood.

And so, lacking anything better to do, I gave Michael DeSanto the same smile I gave lawyers at Chicago Bar

Association events when I didn't recognize them—a sort of *Hi, how are you? Good to see you* kind of smile.

Physically, DeSanto looked a little like Dez Romano, but he wasn't even glancing at his friend right now. His intent stare stayed focused exactly on me. He cocked his head ever so slightly. His face jutted forward then, as if he were straining to understand. And I knew in that moment that it was one of those situations—he'd recognized me, sort of, but he couldn't place me. Yet. I was sure he'd figure it out any second.

I didn't wait for the wheels to start clicking in his mind. Instead, I averted my gaze and hightailed it to the right, then veered back behind him. I glanced across the room at the front door. It was clogged with a huge group of people saying goodbyes, giving each other boozy pats on the back. I could sense Michael turning around to stare at me, so I darted up the staircase and bolted for the bathroom.

I panted inside the stall, trying to work out what to do. *Should I somehow try to say goodbye to Dez? Should I give up on the infiltration job and just take off for the calm confines of my condo?*

It wasn't much of an infiltration job anyway, just a job that required chatting up someone at a bar, a task I used to be rather good at, if I say so myself. However, that skill had gone rusty over the last few years. Who could blame me after my series of, shall we say, unfortunate circumstances. Two friends killed and a disappearing/reappearing fiancé, who was now officially off the map, had caused me to spend a lot of time in my condo, licking my wounds.

Eight months ago, I'd been on top of the world—the highest paid associate at a big, glitzy law firm, en route to partnership not only with the firm but with my fiancé. And then *poof,* all gone, rendering me tired and stunned and jobless. What I'd been doing for the last few months consisted of nothing more than feeling guilty about doing nothing.

Shortly, my funds would literally drop to zero, causing my fears about being forced to sell my Old Town home to become a reality.

And so this request from Mayburn, who believed Michael DeSanto wasn't as squeaky clean as he was telling his wife, led me to Dez Romano. But enough was enough. Heartbroken or not, Mayburn would understand that I *had* to get out of there.

I left the bathroom, went down the first flight of stairs, peeked down the rest of the way, my hands on the silver banister. I saw no one. The large group appeared to have left. I trotted down as fast as my high heels would allow, past the signed photos that plastered the walls—everyone from local judges to international celebrities seemed to have autographed a glossy for Gibsons.

My breath was managing only shallow forays into my lungs, so I stopped once to suck in air. A few more steps and I was at the bottom, the front door only a few feet away.

The maître d' gave me a bored nod as if to say goodnight. But then he glanced to the right, and a questioning expression overtook his face. I peeked to see what he was looking at. Michael. Across the room, Michael was talking to Dez, his arms waving, gesturing.

Right then, Dez looked over Michael's shoulder and saw me. "Hey!" he said, his eyes narrowed in anger.

There were only a handful of diners in the restaurant, but Dez's voice was loud enough to get everyone's attention. They looked at Dez, then at me. Suddenly, Dez and Michael were on their feet and coming toward me, the furious expressions on their faces enough to catapult me into action.

I reached down, pulled off my high heels and dashed out the door onto Rush Street.

"Cab!" I yelled, waving at one. But the taxi's light was off, and it blew by. Same with the next one and the next.

I took off running toward Oak Street, hoping desperately for the shimmering vision of a cab with its light on.

I heard someone shout. Glancing back, I saw Michael and Dez sprinting after me. Behind them was another man, also running, his head down, face obscured by a baseball cap. Was he security for Dez?

I tucked my shoes under my arm and ran faster. When I reached a tiny alleyway, I dodged down it, running until I came to a parking garage.

"Ticket?" a sleepy valet said.

I heard footsteps pounding behind me in the narrow alley. Frantically, I looked around. The garage's entrance was on State Street. I could leave that way, but if I did, surely Dez and Michael and their muscle would see me and keep up the chase. To the left, though, was a steep ramp that quickly curved up and out of sight. If I could get up the ramp before they reached the garage, I could hide and call Mayburn for help. I could call the police if I had to.

I started in that direction.

"Miss!" the valet yelled. "Your ticket?"

"My car is up here," I said as I kept moving.

"No, miss! Only valet here. You have a ticket?"

I hesitated for a moment. I thought about reversing and bolting for State Street, but it would take too much time. They would see me for sure. Then it dawned that if I kept running up the ramp, the valet would probably follow me, which would be a good thing, since he couldn't tell Dez and Michael where I'd gone.

I was about to start climbing the ramp again, but it was

too late. Dez and Michael pounded into the garage. No sign of their security guard.

Dez and Michael both wore blazers; both had that great Italian black hair. And both looked as though they would very, very much like to kill me.

They ran up the ramp as if to do just that. I turned and sprinted off.

When the ramp curved to the right, I figured I had only a few seconds to vanish. There were rows of cars parked in spots marked *Reserved.* I dodged behind a green Jaguar and crouched there, my heart banging violently against the walls of my chest. My dress, made of lavender silk, was damp with sweat and clinging to my body.

I held my breath, afraid to make a sound. But meanwhile, I heard no sounds of Michael or Dez. Surely, they'd seen me. Surely, they were just behind me. I swiveled my head around, feeling exposed. All they would have to do was look around the side of the car and they would spot me. And then what would they do?

I kept holding my breath. Silently, I placed my heels on the ground, bent down farther and tried to see under the carriage of the car. It was so low I had to kneel. Jagged concrete dug into my skin. My curly hair fell over my eyes. I brushed it away, bent lower and looked under the car.

My breath filled my lungs with a rush, almost like a punch. Because there, on the other side of the Jaguar, were two pairs of beautiful Italian loafers. Michael and Dez were standing there. They clearly hadn't heard me yet. But they were just waiting for me to make a sound.

My mouth opened in a terrified O. I began to pant again, this time silently.

I looked behind me and saw a door, maybe leading to an interior staircase. I peeked under the car again, and to my horror, I saw those beautiful Italian loafers start to move.

I stood and lunged for the door. Locked. *Fuck.* I was immediately chastised by my internal swearword replacement monitor, but once again *Frig* just wasn't going to cut it.

I spun around and faced them, shooting frenzied looks around the place, trying to figure out if I could dodge them and make a run for the street. They were still on the other side of the car, moving slowly, almost creeping. Dez was nearly to the front of the Jag.

"So what's your real name, little girl?" Dez said.

"It's not Isabel Bristol," Michael growled. Isabel Bristol was the name I'd used when I first met him.

"And it's not Suzanne," Dez said, no shyness about him now, only a sinister sneer. "C'mere, little girl."

I took a step back, then another. I was backing myself into the locked door, I knew, but the only impulse my body could muster was to recoil from Dez and Michael. My eyes swung wildly. Where was their security guard?

I took another step back. My bare feet stepped on something oily, then on the heels of my own shoes. Swiftly, I reached down and picked them up, thinking of some TV show I'd seen once where a stiletto was used to kill someone. I tucked my purse tighter under my arm. I brandished my high heels like ridiculous satin-covered weapons. There was nowhere else to go.

I tried to think of something to say, but it was clear there would be no chatting with these guys, no talking my way out of the situation.

It didn't matter anyway, because Dez charged around the car toward me. Instinctively, I moved back again, bouncing against the door. And then I was propelled forward as the door opened behind me. I was only a foot from Dez now, Michael behind him.

I felt a hand grip my arm and yank me back, hard, into the stairwell. The security guard. It must be.

"No!" I yelled, thrashing against him. "No!"

But the guy pulled me in farther, and then he did the strangest thing. He slammed the door, right on the puzzled faces of Dez and Michael.

It was black in the stairwell. I could see nothing. Dez's and Michael's fists battered the door from the outside, sounding like tribal drums, loud and menacing and alerting everyone of more danger to come.

I struggled against the grip of the security guard, and to my surprise he let me go.

"You're okay," he said.

I trembled a little, wanting to run but unable to see anything, not knowing where to go. It sounded as if Dez and Michael were pounding the door handle now, trying to break it.

"You have to leave," the man said. "You need to get out of here."

Why did his voice sound familiar, as if I were listening to the note of a song I had heard only a few times?

I felt a touch on my wrist. "Stop!" I yelled out of sheer instinct, pulling it away. In the deep dark of the stairwell, the movement made me feel dizzy, and I willed myself to stand straight.

"Let me show you the banister," he said. "Walk down the steps and out onto the street. Get away from here as fast as you can."

"But…"

Scratching sounded from the direction of the door handle now, as if Michael and Dez were putting something in the lock.

"Hurry," the man said. "They'll be in here very soon."

Enough of a threat to get me moving. I tucked the

purse tighter under my arm and clutched both shoes in my left hand. The man touched the wrist of my right hand again, and this time I let him lead me to the banister.

"Hold tight," he said. "Be careful. But please go as fast as you can."

I took one step, then another. Then I stopped. "Thank you," I said.

"You're welcome." Again, there was a distantly familiar quality to his voice.

I turned and put one foot on the lower step and then the next. I began to get the hang of it, despite the blackness around me. When I got to a landing, I shuffled my feet forward, looking for where the next steps began. Upstairs, I could hear more thrashing at the door.

Then, for a moment it quieted, and I heard the man speak. "Go. You're okay now, Boo."

The pounding at the door continued. An injection of fear kept me moving, finding the staircase, taking the steps faster this time, until I reached the street and pushed open the door, the streetlights hitting my eyes like a blast. I blinked and looked around. No sign of Michael or Dez. Not yet.

I saw a cab, lights on, across the street. I ran to it, yanked open the door and hopped into the back. Breathlessly, I gave my address on Eugenie Street.

It was only when the cab had driven eight blocks that I stopped looking behind me. Then I closed my eyes, laid my head on the back of the seat and let myself hear the last words the man had said.

You're okay now, Boo.

Was that right? Had he actually said that?

I forced myself back to that moment, listening intently to the memory.

You're okay now, Boo.

Boo was the nickname my mother used for me. No one else had ever called me that. Except my father.

And he had been dead for almost twenty-two years.

2

"Let's get tattoos."

I looked at my friend Maggie. "What are you talking about?"

It was Monday, the day after my night with Dez Romano, and needing a warm and welcoming face or two, I had texted my best friend, Maggie, and my former assistant, Q, and was happily surprised when they were both available for lunch. Q, who was also unemployed but living with his very wealthy boyfriend, picked me up and took us into the Loop to meet Maggie at a pub near her office.

Maggie and I ordered the fish and chips. Maggie ate greedily, the way she does when she finally remembers to stop working and eat, while I sort of picked at the fries and poked at the fish with my finger, unable to muster an appetite. Q, who was eternally on a diet to avoid a persistent belly, his personal nemesis to the perfect gay physique, gave a sullen stab at his plain chicken breast and pushed it away.

You're okay now, Boo.

I'd called Mayburn when I got home last night, telling him about the debacle at Gibsons, about being chased, about hearing those words. He wasn't too impressed by the "Boo" thing, but he'd been worried and upset about Michael and Dez being after me. He told me to keep a low profile, to watch for anyone tailing me. I don't think he would consider having lunch in the Loop "low profile," but sometimes you've simply got to be with friends.

"We need something new," Maggie said. "At least I do." She dunked a piece of battered fish into a ramekin of tartar sauce and popped it in her mouth. "And a tattoo is a way to signify something new in your life, like a new chapter."

"Who told you that?" Q asked.

She shrugged. "That's what people say."

"That's what they say *after* they get a tattoo, so they can justify it. So they can live with themselves."

Maggie stopped eating and gave a slightly dejected look.

"Mags," I said. "Your family would kill you if you got another tattoo." Maggie came from a big South Side Irish family, and they barely tolerated the tiny shamrock she got on her ankle during a college spring break.

"I'm thirty," she said. "I can do what I want. I don't care what they think."

Q and I laughed. Maggie did, too. Yes, Maggie was very much an adult, helping to run the criminal defense practice started by her famous lawyer grandfather, trying cases in courthouses all over the state. But her family was as thick as the thieves she represented. They spent most of their free time together, they knew everything about each other, and Maggie very much cared about their opinions.

I bit into a french fry, thinking about my recent exposure to tattoos. The last guy I dated—a twenty-one-year-old wunderkind of the computer world named Theo Jameson—had boasted a plethora of tattoos around his stunning body. A gold-and-black serpent slithered sexily around one arm, a red ribbon on the other. High on his left pec was an Asian-looking symbol. I'd never learned what it meant. We only dated a short time. He'd been too young for me, although that wasn't why we broke up.

Lately, Theo lingered in my mind just as much as Sam, my ex-fiancé, maybe more so because Theo had started texting me again recently.

*I miss you...*he'd say. *I think about you 300 times a day.* And the last one—*I have blood oranges.*

One late night a couple months ago, Theo came to my apartment with a bag filled with small oranges tinged a sultry crimson color. He made us screwdrivers. He squeezed juice on my wrists and licked it off.

I smiled as I chewed now, thinking about it.

Q saw my look. Knowing me well, he asked, "Theo?" before attempting another bite of his chicken breast.

"Yeah."

Q and Maggie hadn't met Theo, but I'd given them a detailed description of him, as well as a somewhat sanitized version of the nights we'd spent together.

"Is he still texting you?" Maggie asked.

"Yeah."

"What are you going to do about it?"

"I have no idea."

"Do you want to see him?"

"I haven't had sex in almost two months. And that kid is sex on a stick. What do you think?"

Maggie groaned, stopped eating momentarily. "I so understand." Recently, Maggie had taken a second shot at a relationship with an older, scoundrel type named Wyatt. And for the second time, Wyatt proved his scoundrel status, landing Maggie and me into singledom at the same time, something that hadn't happened since we'd met our first year in law school.

"A sexual dry spell?" Q said, smiling despite the lunch

he'd pushed away again. "I can't even remember what that's like."

"Shut up," Maggie and I said in unison.

Q kept smiling.

"What about Sam?" Maggie asked me.

"What about Sam?" I repeated, as if by saying the question out loud someone external, or maybe someone deep inside me, would answer definitively. But as usual, only more questions popped up: *Could we ever recapture what we had? Should we stop wondering about recapturing and consider redesigning?* And then came that question, always that brutal question that scared the others, and even the other possible answers, into complete silence: *Was it over between us for good?*

Sam and I had met through Forester Pickett, a Chicago media mogul we both worked for—me as a lawyer and Sam as a financial advisor at a private wealth management firm. When Forester was killed, our worlds spun out of control. And I'm not using that phrase—*out of control*—the way I previously used it when I was on trial or in the middle of a particularly nasty contract battle. *Everything is so out of control,* I would say back then, having no idea what that really meant.

In the aftermath of Forester's death, we tried to put back together the team that was *Sam and Izzy, Izzy and Sam,* but something was missing. And lacking the tools to adequately describe it, or maybe just lacking the tools to adequately ride it out and shift our worlds around, we dated other people and then officially broke up. The breakup came right about the time Theo and I ended, too—right about the time I ended the minor romance that sprung up with my friend Grady.

And so for the last two months, it had been just me. I spent time with Q and Maggie. I saw my family, too—

my brother, Charlie, my mom and her husband, Spence. That friend and family time had helped me to arise from the fog I'd started carrying around, but I agreed with Maggie that maybe we both needed something new.

"Look," I said, ignoring the question about Sam. "Tattoos aren't going to help. We need something else."

"You do," Q said. "It's almost your birthday."

"That's right!" Maggie said. "Ten days from now. What do you want to do?"

I thought about it. "I guess I just want to be around family and friends. Does that sound too boring?"

"Kinda," Q said.

Maggie pushed her plate away. "No, c'mon, you need *something.*" Suddenly, she sat up tall, brushing her wavy, golden-brown hair out of her eyes. "A vacation!" she said. "That's it! We'll celebrate your birthday by getting the hell out of Dodge."

"Shane and I are going to St. Bart's," Q said. "You could come with us."

I leaned back against the booth. "I don't have the cash for a vacation."

Maggie sighed. "And what am I talking about? I don't have the *time.* I'm on trial later this week. But maybe if we just started planning something it would motivate us, give us something to look forward to. We've always talked about going to Prague."

"And Paris."

"And London."

"And back to Italy." Now I sat upright. Maggie and I had done a study-abroad program after our first year in law school.

Maggie saw my excited look and read my thoughts. "Is your aunt still living in Rome?"

I nodded fast. "As far as I know."

"Do you think we could stay with her?" Maggie asked. "That would help with the cost." The truth was Maggie made more than enough to head to Rome for a week or two or four, but I appreciated that she was trying to be sensitive to her newly cash-strapped friend.

"I haven't talked to her in a long time, but I could ask." I could definitely ask, and not only because we wouldn't have to pay for a hotel, but because other than my mother and brother, my aunt was the only person who had also known my father. Elena, my father's sister, had been living in Rome for decades. When Maggie and I went to school there eight years ago, Aunt Elena had taken us to our first meal in Rome—at a restaurant right next to the Pantheon called *Fortunato.* But unfortunately, she had been out of town the rest of that month, and we didn't get to spend any more time with her.

Yet she was exactly the person I wanted to spend time with now.

You're okay now, Boo.

I hadn't told Maggie or Q about last night. Under Mayburn's rules, I couldn't tell anyone about the fact that I was his part-time, off-the-books employee.

I'd started working with Mayburn last fall when Sam had disappeared after Forester's death, and in return for looking into the matter, I'd agreed to freelance for Mayburn. *The whole reason I need you,* he'd said, *is because you're a typical, normal North Side Chicago woman. If there's any inkling that's not the case, if anyone knows you do P.I. stuff on the side, it won't work.* I had argued that I should be able to tell my close friends, but Mayburn wouldn't budge. If one of those people lets it slip to someone else, he'd said, it wouldn't end there; word would get around.

I wasn't so sure I cared anymore about a freelance investigator gig, especially when it got me into the kind of scariness it had last night. I'm a girl who likes to be chased as much as the next, but only in a romantic sense, not in a Mob-is-about-to-kill-you kind of sense.

And yet I couldn't shake the sound of that man's voice, the way he'd called me by my childhood nickname, Boo. Or at least that's what I thought I'd heard. The further I got away from it, the more I doubted myself. But I still wanted to poke around a little, to see if I could find anything out about my father, if there was anything to find out. The man had been dead for almost twenty-two years after all. But no one aside from my mother, used that nickname.

A way to fish around about my dad was to reestablish contact with my aunt Elena.

"Mags," I said, "I think you've got something here." I lifted my napkin and tossed it onto my plate. "I'm calling her tonight."

3

He watched her leave the restaurant, her steps casual, unhurried. And yet her shoulders were tight, her head swiveling. She pivoted once or twice, as if she couldn't decide which way to go, but then he recognized what she was doing. She was getting a feeling, sensing surveillance. And she was right. He watched as she stopped at the window of an office-supply store. To passersby she probably looked as if she was simply smoothing the front of her yellow summer dress, merely tugging a few stray red curls into place. But he knew what she was really doing.

She couldn't identify the source of her suspicion, he could tell, and so after another few fast glances in the glass at the people around her, at the cars on the street, she turned and kept moving. Her body appeared more relaxed now. Apparently, she had decided she wasn't being followed.

She was wrong.

He just hoped he was the only one.

4

I walked home from my lunch date to savor the summer weather—crisp without being cool, sunny without being blazing, breezy without the lake winds blowing your skirt around your ass. Usually, I would be on my scooter—a silver Vespa—but Q had driven me to lunch. With so much time on my hands and considering the fact that Chicago receives approximately four and a half-perfect weather days like this, I figured I had to make the best of it.

The streets were crowded with people. Everyone had a bustle to their steps, it seemed. Everyone had a purpose. You could tell the lawyer types who were dashing to court or a deposition. You could spot the salespeople pulling product in small wheeled suitcases. When I'd been one of those dashing lawyers, I was always jealous of someone like me, someone dressed casually the way I was in flip-flops and a yellow cotton dress, someone who clearly didn't have to rush anywhere. But being on the other side was starting to depress me—knowing that I wasn't just playing hooky for the afternoon or taking a much-needed sabbatical, knowing that I was out of work and out of prospects and almost out of my twenties.

Plus, all those people on the street, and the fact that a crowd made it easy to tail someone, began to make me nervous, made me think about Dez and Michael, and wonder if they knew who I was, if they were looking for me. And of course, thinking about Dez and Michael made me think of that stranger in the stairwell.

It was one night, when I was about five years old, that my father had given me my nickname. I'd woken up crying after a sinister dream. He tried to console me, but nothing worked. In the span of six hours, I'd grown fearful of the dark. My dad told me then that if you were afraid of something, you should look it straight in the eye. I didn't know what he meant, and he must have seen that.

"What are you afraid of in here?" He gestured around my bedroom, lit only by the tiny lamp in the shape of a shell that sat on my nightstand.

I looked around. Nothing appeared particularly scary. "I don't know."

"Ghosts? You're scared that they'll say, 'Boo'?"

"I guess."

"Well, there's nothing scary about that. Nothing scary about ghosts, either. They're just people who aren't here anymore, stopping back in to say hi. Except they say boo."

That sounded rather simple. And not at all terrifying.

"Okay?" Under his round copper glasses, my dad's eyes sparkled, as though a laugh was just about to hit him. I loved when he looked like that. It made everything seem fine.

"I guess..." I said again, the fear still lingering a bit the way bad dreams do.

"You guess? What kind of answer is that?" My father looked at the ceiling and acted as if he was thinking hard. "I'll tell you what. I'm going to call you *Boo.* Just for a little while, so that if you ever do see a ghost and they say that to you, you won't be scared. You'll have heard it before. Okay, Boo?"

I liked it. I'd never had a nickname before. "Okay."

It had been a thing between the two of us, just my dad and me. After he died when I was eight years old, my mother picked up the nickname, as if by using it she could keep him a little bit alive. But I had never seen a ghost, never heard one. Until last night in the stairwell.

When I got to the Chicago River, I began to feel I was being watched. I swung my head around, but it didn't appear as if anyone was following me. I kept walking, paying attention to everyone I passed, and it seemed as if a lot of people were looking right at me, expressions of recognition on their faces. It was hard to tell if any of the people were tailing me or if their expressions were simply the type I'd witnessed frequently over the last couple of months—looks that said, *I saw her on the news, I think. Yeah, she did something wrong.*

The fact was, I hadn't done *anything* wrong, but after my friend died in the spring, the Chicago cops had suspected me of her murder. As a result, my image was flashed across the news stations for a week or so. Thankfully, mine was a flash-in-the-pan story, but I still got those looks with some regularity. I hoped Dez hadn't seen the story, or hadn't remembered it.

I dropped my gaze as I crossed the bridge in front of the Merchandise Mart, not wanting to meet anyone's eyes for too long. I reached into my bag for my cell phone.

"Hey, Iz." My brother answered on the first ring, which he almost always does. He's one of the few people I know who actually answers their phone on a consistent basis.

"What are you doing? Want to take a walk in the park or something?"

"Yeah, meet me at Mom's. I'm over here, using their printer."

"Are they home?" "They" was my mother, Victoria McNeil Calloway, and her husband, Spence. The two were mostly joined at the hip, and mostly at home now that Spence had retired from his business—a real estate development company that provided consulting around the country.

I loved being with my mom and Spence, but I wasn't ready to see them now. You couldn't just waltz up to someone on a beautiful Monday afternoon and say, "Hey, any chance your husband, who died two decades ago, is alive?" I could barely ask myself that question. It was really too ridiculous. But Charlie was hard to fluster.

My mother lived on State Street in an elegant graystone house, a few blocks north of Division Street. Charlie was waiting for me on the steps, his tall frame leaning back casually on his elbows. His loose, curly brown hair glinted in the sun with a hint of red I've always told him he got from me.

He came down the steps and we hugged, then wordlessly started walking down State Street to Lincoln Park. We wandered behind the Chicago History Museum, crossing the street and passing by the entrance to the zoo.

When we reached Café Brauer, we went behind it to the small pond, where paddleboats were rented by tourists or families. Some of the boats were forest-green, others white and shaped like huge swans.

Charlie pointed. "Remember when Mom used to take us on those?"

I nodded. "Mom and I would paddle and let you think you were doing all the work."

Charlie shook his head. "Yeah, and being the sucker I am, I believed it. Thought I was the man of the house."

"You *were* the man of the house."

We both laughed. Charlie has always possessed a lazy streak. It's not that he's stupid. Quite the contrary. Charlie is a reader of history, a lover of art and music. And trumping those things, Charlie is a lover of red wine and naps.

In fact, most of his friends—and sometimes even my mom and I—had taken to calling him "Sheets" because he spent much of his time in bed, a trait that had intensified after college. Charlie had graduated with a degree in English and a desire to do absolutely nothing. A friend's father took pity on him and gave him a job driving a dump truck to and from work sites, which Charlie liked just fine because during down times, he was allowed to doze in the trailer. He might have gone on like that for decades, but one day the truck turned over on the Dan Ryan Expressway when a semi cut him off. He broke his femur, screwed up his back and ended up with a fairly hefty settlement from the semi's insurance company. In his usual cheerful way, "Sheets" took it as a windfall and had spent the last few years sitting around, reading, getting the occasional physical-therapy session and, yes, drinking red wine.

"Let's sit." Charlie pointed to a bench at the side of the lagoon that was shaded by a patch of vibrantly green trees.

He took a seat, his long arm on the top of the bench. I arranged myself cross-legged and looked at him, trying to figure out how to tell Charlie what I'd heard, or *thought* I'd heard, last night. I stared across the pond at a bridge that spanned one edge of it, at the Hancock building and the skyline beyond that.

Ever since Charlie and I were little, I was the more serious, the one who worried enough for everyone, the one who analyzed a situation ten ways before deciding what to do, while Charlie mostly rolled along. I needed him to analyze this one with me, though. I wouldn't tell him about working for Mayburn, but I had to tell Charlie that I thought I'd heard our father's voice.

"So I was on Mom's computer," Charlie said, before I could form my words.

"Working on something for YouTube?" Charlie produced funny little movies filmed on the streets of Chicago. He shot them in black and white and set them to old-fashioned French music. It was kind of hard to explain, but they were really quite charming, and he had developed a coterie of people, mostly female college students, who loved them and as a result, loved Charlie, as well.

"I was working on my résumé."

"Really?" I tried not to sound surprised. Charlie had talked about looking for a job—after years of living off his settlement check, it was starting to dry up—but somehow it was impossible to imagine him getting up and doing something besides deciding between merlot versus cabernet.

"Yeah. Actually, I think I already have the job. They just need my résumé for office purposes, to put it in my file."

"What's the job?"

"An internship at WGN. The radio station."

"The one with the glass studio on Michigan Avenue?"

He nodded.

"Wow." I couldn't hide my astonishment. "That sounds like a big gig."

"No, it's being an assistant—or intern or whatever—to the producer for the midday show."

"So you'll be going there every day?" Somehow this concept seemed impossible.

"Yeah. I'm going to be working, Iz." There was a note of pride in his voice I didn't recognize. He studied my face. "I mean, c'mon, I don't know what I want to do with my life. Actually, I wish everyone would stop asking me what I *want* to do with my life. What does that even mean?"

I shrugged. I couldn't be of any help there.

"But it's time to do something," he continued. "Maybe this radio thing could be for me." He shrugged, too. "You know Zim?"

I nodded. "Zim" was Robby Zimmerman, a friend of Charlie's from high school.

"Well, his dad is in radio sales, and he got me the job. There's no money in it, like no money, but—"

"You're going to work for *free?*" Financially, I was appalled, but this sounded more like the Charlie I knew.

"Yeah. At least at first. Because I have to try something, Iz. I'm *twenty-seven.*" He said this like, *I'm eighty-three.*

Charlie's birthday was just a few days ago, and he was taking it even more seriously than I was my upcoming thirtieth.

"I can't sit around on my ass forever." He frowned and looked out at a duck being chased by a toddler who was being chased by her mother.

"Why not? You do sitting on your butt better than anyone I know." Somehow, this whole notion of Charlie as a member of the working class freaked me out, made me feel as if my world was shifting even more. Things in my life kept skidding around, and I hated the fact that I had no idea where they would all land.

Charlie laughed. "You don't want me to get a job, because you don't have a job."

"Exactly. It's the beginning of summer and both the McNeil kids are lazy good-for-nothings. Let's make the most of it and spend the summer on the lake." Suddenly, I could envision it—Charlie and I walking from my mom's house to North Avenue Beach, maybe sitting on the roof deck of the restaurant that looked like a boat and eating fried shrimp for lunch, lying under an umbrella in the sand for the rest of the afternoon, barbecuing with my mom and Spence in the evenings. Ever since the breakup with Sam—and Theo *and* Grady—I craved my family like never before. Even more so now that it felt as if I was about to lose Charlie somehow. Or at least the Charlie I knew.

"You should do that," Charlie said. "Have yourself a lazy summer. Pretend you're me, and I'll go to work and pretend I'm you."

I frowned. I wasn't enjoying the prospect of suddenly being the sloth of the family. I didn't think I could pull off slothful with exuberance and elegance the way Charlie had. I was pretty sure I didn't want to.

Then I had an idea. "How about we go to Italy? Tell the radio station you can start in a month or even a few weeks." If we could stay with our aunt and I could use my airline miles, it might be doable. Charlie loved the concept of traveling, had been talking about Europe the last year, and if I planned the trip for him, the ease of it all might just push him over the hump and get him to agree.

"Can't. Their other intern quit. They need me on Wednesday."

"Like in two days, Wednesday?"

"Yeah."

"Wow." I hardly knew what to say. "Congratulations, Charlie." I squeezed his hand.

"Thanks." He smiled—that great Charlie McNeil smile that made the few freckles on his face dance and his hazel eyes gleam. If there *was* a famous McNeil smile, as Mayburn had suggested, it belonged to Charlie, not me.

I turned and looked at the pond, at a dad with twin girls on a paddleboat. The girls were laughing, pointing. The dad appeared stressed and was trying to stop them from falling over the side.

"Remember when we got to do things like that with Dad?" I gestured at the boat.

Charlie crossed his arms and studied the family. "Not really. I don't remember much about him at all."

"Really?"

"I remember a few things. I remember what he looked like. I remember what Mom wore on the day he died. Remember that belt she had on?"

I nodded. I could see the scene as if it were playing in front of me.

When I was eight and Charlie five, my mother had to tell us that our dad was dead. We lived in Michigan then. It had been a magnificent, sunny fall day, and Charlie and I were playing in the leaves in the backyard. I would rake and form piles, then Charlie and I would take running, shrieking leaps and dive into them. Then Charlie would sit, and I would rake, and we would do the whole thing again.

We had been doing that for at least an hour when my mother came out of the house. She wore jeans and a brown braided belt that tied at the waist. She walked across the lawn slowly, too slowly. She was usually rushing outside to tell us it was time to eat or time to go into town. The ends of her belt gently slapped her thighs as she walked. Her red-blond hair was loosely curled around her face, as usual, but that face was splotched and somehow off-kilter. I remember stopping, holding the rake and studying her, thinking that her face looked as if it had two different sides, like a Picasso painting my teacher had shown us in art class.

She sat us down on the scattered leaves and asked us if we knew where our dad was that day.

"Work!" Charlie said.

My father was a psychologist and a police profiler. I knew that much, although I really didn't understand what those things meant.

"No, he—" my mom started to say.

"The helicopter," I said, jumping in. My father already had his pilot's certificate and was training for his helicopter rating.

"That's right." My mom's eyes were wide, scared. The helicopter my father was flying had crashed into Lake Erie, she explained. And now he was dead. It was as simple and awful as that.

Charlie seemed to take the news well. He furrowed his tiny brow, the way he did in school when he knew he was supposed to be listening to an adult. But when she was done, he leapt to his feet and scooped up an armful of leaves with an unconcerned smile.

"I'm surprised you remember that," I said to Charlie now. "I thought you didn't really understand what was going on."

"I didn't, not until later. But I remember that day. Always will."

We both stared at the pond. The father had gotten his twins to sit still, and they paddled away from us, all of them laughing.

"Do you ever think you see him?" I asked Charlie.

"Who?"

"Dad. You know, do you ever think you see him or hear his voice?"

"You mean, someone that reminds me of him? Not really."

"I do."

Out of the corner of my eye, I saw Charlie turn his head and look at me. "What are you talking about?"

I said nothing for a moment, then, "I think I saw him last night."

"Are you serious? You think you saw Dad?"

I nodded.

"C'mon, Iz, don't start losing it on me now."

I forced a fake laugh. "Maybe I am losing it. But last night..." How to explain? I took a breath, and in a rush, I poured out the story, leaving out the fact that I was working for Mayburn, making it sound as if I'd had some trouble with some weird dudes I met at a bar, but telling Charlie exactly how the man saved me, telling him exactly about those words—*You're okay now, Boo.*

Charlie said nothing for a while. I could tell he was thinking hard, turning over what I'd said in his mind. Charlie was the type who couldn't be hurried, and he couldn't be shamed into pretending to comprehend something he didn't.

Finally, he looked at me.

I turned my body to face him. "What do you think?"

He gave a one-shouldered shrug. "I think this guy probably said something, and you heard it as 'Boo.' I think it was a stressful situation, and you wanted someone like your father to save you."

It was possible. I'd heard that endorphins and adrenaline could do strange things to your mind. "You don't think it was him?"

"Iz, he's *dead.*"

"Supposedly."

Charlie searched my face.

"I know," I said. "I feel like a prize idiot now that I'm saying this out loud, but there was something familiar about him when I saw him."

"You said you didn't really see him. He had a hat on and then it was dark in those stairs, right?"

"Yes."

"And are you positive he said *Boo?* I mean, it could have been any word. He could have said *you* or something like that."

"I guess. That's what I've been telling myself. It's silly, right?"

Charlie leaned forward and ruffled my hair. It gave me a pang of wistfulness because it seemed like something I would do to him. I was usually the stalwart of common sense, the logical one, and now it was Charlie getting a job, Charlie forcing reality into his sibling's world.

He looked at his watch. "I have to get back to that résumé."

"Right. I'll walk you."

We strolled to my mom's house in silence. We climbed the front steps and went inside. I thought I'd get a glass of water, then go home. But my mom and Spence were there, in the kitchen—a room with an octagonal breakfast table tucked into the big bay window. They were taking food out of grocery bags, talking rapidly as if they'd just run into each other, not two people who spent nearly all their days together.

"Izzy, sweetie." My mom kissed me on the cheek. Victoria McNeil was a graceful woman. Her hair was still strawberry blond, although slightly shorter and more styled than she used to wear it. She had a manner that drew people to her—a sort of mysterious melancholy that made people want to know her, to take care of her.

"Hello, darling girl," Spence said. It was what he'd always called me. Spence was a tall, slightly overweight guy with a perpetually pleasant air. He had thinning brown hair gone mostly white now, which he let grow more on the sides to compensate for the balding up top.

Charlie shot me a look, as if to say, *Are you going to tell them?*

I shook my head no.

Spence glanced at the clock above the fridge. "Four o'clock," he said. He looked around at the rest of us. "Well, it's five o'clock somewhere, right?"

He opened a bottle of wine, and we slid into the evening like so many others. Spence and my mom put out a series of small plates of food—some soft goat cheese surrounded by sliced figs; sliver-thin smoked salmon, small dishes of blanched almonds seasoned with truffle salt—and we sat at the breakfast table and feasted slowly, talking quickly. That table was my mother's favorite spot in the house. She had decorated the living room at the front of the house in different shades of ivory, and the room was beautiful, but in the afternoons as the sun slid around the house, it fell into darkness, and my mother, who was prone to depression, always moved into the kitchen, where she could get a few more hours of the daylight that seemed to feed her. And on days like today, with the windows open, the backyard garden green and lush, my mother's sometimes tight personality seemed to unfurl and relax.

A former business associate of Spence's had died that week, and he told us about the visitation service that morning. "I'll just never get used to it," he said, "seeing a body like that in a casket. I've been to probably a hundred funerals and wakes in my life, but I just can't stand it." He turned to my mother. "Remember, if I die—"

"I know, my love." She gave him a patient smile that said she'd had this conversation before. "A closed casket."

"There was a closed casket for Dad, wasn't there?" I said.

Everyone went still, looking at me. Spence often talked, even joked, about his death, and in general death was not a conversation we shied away from in my family. Except we rarely spoke of my father's anymore. My mother had slipped into a severe depression after he died, and I'd often thought we all still acted afraid, as if any mention of the topic could send her reeling again.

But my mother nodded and answered quickly now. "Yes, a closed casket. That's what they'd always done in your father's family. But it was also required because they never found his body."

"So no one ever saw him? Like, to identify him?"

The silence returned, hardened. I felt Charlie nudge me with his knee under the table.

"I'm just curious," I said, as lightly as possible. "I don't know why. I'm sorry..." My words trailed off.

"Don't be sorry," my mother said. "You're entitled to ask such questions. We probably should have had more discussions like this in the past. But the answer is no. When a helicopter goes down like that, the water is as unforgiving as the ground, and so it shattered on impact." She closed her eyes, as if seeing it, then opened them again. "They found wreckage, which is how they knew the location of the crash. But they couldn't find a body. I was told that's fairly typical for a crash into a large body of water like Lake Erie."

"Something went wrong with the blades, right?"

"From the wreckage and from his last call, it sounded like the blades flexed in a way they weren't supposed to and they cut the tail off."

"Wouldn't they notice a problem like that before he went up?"

"He did an inspection with the instructor and didn't see any problems. The instructor told me later they thought your father had gotten into some kind of problem, something about oscillation. They think he overcorrected and caused the blades to flex."

"Who was the instructor?"

My mother looked up in the air, as if searching for the answer there, then shook her head. "He was with the local aviation company. R.J. was his first name. I can't remember his last." Another shake of her head. "Maybe I don't want to remember."

I opened my mouth to ask another question, but I felt my brother staring intently at me. When I looked at him, he shook his head slowly and gave me a look that seemed to say, *Enough, Izzy. Enough for now.*

5

I climbed the stairs of the Old Town building—a converted brick three-flat—to my condo faster than normal. I didn't stop at the threshold the way I usually did to appreciate the shiny pine floors and the marble turn-of-the-century fireplace with its bronze grate. Instead I walked quickly through the front room, then through the European kitchen on the other side, and went straight to the second bedroom, which I used as an office.

I got on the Internet and did a search for any flight schools in the Detroit area that provided helicopter instruction. There was only one. I picked up the phone and dialed.

The woman who answered the phone said they were about to close, but when I mentioned flight lessons, she launched into a sales pitch to get me signed up.

"I'm in Chicago," I finally said. "I really can't take flight lessons there, but I have a question about someone who did about twenty years ago."

"Oh." A pause. "Well, the owner has been around for thirty years."

"Is he available?"

"Might have left for the day. One sec."

I was put on hold. I stared out the window at my neighbor's side yard, watching a young dad pull a blond toddler on a wagon. Was it even possible that my dad was alive? What would he look like now? Would he still have the messy, curly brown hair that looked so much like Charlie's? Would he still wear the copper wire glasses over eyes that always looked as if they were laughing, or would he have contacts now, or maybe he'd gotten eye surgery? I thought about the man last night. The only time I'd seen him in the light was outside of Gibsons, and his face had been down, his hair covered by the baseball cap. I'd turned so quickly, run so fast that no other details had registered.

I looked at my watch. I'd been on hold for about five minutes and was considering hanging up when I heard a jovial, "Bob Bates, how can I help you?"

I gave him my name, asked if he was the owner and when he gave me a friendly *You bet,* I forged ahead, saying I was looking for information about a flight instructor who used to teach there almost twenty-two years ago. "I believe his first name was R.J., but I don't know the last."

"R.J. Hmm. Sometimes these guys come and go, but that doesn't sound too familiar. I could be forgetting someone, though."

"I'm sure it's hard to remember." I tried not to let my disappointment creep into my voice.

"Why do you ask?"

"Well, my father used to take lessons from your company."

"Who's that?"

"Christopher McNeil."

"Ah, Jesus. You're McNeil's kid? Now, there's a name I won't forget. That's something you never get used to in this business, losing a pilot."

"Do you remember now who his instructor was?"

"Well, yeah, I do remember the guy. He wasn't one of mine."

"What do you mean?"

"He was government. Came in just to train guys when the government needed him to."

I blinked a few times, didn't know what to think about that. "Which government exactly?" I told him my dad had worked for the Detroit police as a profiler. "Was the instructor someone from the county? Someone with the police?"

"No, the instructor was with the Feds. That's all I knew. They paid me up front for the flight time, runways, hangar fees, tie-downs. I leased them the choppers, same way I do to the news stations. Couldn't believe it when he went down over Lake Erie. It's awful when it's on your watch."

"Do you remember the name of the instructor?"

"Hold on, I'll see if I still have any records." He put me on hold for a few minutes, then came back. "Yeah, I found it. R. J. Ohman. *O-H-M-A-N.*"

6

My Internet search for R. J. Ohman revealed nothing.

For the moment, I gave up on finding him and went to the closet in my office, removing boxes of winter stuff—the scarves and gloves that were so prevalent during the winter and seemed like foreign, faraway objects now. Chicagoans are seasonal amnesiacs. In the summer, we literally forget what the winters are like, the warm winds sloughing away our hard-edged memories of January.

At the back of the closet, I found what I was looking for.

For months after my dad died, my mother left his belongings exactly as they were. His ratty blue-and-maroon robe still hung on a brass hook on the back of their bedroom door in Michigan. His shoes—the tan boat shoes he wore so often—were right inside the garage door, as if he might step into them, and back into life, at any moment. His books were still in the office he'd made for himself in a corner of the basement, makeshift shelves lined with psychology texts, but also the mystery novels he loved to read.

When we moved to Chicago from Michigan, my mother got rid of most of those things. She kept some of his books, divided up others between Charlie and me. The clothes she gave to the Salvation Army store. My brother and I used to love to play in that store, trying on goofy hats and ridiculous shoes that someone's grandmother had left behind. But later it filled me with a queer sickness to think of some other kid trying on my dad's ratty bathrobe, laughing at his scuffed boat shoes.

From my closet now, I extracted a cardboard box, reading my mother's handwriting on the side—*Isabel/Christopher.* Seeing my name next to my father's like that always gave me a chill.

Inside the box, I sifted through whatever my hands came across—cards, scraps of notes, a dinged-up metal glasses case my father used to carry with him. I put some items aside, studied others. I thought about the last time I'd seen my father, the night before he died when he put me to bed and he read to me. I searched through the box for the book—*Poems & Prayers for the Very Young.* I remembered the illustration of the boy and girl on the cover; they were looking out the window into a starry night. My father would point to that picture and say, *That's you, Izzy. And that's Charlie,* and I would gaze at him in awe and think that my father must have been the most spectacular man since he could get a drawing of his children on the cover of a book.

I reached to the bottom of the box, and although there were a few more cards there, I realized that I didn't have the book. I only had the memory of it, one that was sharp and vivid. I had other memories, too—of his soft voice reading to me, of the way he sometimes repeated phrases he loved or wanted to make sure I'd heard.

I sifted through the stuff in the box some more. I found a birthday card he'd given me for my eighth birthday, just a few weeks before he'd died.

The card was one that you might give an adult woman, not a child. On the front it had crimson cursive writing rimmed with gold that spelled out *Happy Birthday* on ivory linen paper.

In a few weeks, I would be thirty. If he were alive, my father would have been fifty-seven. *If he were alive. If…*

I read the words he'd printed inside the card.

Happy birthday, Boo.
I am so lucky that God chose me to be your father. You have been my little girl for 8 years, but I love you like it has been forever. Already you live life as if it is yours for the taking, with your big-eyed curiosity, your ability to embrace and overcome anything, and the unfailing kindness toward others that I know you got from your mom. You will be great, no matter what happens to me. Remember, you will always be in my heart.
I love you, Boo,
Dad

When I'd read the card as an eight-year-old, I knew they were nice words. I knew my dad loved me. I was secure in the way children are, sure that nothing will ever change, that happiness will always be at the forefront of life.

And so on that night of my birthday, the last birthday where I felt I was truly young, truly a child, I had put the card aside, moving on to the wrapped gifts that my mother and father had stacked on our kitchen table.

I didn't pick the card up again until six months after his death, and that's when I really read it, studying the words like an archeologist who finds a shard of an ancient urn in the dust.

No matter what happens to me. The words of the card had torn through me, stealing my breath. I kept that card in my nightstand for years after he died. And although it pained me to do so, I took it out of the drawer every few weeks, whenever I was really missing him, and I read it again, marveling at the words he had written, the words that made it seem as if he had somehow sensed his approaching death, although no one could ever have predicted a helicopter crash.

After a few years, I put the card away. It was too sharp, caused too many knife slits in the still delicate skin of my psyche. But now, I looked at the card and examined it from more of an emotional distance. Had he told anyone about this sense of foreboding? Or did he carry it around by himself, thinking it too morbid, maybe embarrassed to be having such thoughts. He wasn't sick. So why that wording, as if he were reassuring himself that I would be okay without him when he was gone?

I thought back to my phone call with the owner of the airport, and then I thought about my dad's profession as a psychologist and a profiler. The pilot thing was something I understood he did on the side, a hobby. But then why the government instructor? Was he working for the federal government? Did that mean the crash had something to do with his job? Maybe he'd been working on a case when he died; maybe it had to do with a helicopter? And…and…then what? It all seemed so vague.

I flipped through some of the other cards and letters I'd taken out of the box and found those from my aunt Elena, my father's only sibling. Most were postmarked from Rome. They all bore her small, pristine handwriting. In the left corners, she'd written her married name, Elena Traviata.

When I was younger, she had sent me a card every year for my birthday, beautiful cards with Italian words that she would translate in her tiny penmanship, as if she hoped that from afar she could teach me Italian, that I could share her passion for the country and the language.

There were other cards from her, too—some for graduations and other big life events. The last one I'd received was for my law school graduation. It was hard to believe we hadn't shared any contact since then, but the years had slipped away, and I hadn't been good about keeping up my end of things, either.

I stood from the floor, groaning a little at the stiffness in my legs. Holding one of her cards, I moved to my desk and switched on the small light against the encroaching darkness outside. I looked for my date planner. Most of my friends, and nearly all the lawyers I knew, kept their calendars on their BlackBerrys or computers, but I liked the old-fashioned hard copy, liked seeing my days laid out in front of me. Those pages used to be chock-full of meetings, depositions and conference calls. Now there were only a few tragically mundane things. *Take Vespa to get headlight changed. Buy tampons. Teeth cleaning.*

I found the date book—thin with a maroon cover embossed in gold—which my former client, Forester Pickett, had given me before he died. I kept some contacts written in the back. Flipping there, I found Aunt Elena's phone number in Rome. Hoping it was still the same, I began to dial, but then I looked at my watch. Eight-thirty. Which meant it was three-thirty in the morning Rome time.

I hung up the phone and sat back, disappointed.

My cell phone rang. Mayburn.

"Meet me for a beer?" he asked.

I looked at my office floor, strewn with cards. "Don't think so, but thanks."

"C'mon. Just one. I just need to get out. I'll come to your hood. Meet me at Marge's. Half an hour. One beer. Please."

I'd never heard him say please. *He must be in a bad way.* "All right. Just one."

Twenty minutes later, I walked down Sedgwick to Marge's, a bar that had been in the hood for years and years, but had undergone a recent renovation. Inside, it was clean, the tin ceiling sparkling. Being a lover of dive bars, I missed the atmosphere it used to have.

Mayburn was sitting at the bar. He turned when I came in and gave me a little wave.

Mayburn was in his early forties, although he looked younger and acted older. He was cynical and sarcastic in that way people are when they're using such traits as a shield. The only person I'd seen penetrate that defense of his was Lucy DeSanto, and now that she was back with her husband, Michael, it was as if Mayburn's shield had been ripped away, leaving him a little colorless, a little flat.

"Hey," he said, when I reached him. "Thanks for coming." His sandy-brown hair, which was usually styled well, was slightly messy. During the week he wore suits and jackets, but on nights and weekends he wore cooler clothes—great jeans, beat-up brown boots, stuff like that. At Marge's now, he wore old jeans and a black T-shirt that had a skull and crossbones on it.

I pointed at his shirt. "Feeling chipper today?"

"Yeah. Really fucking chipper."

I sat and ordered a Blue Moon beer with an orange. It was what Sam used to drink, and recently—maybe I was missing Sam—I'd adopted Blue Moon as my beer of choice.

Mayburn turned toward me on his stool. "So. Any other problems?"

He meant the debacle at Gibsons, about being chased. "No."

"No one lingering around you? No cars tailing you?"

"I don't think so. I walked around all day and—"

"You walked around all day?" His face was irritated. "Jesus, Izzy, I told you—"

"You told me to keep it low-key, keep a low profile,

whatever. But how am I supposed to do that? I'm looking for a job." I thought of my day, which had consisted of lunch, sitting by a pond and drinking with my family. "Sort of. I mean, I can't hang out in my condo all day, just because *you* got me into trouble last night."

He sighed. "I know. I'm sorry. But you have to be careful."

"I am. I kept my eyes open. Believe me, I don't want those guys finding me any more than you do."

"But you're hoping someone will find you," Mayburn said. "You're hoping your dad will step out of the shadows and introduce himself."

I hated that I was so transparent, but the tone of Mayburn's words was kind.

I took a sip of my beer. "I guess you can understand wanting someone to come back to you," I said softly.

A pause, a pained one. Mayburn turned back to his own beer. "I do understand. But, hey, let's not lose sight of the fact that my someone is alive."

I said nothing.

"Izzy, don't get your hopes up here."

"Hopes? I have no hopes. Hell, if anything, I hope I'm wrong. Because if he's really alive, what does that mean? What would that say about him?"

He certainly wouldn't be the man I knew, the father I thought I'd had. And somehow that would be worse than having him dead for all those years.

"Did you talk to Lucy today?" I asked, changing the subject.

He groaned a little. "Yeah. She isn't real pleased with me. Michael came home last night, yelling about the friend she brought into the house, the one who sent him away to prison. She knows I sent you to investigate them."

"Does Michael know that you and Lucy had a relationship while he was in jail?"

"She told him she dated someone when he was inside, but she wouldn't tell him who. She wants me to back off now. She wants to give her marriage a shot."

"Even if Michael still seems pretty tight with Dez Romano?"

"He tells her he's not. Says he just went to see Dez to clean up some stuff, to tell him he's out for good. I don't believe that, but she does. Or at least she wants to."

I patted his hand, and surprisingly he let me. "You have to let her do whatever she thinks is best for herself and her family. If you don't, you could lose her."

"She could get trapped again. She could get trapped with this guy forever."

"It's her call, Mayburn. Let her make it."

He pulled his hand away, went silent for a second. "I don't know what to do with myself."

"How about helping me look for my father?"

He gave me a smile. "Even though I think you're a little delusional, sure. Tell me what you need."

I told him about my dad's flight instructor being someone from the federal government, someone named R. J. Ohman. "Can you find him?"

"I'll kick it around."

My cell phone rang. I looked at the screen. *Theo.* My pulse picked up. I answered. "Hey," I said, trying to sound calm. I stood and moved away from Mayburn.

"Girl." He'd been texting me, but I hadn't heard his voice in months. And with that one word, I felt a little short of breath.

"Hey," I said again. I went to the front window. The night sky was a sexy, deep orange from the last bit of the sunset.

"I'm by your house," he said.

"Oh, yeah?"

"Had a beer with a friend at Border Line."

"That's not near my house. It's in Bucktown."

"But it's on North Avenue. And your place is *near* North Avenue."

"And so this is what? A booty call?"

"Like you'd let me get away with that." He laughed. "I had to drink a beer to get up the courage to call you since I screwed things up with you last time."

"You didn't screw up. You just didn't tell me something that I wish I'd known about."

"Exactly. I wasn't totally honest, and I don't feel good about it. Give me another chance."

I turned away from the window and leaned back against the wall. "At what? Theo, I'm about to turn thirty—"

"When?" he interrupted.

I told him the date. "But that's not the point. I'm almost thirty and you're *twenty-one.*"

"Twenty-two."

"When was your birthday?"

"May."

"I cannot believe you were born in the Eighties."

"You owe me a birthday present."

"I *owe* you?"

"Let me say that a different way. You want to know what I want for my birthday?"

"The ability to rent a car by yourself?"

He laughed. That was one thing, among the several, that I enjoyed about Theo. Unlike many men, he had the ability to see himself with a sense of humor. Maybe it was due to the fact that he was gorgeous. And smart. And sexy. And wealthy.

"I want to see you," he said. "Just see you. Let me stop

over and say hi. We can sit on your front stoop if you don't want me to come up."

"We never did get to sit on the stoop last time, did we?" When we'd dated in April, my friend's murder and me being a suspect meant the media had been camped out on my front lawn much of the time.

"So what do you say?"

I walked back toward Mayburn. I decided not to think too long about Theo, but rather to go with what I wanted. A baseline want, maybe, but I really didn't care. "I'll see you outside my house," I told him.

Fifteen minutes later, truly night now, and I was sitting on the stoop with a glass of water, moisture beading on its sides, waiting for Theo. Mayburn had given me crap about dumping him for, as he called Theo, "a twelve year old."

"He's not twelve," I said.

"Sounds like he might as well be."

"He's cool. Really."

"Oh, I'm sure your boy toy is cool."

"He's not a boy toy! He's—"

"Look, Iz, you don't have to explain it to me." He pulled my beer toward him. "I'm going to sit here and finish the rest of your beer and then I'm going home."

"And you're not going to call Lucy."

"Right," he said. Then, again, "right," as if he needed to convince himself.

I put Mayburn out of my mind when I saw Theo turn onto Eugenie Street, a tall figure, solid and dark with the streetlights behind him. I could see the outline of his muscled shoulders, the rounded dip and curl of his biceps. I pushed my sundress between my legs and closed them.

I waited until he was standing before me—looking down, his chin-length hair falling forward onto his face—

then I said hello. I put my water down. He held out a hand and pulled me to my feet. He wrapped his arms around me and I thawed, curving myself around his abdomen, his chest, hugging him tight, surprised at the relief. The feeling was quickly followed by desire—shots of it, stinging through me, hitting my brain, my body.

Theo looked up at the building above us. "Are your neighbors home?"

I looked up with him. The lights were on in all three condos. "Yeah."

"Think they'll come downstairs?"

"Why?"

"You think they'll come downstairs?"

"No. My neighbors usually have to be up early. They both work." *Unlike me.*

Theo reached an arm out and pushed the front door, which I'd propped open with a rock. He kicked the rock away and pulled me into the stairwell, a place constantly too dark, a complaint I'd made more than once to the management company. But now, with the door shutting behind us, Theo pushing me against the wall, kissing me deeply, I didn't mind that the stairwell was shadowy and hot.

Desire turned into frantic craving. I kissed him back hard, threading my hands through his hair, hearing myself pant, gasp.

He lifted me up, legs around him, then pushed me back against the wall. I kissed him deeper, gulping at his mouth. I felt my body temp soar, my mind open.

"Should we go upstairs?" His words were muffled by his mouth on my throat, my collarbone.

"No. No way." I yanked at the skirt of my sundress, pulling it up, and I wrapped my legs around him tighter.

7

The next morning, Theo was up by six and ready to leave ten minutes later, kissing me on my closed eyes, his soft hair brushing over my face.

"I've got to get to work," he said. "Bunch of meetings today." Theo had founded a Web design software company while he was in high school. He went to Stanford on a full-ride scholarship, but dropped out after a year. I'd been told he was making millions and millions now. We didn't much talk about work. Truly, we didn't *talk* much at all.

I pulled him toward me and kissed him, then we murmured our goodbyes. When he was gone, I lay in bed, eyes still closed, replaying the night. My bedroom felt thick with heat from the memories.

I fell back to sleep, and when I woke up at eight, my mind drifted to my dad. Or, should I say, to that man in the stairwell.

I called my brother. "How are you?"

"Nervous. I have to go into the radio station today to fill out paperwork and meet with the head producer."

"Don't be nervous. Everyone loves you."

He laughed. "Thanks, Iz, but c'mon, everyone loves me at a party. Everyone loves me at a bar. This is a *job*."

"It's so weird to hear you say the *J* word. You *want* to do this, right?"

"I do. I really do. I was up all night thinking about it."

"You were?" I couldn't hide the surprise in my voice. Charlie never stayed up all night—not to party, not to be bothered about girls, not to fret about anything. If Chicago were in the grips of a natural disaster, the city being swept into Lake Michigan by a violent, massive tornado, Charlie would land in the lake, find something to use as a raft and lie down for the night, happy to let the jostling waves put him to sleep.

"You'll be fine," I said. I told him what I used to look for when I was searching for a new assistant. As I thought of working at the law firm and how I'd eventually hired my amazing assistant, Q, I felt rather misty-eyed about those days in a way I hadn't when going through them.

Then I asked Charlie about the book, the one our dad used to read to us. "Do you have it?" That book was one of the few objects that reminded me sharply of my dad and made me feel close to him, or the man he used to be. After the other night, I wanted that.

"I think I left it at Mom's house with a bunch of other books the last time I moved."

"Perfect." My mother had other books of my father's, too. Maybe looking at them would give me some sense of him, tell me something about him.

A pause. "Iz, be careful with all this."

"All what?" I threw back my sheets and stood up. The image that greeted me in the mirror over my dresser was comical. My long red hair was stringy in parts, extra curly in others, springing from my head and falling around my shoulders in crazed coils. My neck was splotchy from being kissed so many times. I tugged down a corner of the T-shirt I slept in. There was a red spot—a bite mark—on the top of my left breast. *I'm scarred,* I thought. And I was not unhappy about it.

"You know Dad is dead, Iz," Charlie said. "Has been for a long time."

"There was no body."

"When you crash a helicopter into a huge lake, there's a good chance the body won't be recovered. Seriously, Iz, don't let being out of work and away from Sam make you nuts."

"I'm not nuts." I looked at that bite mark. "And right now I'm okay about Sam."

"I know. But, hey, learn from your brother. *Use* the time you have when you're out of work. Go have a glass of wine."

"It's 9 a.m."

"Exactly. You're already an hour late."

We hung up, and I walked to the kitchen, opened my fridge. I thought of Charlie's words and considered a half-full bottle of pinot grigio. The thought made me nauseous. Charlie and I were simply different. We'd always known that. No reason to take my unemployment and turn it into alcohol dependency.

An hour later, I was at my mom's. It was one of my mother's greatest pleasures to give or loan her children something, even something mundane, because it meant she was a part of our lives; it meant she was needed.

If I was, for example, on the phone with my mother and casually mentioned I needed lightbulbs, my mother would inevitably say, in a quick voice, which counted as excited for her, "I've got lightbulbs. What kind do you need? What wattage?" I would tell her that the hardware store was closer than her house, that I would get them there, and inevitably she would be disappointed.

So that morning, I called and asked if I could borrow a pair of earrings I liked and maybe a book.

"Of course!" she said quickly, before giving me a summary of the three books she'd finished in the last week.

When she opened her door, she was already showered and dressed for the day in a cream skirt and silver silk blouse. She hugged me. "Do you want me to make you some green tea?"

I held up my Starbucks cup. "Already got it."

"There are four pairs of earrings on the counter in the kitchen. Take all of them. Meanwhile, I have to help Spence with something." She stopped. "Oh, and take anything you want from the library."

I walked through her house to the library, a cozy, winter-hideaway room off the kitchen where none of us went in the summer. It was loaded with bookshelves and plump leather chairs. Although it had French doors that looked onto the back garden, they were partially obscured with yellow velvet drapes.

My mother had a desk in there, where she worked on her charity, an organization called the Victoria Project, which helped widowed women with children. A few stacks of paper sat on the desk, but it was the slow time of the year for the project, and so the library was as pristine as the rest of my mother's house. I drifted to her fiction section and perused some novels, but my eyes kept moving upward, to the shelf at the top right, the one above the autobiographies, the one that required a step stool to reach.

A wooden stool with two steps was tucked to the side of the shelves. I pulled it over and climbed the steps. I felt a little dizzy as I did so, part of me remembering climbing down the dark steps the other night, another part of me woozy with the sense of climbing now into the past.

These were my father's books. I easily found the one Charlie and I talked about. *Poems & Prayers for the Very Young.*

I took it off the shelf and stepped off the stool, drawing my fingers over the cover, over the drawing of the two children on the front. I felt flooded by snippets of recollection—my dad's hands opening that book; me, excitedly pointing to a poem I wanted to hear.

I flipped, reading the first lines. *I wake in the morning early. And always, the very first thing…*

What did my dad do first thing in the morning these days?

I chastised myself a little for asking the question. What were the chances that he was really alive? Was this something I'd concocted from the recesses of my mind to distract myself from the fact that my life was stuttering?

Yet here I was on a Tuesday morning, when I should have been working (or at least looking for work), idly perusing my mother's bookshelves, stepping back in time. Later, I told myself. Later I would look for a job, then I would sort through the night with Theo and what it meant, if anything. I would call Sam for the first time in weeks and see how he was doing, how *we* were doing.

I put the book down on my mother's desk and stepped back up on the stool. A few of my dad's textbooks were there, a couple of those novels he used to read and some historical books dealing with the history of Southern Italy and others on uprisings in Italy and Greece.

My father was half Italian on his mother's side, and he always had a taste for learning about his heritage. I opened the history books one by one, flipping through them. The pages were golden with age. I searched for notes my father might have made, passages he might have underlined, but there was nothing like that.

I looked at a book about urban regeneration in Naples. I flipped through the pages the way I had with the other books. Again, no idle thoughts were scribbled into the margins, nothing that told me what my dad was thinking as he read the lines. But at the end, I found something sandwiched tight between the back cover and the last page. A newspaper clipping, dated February 1970.

The clipping was small, almost ashy to the touch, and like the book pages, it was yellowed. I unfolded it and read the headline. *Thieves Kill Man at Shell Station.*

I began to read the text and flinched when I saw the name of the victim—Kelvin McNeil. Suddenly, I remembered my dad talking to me one night, telling me a story, but this one wasn't from a book. It was about his own deceased father, the one who would never meet his grandkids.

You would have called him Grandpa Kelvin, he'd said, *and he was a great man. He loved your grandmother very much. He always said the best thing he did was marry her.*

Grandma O? I asked.

My father had nodded, smiled. Grandma O was Oriana, my dad's mom. She lived in Phoenix, having moved out there from the East Coast when it was still a desert and not a suburb. Because of the distance, I only saw her about once a year. She'd died in a car accident a month before my father.

I got down from the step stool, held the article closer and read it.

Kelvin McNeil, it said, had pulled his vehicle, a 1969 F100 truck, into a Shell Station. Five minutes later, a neighbor screamed from an apartment next door. Police arrived at the scene and found McNeil lying dead beside his truck, the victim of a stabbing to his chest and abdomen, his wallet stolen. The keys were still in the ignition.

8

Dez Romano watched Michael DeSanto pace his office.

"We've gone over this," Michael said, "but there's got to be something I'm missing, you know?"

Dez decided to say nothing.

Michael kept pacing. "When my wife met her last year, she said her name was Isabel Bristol. She said she was a lawyer who moved here from L.A."

"Did you have someone check the California Bar records?"

"Yeah. No one with that name."

Dez reached forward to his desk and picked up a program from the Naples opera house, which he'd gotten on his trip there two weeks ago. The opera had been Puccini's *Turandot.* He leafed through the program, remembering the heat in the opera house, the women waving fans in front of their faces, the swell of the orchestra's music, the lone, clear note of the alto that cut through the heat and made everyone think of no one but her.

Michael kept pacing, kept talking about the redhead. Even though he was out on bail for the money laundering he'd done for Dez and the Camorra, the case, from what Dez had heard, was nearly lock solid. Michael would most likely be heading to a federal pen for something like ten years. Dez's source had also told him that although the authorities could prove Michael had been laundering funds for a company in the suburbs called Advent Corporation, they couldn't tie the ownership of the company to Dez or anyone in the Camorra. The attorneys Dez had originally paid to structure Advent Corporation had charged him astronomically, but they'd been worth every penny.

As far as Dez could tell, it was only Michael, and his word, that could bring Dez down, and so Dez wanted to keep Michael as happy as possible, until he could pat him on the shoulder and tell him he'd see him after prison. He had promised Michael that he would always have a job with him, a place in Dez's system, and a hell of a lot of money when he got out. And Michael was happy to be a cog in the wheel.

So now Dez watched Michael stalk and talk in front of his desk. It was tough to take Michael's energy. Dez tuned him out. He was thinking of that alto, and yes, he was thinking of the redhead. In fact, he'd been thinking of little but her since Sunday night when he'd first seen her at the bar, her head dipped down toward her cell phone, her face grimacing at what she read there, the way the purple silk of her dress had slipped down one shoulder. At that moment, she struck him as exactly the kind of woman he wanted now that he was divorced. She looked educated, well brought up. But she also looked like a hell of a lot of fun.

And he'd been right. Dinner was a blast. And a turn-on.

But sex wasn't why he was thinking about her now. No, not at all. Another emotion drove his thoughts, one just as primal, but much more violent.

9

"What was dad working on when he died?"

My mother turned from the kitchen counter, where she was collecting her cell phone, putting it in her purse. Since I'd come out of her library, she had been talking about Spence, how it was so funny that sometimes he couldn't seem to dress himself. I hadn't known how to segue into the topic again, so I just blurted it out.

My mom cocked her head. I watched her intently for her reaction, not wanting to upset her, but she just blinked a few times, shook her head a little as if she was surprised, and said, "Why these questions all of a sudden?"

I was sitting on a tall chair at the island. "I don't know. I've just been thinking about him, I guess."

She turned back to her purse. "It makes sense, I suppose."

"What do you mean?"

"Well, you're at a transition point in your life, a time when you can go one way or another, and it's usually at those times that we look back and try to make some sense of it all, see if we've done the right things, if we've ended up with the right people. And we remember people who aren't with us anymore."

"Is that what you do? I mean, do you think about whether you ended up with the right people, wonder if you did the right things?"

My mother turned around again and looked at me. She put her hands on the counter behind her and leaned back.

In the last year, I had learned something about Victoria McNeil, something she thought no one else would ever know. We hadn't spoken about it since. Not directly. But now, I think we both knew I was referring, obliquely, to the topic, and yet we both knew the specifics would remain unspoken. My mother was from the school of holding your emotional cards close to your heart, and after all she'd been through in her life, I respected that.

A thump from above us, then another. Spence dropping something upstairs. He could be clumsy, especially when he was distracted and running late. My mother smiled at the sound. "I ended up with the right people," she said. "And you?"

"Well, since I haven't ended up with anyone, it's kind of hard to say right now."

"What about that young guy you mentioned?"

I laughed a little. I hadn't told my mother how young he was.

"What?" she said.

"Nothing. I saw him last night."

"Fun?"

I remembered the feel of my legs around him, my back against the rough wall of the stairwell. I thought of him later in bed, curving around me, how he fell asleep first and I traced the ribbon of red tattooed in a trail down his arm. "Yeah, it was fun."

"And so?"

I shrugged. "Who knows?"

Theo hadn't said anything specific about getting together again. It gave me a tickle of discomfort. Was all that stuff about dying to see me just about one thing—sex? Then again, what did I care?

"And how's Sam?" my mom asked.

"We haven't spoken in a few weeks."

"Do you miss him?"

I shifted around on the chair. "Yes. And no. I mean, I miss lots of things about him, and I miss having someone in my life, but sometimes I don't mind being alone. I don't mind deciding what *I* want to eat for dinner and what I want to do for the weekend. I like that part a lot." I looked down at the book my dad used to read me, played with its cover. Inside, I had tucked the clipping about my grandfather's death. "But then again, sometimes it's lonely."

My mother chuckled. "And so goes the circle of life." She nodded at the book. "So all this about your dad…"

"Yeah, I don't know." *You're okay now, Boo.*

My mother stood away from the counter, collecting other things in her purse—her keys, a small water bottle. "You asked what he was working on when he died. I don't know all the specifics. I really never did. Your dad didn't talk much when it came to his work."

"Didn't that bother you?"

"No. I knew he had to keep quiet because he was working sensitive cases."

"He worked for the Detroit police, right? Wasn't it just the usual robberies and stuff?"

"Your father worked out of the Detroit police office, and yes, he worked on things like robberies and even a serial killer, but he also profiled for the federal government. The primary case he was working on when he died was federal."

"What was it?"

"A Mob case. The killing of the Rizzato Brothers."

"A Mob case?" I repeated. I thought of Dez Romano, Michael DeSanto.

"Your dad had a certain knack for organized-crime cases. They were always asking him to consult."

"Did he ever get any threats from them?"

"From whom? The Mob?" My mother shook her head. "He was just an average consultant. Never in the forefront."

I thought about the man running behind Dez and Michael as they chased me out of Gibsons. He hadn't been at the forefront there, either. But somehow, whoever he was, I doubted that he was just an average consultant.

10

Louis ("Louie") and Joseph ("Big Joe") Rizzato were born and raised in Chicago after their parents emigrated from Ischia, Italy, an island off the Gulf of Naples. The Brothers Rizzato, as they were sometimes called, became involved in criminal activity early in life, eventually became Mob enforcers and were known for their violent and often cruel tactics. Louie rose to the position of Mob boss, but roughly six months after that, both brothers disappeared on the same night.

I looked away from the computer for a moment.

I had gone home from my mother's and called Aunt Elena. No answer. I hung up without leaving a message. I wanted to get her on the phone, rather than crisscrossing with messages for weeks.

I looked then at the stack of résumés by my keyboard, copies of ones I'd sent out and now just waiting for me to follow up on them. When I worked at the firm of Baltimore & Brown, I specialized in entertainment law, mostly because Forester Pickett, the media mogul, had taken a shine to me and given me a large chunk of his work—negotiating contracts for radio and TV personalities, defending the company or hiring local counsel, when cases of all kinds were filed against it. The phrase "trial by fire" had never been more apt. I hadn't known what I was doing when I started, but I learned, and I learned fast, if only because there was no other way to stay afloat.

When Forester died and I lost all my work, I'd been set adrift, and unfortunately the city didn't have much entertainment law work to go around. When actors, musicians and directors from Chicago hit it big, they usually headed for one of the coasts. And so, unless I wanted to move, I was going to have to start thinking creatively about my employment possibilities. I'd already contacted most of the big law firms months ago, and after that attempt rendered nothing I could get excited about, I tried a gig as an on-air legal analyst. I even initiated an investigative report on a very wealthy but very crooked attorney, and that investigation eventually uncovered a class-action lawsuit scam. But after my bizarre run-in with the law as a murder suspect, no station was jumping at the chance to put me back in front of the camera. Hence the pile of résumés I'd sent out for in-house positions at different corporations.

But I was too curious about that newspaper clipping about my grandfather, and what my mom had said about my dad, to make follow-up calls. I had pushed away the stack of résumés and done an Internet search for the Rizzato Brothers. And found that description of them—*known for their violent and often cruel tactics.*

I sat back, away from the computer, and tried to think.

My father had been working on a Mob case—that of the Rizzato Brothers—when he died. The Rizzato Brothers were Mob enforcers, one eventually a Mob boss, and they had disappeared. Meanwhile, I had been hanging out, rather innocently, with a Mob figure and was being chased by him when suddenly a vision appeared—an auditory one at least—of my dead father.

It sounded like a load of crazy.

Enough of this. I turned off the computer monitor and lined up my stack of résumés, then started making job-hunting calls.

I got a lot of *Sorry, nothing right now* kind of responses. I got a few vague *We haven't decided anything yet, but we'll let you know* kind of answers. I got a lot of anxiety as it seemed that nothing was opening up and nothing would anytime soon.

I looked at my watch. Six o'clock in the evening Rome time. I picked up the phone and dialed the number for my aunt Elena.

She answered this time. "*Cara!*" she said, hearing my voice.

It had been so long, and we chatted about everything—Charlie, my employment status, Chicago. We got into that seamless conversational space that weaves around in a pleasantly aimless way. I had always loved my aunt, and the older I got, the more I enjoyed her.

But as with my mom, I couldn't just dive in and say, *Is it possible your brother is alive, or do you think I'm losing it?* And although I'd told Maggie I would contact Elena about visiting, I hadn't spoken with her in over a year. It seemed awkward to suggest a houseguest too quickly.

Instead, it was less uncomfortable to say, "So, tell me about your mom and dad." I had the book my father used to read on the edge of my desk. I pulled it forward, opened it and took out the yellowed clipping. *Thieves Kill Man at Shell Station.*

"What about them, *cara?* They were wonderful people. I guess you never got to meet my father."

"No. And I've been thinking about family lately. Grandma O was Italian and Grandpa Kelvin was Scottish, right?"

"That's right. Their love affair was something of a scandal. No one in my mother's family had been involved with anyone who wasn't Italian. Actually, no one had ever been involved with someone who wasn't originally from Naples, if you can believe that. She met my father at a drugstore. It was in the winter, and they were both buying cough drops. My mother, Oriana, was a few years out of high school. My father was a few years older than her. It was one of those things you hear about—they saw each other, they both looked at shelves without talking, and when my father finally got up the courage to speak to her, they didn't stop. They talked for hours in that aisle."

"And that was that? They were just in love and they lived happily ever after?" *When had I gotten so cynical?*

"Well, no. There was resistance to them dating. Her family wasn't happy at all, especially when they got engaged only six months later. But like I said, they were in love."

I thought of Sam. We had been in love once. There had never been a doubt about that.

"Did they stay in love?"

"Yes, always." She sighed a little. "I used to wonder if I was only seeing that love through the eyes of a child, if maybe it didn't really exist, or maybe as an adult I would realize that it was very different than what I'd thought. But no, now that I am an adult..." She laughed. "*Incredibilemente,* I am much more than an adult. Well, I see how pure their love was. It wasn't always easy for them, especially my dad, coming into this Italian family. His family was already scattered around the country and didn't see each other often, but my parents had this powerful connection. Everyone could see it."

I drew my finger over the news clipping. "And then Grandpa Kelvin was killed."

Elena was quiet, then, "Yes, he was stabbed."

"At a gas station."

"How did you know that?"

"I found a news clipping."

"Ah. Well, yes, you're right. He was putting air in his tire one night at the side of a gas station, and he was killed." A pause. "Did your father ever talk about that?"

I got a zing through me—*your father.* "No. He never mentioned it. I guess we were too young."

"Yes, too young," she repeated. "And you and I never spoke about this, either."

"No. How old were you when your dad died?"

"Sixteen."

I felt envious for a second, thinking that she had eight more years with her father than I did with mine. "And my dad was eighteen then."

"That's right."

"I know he went to college." I could remember my father telling me this. "And you moved to Italy to be with family, right? After Grandpa Kelvin died?"

"Yes. My mother was having a very hard time. She went to Phoenix to try and forget. Her family thought it would be best if I finished high school somewhere else instead of going with her. They thought it would be good for me to be away, too, somewhere new where everything wasn't about my father."

"So you went to Naples?"

"No, I lived with a cousin in a lovely area, in Frascati, in the hills, outside of Rome."

"Was it hard for you to be away from the U.S.?"

"Yes and no. Italy is certainly different from the United States, different from every country, in fact. But throughout my whole life my mother had been telling us about Italy. The stories about Italy were our nighttime tales. I found much of that had sunk in and made a difference when I moved here."

"How often did you get to see my dad after that?"

"Not very often." Her voice was somber. "That was one of the hardest things."

"Were you not close?"

"It wasn't that." She said nothing else.

"So what was it?"

"I suppose it was simply that he lived in the States, and I lived in Italy. I fell in love with the country, and I stayed."

Could he be alive? "What do you know about how he died?"

"He died in a helicopter crash, Isabel." She said it like *Ee-sabel.* "You know that." A pause. "Did your mother not talk to you about this when you were young?"

"Yes, but I suppose that as an adult, I wonder about the details."

"Such a tragedy. It was horrible."

"Do you still think about him?"

"Of course. All the time."

Do you ever see him like I did? Do you ever hear him?

But before I said anything, Elena was suddenly saying she needed to go, that it was lovely to talk to me.

"I had some other questions about my dad," I said.

"And I'd love to answer them, but right now I must go. I have a work dinner."

"Where are you working?"

"I'll tell you next time we talk, *cara.*"

It was obvious she wanted to get off the phone. "We should stay in better touch," I said.

"Yes, *cara,* you are right."

"Do you have an e-mail address?"

"Of course. We e-mail, we text. We're very forward in Rome. Everyone walks around the city with their cell phones attached to their cheeks." She gave me her e-mail address. "Must go. *Ciao, ciao.*" And then she hung up.

I leaned forward and turned on the monitor again.

Although their bodies have never been found, copious amounts of blood (identified as blood from both Louie and Big Joe) were found in the basement of their parents' home the day after their disappearance. No arrests have ever been made in the disappearance of the Brothers Rizzato.

11

The next few days skidded by quickly, an inefficient bunch of days where I thought of little but my father and checked my BlackBerry religiously for a call or e-mail from my aunt.

I had e-mailed her the morning after our talk, mentioning that I might visit Italy. I heard nothing back. I called the next day and left a message this time. Again nothing.

I sent out some more résumés, made follow-up calls and a few halfhearted attempts to establish new contacts. Still nothing.

I grew frustrated, short-tempered. I could think of little else to do about my job search *or* my dad search. I talked to Mayburn but he was in too much of a twist about Lucy and the fact that she was living with Michael to be of much help. I couldn't shake the feeling that if I could just speak to Aunt Elena again and find what else she knew, if anything, about my dad's death, then maybe I would know where to go from there. Or, even better, I could just put the whole thing away. I didn't want to go any further with my mother because she had endured a lot of loss over her life. The last thing she needed was her bored, out-of-work daughter shooting around assertions about what she'd *maybe* heard in a dark stairwell.

Meanwhile, the one thing getting me through my week was someone else on a dark stairwell, and it wasn't my dad.

Theo had called Tuesday night, and again Wednesday and Thursday, and each night I met him on the stairwell, and each night it was the same. And yet even better.

He worked during the days at his software company, and so he was gone every morning, leaving me flushed and sleepy and satisfied. It was as if Theo rounded down the sharp angles that I collected every day and that I'd been collecting from my months off work.

Friday morning, I got up an hour after Theo left and found a message on my voice mail. It was from Elena. She'd left it at three in the morning Chicago time, a vague, "Hello, *cara.* I am sorry I haven't been able to get back to you. Let's chat soon." And that was it. She didn't mention my possible visit.

I called her again. Heard nothing back. I e-mailed again, telling her once more that I was considering a visit and mentioning a few dates. I didn't go so far as to inquire if I could stay with her. Even though we were family, our contact had been so minimal over the years it felt rude.

On Saturday morning, I received an e-mail. *Cara,* she wrote, *I do not think you would enjoy Rome in the summer. There are so many tourists, and it is about to get very hot. Also, I am busy working in a new* galleria *that has just opened in the last few years. It is a personal passion of mine, very close to my heart. Perhaps you should come in October or November?*

I sat back from the computer as my cell phone rang.

"Izzy?" a woman's voice said when I answered. "It's Lucy DeSanto."

"Lucy!" My voice went high. She was about the last person I expected to hear from.

In my mind, I pictured her—a tiny, toned blonde with a pixie haircut and a big smile.

"Hi," she said. "So, I heard that you ran into Michael."

Michael ran after *me,* I wanted to say, but instead I just mumbled a chagrined, "Yeah, I did."

Lucy and I had a brief but complicated history. The cold fact was that I'd originally met her because Mayburn asked me to pretend I was a neighborhood mom (and wanted to be her friend) so I could get inside her house and onto her husband's computer. The ruse worked, and the evidence I collected landed Michael with a federal indictment. But it also worked its guilt on me. I genuinely liked Lucy, and I felt bad duping her. When she found out what Mayburn and I had been doing, I thought she would be pissed as hell. But instead, Lucy—sweet, elegant Lucy—had been forgiving. She'd always been in love with her husband, but she hadn't known he was involved with the Mafia. That knowledge had devastated her, and yet she was glad the secret was out. Then she'd started up with Mayburn, and the last few times I'd seen her they'd seemed over-the-moon happy.

And yet now here we were, back on familiar territory, where I found myself apologizing, once again, for messing around in her life.

"That's okay," she said. "I know you did it for John."

I chuckled. "It's funny to hear him called John." I'd met Mayburn because he was the private investigator often hired by my former law firm. And no one called him anything but Mayburn. "He misses you," I said.

"I miss him." She sighed. "But, Izzy, I have kids. And I want the kids to grow up with their dad, with a family that's a whole unit. I loved Michael for a long time, and he says he's done with that business."

I thought of Dez and Michael standing in Gibsons,

looking so similar. "I hope I didn't complicate things for you. Mayburn just wants to make sure you're safe."

A moment of quiet. "I want to talk to you about John."

Suddenly, there was a shriek in the background.

"Lucy?" I said, alarmed.

Another sigh. "It's my kids. I've been promising to take them to the nature museum for weeks now, and we're finally going this morning." She paused. "Is there any way you'd want to come with us?"

"I'd love to see you, but…"

"What?"

"Well, does Michael know you're asking me?"

"No. He's already gone this morning. He's networking to try and find a new job."

"Hmm, that's what I'm supposed to be doing, too."

"Look, I'll tell you one thing. I'm trying to make this work with my husband, and I'm trying to be honest with him so he'll be honest with me. But I am *not* going to tell him I'm seeing you. No way. I'm just so confused." A pause. "I really need a friend. Someone who knows John."

I trusted Lucy. It was impossible not to. But still… "I'm not sure, Lucy."

A pocket of silence. "I understand." Then a tiny sniffle. "I just feel like I'm going crazy. *Crazy.*"

"God, I'm so sorry."

One of her kids yelled in the background. "Noah, give me one minute!" she said, sounding as if her voice might break. "I have to go, Izzy. Don't worry about it."

The heartache in her voice killed me. "Of course I'll meet you."

"Really?"

"Sure."

"Oh, thank you. *Thank* you. We're going to the nature museum at ten. Do you know where it is?"

"Fullerton, near Lake Shore?"

"That's it. Inside, there's a big stuffed bear to the right. My kids love it, so we'll be there for at least fifteen minutes." Another shriek in the background. "I'll see you there, Izzy."

I called Mayburn and told him. "She wants to talk to me about you."

"What about me?" he said quick, anxious.

"I'm not sure."

"Well, as much as I want to hear what she says, I'm not sure I like this. What about Michael?"

"She said he'd left the house. And she's not telling him we're meeting. Do you trust her?"

"Hell, yes."

"Me, too. I'll call you when we're done."

At a few minutes before ten, I parked my Vespa outside the Peggy Notebaert Nature Museum, an oddly unnatural-looking structure made of glass and sand-colored steel. It was surrounded, however, by the rolling, green lawns of Lincoln Park and gold ornamental grasses that fluttered in a balmy breeze. Behind the building, ducks in a pond glided by a snapshot view of the skyline.

The North Pond Café, once a favorite of Sam's and mine, was at the other end of that pond, and I stood outside the museum for a moment, gazing in that direction, thinking of the last time we were there. It was a few months ago, when we were trying, and failing, to patch up our relationship.

I made myself shut down the memories. Inside the museum, the sounds of children's voices filled the place. I paid and made my way past parents corralling kids inside the entrance. A few steps down the hallway, I easily found the giant white polar bear standing on its haunches, its mouth open in a ferocious, silent roar.

I looked around, didn't see Lucy or her kids. I checked my watch, wondering if I'd misunderstood her. I was about to call her cell phone, when I heard someone shout my name.

Lucy was hustling down the hallway, wearing white jeans cuffed at the bottom and a light blue cotton blouse with short sleeves. She had a kid by each hand. Noah, a boy of about five or six, had a smear of something red on his face, which was also red with frustration. "I don't want to see the bear again!" he whined. Noah's little sister, Belle, was a three-year-old mini replica of Lucy, who looked at her big brother with a calm kind of wonder that said, *What's all the fuss about?*

I hugged Lucy when they reached me and took Belle by the hand. Lucy, in turn, hauled Noah up and onto her hip, although the kid looked too big to carry around.

"Can you say hi to mommy's friend?" she said.

He shook his head hurriedly. "I don't want to see the bear!"

"How about the butterfly room?" I said. I'd heard lots about the museum's famous butterfly exhibit but had never seen it myself.

Noah's eyes got big. He looked at his mom for confirmation. "Butterfly room?"

She nodded, wiped at the red spot on his cheek and set him back on the ground, where he took off. He obviously knew the place.

"Thanks," Lucy said as we tailed Noah, pulling Belle along with us.

We followed Noah upstairs, down a hallway, past exhibits of stuffed prairie animals to a dimly lit hallway with two sets of swinging rubber doors at the end.

Noah jumped on his toes outside the first doors where a sign read *Enter.* "Can I, Mommy?"

Lucy laughed, nodded. Noah pushed the doors open, and we followed him into a bright humid room full of lush green trees, shrubs and plants. And on every surface—butterflies. Some were small and bright yellow. Others were the size of a fist with complicated zigzag bolts of color on their backs. Some were as large as a human head, their wings spread wide on the high glass ceiling of the room.

"Mommy, look!" Noah dashed into the room and grabbed a laminated card that was essentially a butterfly menu. "I see this one!" He gestured excitedly at a picture of a black butterfly with iridescent blue and white markings, then pointed at a bush where the real-life butterfly perched and fluttered.

"I see one," little Belle said, waving at a blue butterfly on a plant frond.

Noah pointed at the huge butterflies on the ceiling. They were gray but with a glistening green sheen to them. "Look, Mom, those are moths."

"Let me see," Belle said. She tugged at the card, trying to snatch it from her brother's hand. "It's mine!"

"Belle Josephine, you play nice," Lucy said. "Share with your brother. Now go find more butterflies."

Off they went, clutching the laminated card between them, two blond heads swiveling, four little hands pointing in awe.

Lucy and I walked to the side of the room and took a seat on a stone bench.

"Great to see you," I said.

"You, too."

"I'm sorry if I caused any trouble when I saw Michael the other night."

She ran a thumb over a fingernail on the other hand that was perfectly painted shell-pink. "John has to let me make decisions for myself. He has to respect me right now and give me space."

I nodded. "I know. I told him that, too. I think he's just afraid to lose you forever."

"I'm afraid to lose him, too." Tears popped into the inside corners of her eyes. She squeezed her eyes shut and wiped the tears swiftly with her hand. "But I need to do this for myself. I knew Michael still saw Dez socially. So telling me that they're meeting at Gibsons doesn't change anything. *I* need to be the one who decides if Michael is good for me or not, whether we can raise our family together or not." She gave a sad laugh. "All I've ever wanted in my life is to marry one wonderful man and have a few wonderful kids and live a simple, happy life. For a while, I thought I had that. Then everything changed, and now I'm trying to put that dream back together..." She shrugged. "But the truth is I'm no longer sure what I want."

"I know what you mean. I had Sam, and I wanted to be married, and I didn't think much about what would come after that, because it just seemed like our whole life was lined up—my work, his work, us together. And then the plug got pulled and now I have no clue what to wish for or what to plan."

"Are you and Sam talking?"

I shook my head. "Not really." I gently batted away a reddish butterfly that was flapping around in front of my face. "We've tried talking, and we've tried acting like we were back together, but neither seemed to work. It's like we've lost this thing we had. This *thing* that was uniquely us. I've been meaning to call or stop by and see how he's doing."

"So you miss him, and you love him, but you're not sure if it's right to be with him right now?"

"Yeah."

Lucy nodded, her blue eyes scanning the room for her kids. "That's what it's like for me with John."

I studied her. "He's in love with you, you know."

Lucy's eyes zeroed in on mine. They gleamed with tears again. A huge, orange butterfly sailed by. "I love him, too. He knows that."

"I think he's also afraid that Michael could be involved with those guys again."

"Mom, Mom!" Belle ran up to Lucy, waving the card. "I saw five butterflies!"

"Good job, Belle," Lucy said.

Belle turned and toddled away again.

Lucy looked at me. Two white butterflies quivered behind her head. "What do *you* think?"

"I didn't get a chance to chat with Michael that night." I swallowed hard, thinking of the fear that had shot through my belly as I'd crouched behind that car. "But I think they looked like two men who worked together pretty closely. *Now*. Not like two people who *used* to work together."

Lucy shook her head, her light hair shimmering in the bright lights of the room. "He was just there to tell Dez a few last things." She squeezed my hand. "By the way, Izzy, be careful. Dez is a bad guy."

"How so?"

"I don't know how to explain it. I mean, he seems charming, don't you think?"

I nodded. "If I hadn't known he was shady, I would've definitely gone out with him."

"But there's more beyond that charming front. For one thing, he can be really cruel, especially to Michael."

"Michael doesn't seem the type to take shit from anyone."

"Well, that's usually true. Michael can be obstinate and even scary when he's angry."

"Oh, I know that. I remember when I was in his office, trying to get onto his laptop."

Both of us were silent for a moment. We had never talked specifically about how I had helped to bring her husband down.

Lucy shook her head as if not wanting to think about it. "Anyway, Dez is incredibly arrogant. He expects everyone to jump around and do whatever he wants. It's like he thinks he's a king, and he's *entitled* to being treated like a king." She wore an irritated scowl on her face. "I wouldn't see him again, Izzy."

"Trust me, I'm *not* going to be seeing Dez again. He doesn't even know my real name."

"And I've never told Michael your name. I never even told him that we saw each other when he was in jail."

I started to reply, but something across the room caught my eye. Something dark. Something almost hidden behind a huge fern. I looked closer, jutting my head forward as I squinted across the room.

It was a man, I realized. A man wearing black jeans and a black jacket. He moved to the left, blocking the doors we had come in. My eyes searched for the exit doors, saw another man.

And right then I realized I was wrong. I *would,* in fact, be seeing Dez Romano again. He was standing right in front of the exit, his arms crossed, and he was looking right at me.

12

My eyes shot around the place. There had been at least six other people in the room when we entered. Now it was just Lucy and me and the kids, who were bending over a fern in the corner, pointing at hovering butterflies.

"Lucy," I said, my voice low.

Her eyes narrowed. She looked at the man by the entrance. She called quietly for her kids to come to her.

"Lucy," I said again, pointing as surreptitiously as possible to Dez Romano, who stood, blocking the exit, giving a hostile, cold stare that scared the hell out of me.

She stood. "Dez, what are you doing here?"

He took a few steps toward us, arms still crossed. He wore soft-looking camel pants and a houndstooth jacket. "I came to say hello to Suzanne. Or is it Isabel? Or should I say 'Izzy'?" He gave me a cool, level stare. "Or wait. Should I say Izzy *McNeil?* That's right, isn't it?"

I stood alongside Lucy. We looked at each other; her eyes were pained.

"I'm sorry," she said, her voice still low.

"Did you know this was going to happen?" I whispered.

"No!" Her eyes went big, scared. "God, no."

"Then how?"

"Michael must be taping my phone conversations. Or maybe everything in my house." Her voice was anguished.

"Lucy, you should get the kids out of here."

She glanced around, and raising her voice said, "Noah. Belle. Come here."

The humidity in the room seemed to be pushing downward, making it hard to breathe.

Dez smiled at me. A triumphant smile. "You and I have some talking to do, little girl."

The kids ran up to Lucy. They were quiet, eyes big, as if they'd just noticed the heavy, frightening weight in the room. Lucy wrapped her arms around them. "Where's Michael?" she said.

Dez shrugged, didn't take his eyes off me. "No idea. We don't work together anymore. Why don't you take off, Lucy?"

"I'm not leaving my friend."

"Oh, you're friends, are you?"

I turned to her. "Just go. If something happened to the kids I'd feel terrible."

Lucy looked conflicted.

"It's okay," I said. I leaned toward her and whispered, "Call Mayburn when you're outside." My whisper sounded calm, even authoritative, but panic was thumping in my chest.

Dez glanced at the guy in black and nodded. The guy took a few steps into the room. He looked about my age, maybe thirty, but his face was twisted somehow, as if he'd seen centuries of wars and strife. His neck was tattooed with a multitude of what looked like grotesque images—bloody knives, disembodied heads and a large circle with a capital *A* inside it.

"Mommy?" Belle said, her voice a scared whimper.

"Lucy, go," I said.

The guy in black took another step into the room. So

did Dez. He waved a hand behind him at the exit. "See ya later, Lucy. We've got everything we need here."

It was said in such a demeaning tone that I could feel Lucy bristle. She threw her shoulders back, then hugged her kids closer, hesitating.

"Mom?" Noah asked.

"We're going home," she said. "And Izzy is coming with us." She started to move forward. She put a hand on my arm, tugging me with her.

"Oh, no," Dez said, laughing. "*Izzy* is not going anywhere." Beyond one of his shoulders, two black butterflies circled lazily, like tiny vultures around a corpse.

What did he want? What was he going to do?

"We're leaving," Lucy said, "and you're going to leave all of us alone."

Another chuckle, then the smile dropped. "Get the fuck out of here, Lucy, and take those kids, or I'm going to stop being nice about it."

A deafening siren pierced the room. The kids threw their hands over their ears.

Dez pulled a cell phone from his breast pocket, opened it, typed something in as if he was texting. The siren stopped in the room, although we could still hear it outside.

"The whole place is being evacuated," Dez said. "Small fire apparently."

Lucy and I looked at each other.

"Go." I nodded. "I'll be right behind you." I didn't know if I believed it, but she had to get the kids away from these guys.

She took the kids, walked toward the exit. She shot a scared look over her shoulder.

"Thatta girl, Lucy," Dez said in the same demeaning tone. He tried to pat her on the shoulder, but she flinched and glared at him.

She kept the kids moving and pushed through the exit doors.

Dez looked at the guy in black. "Make sure she gets all the way outside."

The guy left. Dez flashed that cold smile again. "Finally. We're alone. Just where I wanted you the other night."

His tone slithered. It seemed to wind through the heat to reach me. Why had I thought him fairly harmless on Sunday?

I coughed and forced my mind into the mode I used when I was nervous about a case and had to step up in front of a judge. "What can I do for you?"

"Oh, you're going to do a lot for me. A lot. You're going to start out by telling me who you work for."

"What makes you think I work for someone?"

"A girl like you isn't smart enough to try and fleece me on your own."

It was my turn to bristle. I'd rather be called anything other than stupid.

Dez saw it. He smiled, then looked me up and down slowly, lecherously.

I glanced at the exit door. The sirens outside kept screaming.

"You know what?" I started to walk right toward him. "Let's just cut the shit. I wasn't trying to fleece you. I work for the federal government. You're under surveillance." I had no idea what I was talking about, but the words had the effect I wanted. An uncertain look crossed Dez's face.

"You don't want to harm a federal agent," I continued. I thought of all the times Maggie had talked to me about sentencing hearings. "That'll get you another eighty-six months in prison." My heart was banging in my chest now, but still I kept walking toward him. "Leave me alone and you'll be fine. I've got nothing on you anyway."

Again, for a moment, he looked unsure. But he was still blocking the path to the exit. I seized the moment and veered to the right, toward the entrance doors.

Apparently, Dez wasn't as unsure as I'd thought. He moved fast, grabbing me by the arm, twisting it behind my back. "Don't walk away from me," he said. "Don't *ever* walk away from me."

I started shaking. I couldn't help it.

"Yeah, baby," Dez said in my ear, twisting my arm tighter behind me so that it felt it would pop out of the socket. "That's how I like it. I like you scared. I like you trembling. That's going to make this so much more fun."

I'd taken a self-defense class once in college. My mind scuttled about, trying to remember what I learned, what you were supposed to do. "No!" I yelled. That was the main thing I remembered from the class. "No!" I yelled again. It wasn't super helpful given that the fire alarm was still shrieking outside the room.

Yank. Dez twisted my arm tighter. I tried not to whimper, but a grimaced moan escaped from my throat.

"Yeah, that's it." Dez pulled my arm up and even tighter. "Feels nice, doesn't it? You're into pain, aren't you? That's good." His breath was hot, moist in my ear. "I don't care who you work for. I really don't. You stepped into the wrong pile of shit here, because I make an example of people who mess with me. I am going to fuck you up, girl. Bad." He chuckled. "I mean really bad. But you'll love it." His wet breath was whispering in my ear now. *Yank* again with my arm.

I turned my face away from his, then decided to try and use the momentum to my advantage. I swung my face back, and before he could react, *Crack!* I hit my forehead hard against his nose.

"Goddamn it!" he said. One arm still clenched mine,

but he raised his other hand to his face as if searching for swelling or blood. Suddenly, I remembered another tactic from that self-defense class. I raised my foot and brought it down hard on the top of his.

"You cunt!" The blow to the foot seemed only to anger him, not to slow him down. The arm he'd raised to his face shot to me now, but in that second, I ducked fast and managed to squirm out of his grasp. A huge urn with an exotic tree was just to my left. It was about as tall as me. I grasped it at the top and heaved it. I couldn't lift it, but I managed to get it rolling on its base, right at Dez.

It hit him, but he deflected it and the urn crashed to the floor, breaking into hundreds of shards of pottery, water pooling around our feet. I turned to run toward the entrance doors, but right then they opened. The guy dressed in black stepped inside. He looked over my shoulder for a second at Dez, then lunged toward me, pulling both arms behind my back, and facing me toward Dez.

Dez grinned coolly. "Isabel McNeil, meet Ransom. Ransom likes redheads, don't you?"

The guy behind me murmured something I couldn't exactly understand, a garbled, guttural string of words.

"After I get you, he gets you," Dez said. "And he likes pain as much as you."

I started trembling again. *What in the hell should I do?*

Dez took one step toward me, then another. I kept shaking, and Ransom kept gripping his meaty hands tighter around my arms, pulling me back against him.

Just then I saw something above Dez—one of the massive moths that had been on the glass ceiling. It fluttered behind Dez's head, almost as if it were dazzled by the sheen of his overapplied hair gel.

"Dude," Ransom said, followed by more guttural-sounding words. I could only make out, "*You got some—*"

"I got some what?" Dez said, his voice coy but menacing. He stared at my breasts. Took a step toward me. But then the moth decided to land. Right on Dez's head.

"What the fuck?" Dez screamed, batting at his hair. "What the fuck?"

But the moth wouldn't leave. In fact, it fluttered up for a second, then landed again, this time on his face.

"Fucking bug!" He squashed the thing with his hands, but it was as if he'd angered the moth's posse, because suddenly there were four of them, all flapping around Dez's face, while he swore and smacked at himself.

Ransom tried to drag me over to Dez, I guess to help him, but the minute his grip lessened the tiniest bit, I surged out of his clutches and dashed to the doors. I pushed through them and started running, yelling for help. But there was no one in the museum, just the screams of the fire alarm. I heard another sound behind me, though, and I looked over my shoulder. Dez and Ransom, sans the moths, were running after me and fast. I turned and kept hauling.

"Help!" I yelled once or twice, but I knew it was pointless. I ran downstairs, past an exhibit about rainwater. I could hear the footfalls of Dez and Ransom at the top of the stairs. I had to find somewhere to conceal myself before they got to the first floor. My eyes careened wildly around the place. But the floor plan was open—made so children could enjoy themselves and their parents could keep an eye on them. There were no nooks or crannies.

I kept running. I had to get outside before they did. I turned a corner and just then an arm shot out from a photo booth and pulled me hard. *Shit! Was it another one of Dez's guys?* Then I thought, *Dad?*

Still, my instincts made me struggle against it, until I heard a fierce whisper. "Jesus Christ, McNeil. Relax."

"Mayburn?"

He clamped his hand over my mouth and pulled me into the booth, one of those old-fashioned ones that print little strips of photos. Over the sirens, we heard footsteps pounding down the hallway.

"Quiet," Mayburn whispered.

I held my breath, froze my body.

The footsteps stopped. Where were they? What were they doing? With the sirens still ringing, we couldn't hear them now that they weren't running.

I held my breath so that I wouldn't move. With Mayburn's hand still over my mouth, I felt I was going to pass out. I shook his hand away from my face. Sucked in quiet lungfuls of breath.

"Hey, Ransom," I heard Dez say loudly. He must have been fifteen feet from us. "Ever get your picture taken in one of those booths?"

Ransom gurgled a response, which sounded like a sickening laugh.

"Yeah, let's get a picture." Dez's voice was closer now. "We've never had our picture taken together."

Ransom gurgled again, sounding closer, too.

I tried to turn to see Mayburn, so we could figure out what in the hell we were going to do, but then we heard a crash of glass, followed by shouting.

"It's the Chicago Fire Department!" someone yelled. "Is there anyone in the building?"

We heard the banging of boots on the floor.

"Sir! Sirs!" It must have been one of the firefighters yelling at Dez and Ransom. "Sirs, we have to evacuate the building. This way."

"We're okay," Dez shouted.

"Exit this way, sirs."

"Yeah, just a minute."

"Now!" yelled the firefighter. "We need you out of here." Boots pounded closer.

"Hey, don't touch me," Dez said.

"We're just evacuating you, sir. Follow me and I won't have to touch you."

Boots passed by the booth.

"We'll go," Dez said.

Mayburn and I sat frozen for a few minutes, the sounds of boots trailing down the hallway. When they were gone, I extricated myself from Mayburn and turned around. He wore jeans and a gray T-shirt with a Buddy Guy logo.

"Why didn't Dez tell the firefighters we were in here?" I asked.

Mayburn shrugged. "Probably because then he'd have to explain why someone was hiding from him and that would look suspicious. Might make the firefighters hold him for questioning, and I would guess that a guy like Dez doesn't like being questioned by the authorities."

"But he could be waiting outside for us right now."

"Yeah. We've got to get out through some other exit." Mayburn poked his head out of the booth. "It's clear." We heard footfalls from the floor above us. Probably more firefighters. "Let's go."

Mayburn and I ran down the hallway, farther into the museum. Most of the sirens had been turned off, although there were a few still shrieking. We found a glass door at the back of the building with a sign above it that read, *Emergency Exit Only.*

We pushed through it, and it set off another alarm. But finally we were outside. We ran along the footpath that hemmed the pond.

I glanced over my shoulder. "Oh, no!" Dez and Ransom were a hundred feet behind us, running, pissed-off looks on their faces.

Mayburn saw them. "Faster! My car is just on the other side of the bridge."

We sprinted along the path, past joggers and waddling ducks. We bolted in front of the North Pond Café. This time, I didn't stop to reflect about Sam. We ran under a fieldstone bridge.

"There!" Mayburn yelled, pointing at a tiny silver car, his late '60s Aston Martin coupe.

"You know I don't like that car," I said, hoofing toward it. "It's impossible to get in."

"Just shut up and get your ass inside, and this car will get us out of here." He ran to the driver's side and opened it, sliding in.

I was still standing outside the car, and when I looked behind me, Ransom and Dez were running under the bridge. "Hurry!"

Mayburn opened the door, and I folded myself into the low, little car.

Bang! Bang! Bang! Dez and Ransom had reached the back of the car and were slamming it with their fists. Mayburn started the engine, but Ransom and Dez were on either side. Dez was next to my window, and he grinned that lecherous grin, before he raised his fist and smashed it against the glass. The window cracked like a spiderweb.

I cried out, but it was nothing like Mayburn, who bellowed, "You motherfucker!" Mayburn really did like his car. He jerked the thing into Reverse. Ransom smashed the driver's side window.

"That's it," Mayburn said, shifting into gear. "I don't like to hurt people but the hell with it."

He put his foot on the gas, and the car shot into the street. And, apparently, right over Ransom's foot. You could hear the guy howl in pain.

Mayburn zipped up the street, and at last, we'd lost them.

"Thank you for saving me!" I said, but Mayburn was just muttering about his car, his face flushed.

"Lucy called you and told you to find me?" I asked.

"Yeah. I was already outside the museum, so it was easy."

"What do you mean you were already outside? Like you were following Lucy?"

He nodded, his face more chagrined now than pissed.

"That's not going to make Lucy very happy."

"She's definitely not happy. She said her husband is probably taping her conversations, and now I'm following her. She told me not to call, not to text."

"Ouch. Sorry."

"Me, too."

"I warned you about that."

"Shut up."

"Sorry."

Mayburn sighed, turned the car onto Clark Street.

"Where are we going?" I asked.

"I'm taking you to your house, and then…" He paused, looked at me. "Is your home phone number and address listed?"

"No. When I moved in years ago I'd just finished dating a guy who was a little too enthusiastic, so I unlisted it."

"Good. I'm going to wait while you pack and hope that those guys didn't find where you live some other way, then I'm taking you to the airport."

"Where am I going?"

"Out of town. Anywhere you want. The farther the better. Dez Romano is serious business."

"Then why did you send me to hang with him at Gibsons, for Christ's sake?"

"I shouldn't have. I'm sorry. I'm just so screwed up about Lucy. It's clouded my judgment."

"Maybe it's clouding your judgment now. Maybe I don't have to get out of town."

He stopped at a light and looked at me. His face was as serious as I'd ever seen it. "You're leaving. I'll work things on this end. I'll try and dig up some stuff on Romano. See if I can get behind the layers of reputable businesses he hides behind, and if there's anything to find, I'll turn it over to the authorities."

"Can you also look into Kelvin McNeil? That's my grandfather." I told him how he was killed, about the clipping I found in my dad's book.

Mayburn shrugged. "I'll look into it, but it's not strange that your father would have a clipping of his own father's death."

"I know. I just want to know more about it."

"What if there's nothing to find?"

"Then there's nothing to find. And what about Dez Romano? What if there's nothing to find there, either? He obviously covers his tracks. It was Michael they prosecuted, not him, because he covered them so well."

"Then we'll talk to the Feds about getting you an order of protection. I just don't want him looking for you while we're trying to get all these things done. These guys specialize in making people disappear. You need to do that before they get the chance. No discussion. You're going. So, you got some place in mind?"

I looked through the windshield at girls in sundresses crossing the street, towels in hand, on their way to the beach. I loved Chicago in the summer. Old Town Art Fair was starting today, and the street fairs would continue every weekend from one quirky neighborhood to the next until September. But I'd spent one summer in another place, a place I had loved, too—a sticky, hot, glorious city with an array of streetside cafés, *enoteche* and *ristoranti.*

Plus, the questions about my dad wouldn't wait until October.

I looked at Mayburn. "I've got someone to see first, then I'm going to Rome."

"Oh, that's brilliant, McNeil. You're running from the Mob, and you're going to head to their homeland?"

"You think these guys will expect me to go there?"

"No, it's probably the last place they'd expect, and they—"

"Exactly. I'm going to the *last* place they'd think I'd go."

13

It all happened fast. Still in Mayburn's car, I made a call to the airlines and found an open seat on a 3:30 p.m. flight to Rome that afternoon. When I heard the price of that seat I must have looked as if a truck had hit me, because Mayburn quickly said he'd handle the cost as payment for sending me to Gibsons to meet Dez. He also made me hand over my Vespa keys and said he would pick up my scooter from the museum.

When we reached my neighborhood, Old Town Art Fair was in full swing, the streets lined with canvases and beer tents. It made me wistful. I should be getting together with Maggie, heading to the annual party outside St. Michael's church, drinking beer from a white plastic cup and laughing in the sun.

The good thing was that if Dez and Ransom knew the neighborhood where I lived, it would have been hard to search for us through the hundreds of people strolling the streets. To be safe, I got out of the car and bought a scarf at a tent to throw over my hair. Two minutes later, Mayburn had checked out my place, found nothing and said he would stand downstairs while I packed.

"And don't call anyone," he said as I began to climb the steps to my condo, thinking of Theo on those steps, missing him already.

"I should tell my mom I'm leaving."

"You'll call her from a payphone at the airport. Give me your phone."

"Why?"

"I want to check it out."

"I really should call my friend Maggie."

"No."

"I have to at least text…"

I was about to say Theo, but Mayburn cut me off. "No texting, no e-mailing, no calling. I don't know yet how those guys found you or if they've been watching you."

"You think they've tapped my phones?"

"Your house phone, maybe. Your cell, unlikely. Very unlikely. Now, give me your phone."

I handed it to him and he flipped out the battery, poked and prodded. "It's clean," he said, handing it back to me. "But I still don't want you on any phones or sending out any smoke signals. I just want to get you out of here. Now, go upstairs and pack."

"Jesus, no wonder Lucy broke up with you. You're demanding as hell."

"Only when I'm worried about people I care about."

I put my hand on my hip and looked down at him. His eyes were squinting as if he were thinking too hard. Worry lines cut across his forehead. "You care about me?" I said.

He groaned. "Please. Please go pack."

"That's only the second time I've heard you say please."

Upstairs, I made sure my passport was up-to-date, then packed it along with outfits I'd been wearing lately in Chicago—a few dresses and skirts, a pair of jeans, a bathing suit, a couple of T-shirts. I threw in some slacks and three pairs of sandals of varying heights. I was about to zip up the bag, when I remembered the twisted ankle I'd gotten in Rome years ago from attempting to wear high heels on the very cobbled streets of Trastevere. (I'd heard that only Roman women could pull off such a feat, and I should have listened.) I opened the bag again, took out the pair of stiletto heels and replaced them with wedges.

As I pulled the bag to the front door, I felt a release of energy inside me—a kind of nervous force, unsure and yet thrilling. Because although Dez Romano had tracked me down, and although I was technically running from him, I was also running toward Elena, and I could ask her whether there was any chance my dad was alive.

When I got downstairs, I asked Mayburn, "When can I use my phone again?"

"Once you get overseas. Then it'll be nearly impossible to tap it or trace any calls." He stared at his own phone.

"Mayburn," I said, as kindly as possible. "I know you're hoping Lucy will reach out, but when someone tells you they need some space, they usually need space."

Yet even as I said it, I thought of someone who had told me he needed space. Sam. It was Sam who made the call that we were done for now, because he wanted us to be firmly *into* our relationship, no in-betweens, no *maybe we're dating, maybe we're not, we'll figure it out, we'll see how it goes* kind of thing, while I had grown more fond of, or possibly more comfortable with, the maybes and the in-betweens.

But Sam was still the person I had checked in with every day for years; the person who, for years, had made all life decisions with me. And even though we weren't together anymore, I wanted to tell him that I was leaving town. It was a courtesy he hadn't given me last year when he'd disappeared, but what was done was done, and I didn't believe in punishing.

I looked at my watch. It was Saturday, which usually

meant Sam was with the Chicago Lions rugby team. Sam wasn't one of the starters, but he was one of the guys who trained with the team or helped out when they traveled locally. The Chicago Lions schedule was still in my datebook, because I used to have to plan our social stuff around it. I glanced at the schedule. The team was on a road trip to San Francisco, and Sam didn't usually attend cross-country games. Instead, he was probably at his apartment, strumming his guitar, maybe having a Blue Moon beer. Just the thought made me miss him.

I told Mayburn Sam's address. "I need to stop by on the way to the airport." When he opened his mouth to protest, I held up my hand. "Look, if I can't make any calls, then I have to stop by. I'm not getting on a plane unless I talk to him first."

Sam's apartment was in Roscoe Village, sandwiched next to a bar called the Village Tap. He'd been there for years, to the chagrin of his mother, who, every time she visited, told him he should move out of his bachelor-esque pad and head downtown into a place more "grown-up." The plan had been that Sam would move in with me when we were married, but since that hadn't happened, the apartment with the funky gray door was still his home.

"Hurry up," Mayburn said, pulling up to the curb, putting on the hazards and focusing nervously in the rearview mirror. I jumped out.

"The Tap," as everyone in the neighborhood called it, already had a hopping lunch crowd. You could hear happy outbursts of laughter from the beer garden in the back.

Sam had stopped carrying my keys a few months ago, a fact that had surprised and wounded me, but I'd never stopped carrying his. I guess I wasn't ready to put away the idea of Izzy and Sam.

If he was home, I'd tell him I was going out of town, and if he wasn't, I'd leave a note and call him when I landed. But at least I'd make the effort. He would know that I still missed us. I still thought about us. I still thought there was a chance for *us*.

I got out my keys, opened the street door and walked up the flight of stairs. I rapped lightly on the door, the way I used to, then let myself into the apartment. The living room was dark and looked the way I remembered it. His leather couch was slouchy and slightly dusty looking. The blue afghan with the Cubs logo, which Sam's grandmother had knitted for him, was tossed over the side of it. On the coffee table were financial papers and magazines like *Barron's* and the *Fenton Report,* and next to those were two empty Blue Moon beers. Sam had stayed home last night apparently, a fact that made me feel slightly sick with guilt, since I had spent the night, and the last few, with Theo.

Something glinted on the coffee table, something next to the beer bottles. I looked closer and saw they were two tiny diamond earrings, set in gold. I picked them up. For a moment I thought they were mine, but my diamond earrings were fake and set in silver. As I held them up to the sunlight filtering through the window, I could see that these were clearly the real thing.

Sam didn't wear earrings.

A shuffle from one of the bedrooms. I froze, irrationally scared for a second. What was I scared of? I looked down at the earrings. I thought I knew.

The door to Sam's bedroom opened, and there he stood. He was wearing boxer shorts, only that, over his short powerhouse of a body. He wiped sleep from his eyes, despite the fact that it was already noon.

"Iz?" He pushed up at his cropped blond hair, making

it sexily jagged with angles. He blinked his eyes, which were a sparkly olive color, so much so that I'd always thought of them as *martini-olive eyes.* But he was staring curiously at me now, and his eyes didn't seem to be sparkling so much as squinting. "What are you doing here?"

He pulled the bedroom door closed behind him as he asked the question. And it was that movement, more than the earrings, that told me everything.

"So, you have a date?" I said.

More blinking. "Something like that. Were you and I supposed to meet or something?" He said it in an irritated way. He knew we had no plans to meet.

"I'm going out of town. I wanted to let you know, and they told me not to make any phone calls."

"Who's 'they'?"

I shook my head. "It's a long story. But I'm going away."

"Where?"

I could almost hear Mayburn screaming, *Don't tell anyone where you're going!* "I'm not exactly sure yet."

"For how long?" He shifted his arms over his chest as if he were suddenly embarrassed to be seen by me—by *me!*—in his near nakedness. He was so cute, though, his trim, compact body so delicious in person—and in my memory—that I couldn't get worked up about his modesty.

But what happened next made it easy to get worked up.

Yes, of course the bedroom door opened, and yes, of course a girl in panties and Sam's Jeff Beck T-shirt, the one I used to sleep in, poked her head out. But that wasn't what left me speechless.

It was the fact that it was *Alyssa.*

Alyssa Thornton was Sam's ex-girlfriend, the one I'd been crazy jealous about since I met her at their high school reunion and had seen two things. One, she was ethereal, stunning, and, as I'd always said, thin as a bag of doorknobs, which, with my curves and my envy, was not intended as a compliment. With her white-blond hair, Alyssa almost looked like a miniature, female version of Sam. The second thing I had noticed at that reunion? Alyssa still loved Sam. She glowed when she gazed at him. Just like I did. But Sam had told me he was the one who broke up with her a few years into college, that they were just friends, only that.

After the reunion, I tried to put a lid on the jealousy, but it kept bugging me, especially because I knew they e-mailed often. Finally, I asked Sam if he'd stop e-mailing her. I knew my jealousy was irrational, I told him, but it wouldn't go away. Sam had smiled at me. And he agreed.

As Sam and I continued to date and then got engaged, I got over the thought of Alyssa. But then Sam disappeared, and I found out that he went straight to her for help when he did so. I later learned his reasons. But still. But *still.* I hadn't gotten over that.

Clearly, Sam hadn't, either, because there she was. There she was positively glowing at him again as she peeked from behind his bedroom door.

If my insides had been slightly twisted with guilt over the fact that I'd spent the night with Theo, my stomach filled with bile now. It's one thing to learn your ex is dating someone else. It's another thing to find out that "someone else" is the girl you always had the bad, bad feeling about.

And it was a whole other bag of cherries to see them post-romp.

"Hi, Alyssa," I said.

"Hi." There was no triumph in her voice. "I'll give you guys some time."

She pulled her head back inside the room. *Click* went the door of Sam's bedroom, then *click* again, because it had to be pushed twice to keep it closed. The fact that Alyssa knew that slayed me. Tears sprang to my eyes as I stood there looking at my fantastic, adorable, beloved *ex*-fiancé, who had clearly moved on with his life.

"I thought she lived in Indianapolis," I said.

"She moved here a few weeks ago."

"To be with you."

"No, to work at Rush Medical Center. She's in geriatric—"

I cut him off. "I remember." Alyssa was a researcher in the geriatric field, working to improve the quality of life for the elderly, particularly those who were bedridden. She was, essentially, an angel of mercy. Which, I'd always said, made it pretty tough to compete with her as an ex-girlfriend. Or maybe she wasn't the ex anymore. It appeared *she* was the girlfriend now, and I was the former.

The energy I'd had in my apartment crashed, replaced by a sorrow so deep I took a few steps to the couch and sank into it, putting my face in my hands.

"I'm sorry, Iz." He sat next to me and put his arm around me.

I didn't think there could be anything worse than finding Alyssa in Sam's apartment, but this—*this*—was worse. Sam awkwardly patting me on the shoulder, trying to comfort me, sure, but making it somehow clear in his stiff body language that his body didn't belong to me anymore, nor, apparently, did his heart.

And what of my heart?

I thought of Q, my former assistant. Q had just entered the gay world when we'd met, and as such, he took any and all breakups hard.

One day we were discussing his latest, and he had asked me when my heart had last gotten broken.

"Never," I'd told him. And it was true.

The guys I'd dated before Sam—Timmy, my boyfriend in college, and Blake, the one I dated during law school—had been such insignificant relationships compared to the one I had with Sam. I was the one who broke up with Timmy—his love of beer bongs got old after freshman year. And Blake and I were on again–off again and had finally decided to part when we couldn't find time to get together with our busy law school schedules and also found we really didn't care. And when Sam and I split, well… How to explain it? I guess I never saw it officially as a split. Even when he disappeared and even after that, when he said he needed to move on, I didn't *really* expect him to move on. I assumed that *Sam and Izzy, Izzy and Sam* was still an option that hung in both our horizons.

Now I felt the heat of his skin as he sat next to me. I breathed in that Sam smell. Both of these things had brought tears to my eyes in the past, and this time was no different. And yet those tears definitely were different. They weren't the sweet tears that glitter from your eyes when a deep connection makes you so happy, so filled with joy. No, those were tears I'd never felt before—hot, almost burning tears that must have come from the skin that protected my heart, the skin that felt sliced now, carved deep.

"I'm sorry," Sam said again. He turned and gave me a half hug, and the self-consciousness of it cut me even deeper.

"It's okay." I stood, wiping tears. They splashed on my cheeks and chin. They felt as if they were leaving marks, burning me. "I have to go." My voice sounded like someone else's. And as I looked at Sam, my eyes clouded, making him look different, too. "I'll talk to you later." My voice sounded strangled.

"God, Iz." He started crying now. He stood, grabbed me fiercely, wrapped his arms around me in a way that felt *so* Sam, *so* us. We stood together, a tight mass, quietly choking out sobs.

I heard a persistent *bleat, bleat, bleat, bleat.* Mayburn honking from outside.

"I have to go."

He nodded, sniffed, stared into my eyes. And that stare said it all. It said, *Goodbye.*

PART II

14

"Ciao, ciao," the porter said to me, as I left.

I waved at him, went out into the courtyard and walked a pathway lined with stone busts.

My first day in Rome, and I felt as if I was in the middle of one big flashback.

When I had arrived at O'Hare yesterday, my flight wasn't leaving for a few hours. Using one of the public computer kiosks, I got on the Internet and searched for hotels in Rome. The rates were astronomical. Since Mayburn picked up my flight, I was willing to take on some credit card debt (something I'd never done before), but if I stayed a week in the Roman hotels, even the modest ones, I'd have to live in a cardboard box under Lower Wacker when I returned.

I kept thinking about the summer I'd spent in Rome years ago. It was during that time that my friendship with Maggie solidified into sisterhood. Maggie and I immersed ourselves in *Roma,* in our fellow students, our professors, the tenets of international and comparative law, and it was as if a happy bubble had sprung up around us. Of course, there were the usual traveler's woes—blisters adorning our feet, having to wash your underwear in a dorm sink—but I loved every bit.

As I remembered that time, a thought occurred to

me. I found the Web site for Loyola's Rome campus. It was in *Monte Mario,* a neighborhood on the outskirts of the city with upscale apartments and a few piazzas full of shops.

I scrolled through the Web site. And there, on the bottom of the Housing page, it said, *Alumni: Rent a Room! Low Occupancy in the Summer Means We Welcome Visitors!* I scrolled to find the cost—less than half of what the hotels were charging. I could put up with dorm-style living in order to save money and to be, once again, in Rome, where I could escape Dez Romano and where Elena couldn't escape the questions about my father.

The campus was set on a long, narrow, grassy plot of land, the main building a three-story unassuming brick affair. But if the architecture and the setting were somewhat unremarkable, the feel of the place—the energy—wasn't. Rome is a seen-it-all kind of place. No matter how much the Italians delight in things—food and wine and sex, to name a few—the fact remains that their cultural DNA includes a world weariness of it all. And yet the American students who studied at Loyola were visiting Italy, and sometimes Europe, for the first time. They were wide-eyed, eager to see, to learn, to live. And so the campus with its otherwise sleepy appearance hummed with that energy. It vibrated at a low level but with a certain light that colored everything a pretty ochre, that made the place soothing and yet made it sing.

Thank God, because dorm living and me really weren't made for each other. But I let the energy of the place take me, happily, to the showers that scalded in such a familiar way and then turned suddenly freezing, to the teeny bed that was really just a cot with sheets that felt like paper towels. I slept a dreamless sleep—a godsend—and in the morning, I left my dorm room and strolled past the campus's stone busts. I pushed through the tall metal door set into the high brick wall and walked onto the street.

A bus took me to the Balduina subway station, and I rode a couple trains until I landed at the Barberini stop. I got out there simply because I couldn't remember seeing the piazza during my last visit. When I got to the top of the subway steps, I chose a cloth-covered table at a restaurant, essentially because it was the first one I saw, and I was bleary and hungry from the overnight flight.

Even though I normally avoided caffeine, I knew I should probably get a cappuccino, something to power through my jet lag. But when in Italy one tries to do what the Italians do, and the Italians don't drink cappuccino with their midday meal, they drink wine. I ordered a glass of Greco di Tufo.

Then I got out a notebook I had brought with me, opened it to the first page and wrote at the top: *Christopher McNeil, Things to Do.*

Under that, I wrote:

1. *Find Elena, get her to talk*
2. *Bug Mayburn to find R. J. Ohman, flight instructor. Ask him why Fed instructor needed for McNeil and also what was cause of crash*
3. *Learn who killed Grandpa Kelvin*
4. *Find out more about the Rizzato Brothers*

I put the pen down and looked up *via Veneto,* the street that the restaurant faced. It was a wide, stately avenue flanked with regal *appartamenti* decorated with stone balconies and potted plants. It ended at the Piazza Barberini. A hotel sat at one side of the piazza. Its unimaginative brick front looked more like an American hotel, but surrounding it were stuccoed buildings painted brick-orange, their windows and shutters thrown open. Taxis and scooters and the tiniest of cars zipped around the circular piazza. And not just any scooters. Vespas! Rome wasn't just the capital city of Italy, it was the capital city of Vespa country. They skirted the fountain and shot up *via Veneto.* I itched to get my fingers on the handgrips of one of them.

I took my cell phone from my bag and set it on the table, hoping my aunt Elena might call. I had followed Mayburn's recommendation that I turn on my international service while in the car on the way to the airport, and so my phone worked. Since I didn't know where she lived I had called Aunt Elena three times since landing in Rome. Each time, the phone was answered with a quick message in Italian. I couldn't understand whether it was Elena's voice telling me to leave a message or a recorded message notifying me I had dialed wrong.

I had decided I would keep calling and, meanwhile, forge into the city. If there was one thing I learned on my previous visit to Rome it was how much I didn't get to see. The treasures, the hidden courtyards, the historic sites—these are endless in Rome. And according to a guidebook I'd picked up, a rash of new *musi,* galleries and *palazzi* had opened.

I pulled out that guidebook and flipped through it now, setting my sights on the Barberini Palace, right around the corner from the piazza. I kept studying the book, hoping I could divine the gallery Elena had mentioned, the one where she was working and which she said was close to her heart. The problem was, I didn't know Elena very well. I didn't know what moved her heart. Come to think of it, I wasn't sure what moved my own heart these days.

The sight of Alyssa in Sam's apartment—in Sam's *T-shirt*—nagged me, kept showing up in my mind like a neon-lit image. I let that image linger and filled it with more light, because sometimes that chased away the feel of Sam's farewell embrace.

To get rid of both of them, I perused the menu.

I ordered a pasta I'd never heard of and watched the Sunday foot traffic on the street, hoping in vain that somehow Elena might walk by, fearing that if she did I wouldn't recognize her.

I looked at my watch. It was early in Chicago, but that was probably the best time to catch Q. He would make me laugh about my whole situation somehow. He would encourage me to enjoy this time.

I called his home phone, at the apartment he shared with his wealthy boyfriend, but their voice mail picked up right away. *We're not in right now,* I heard Q's recorded voice say. *In fact, we're in St. Bart's, and we're not checking messages, but leave us one, and we'll call you when we get back.*

I hung up, suddenly wistful at the thought of how much time Q and I used to have together and how our life paths had diverged so sharply. I went back to watching the foot traffic pass my table. The longer I stared at the parade of pedestrians, the more I noticed that Rome was different from when I was here eight years ago. Or maybe it was just the Roman men.

When I was last in Rome, if a reasonably attractive woman stopped on the street to consult a map or much less ate alone at a restaurant, as I was doing, it would invite a torrent of male attention. The men would literally surround you—touching you, shouting come-ons in a desperate mix of Italian and English. It became one of Italy's few liabilities.

As I sat near the Piazza Barberini, alone and unapproached, it was clear things had changed.

My pasta was delivered—green-and-white striped noodles in a mushroom-y broth. Delicious.

I kept eating my pasta and sipping my wine, depressed a bit about the change in the Roman men. Being single for the first time in years, I had envisioned a bevy of male attention that, although largely unwanted, would serve to lift me away from my questions about Sam, from a lingering taste of fear at the back of my throat every time I thought of Dez and Michael.

In fact, most of the men strutted by, not noticing any women. The men were dressed in exquisite fashion, their heads held high. Most of them were in perfect shape, their black hair tousled to perfection. It was almost as if they expected to be watched now, expected that *they* should be the admired ones. They were preening peacocks, full of bravado, no longer reduced to preying on tourists.

I picked up my phone and called Maggie.

"What courthouse?" she barked into the phone. I could imagine Maggie in her South Loop apartment, her body only a tiny bump in her big bed. "What's the bond?" Maggie loved to sleep as late as possible, but was constantly awakened by drug clients who often landed in holding cells over the course of the night.

"Sorry, Mags," I said.

"Hey, just because you're not working doesn't mean the rest of us aren't." A pause. "Well, actually, I was going to be working because of my trial but I got directed verdict on Friday. Which means I'm going back to bed. Call you later."

"I'm in Rome!" I tossed out before she could hang up.

"What?"

"Yeah, I got here yesterday."

"You're kidding me? Did you get a hold of your aunt Elena?"

"Not yet. But I just felt like getting out of town." *And away from Dez and Michael.*

"You're in *Rome?*"

"Yeah. I'm sitting outside near *Piazza Barberini* right now."

"How is it?"

"As beautiful and chaotic as always. You should get on a plane and get over here."

"Oh, I don't know. My trial is over, but I've got to dig myself out of the mountain I let pile up while I was prepping for it."

I told her I was staying at the Loyola campus.

"You're kidding?" she said.

"You have to see it again. C'mon, Mags. How often are we going to get this chance? How often are we both going to be single at the same time? I mean, in a couple of years you might be married with a kid." Maggie very much wanted a family. It was the husband part of that proposition that was causing her trouble.

"You're right," she said, her voice excited. "And we could celebrate your thirtieth."

"I've got a glass of wine in front of me and a spot across the table for you."

"I'm calling my travel agent."

"Seriously?"

"I'm going to make this happen. I'm coming to Rome."

15

I hung up after the call with Maggie, a smile on my face. I asked for my check, then went back to watching the Italian men. Many wore tailored jackets. Nearly all wore beautiful Italian shoes. And those shoes reminded me of Michael and Dez.

I called Mayburn. He answered with a groan.

"What's up with you?" I asked.

"Time change," he growled. "Think about it before you call."

"Oh, please. Get up, you lazy ass."

"This *ass* was up late last night. You know how you wanted info about the people who killed your grandfather?"

I pulled my notebook closer to me and put a star by item number three. "Yeah. Find something?"

"I thought you were stretching to look that far back, but there's something interesting."

"Don't tell me my grandfather isn't dead, either."

"No. Sorry to say, two guys did kill him at that gas station. Their names were Dante Dragonetti and Luigi Battista. The cops arrested them, but both escaped from jail before they could come to trial."

"Escaped? How did they do that?"

"I tried to find that out, but the details are sketchy. It looks like they were kept in a simple holding cell in a small town out East, but these guys weren't simple criminals. And they probably had help. The authorities think they returned to Naples, where they were from. Tried to extradite them, but they apparently went deep into hiding, maybe changed their names, because the U.S. authorities couldn't prove exactly where they were. So no extradition was ever granted."

"And no one was ever tried for my grandfather's murder?"

"Nope."

"Sad." I drew a line through item number three, thinking about how that must have made my father feel—and Elena and my grandma Oriana—to have those men living free somewhere, the same men who had stopped the life of Kelvin McNeil. Then I looked at number four on my list. "Have you ever heard of Louie and Joe Rizzato?"

"The Brothers Rizzato? Sure. I saw a documentary on PBS about them. Disappeared. Never found the bodies."

"That's the case my dad was consulting on when he died. He was a police profiler for the Detroit police force, but he worked some federal cases, too, and that was one of them."

Mayburn was silent.

"What are you thinking?" I asked.

"I'm thinking I better educate myself a bit about the Rizzato Brothers. Call you back."

I left the piazza and walked up a steep street to Palazzo Barberini, where the *salone* took my breath away. The three-story stone walls were mostly unadorned. The true draw was the fresco on the domed ceiling.

Only one other person was in the salon when I entered, a man lying on his back on one of the four gray chaises in the middle of the room. I sat on another chaise, then feeling a little cautious, I lay back, too. The fresco, called

Divine Providence, depicted historic figures frolicking across a luminous, heavenly blue sky. I thought about my father, who always resided in a similar place in my mind—in a beautiful, warmly lit other-universe where he floated about, with no worries, but always able to see Charlie and me, always watching us.

When I left the *palazzo,* I kept calling Aunt Elena, and eventually I was able to translate the message. It wasn't Elena's voice, I realized, but a standard greeting from the phone company inviting callers to leave their own *messaggi.* Because Elena had seemed skittish when I'd spoken to and e-mailed with her from Chicago, I simply left a message, asking her to please call me back. In the meantime, I kept walking around the city, stopping at places I hadn't paid enough attention to before—the Capitoline museum (reached by climbing stairs next to Vittorio Emanuele), the Jewish ghetto, the Napoleon museum by the Tiber river.

On *via del Banchi Vecchi,* a medieval-looking street, I found a wine bar with a sign out front that only said *Vino Olio.* It was a tiny place where people spilled onto the sidewalk to smoke. I lucked out and found a single seat at the bar. I sat there and kept checking my cell phone, in vain, for a sign that Elena had called. I didn't want to be rude. I didn't want to just drop in on her, in her city, when she clearly didn't want to see the niece she barely knew, but finally, sitting at the rough wooden bar, I decided to text her this time. I wrote, *Hi Aunt Elena it's Izzy. I'm in Rome.*

Fifteen minutes later, as I was making my way through my second glass of Falanghini wine, she called. "Oh, *cara,*" she said. "Why are you here?" She didn't say it in a rude way, but rather in a manner that was both fond and weary.

I swirled my wine, watching the smooth yellow-gold liquid swish against the clear glass. I thought about what to say, decided that there was nothing to say but the truth. "To talk about my dad."

A pause. "Where are you?"

I told her.

"I am just leaving work. Do you know this hotel?" She mentioned an address.

I'd seen it in my strolls. "It's a few streets from here, right?"

"Yes. *Mio amico,* my friend, runs the hotel. It has a rooftop terrace bar. It is closed for remodeling, but he will let us use it. Meet me there at half past."

I looked at my watch. "In twenty minutes?" I wanted to make sure I understood.

"Yes."

I said goodbye. I didn't ask why we had to meet on a roof deck that wasn't open to the public. I took another swallow of the wine, but it had gone a little warm and tasted slightly sour instead of refreshing.

I pushed it away, left Euros on the bar and then left to see my aunt for the first time in eight years.

16

We made small talk at first. How was my mother? Elena asked. What about her husband, Spence? Were they happy? She hoped so.

"She was very much in love with your father," Elena said.

And there it was—*your father.*

We were sitting at a high table on a sixth-floor roof deck. The hotel was small and beautiful with a lobby library and wine bar. The place had once been a convent, Elena had told me.

I looked at her now and noticed that her posture was still dancer-straight, her hair still a shiny chestnut, her skin faintly lined but supple. Behind her, the dome of St. Peter's Basilica glittered a serpentine gray-green as the sun began to disappear.

Neither of us said anything for a moment. I couldn't read her expression because of the large black sunglasses she wore. They had a silver braid on the side that glinted in the sunlight whenever she turned her head.

"And what about you?" Elena said, skipping over the topic of my dad. "How is your love life?"

Now I was the one who wanted to skip over the question. I raised my left hand, the ring finger conspicuously unadorned. "I was engaged."

"And now you are not."

"No."

"Why?"

"A lot of reasons." I suddenly felt tired of explaining my breakup with Sam, or the need to put a neat narrative spin on it.

"It's hard to explain," Elena said, as if answering her own question.

"Yes." I looked at Elena's hands. They were the only parts of her, really, that gave away her age. She wore a thick gold band on her wedding finger. "And you?" I asked. "How is Maurizio?"

My mother had once encouraged me to call him Uncle Maurizio. He had, after all, married my aunt long ago. But I'd never met him. They hadn't come to the States for my father's funeral—I don't remember hearing the reason why—and when I'd visited Italy during law school, Elena had spoken of him but he'd always been busy.

She looked down at her wedding ring. "Did you know…" Her words died away, as if rethinking them. She sighed. "It's very *italiano* to have affairs."

"I've heard that."

She chuckled. "Yes, I suppose it's a cliché by now. And believe me, it's not something that every Italian gets involved in. There are many people now who don't, but…"

I felt a sear of pain for her. Whatever Sam and I had been through, even seeing Alyssa at his house, at least he hadn't cheated when we were together. I had learned a lot about infidelity lately—the different kinds, the different reasons—but it was still the one thing I didn't think I could tolerate. "It's part of your culture," I said.

She nodded. "It is."

We said nothing else about the subject.

"Do you and Maurizio still live together?" I asked.

"Yes, of course."

"And is he good to you?" I almost held my breath as I asked the question. It seemed so adult, somehow, to be asking such a personal thing of my aunt.

"He is. In his own way." She smiled a small smile. "You know, I was a couple years younger than Christopher, your father, and he was always the one who took care of me."

Elena had apparently decided that we were done chatting, and she was ready to deal with the topic I wanted to talk about.

"Your father was usually very serious," she said, "but he could be wickedly funny."

"I remember that," I said. "He had that way of laughing—"

"And his eyes laughed, too," Elena finished for me.

"Yes!"

"And he always wore glasses, but you could still see *the life* in his eyes. Always."

The words *the life* halted me for a second. I had no idea how to have this conversation, this *Is it possible he's alive?* kind of discussion.

And so I just came out with it. "I think I saw him."

She shook her head fast. "What?" Her tone was incredulous, but I couldn't see her full expression because of the sunglasses.

"I guess I didn't see him so much as I heard him."

"What do you mean?" She kept shaking her head. The braided silver arms of her glasses sparkled with the motion.

I looked away from her, over the rooftops and through the mustard sky to the oxidized green dome of St. Peter's. "I got into some trouble the other night." I shrugged, as if shrugging off the details. "Some guys were hassling me, and I ran away from them. They caught up to me, but a man pulled me into a stairwell and got me away from them. He came out of nowhere. And it was black in the stairwell. I couldn't see a thing." I turned back to her. "But he said something to me."

"What?"

"Well, it wasn't what he said, exactly. He said, 'You're okay now, Boo.' It was that Boo part. That's what—"

"What your dad used to call you," Elena said. "I remember."

"Right. And no one else calls me that except my mom. So…" I shrugged again.

Elena took off her glasses. Her eyes were deep brown, but there were flecks of green in them and something else. It looked like sympathy. "Did this man say anything else?"

"That was it, really. He told me how to take the stairs. He told me to get going."

"Did he call you by your name?"

"No."

"Did you see his face?"

"No, not really. When the guys were chasing me, he was behind them, but he had a cap on, and he was looking down."

"Could you tell how old the man was who had this cap on?"

I shook my head.

"Isabel." Again, she said it in the Italian way—*Ee-sa-bel.* She frowned, but her eyes carried some humor. "It wasn't your father."

"How do you know that?"

She laughed. "Because your father died many years ago. It was a stressful situation that you were in that night, and you manufactured a response to help get through it."

"It *was* stressful." I got a flash of Michael and Dez across the car from me. Dez saying, *C'mere, little girl.*

I must have made an expression of distaste or fear, because Elena looked at me with even more sympathy now. "Who were these men that were chasing you? *Why* were they chasing you?"

"Oh…" I waved my hand. "No one. It was nothing. I was talking to them in order to help a friend out. It's a long story."

She smiled. "I don't like the idea of my sweet niece hanging out with dangerous characters."

"I usually don't." I thought of Theo with his constellation of tattoos. "Well, I've been dating—sort of dating—a young guy who looks like he could be dangerous, but he's actually the sweetest person. And those guys that one night, they were just…" I trailed off. Repeated, "It's a long story."

Elena patted me on the hand. She put her sunglasses back on. "How long are you in town, Isabel?"

I told her my trip was open-ended.

"I would like to show you something tomorrow. The gallery where I work."

"I'd love that."

"Good. I must go now."

Elena pulled a small crocodile notebook from her purse then a tiny, gold pen. She uncapped the pen, wrote *Palazzo Colonna,* a time and an address on a small sheet of paper, then ripped out the paper and handed it to me.

"*A domani, cara,*" she said. "I will see you tomorrow."

A bleating sound woke me in the middle of the night. I sat up, looked around, struggled to get my bearings—Italy, Rome, dorm room. Got it. I looked at the small faux wood cabinet that served as a nightstand in the room. My cell phone sat there. It was ringing, I realized. I looked at the screen and recognized that number. Mayburn.

I sat up against the headboard, drew my knees up. "Yes?" I said, sleepily drawing the out the word.

"You were asleep. I know. But you gotta hear this. The Rizzato Brothers? They were from Naples."

"And originally from some island called Ischia. I know. Is that why you woke me up? You can find that out on Wikipedia."

"Hold off with the sarcasm, will ya? Did you find out from Wikipedia that the Rizzatos were Camorra?"

"Camorra, the organized crime syndicate?"

"Yeah."

"The one that Dez Romano is a part of?"

"Yeah, and you know who else was believed to be Camorra? Dragonetti and Battista."

I pushed myself up straighter, kicking off the covers from my legs. "The men who killed my grandfather?"

"Right. And I got one more doozy for you. You know who else is Camorra? At least technically."

Why did I feel right then that the dorm room squeezed in on me, the linoleum floors contracting, the walls shrinking? "Who?" I said, although you could barely hear my voice.

But I heard Mayburn clearly. "You."

17

The Palazzo Colonna was on an odd cobblestoned lane across the street from a high wall with a garden at the top. Like so many places in Rome, the front door of the palazzo gave no indication of what was behind it. A discreet plaque said that the palazzo was only open on Saturday mornings. It was Monday.

I checked the address again from the sheet where Elena had written it, then raised my finger to the buzzer, hesitating only for a second before I pushed it. Nothing happened. It was hot outside. I lifted the hair off my neck, wishing I had a barrette so I could put it up.

I tried the buzzer again. No sounds came from inside. I couldn't tell if it was working. I laid my finger on it again.

And then the wood door clicked open.

The heat receded when I stepped inside, almost as if it had been sucked out by a vacuum.

The first floor was a small foyer. On a nondescript desk, brochures and pamphlets were laid out. Next to that was a circular staircase, its walls holding shelves with paintings, tiles and statuettes from different eras.

I heard a soft *tap, tap, tap* and saw a pair of black patent leather heels coming down the stairs. Aunt Elena was dressed in red pants and a stylish, asymmetrical black shirt.

"Isabel." She walked over and embraced me.

I heard sounds from behind her and saw a woman in her twenties coming down the stairs. Elena introduced the woman as her assistant, Justina. She pronounced it *Juice-tina.* "Now, come," Elena said, "let me show you around my second home."

I followed her up the winding iron stairs. At the top was a small room with a few red velvet chairs and stands displaying enormous art books. Elena opened one of the books and fanned the pages. "These show all the art."

"The art in Rome?"

She smiled. It was a secretive and yet jubilant smile, as if she couldn't wait to let me in on something special. "No. The art from here."

I looked around the room. The walls contained sketches and paintings, all framed in gold, but they would only take up a couple of pages of the book.

"Let me show you," Elena said.

She crooked a finger and stepped to double doors at the side of the room. I stood behind her.

Elena took a set of keys from her pocket and used them to unlock the doors. She slid them open, stepped forward and then turned and threw her arm out as if to say, *It's all yours.*

I gasped. I walked through the doors, looked to the right and gasped again.

How to describe that place? What I was looking at was a gallery, clearly, and yet the word *gallery* is too small, too pedestrian, too quaint for the grand, ostentatious and stunning salon that lay before me. Its floors, fashioned from all different types of marble—yellow trimmed in green, white striped with gray, red that was deep and rusty—stretched out hundreds of feet. The ceiling was at least four stories high, barrel vaulted, rimmed with gilded gold and painted with a vibrant fresco. The walls were lined with paintings, and before them stood white marble sculptures of Roman figures. Sunlight flowed into the room from a few high windows on one side, making the gold gleam, the marble sparkle.

Elena walked me farther into the room and we stood at the top of a few stairs between two massive, vividly yellow columns.

"All this art was collected or commissioned by the Colonna family, one of the grandest aristocratic families in Rome." Elena pointed at the ceiling, where ships battled and knights clashed and angels flew above it all. *"The Battle of Lepanto,"* she said. "By Giovanni Coli and Filippo Gherardi."

"Amazing" was the only word I could come up with.

We walked down the stairs. I was surprised to see that on one step, the marble had splintered, and in the center was a pewter-colored ball about the size of a large grapefruit.

Elena saw me looking at it. "A cannonball," she said. "It was shot in here during the siege of Rome in 1849. You can pick it up."

I lifted the heavy ball of iron, its surface slightly mottled, and wondered at the other hands that had touched it—the man who made it, the one who put it in the cannon and shot it here. I bent down and replaced it. "Why is it still here? I mean, I'm surprised, because the rest of this place is so well-maintained."

Elena nodded. "Thank you for the compliment. But the cannonball is history, and if there is one thing we try to do in Rome, it is leave space for history."

She walked me through the rest of the salon, noting different works of art, telling me about a chest that was carved with a hundred tiny drawers and studded with precious jewels. "Amethyst," Elena said, pointing. "Topaz. Garnet. Chrysolites. Cornelian. Cat's-eyes."

We took a few steps away and looked back through the salon, as magnificent from that end as it was at the beginning.

"As you can see, most of the works here are not from famous artists," she said. "But that wasn't the point of the Palazzo Colonna. These were amassed to give a *collective* impression of beauty. The intention is that one doesn't need to be an art historian to appreciate this place. You don't need to study each little brush stroke, every inch of gold." She waved her arm and spun around, and in that moment I could see her as a young girl, joyous and inquisitive and free of any sadness. "I think it is important what this place teaches," she said. "I am not a historian, but I learn from the palazzo every day. It teaches you to look at the whole. Not one individual masterpiece."

"How did you come to work here?" I said.

She smiled, as if remembering. "I got the job the way you do anything in Italy. You ask and you ask and you ask. And they look at you like you are crazy, and they tell you *No, no, no* over and over again, and one day, just one day, they look at you, and instead of saying, *No, no, no,* they say *Okay, okay, okay.*"

"And you fell in love with the place, because the entire thing is a work of art." I spun around the way she had, trying to take it all in, the splashes of color, the glinting gold.

"Exactly," she said, clearly pleased. "That is why I love Rome, too, and that is what keeps me here." She pointed to the cannonball and smiled. "The flaws are many when you look. Mistakes have been made. And yet the overall effect is one of true beauty, a beauty that transcends any mistakes."

I looked in her eyes. "Do you believe the same about people?" I asked. "That they can be flawed and make mistakes and still have a transcendent beauty?"

She nodded. "Yes, a beauty inside them, not just out."

We were quiet for a second, and as we stared at each other, the gold and the colors and the marble dimmed, and the only thing for me to study now was my aunt Elena.

"Are you referring to any specific person?" I asked. C'mon, I thought. *Tell me. Tell me what you know.*

"You remind me of your father," she said.

I made an inquisitive face, but inside I was saying, *Yes, yes, yes. This is it.*

"He was curious like you," Aunt Elena said.

"That sounds more like my brother, Charlie."

Elena gave me the slow grand shrug Italians have mastered. "Maybe. Christopher wanted to know everything." She held up a finger. "Correction. He wanted to *understand* everything. There is a difference." She looked at me for a sign of comprehension.

I nodded slowly, thinking about what she'd said. "There is a difference between knowing something or memorizing it, and truly understanding it."

"Yes, that's right. And true understanding requires a much deeper curiosity, a willingness to seek for motivations and appreciate subtleties. But that kind of curiosity can be dangerous."

"Why?"

"Because you begin to think that maybe the world isn't so black and white, maybe people aren't, either. You don't realize that some people truly are black. Just black."

She'd lost me now. Was she talking about my father? Had he done something so terrible that even she, his sister, couldn't see anything but evil?

"Is he alive?" There. I'd said it. It was the real question I'd wanted to ask all along, but I had been afraid it would scare her off. But I'd come this far, and now in this jewel of a room, it was just she and I and the memory of my father. And I needed to know if he was more than a ghost.

Elena looked around the salon, then up at the ceiling. Was she looking for someone or something in particular, or was she just drawing strength from this place that she loved?

She looked back at me. "Your father died when you were eight years old."

"I was *told* my father died when I was eight. But then a week ago I heard him on the stairs. I heard his voice, *his* voice, and he called me by my nickname, the one he gave me."

"You are young." She gave a shrug that was purely Italian. "You still want your father to be around."

"I'm not so young. I'm almost thirty."

"That's right. You have a birthday this week."

I nodded. "In a few days."

"*Buon compleanno,* Isabel."

"Thank you. But, Aunt Elena, I have to tell you, I long ago stopped wishing my father were still alive. Somewhere along the way I completely accepted his death."

"Good."

"But I heard him that night."

"People invent comforting things when they are in trouble."

I crossed my arms and widened my stance. "I didn't invent it." I certainly wasn't going to tell her my doubts about that night, because if my father truly was dead, then why wasn't she, his sister, more appalled by my questions? If Charlie died—*God forbid, knock on wood, please, please no*—and someone later suggested to me that he might not really have died, I would unleash on them. I would go mad. But Elena was calm, answering these questions matter-of-factly, the way she might if she was leading a tour of this place.

Our conversation reminded me of the one we'd had the night before on the roof of the hotel. She had been surprised, initially, at me saying I thought I'd found my father; she'd been full of questions, but then she'd dropped the topic, simple as that, as if it were normal or not so surprising at all for a grown woman to be saying she thought she'd heard her father, who had been dead for two decades.

Elena looked around the gallery, giving another unconcerned shrug.

I decided to try a different tactic. "Am I Camorra?"

Her head snapped back, her eyes zeroed in on mine. "What did you say?"

"I was talking to a friend, and he told me that we're a Camorra family, or that at least Grandma O's family was."

"Who is this friend?"

I shook my head. "It doesn't matter. I'm not even sure what it means—the Camorra."

She flinched a little. "Justina!" she called out suddenly, her voice cutting through the stillness. "Justina!" she yelled again. She paused. There were no sounds—not an answer or the patter of footsteps. "Good," Elena said. "She has gone." She placed a hand on my arm. "And we must talk."

18

Elena led me from the gallery through a few smaller rooms to the other side of the palazzo. She opened a door using a set of keys.

"Wow," I said, following her through the doorway.

She glanced around as if seeing what I was seeing—a series of rooms that led one to another. These rooms were also trimmed in gold and laden with paintings, many of them landscapes of Rome, but there was furniture, too. "Yes, I was going to surprise you with this," she said. "These are the private apartments of Princess Isabelle, one of the Colonna daughters. I was thrilled when I came to work here, because they made me think of you." She looked around a little more, and said distractedly, "Part of *Roman Holiday* was filmed here. With Audrey Hepburn. But this is not important now. Let me show you something."

She drew me across the room. At the far end, the wall was painted with tiny strokes. When I looked closer, I saw it was a miniature frescoed ballroom scene.

"What do you see?" Elena said, pointing at the wall.

I looked from her to the wall and back again. "What do you mean?"

"Do you see anything in particular? Anything special?"

"It's beautiful."

She nodded. “It is that. But no, I want to show you something else. Something that is very special to me. She pointed toward a depiction of a woman in a pink flounced skirt, then reached out and touched the skirt. And suddenly the painting seemed to move. The skirt popped out in her hands.

“Oh,” I said, surprised.

Elena turned and smiled at my reaction, which made her appear younger, more carefree. Holding on to the skirt in the painting—the edge was still connected to the wall—she twisted it, pulled it, and suddenly the entire wall moved, slid aside under her grasp.

“A hidden door,” I said. Beyond the door was a room, small with two high windows, the sun streaming inside.

“My office.” Elena gestured me in with a hand.

I took a few steps inside. “So this is where you do all your work for the *galleria?*”

She shook her head. “No. No one knows about this. It was a closet of Isabelle’s, used for undergarments and such. Have you heard that every woman should have her own space, a room of her own?”

I nodded.

“Well, this is mine. I have an office, officially, downstairs with all the other *galleria* employees…” She shrugged. “There are not so many of us, really. Just my assistant, my two events planners.”

“So why do you need this room?”

“When I first worked here, the palazzo was not open to the public. It was something I worked hard at. I *wanted* this beautiful place to be seen by everyone. But sometimes it is sad for me to see strange people in the place where I worked for such a long while by myself.”

“It’s not just yours anymore.”

“Yes, exactly. So this is where I come to escape, to think.”

I wondered what she had to escape from, but didn't ask. I looked around the office. Two upholstered chairs in a soft blue had been placed below the tiny windows. An eclectic assortment of sketches—historical fashion drawings apparently—decorated the walls. A little marble table with tapered, spiraled legs sat near the wall, obviously used as a desk.

Elena took a seat behind the desk and opened a round, lacquered box using a set of keys. She reached into the box and removed another smaller box, this one made of brown velvet. "I want to give you something, Isabel."

I had grown to love how she said my name—*Ee-sabel.*

She put the box on the desk and pushed it across, nodding at me.

"What is it?" I asked.

She nodded at the box again.

I pulled it toward me. It was heavy, as if weighted. I opened it. Inside was a delicate yellow gold chain with oval links. Dangling from the chain was a stone, about the size of a small egg. The stone was amber and intricately beveled so that the sun from outside hit it and sent spikes of orange light around the room.

I gasped a little as I lifted the necklace from the box. I looked at my aunt.

Elena smiled. "It was my mother's."

"Grandma O's?"

She nodded. She got up from her desk, walked around it, and took the necklace from my hands. She undid the clasp and stood behind me, fastening it behind my head.

The necklace fell between my breasts, and the stone hit my ribs with a light thud, the sun glittering through it again. I was mesmerized by it. "It's beautiful. Are you sure you're okay to give it to me?"

"Absolutely. It's almost your birthday, and I do not wear it anymore." She took her place behind her desk again and looked at the necklace, cocking her head a bit. "It makes me too sad to wear it."

"Why?"

"It is difficult when your family is gone, when you are the only one left."

We both were silent, I met her eyes. I wanted to say, "*Are* you the only one left?" but I had already asked that question. So I returned to the one left unanswered. "Are we Camorra?"

She gazed at her hands, squeezing them into fists, then unclenching them. "Isabel, please be careful when you say—" she cleared her throat "—Camorra."

"Why?"

"The Camorra is not something to play around with."

"I'm not playing. I'm just asking you, are we Camorra?"

Now she looked annoyed; her mouth pursed. "What do you know of this, the Camorra?"

It was my turn to give the Italian shrug. "I know it's an organized-crime syndicate. Kind of like the *Cosa Nostra* group from *The Godfather.*"

She laughed but without mirth. "The Camorra is not like *Cosa Nostra.* Not at all."

"What are they like?"

"Dangerous." She said the word plainly. "You must be very careful."

"Of what? I'm not even sure what we're talking about here."

She sighed. "I wanted to give you that necklace because it is true that it makes me too sad, and I do not wear it anymore. But also I wanted you to remember your grandmother and her family. That stone has been handed down for generations. And yes, my mother's family was traditionally a Camorra family. When they lived in Naples, they were one of the leading families of the Camorra. But ultimately, many members of the family did not want to be defined by the Camorra. Oriana's mother and father were such members and they moved to the United States. They wanted their daughter to be raised differently. Which is why they allowed her to marry Kelvin, who wasn't Camorra or even Italian."

"But Kelvin was killed by two Camorra members."

She glanced around, as if someone was listening. "Who told you that?"

"My friend."

"Yes, well, your friend is correct. The men who killed my father were Camorra."

"Why did they kill him?"

"I do not like to talk about the Camorra, Isabel." She cleared her throat. "But in answer to your question, *Are you Camorra?*—the answer is no. You are not born into the Camorra. You choose to be involved or you don't. And you do not."

"I still don't understand what it means, the Camorra."

"Nor do you need to know, Isabel. Please just leave it be. It's what we all should have done."

"We?" I said. "Who do you mean by 'we'?"

She shook her head, looked at me sadly, then glanced at her watch, a small, exquisite piece of jewelry with a black face studded with little diamonds. "We must go. The princess's apartments are only shown to certain groups who book a tour in advance. And I have such a group coming in right now."

She stood. Reluctantly, I did the same. "Could we get together later?" I asked. "For coffee or dinner?"

"I am not sure, Isabel. I will let you know."

"Or tomorrow?"

She led me from the room, locking the door behind her. "Yes, possibly tomorrow."

Our heels clacked on the marble floor as we passed through the gallery. It seemed less majestic, less fascinating somehow now that Elena didn't have the spring in her step, the joy in her eyes.

A minute later, I was outside on the street. "Goodbye, Isabel," Elena said. And then she closed the door.

19

When I got back to the campus, most of the students were studying for an exam. The place was quiet, the campus snack bar filled with students staring into their laptops. I decided to follow suit and do some studying of my own.

I brought my laptop into the snack bar and found an empty table at the back. As I waited for it to power up, I lifted the necklace that Elena had given me and studied the amber stone. It was beautiful, seemed mysterious. I liked that I now owned something that had been in my family for a long time.

Once my laptop was up and running, I did an Internet search for *helicopter crash.* Even though such a crash sounded like a rare thing to me, I learned that they happen every day somewhere in the world. They almost always resulted in serious injuries or death. There were even lawyers who specialized in nothing but helicopter crashes. Usually pilot error was the cause of the crash, although it could also be a defective part or design, particularly if the helicopter was made from rebuilt or worn parts. And what my mom had been told—that crashes into large bodies of water often result in the human remains being unrecoverable—was true.

I read some more and studied photos of crashes until

I began to feel ill, imagining my father inside those wrecked twists of metal.

After I closed the search engine I checked my e-mail. There was one from Maggie, and the subject line read, *I GOT A TICKET!!! I'LL BE THERE TOMORROW!!*

I clapped my hands, drawing a few frowns from the studying students. I read quickly through Maggie's e-mail, jotting down the information about her flight. At the end she'd written, *There's one thing you have to do for me—book us a hotel. I love Loyola, but I am too old to be staying in a dorm, and so are you. I know, I know, you don't have any cash but I do. Consider it a birthday gift. Pick any place you want.*

I thought of the hotel where Elena and I had met. I found their Web site and booked a room for the next day, wincing at the rate and thanking God for good friends.

I went to the vending machines and bought a bottle of water. When I got back to my table, a message light had popped up on my phone. I called my voice mail. The message was from Mayburn. "I've been trying to find Dez Romano," he said, with no other greeting, "but he's keeping a low profile. Been looking for someone named Ransom, too, but I'm not getting anything. Probably a nickname. I did find that guy—R. J. Ohman. He wasn't technically a Fed. He was a flight instructor who did civilian contracting for the FBI. Retired now. Lives in Bozeman. I've got a number for you." He listed it. "Let me know if you want me to call him."

But this was one call I wanted to make myself. I looked at my watch. It was morning in Bozeman. I took my cell phone outside and called. The phone rang and rang and rang. No answer. No voice mail. I tried it again. Same thing. I went back inside and texted Mayburn. *You're sure that's the right number? I tried it but it just rings and there's no machine.*

A minute later, he texted me back. *I just tried, too. Got the same thing. I'll see if I can dig up another number or e-mail, but it was pretty tough to find that one.*

I sat back in my chair and tried not to be frustrated. I picked up my cell phone again and went back outside. A basketball court of sorts had been set up there. The hoops were literally baskets with the bottoms cut open. The court itself was red earth, and the guys playing on it kicked up puffs of red dust.

I sat on a stone wall and watched them for a minute, then tried R. J. Ohman's number again. I kept getting the same endless ringing.

I called my mom on the private phone number for her charity. So few people knew about that number that I figured if Dez and Michael were tapping any phones that wouldn't be considered a place I might call.

"Izzy!" she said, "I was just about to call you. Do you want to come over for brunch? We have pastries from Red Hen Bakery, and Spence is going to make those decadent cream-cheese omelets." There was a shout in the background. "What's that, Spence?" my mother called. "Oh, yes," she said, speaking into the phone again, "and he says to tell you later that he's making some kind of cocktail that's got kiwi juice in it." She dropped her voice. "That doesn't sound good, but you know Spence when he gets on these kicks."

I looked around the snack bar, full of students a decade younger than me, and suddenly, I missed Chicago. "I can't come over, Mom. You won't believe this, but I'm in Italy."

"What? Italy? When did you leave town?"

"Saturday afternoon. I didn't have anything going on with the job search, and I found out the Loyola campus in Rome had cheap rates for alums so I just went for it."

"Spence, Charlie," she said, sounding as if she was calling over her shoulder. "Izzy is in Rome."

"Fabulous!" I heard Spence say.

"What?" Charlie said, then he got on the phone. "Hey, Iz."

"How's the new job at the radio station?"

"Awesome. I love it."

"That's great."

"Yeah, it is." A pause. "What are you doing over there?"

"Visiting with Aunt Elena. And Maggie is coming over tomorrow."

"Find out anything I should know?"

"I'm working on it," I said, not wanting to get into anything when he was in front of my mom. "I'll keep you posted."

"Let me say hi!" I heard Spence say. Then he was on the phone. "Izzy, you must, and I mean you *must* go to Obika. It's a great restaurant."

"That sounds Japanese."

"No, no, it's a mozzarella bar. And it is heaven." Spence rattled on about making reservations, and recommended about thirty other restaurants. "Your mother wants to talk to you, but I'll think of some other places."

Then my mother was back on the phone. "I can't believe you just picked up and went to Italy. What made you decide to go?"

Two men trying to rough me up in a butterfly room. "I just decided to take advantage of my time off." *And I'm hoping to find out about Dad.*

"Well, I think it's wonderful. Absolutely wonderful. Have you called Elena?"

"I saw her today."

"Fantastic. How is she?"

I told her that Elena looked well. I explained about the

gallery and her job. I didn't mention that Elena had all but given me the bum's rush out of there. "There's something I meant to ask her today, and I forgot—why was Dad taking helicopter lessons? I mean, his job didn't require it, right?"

"No, it was just a hobby. Something he wanted to learn."

"Had he always had that desire? I mean, had he talked about it a lot?"

"Not really. He'd gotten his pilot's license in college. He kept it current but didn't use it that often. Then one day he started talking about flying helicopters, and your father was very determined when he wanted something. Within days, he was taking lessons."

"How long after that did he die?"

"A couple months." She sighed. "Time goes so fast. And then he was gone."

20

About the fifty-third time I called Bozeman, Montana, the phone was answered. By that point, I was back in my dorm room, jet lag catching up with me, getting ready for bed. As the phone rang at the other end, I was barely paying attention. Somewhere along the way, I'd stopped believing that anyone would ever answer, and yet, my finger kept hitting the redial button.

"Ohman here," a brisk but friendly male voice said.

"Mr. Ohman? R. J. Ohman?"

"You got him."

"This is Isabel McNeil." If there was any recognition of my name, he said nothing. "I'm calling from Italy," I said. "I wondered if I could ask you a few questions about my father."

"Who's that?"

"Christopher McNeil."

Still nothing.

"He died in a helicopter accident twenty-some years ago. I think you might have been his flight instructor."

"Ah, hell, sure. You're Chris McNeil's kid?" He tsked. "That still bothers me."

"What do you mean?"

"Well, helicopters are more dangerous than planes,

but you don't expect to lose a student. I trained him well. I train everybody well."

"Was he a good student?"

"Hell, yeah. Always came prepared. Took it very seriously. But there were concerns about the R22s back in those days."

"What's an R22?"

"The chopper. Could be kind of a swirly bird. Damn near lost one myself."

"So there were problems with it?"

"Well, the lawyers told me not to say this—they were afraid we'd get sued, I guess—but I was never very good at holding my tongue." He grunted. "But anyway, yeah. The R22s used to have problems because they would start oscillating and student pilots would sometimes overcorrect. That would make it worse and the blades would flex and slice the tail rotor right off."

"What happens then?"

"Once that tail rotor comes off, it's a quick trip to the undertaker. You go into auto rotation. And then you're going down."

I winced. If he had died, what must my dad have gone through? Had he been scared? "Do you think it was excruciating for him?" My voice came out soft.

"Honey, he probably never knew what happened. I'd guess he didn't even have time to think about the fall, and when you hit that water, you have nothing more to worry about anyhow. He didn't suffer."

"Did you inspect the helicopter before he took off?"

"Yep. Nothing wrong that I saw. We both did the pre-flight inspection."

"What does that entail?"

"A long checklist. We pilots do almost everything from checklists. I always tell my students, you might think you're pretty smart, but a checklist has a hell of a lot more intelligence."

"And what did you find during the inspection?"

"Everything looked good to me. To your dad, too. This was one of your dad's solo flights, so he spent a lot of time around the chopper before he left."

"Is it typical for students like him to fly over bodies of water like Lake Erie?"

"Well, in order to get their certification, they have to complete a number of solo cross-country flights. Up to him to chart his course. And I checked it with him. Also, the helicopter was equipped with pontoons so he could practice water landings if he wanted."

"Did he file a flight plan?" I thought of some of my Internet research, which mentioned flight plans.

"Yep. And didn't look like he was off course."

I sat down on the dorm bed, pushing a toe back and forth across the black-and-white patterned linoleum floor. "Mr. Ohman, you worked with the FBI, is that right?"

I thought he'd hesitate, maybe be secretive, but he answered with a quick, "Yep. Civilian contractor with them for over thirty years."

"I know my father did consulting for the federal government. What I don't understand is why he would need helicopter training."

"Didn't need it from what I knew. Just wanted it. And at that time, if you worked with the Feds, they encouraged all kinds of skill-set enhancements. I was told your dad simply wanted to learn how to fly a helicopter. He was already a pilot. My job was to go around the country and train federal employees how to fly better or fly different aircraft."

"He worked for a city police department and consulted for the Feds."

"Well, he had something more than consulting to do with the Feds if they hired me."

I didn't know what to say to that.

"Was he a good pilot?"

"Absolutely. Conscientious and thorough. I was surprised as hell when we lost him."

I thought about the question that had been playing in my mind. I wasn't sure whether to ask it. If I did, and I was right about my hunch, would it signal something, start some chain of events?

But I've never been good at holding my tongue. "Is there any chance my father's death was faked so that he could enter the witness protection program?"

He actually laughed at me. It wasn't an unkind laugh exactly, more of a chuckle. "Why do you think your father was in the witness protection program?"

"Because his body disappeared and…" I figured I might as well say it. "I think I saw him recently."

He didn't laugh at that. "What do you mean?"

I told him what had happened in the stairwell. I told him I thought I had heard my father's voice. He listened, then said, "What did you say your first name was?"

"Isabel. Izzy."

"Well, Izzy, I'd never thought about that possibility before. Really hadn't. The fact of the matter is if he was entering a Fed protection program, they wouldn't have told me. But thinking about it now, seems like it's not a bad guess."

21

I called Mayburn right away. It was nine o'clock Rome time, two in the afternoon in Chicago. "What do you know about the witness protection program?"

"Nothing, really," he said.

"Know anybody who does?"

"Well…" I heard him making a clicking sound with his tongue, as if he was ticking off the potentials in his head. "Hey," he said then, his voice a little excited, "I do know this journalist in town. Pulitzer prize winner, all that stuff. He wrote a bunch of articles and then eventually a book about this guy in the witness protection program who saw the murder of a senator. He hired me to dig up background on some of the people in the book."

"Think he'd talk to us?"

"What do you want to know?"

"If my dad was in the witness protection program. Or if it's a possibility."

More clicking of the tongue.

"What?" I said.

"I'm wondering if you should be leaving this whole thing alone."

"Like you're leaving Lucy alone?"

"Different situation."

I got up and walked to the window, looked down at the dimly lit path that wound through the stone busts. It struck me at that moment, looking at those statues, those torsos of the dead—was making them a way to try and keep the person alive? To remember them? Was that what I was doing here in Rome, figuratively creating a stone bust of my father as I pushed at what might be nothing?

"Will you call the journalist for me?" I asked Mayburn.

"I'll try him," he said. "You going to be around for a while?"

I looked around the dorm room. I should have been out in the midst of a Roman night. But as magic a city as Rome is, the thought of finding my father was more so.

"I'll be here," I said again, and hung up.

I lay back on the hard, thin dorm bed and finally thought about Theo. I take it back. It wasn't that I hadn't been thinking of him. I'd gotten a text from him, the day I left. *You around?* he'd written. *It's the weekend, and the only place I want to be is with you.*

Today, after he hadn't heard from me, he'd texted, *How was your weekend? I missed you.*

I hadn't answered either text. I wasn't ready to let go of my farewell with Sam, and if I texted with Theo it seemed like moving on. And as much as I knew I needed to do that eventually, I wanted to make sure I was thinking about the goodbye with Sam, feeling it and what it meant for us. It wasn't hard. Those few minutes in Sam's apartment were unrelenting. It wasn't so much the memory of Alyssa (although that thought tortured me when I let it) but rather the recollections of us—of his arms, our clinging to each other like the last survivors of a boat crash—that were making me sick. So sick that aside from my first big meal outside the Piazza Barberini, I'd eaten little. It was why I was fine to simply spend time in a dorm, searching around on the Internet for clues about my father, to spend my night in a tiny room wondering.

And now that I was waiting for Mayburn to call, now that I couldn't think of anything else to do, all I could really focus on was this big, hollow-as-hell feeling and the memory of that moment with Sam, that moment that said, *It's over. Truly, truly over.*

I looked at my cell phone, thought about calling him, but then I realized that a message had come in sometime during my call with Mayburn.

"Izzy," I heard when I checked my voice mail. I knew that kind, soft voice. Lucy.

"I'm not sure where you are," she said, "and you probably won't recognize this number. I'm using my sister's cell phone. She's in town, visiting me. I don't feel like being alone with Michael, even though we're trying to patch things up. He swears he didn't tape my conversations or anything in the house, but he admitted he heard me talking to you, making plans to meet you at the nature museum. I guess he'd come back in the house and I didn't know he was there. He says he might have mentioned it to Dez. He can't remember." She laughed under her breath. "That sounds like such a bunch of crap when I say it out loud, but I'm still back to wanting to be a hundred percent sure before I end things with him." A sigh. "Anyway, I wanted to see how you were. I've been afraid to call you because I feel like I made that whole thing happen at the museum. I shouldn't have involved you. I'm really sorry."

Holding the phone, I shook my head at it. It was *me* who had involved Lucy. I had only brought trouble into her world with the work I'd done with Mayburn. Because of me, her husband was awaiting trial on money laundering charges and a host of other things, and she was poised to be a single mom. On the other hand, Lucy had told me after Michael was arrested that she was relieved, because he had been a nightmare to live with, emotionally abusive to say the least, and when he was gone she felt she could breathe for the first time in her life.

I was staring at the phone, thinking, when it rang.

"Hey," Mayburn said. "He's around, and he'll talk to us."

"Who?"

"The reporter. Weren't we just talking about that?"

"Yeah, but I just got a message from Lucy."

No response.

"Mayburn?"

"What did she say?" His voice was quick, flat.

"She was calling me from her sister's cell phone. She wanted to check on me. She was apologizing to me."

"Jesus."

"I know. She's the sweetest person on the planet."

"In the universe."

"You miss her."

"Yeah. But it doesn't help to talk about it. Give me the sister's cell-phone number."

"Has she given it to you?"

"If she had, then why would I be asking you?"

"I'm not giving it to you. You need to let her have her space."

"I need to make sure Lucy is okay."

"She's okay. You know that. You just want to call because of you, not her. You can't take being apart from her. Believe me, I understand."

Silence.

"I'm not giving it to you for your own good. But I'll hold on to it, I promise. So, this reporter," I said. "How do I talk to him?"

Mayburn exhaled. "I'll call him and conference us in."

"Damn, you know how to make things happen," I said. "I appreciate this."

"Yeah, yeah. Hold on." There was quiet for a moment and I took a breath, staring at an old photo, cheaply framed, that hung on the dorm wall—a shot of the sun hitting the dome of a Roman church in a silvery green stream of light.

"Iz, ya there? I've got Stephen Gooden on the line. Steve, can you hear us?"

We all said our hellos. "So, what can I help you with?" Stephen said. He had a resonant, academic-sounding voice. "Something about the witness protection program?"

"Yeah," I said. "It's something to do with my father. I guess I'm just wondering exactly how the witness protection program works."

"Well, for starters, there are a couple of different kinds of programs. The federal marshal program, the U.S. Attorney's program and the state level."

"What's the difference between those three?"

"Well, the federal marshal's program usually involves a witness in a case with the Justice Department or the FBI. The U.S. Attorney's office has separate funding to protect people who might be witnesses in an upcoming case or something like that. And then there's the state version. Local police or almost any law enforcement can put someone into protection mode. None of these programs are much fun."

"What do you mean?"

"They're essentially social services. They set someone up with an identity, give them a little cash or a new job and turn them loose. After a year, no more financial assistance. Used to be they didn't even provide any papers or documentation. Today, there's still very little follow-up."

"So, does that mean that the person can come out of hiding at anytime?"

"It's not exactly hiding. But, yeah, it works something like that. I mean, a federal employee can't stay with someone twenty-four hours a day in order to make sure a witness doesn't get themselves into trouble after the case is over."

"How do you know if someone is in the witness protection program?"

"You don't. That's the whole point."

"So they just go away forever?"

"Look, do you want to tell me what drain we're circling around? I mean, is there something more specific you want to know?" He didn't say this unkindly. In fact, he sounded as though he wanted to help.

So I told him about my father's helicopter accident. I told him what the flight instructor had said. "From what you've heard, Steve, is there any chance they faked his death and put my father in the program?"

"Doesn't sound like it to me. In every case I've heard of they take the whole family."

"What do you mean by that—'take the whole family.'"

"That's not the right way to say it. What I mean is that they'll usually put the entire family unit in the program. The point is to keep everyone safe. The whole faking of the death thing is really just a myth. In actuality, you disappear. They don't tell people you died. It's too complicated to find a body and have a funeral."

"There was no body in this case," Mayburn said, speaking up. "Does that red flag anything?"

"No. Like I said, they wouldn't usually just eliminate one person. They'd make the whole family disappear."

"The family just takes off?" I asked.

"Essentially. They say they're moving out of town to take a new job. Sometimes, the program doesn't let them talk at all—they just move 'em in the middle of the night.

But faking deaths? The government doesn't do that. I mean, your father would have to have been so instrumental, so key to a massive case or a huge federal program. Even then…I really doubt it."

The disappointment, layered on top of the sagging sadness of what was left of Sam and me, made me take a few steps to the bed and fall back on it. I held the phone to my ear. I heard Mayburn asking the guy a bunch of other questions. I thanked Steve, thanked Mayburn, said it was late Rome time, and hung up.

A bouquet of sounds came from the room above me—music with loud bass, footsteps, scraping of furniture, laughing. I could almost see the group of students who were up there—I'd been one myself years ago. They were drinking Moretti beers and pulling off hunks of bread from the local market, gesturing with the bread while they talked about politics and international law and the professor who would administer their exam tomorrow.

The music got louder. More scraping and shouts of laughter. As much as I wanted them to shut up, I was envious of them. But then I remembered my own friend. Maggie was coming tomorrow. The thought gave me a burst of energy.

I sat up, turned the lights up brighter, put my own music on—blaring a Wilco tune—and got back on the Internet.

The Camorra, I learned from my research, became a powerful force in Naples in the 1800s, when its members acted, essentially, as law enforcement for the Bourbon monarchy. When Naples officially became a part of Italy, the Camorra was forced aside. But they were never eradicated from the city of Naples and the Campania region, and they once again became a powerful presence in the mid-1990s with control of the area's garbage disposal.

Apparently, they hadn't done such a good job—no regard for the environment, much less the health of residents—and yet officials couldn't get them out, couldn't put an end to the warring clans of Camorra, who all kept fighting each other for control, making it unlike the *Cosa Nostra* in Sicily, the *Sacra Corona Unita* in *Puglia* or the *'Ndrangheta* in Calabria. The Camorra infighting led to massive violence in Naples, most notably drive-by shootings which often killed civilians, as well as *Camorristi.*

I sat back from my computer. I thought of my aunt Elena's words that morning. *Dangerous,* she had said about the Camorra. *You must be very careful.*

Was it just the Camorra in general that she feared? Or specific people inside the organization? Could it be that one of those people was my father? And why hadn't she been more surprised or alarmed when I'd talked about hearing my father, wondering whether he could be alive?

I leaned forward and typed a search for *Camorra* and *United States.* The site I found mentioned the Rizzato Brothers. They had been Camorra, but since their disappearance, no one knew whether there was any Camorra left in the country. *The exact nature of the Camorra's presence in America currently is unknown,* said another site. Another final site stated simply, *The Mafia in America, the* Cosa Nostra, *is almost wholesome compared to that of Naples's Camorra.*

22

Tuesday morning I was up long before the sun, checking the Internet religiously for Maggie's flight. *Delayed,* it kept saying, but then finally it reported she was in the air. She was hours away, and I could not freaking wait to see her.

That intense desire to see Mags, to talk to her, was something new, something different from the last few years. Going through this roller coaster of a search for my dad—*it's stupid, it's not, he might be alive, of course he's not*—and not having Sam to talk to, I realized just how much I'd turned to him over the years and how much I'd turned away from Maggie. It was unintentional, of course, the usual fallout from getting into a serious relationship. But now, I wanted to talk to her more about her breakup with Wyatt and how she was feeling. I wanted to tell Maggie everything about my dad. I needed to tell her about Sam, too. I hadn't talked with anyone about our breakup—what felt like the real one—and the memory was starting to fester and rot in my mind, needing to be dissected, just to make sure I was reading it tragically right before it disintegrated entirely.

I took a shower and dressed, then got back on the computer. In my research the night before, I'd found that there was something called the National Antimafia Directorate in Italy. In fact, the headquarters were in Rome. So

I started to do some more in-depth research on the directorate. After half an hour of trying to convert Italian words into English, I finally found an address for the place, apparently not too far from the hotel, the one I'd been to with Aunt Elena, the one Maggie and I would be checking into today.

I went downstairs to the porter and asked for exact directions to the hotel and from there to the directorante. When I mentioned that place was the "antimafia office," he raised his eyebrows then shook his head in sort of a silent *no-no-no* kind of way.

"Yes," I said, "please tell me how to get there."

Again that shake of his head. "You no want to go there. Go to Colosseum, go to Pantheon."

"Per favore," I said pleadingly. Then for good measure, I put my hands together in a prayerlike position, the way I'd seen the Italians do, and said it over and over…*Per favore, per favore, per favore.*

Finally, he laughed, shrugged. He took my map and circled a location.

I flashed him a smile and tipped him some euros. Tucking the map under my arm, I went upstairs to my dorm room. I looked around once more. It had been wonderful to visit Loyola Rome for a few days. But it was time to go.

In the still, dusty-yellow quiet of the Roman morning, I packed everything into my suitcase and took a cab to the hotel. Once there, I stowed my luggage in the hotel's lobby, since it was too early to check in, and left. When I reached *via Giulia,* the street the antimafia office was on, I stopped to consult my map and read about it in my guidebook. It was a wide-laned avenue, much bigger than the usual Italian streets, and it had been created during Renaissance Rome to connect all the major governmental institutions. During the sixteenth century, it had been fashionable to live there, the guidebook said, and I marveled at that one phrase—*during the sixteenth century*—since very little had been fashionable in the U.S. then. *Via Giulia* was now a cobbled, shaded street that seemed to house mostly antique and jewelry shops.

After fifteen minutes of strolling and glancing at the map, I found the directorate. The building itself was medieval-looking, brown with steel bars on the windows. A black stone sat near the entrance. On it, written in red, was *La Direzione Nazionale Antimafia.* There was a bell. I rang it. Once, then again. A few minutes later, a *carabiniere* stepped outside. He looked me up and down, raised his eyebrows.

"Buongiorno," I said. *"Parla inglese?"*

A nod. *"Sí."*

"Great. I'd like to speak to someone in the Antimafia Directorate."

The policeman turned and opened the door, holding it for me. Inside, he led me through a courtyard garden. In Italy, apparently even the government knew how to do a courtyard right.

On the other side we entered another door, and the *carabiniere* gestured at a desk. No one was behind it. A logbook sat open on top of it, and the man nodded, as if saying, *Sign it.*

I picked up the pen that sat there, held my hand poised over the book. Should I give my real name? I didn't see any way around it. If I was going to ask about my father, I'd have to give *his* name. And they might ask for identification. And if I got anywhere with these people and they found out I had lied, that wouldn't be good.

I signed the book, then looked at the *carabiniere.*

"*Uno momento,*" he said. He stood silently, arms behind his back.

A woman in a suit and a scowl came to the desk. She looked at my name in the book, then rattled off a few Italian words, her tone giving me the impression that she was saying, *What in the hell do you want?*

"Is there someone I can speak to?" I said.

"Perché?" Why?

"I'd like to ask some questions about the Camorra."

Silence.

I glanced from the woman to the *carabiniere* and back. Neither moved a muscle. "I think I might be from a Camorra family," I said. "Technically anyway. And I'm trying to find my father. He did consulting for the U.S. government. And I know he was involved in the case of the Rizatto Brothers."

She frowned deeper. "You are *americana?*"

"Yes."

"Your name, *per favore.*"

I pointed at the box I'd signed. "Isabel McNeil."

"Do you understand where you are?" She gestured around the office. It was fairly nondescript, looked like a reception office anywhere.

"The National Antimafia Directorate."

"Yes. And do you know what is here, what we do?"

I felt the urge to say *Mafia hunting?* I ignored it, kept quiet.

"We are prosecutors," she said. "You understand?"

"Yes, I'm a lawyer."

"Okay, so you understand. We do not answer questions, we prosecute. We do not give out information."

"Well, where would I get information? I mean, is there…" What *was* I looking for exactly? A Mafia museum? "…a place to do research about someone from the United States, someone I know who was working on a case involving the Camorra and then—" I was about to say *died,* but instead said, "—disappeared."

"Not here." She gave a brusque shake of her head. "You will not get that information here."

She gestured at the door. The *carabiniere* stepped forward, ushering me toward the door and back through the courtyard. Once again, I found myself standing outside the building.

And that, apparently, was that.

I stood another moment, looking at the door. I was about to turn away when it clicked open. I expected to see the *carabiniere* frowning, telling me to *move along* or whatever they say in Italian, but instead a young man stepped outside. He looked about my age. He had sandy-brown hair and gleaming blue eyes. Unlike the *carabiniere*'s and the woman's, those eyes were smiling.

"You said you were here for what?" he asked.

When I hesitated, he pointed to the camera above the door. "They are everywhere in the building. We see and hear everything."

"Oh," I said, a little uncomfortable, "I was just here to ask some questions…."

"Come," he said, gesturing away from the camera. We took a few steps up the street. He nodded at me, encouraging me to continue.

As I spoke, the man nodded, his eyes gleamed some more. "You are in *Roma* for how long?" He smiled, showing lots of teeth.

"I'm not sure."

"Well, come." He waved an arm up the street. "Let us take a coffee, and we will talk."

23

He didn't ask my name. But then, he'd heard everything I'd said at the office. He already knew that. Still, I offered my hand. "Isabel McNeil."

He shook it, bowing slightly. "Alberto Giani."

He began walking, sort of casually strolling. Hesitantly, I followed. I was here to ask questions, after all, and hopefully, he was here to give me answers.

We walked to the *Campo de' Fiori,* a big piazza that hopped at night with tourists since it was lined with bars like the Drunken Ship and Sloppy Sam's. But in the morning, aside from the fruit and vegetable markets, many establishments were closed. The smell of old cheese wafted through the piazza and newspapers blew haphazardly.

I looked at Alberto. He smiled again, gestured at one of the places that was open. We went inside. Patrons stood at the bar, sipping, or in some cases sipping-disguised-as-slugging, from white cups topped with foam.

Alberto stepped up to the cashier and ordered two cappuccinos.

"No, no," I said, moving beside him. "Tea, *per piacere.*"

"Tea?" both the cashier and Alberto repeated. They both pronounced it like *tay.*

"Sí," I said. "Decaffeinated, please."

Now they both stared at me with puzzled faces.

"Decaffeinato," I said. Since I'd been out of work, I'd noticed that the caffeine in my usual green tea was making me jittery, as if my body didn't have enough daily running-around-stress to soak it all up. So, I'd switched to decaf. It wasn't much fun to be a decaf tea drinker, I'd found, at least not when you went to a coffee shop. The clerks always looked disappointed at the order. There were usually only a few lame selections, like chamomile or lavender, to choose from. But if I felt marginalized as a decaffeinated tea drinker in the U.S., I knew Italy would be fifty times worse, and so before I'd left, I'd learned to say *decaf* in Italian.

Almost defensively, I repeated it now. *"Decaffeinato."*

Alberto nodded, as if to say, *Okay, then,* and he and the cashier had a flurried, indecipherable conversation before the cashier seemed to cave.

When we sat on barstools near the window, I thanked him for talking to me and launched into my questions about the Camorra.

But he wasn't responding. Or suddenly, I realized, he wasn't listening. He was just bobbing his head, his gaze bobbing somewhere lower than mine.

"Can you help me with this kind of thing?" I asked, bending down a little to try and catch his eyes. "Can you tell me about the Camorra?"

He gave what seemed a blasé shrug. "There are some Camorra in Rome, but mostly they are in *Napoli.* You want the Camorra, you go to *Napoli.* But you no want the Camorra. So, what do you do in America? For a job?"

"Well, you heard me in the office, right? I'm a lawyer." I didn't feel much like a lawyer right now, but hoped it would lend me some cred.

"What kind of lawyer?"

"Entertainment."

His eyes went big. He named a few pop bands from America. "You are their lawyer?"

"No. Look, if I wanted to find out about someone in the United States who was working on something long ago, maybe something involving the Camorra, could you help me with that?"

"How long ago was this person working on it?" he asked, although he didn't sound particularly interested.

"Almost twenty-two years."

He gave me that big Italian shrug. "Twenty-two years? Ah!" He shook his head, leaned in a little. "So. Where are you staying in *Roma?*"

I was about to mention the name of the hotel, but something made me lie. "The Hassler," I said, naming a hotel atop the Spanish Steps.

"Ah, Hassler! They charge too much for drinks, but the courtyard..." He snapped his fingers. "*Bellissimo!* Have you been to the courtyard?"

I squeezed my lips together, trying to figure him out. What was with all the personal questions? "Not yet," I muttered finally.

"We will go." He gestured between the two of us, then cocked his head to one side and looked at me. "You are how many years?"

"Excuse me?"

"You are twenty-five years?"

"Twenty-nine."

"You have a boyfriend?" he asked.

And suddenly I got it. He was *hitting* on me. At *last*—an Italian guy who still knew how to chase women no matter what the circumstances.

I flashed a smile. "No. No boyfriend." I leaned in, and then I charged forward with my questions.

But the guy couldn't be budged. By the time he'd finished downing his cappuccino, he was already trying to get me back to his apartment.

"I can't," I said. "Thank you. Can you tell me anything about the Camorra?"

He made a hand-waving gesture. "I already tell you. The Camorra is in *Napoli.* You want the Camorra, you go to *Napoli.*"

"But they prosecute them here, right? The directorate does?"

"*Sí.* Here and in *Napoli.* But I am not prosecutor."

"Then what is your job?" I waited to hear *detective, investigator,* something like that.

"I am notary."

"You're a *notary?*" I leaned back, deflated.

"Yes. Yes, I am." Now, he was the one who sounded defensive. "Notary here is much bigger job than in the United States. It is an honorable position."

"I'm sure it is. But do you work with the Mafia at all?"

"Not so much." He beamed at me, flashed his teeth. "You meet me tonight?"

I pushed my tea away. "Not so much."

Ten minutes later, I was back at the hotel, alone and with no questions answered. I would have to keep going back to one source for them—Elena.

I looked at my watch and figured Palazzo Colonna was open for the day. My aunt would be at work, and it was time for more questions about this Camorra business and my dad. It all seemed too bizarre that my grandmother was Camorra, my grandfather had been killed by Camorra members, my father had been looking into a pair of brothers who were Camorra when he died, and *I* had been chased by another alleged Camorra member and saved, I thought, by my father.

I called the palazzo. No answer. Not even a machine. Typical Italy.

I tried again, and again, and finally at nine-thirty, the phone was picked up and I heard a pleasant, *"Pronto."*

"Elena?" I said.

"Justina."

"Oh, Justina, this is Isabel. Elena's niece."

"Chiè?"

I tried again to explain who I was. What was the Italian word for *niece?* I had no idea. Finally we managed to connect.

"Elena is no here," she said, switching to English.

"Do you know where she is?"

"She went to Poseidon."

"Poseidon?"

"Poseidon is waters. How do you say…healing waters. *Sí.*"

"And where is that?"

"Ischia."

Ischia. That was where the Rizzato Brothers were from. "It's a little island," I said. "Is that right? Outside *Napoli?*"

"Sí." Justina kept talking, saying Elena wouldn't be back in the office for a few days, in fact, she wasn't even sure when she would return.

In my mind I kept hearing Alberto—*You want the Camorra, you go to Napoli.*

When Maggie finally got into town, I was standing at the Fiumicino Airport, just outside the baggage area.

She emerged, blowing her honey-colored bangs out of her face, her tiny body about the same height as the large teal-blue suitcase she lugged behind her.

"Mags!" I shouted.

Her mouth opened in a wide grin. She ran around the fencing and hugged me tight. "Happy almost birthday!"

"Thank you. I'm so glad you're here!"

"Me, too!" She hugged me again, standing on her toes the way she does.

I pulled the luggage out of her grasp. "Jesus, what do you have in here?"

She laughed. "I had no idea what to pack for Rome these days. I mean, what do people wear now?"

I stopped, looked her in the eye. "What if I told you it didn't matter?"

"What do you mean?"

"Well, we're not staying in Rome. Don't kill me, but we're going to Ischia."

She opened her mouth. She seemed stumped for words, finally settling for, "What?"

"It's an island off the coast. It's not that far." I put my hand on her arm. "Mags, we're getting a train to Naples."

24

Dez Romano's man from the antimafia office called at 10:00 a.m. It was good to have his people everywhere, especially in organizations that were trying to fuck him.

"It's me," his mole said in Italian.

"*Sí.*" Dez gestured to his secretary that she did not need to leave his office. This mole wasn't important, wasn't any kind of *clandestino* supersleuth, just a watcher, there to report on certain topics when he came across them. The mole was Antonio Sandello, not that his name was of any significance. It was his heritage. He'd grown up in the System—what everyone on the inside called the Camorra—and although he now worked for the other side technically, as a video tech for the antimafia office, the kid harbored a dream to move to America, to live a big life there. Dez had promised to help him do that someday in return for a heads-up when information came through the office, usually from feeds from office cameras, dealing with anything that had to do with the Camorra and the United States.

"An American came into the office today," Sandello said.

"Is that right?" The System had never been successful at establishing a strong foothold in America, but Dez was going to change that. And people like Sandello were going to help him.

"Said she was looking for her father, someone working on a Camorra case when he disappeared."

"What kind of case?"

"Rizzato Brothers."

"Who was the person working the case?"

"Didn't say."

"Did the office give her anything?"

"Just the door. You know they do not hand out information."

"Certa," he said. *Obviously. Of course.* It would be so much easier for him if the office was loose with their information. "Did she come in cold?"

"*Sí.* She did not have an appointment. Walked in off the street."

"Interesting. Name?"

"Isabel McNeil."

Sandello pronounced it all wrong, but Dez recognized the name right away. She'd been on his mind for days.

He put down his pen and gestured for his secretary to leave. He asked Sandello a multitude of questions and learned that after being turned away, Isabel McNeil had walked down the street with a staff member of the office. A notary. The office's cameras recorded the direction they were heading, but then she'd gone out of range.

He told Sandello to talk to the notary, told him exactly how to do it, then he hung up, a little disappointed. She had seemed quite intelligent to him, but how fucking *stupida* did you have to be to run from the Mob and head straight for Italy?

Then again, maybe *he* was the stupid one. Could there have been any basis to the words she'd thrown out in that goddamned butterfly room—that she was a federal agent? Was *she* the one playing him?

25

Maggie and I took a seat in front of the travel agent's desk. In Italy, travel agencies are as plentiful as tomatoes, and they're always the most orderly places to book a trip in a very disorderly country.

"Tickets to Naples, please," I said, telling the agent we wanted to leave as soon as possible.

"Sí," the agent said. *"Napoli Centrale.* Regular or Eurostar tickets?"

Maggie sat, rubbing her head. "I still can't believe all this. I cannot believe it."

I'd told Maggie everything in the cab from the airport. The night on the stairwell, Dez and Ransom chasing me from the museum, finding Alyssa in Sam's apartment, our teary goodbye. I even told her about the fact I had been working for Mayburn. Mayburn would kill me, but I simply could not hold it back any longer. And it felt damn good to have my best friend once again knowing all.

But Mags was having a hard time wrapping her head around it. *"You?"* she was saying now. *"You* have been doing undercover work?" More rubbing of the head. "And your *dad?* You think he might be alive?"

I asked the ticket agent about the Eurostar price, did the math. "Shazzer," I said.

Maggie frowned. "What's *shazzer*? Is that an Italian word?"

"My replacement word for *shit*."

"Are you still on that kick? It's not working, by the way. You always end up saying the swearword because you have to explain it."

"Allora," the clerk said, "regular or Eurostar?"

"How much is the Eurostar?" Maggie asked.

"I can't afford Eurostar," I said.

Maggie dug a credit card out of her purse. "I'll get it."

"Wait. Mags, I don't want you paying for everything."

"Well, I'm paying for this." She gave the agent her card. "Do you remember the time we went to Florence on a 'regular' train? 'Regular' means the local line, in case you've forgotten."

I had a flashback—Maggie and me, an un-air-conditioned train car, the press of bodies around us. People were packed onto the seats, some standing one after another in the aisles, some huddled at the end of the cars, near the broken, powerfully smelly bathrooms. The heat had been junglelike, the moods of all the passengers beyond surly. When the train finally spat us out in Florence, Maggie and I had practically kissed the ground. We'd stayed an extra three days just to recover.

"Eurostar," I said definitively to the agent.

She nodded. "*Passaporti,* please."

After we gave them to her, Maggie nodded at my chest. "I've been meaning to ask you. What is that necklace?"

I lifted the amber stone and gazed at its bevels, which seemed to manufacture sunlight. "Elena gave it to me. It was my grandmother's."

"Stunning," Maggie said. "It suits you."

At the *Termini,* the main Rome train station, the heat was thick and the crowds thicker. The open-air nature of the place only supported humidity and prolific sweating, and yet the *Termini* was nicer than when I was last in town. A huge Nike store and other designer shops resided next to the *tabacchi,* and the place had a little sparkle where before it had been gritty-city.

Maggie breathed out hard as we walked through the *Termini,* throwing her shoulders back in an exaggerated way and squinting her eyes a little.

"What are you doing?" I asked.

"Getting ready for the onslaught."

"The onslaught of what?"

"The Italian guys." She sent a couple suspicious glances over her shoulder.

"You mean, the flirting and the harassing? They don't really do that anymore."

"Seriously?"

"Yeah. Just the notaries from the antimafia office."

On the train, we boarded a blissfully chilly car and began searching for our seats. Maggie struggled with her suitcase, muttering lots of *scusi, scusi* to the patrons she kept knocking into. When we found our seats, we looked at her bag, then back up at the overhead compartment, which seemed about nine feet high.

"How are we going to get that thing up there?" I asked.

Maggie exhaled determinedly. She'd never seen a task she thought she couldn't do. She squatted and began tensing her arms. I sighed and bent to help her.

But then we heard, "Let me get that."

We turned to see a huge Asian guy wearing an orange golf shirt and baggy jeans. He scooped up the massive suitcase with one hand, like a socialite picking up a kicky little purse, and slipped it into the overhead compartment.

"Thank you!" Maggie said.

"No worries."

Oddly, Maggie was wearing an orange-ish tank top and the same color jeans as the guy. She pointed at him and laughed. He laughed back.

The man dumped a beat-up leather shoulder bag on the seat across the aisle from us.

"Are you from the U.S.?" Maggie asked.

"Yeah, Seattle. You guys?"

"Chicago." Maggie held out her hand—she had to hold it at her eye level since the guy was so tall—and introduced us.

"Bernard." He had kind eyes, a wide nose and a full head of shiny, shaggy black hair. When he smiled at us, it was one of those smiles that made you want to know him.

I moved into the window seat. Mags sat next to me. When Bernard settled his big frame into the seat across the aisle, Maggie asked him, "What are you doing in Italy? Vacation?"

"I'm teaching a master's class in music."

"What do you play?"

"French horn."

"Oh, how cool," Maggie said. "It's such a beautiful instrument. I've always loved the sound of it. My grandfather has been taking me to the Chicago Symphony Orchestra since I was little."

"I've played there."

"You're kidding?" Maggie crossed her legs and turned her body to face him. "What did you play?"

"Mozart. *Horn Concerto Number Three.*"

"I love it."

"You know it?" He grinned big.

"Yeah, sure. And aren't there some Schumann pieces for French horn?"

He blinked. "Yeah. I can't believe you know those." He shook his head. "That's amazing. I hardly ever meet anyone who knows the horn." He shifted around in the seat, trying to find a comfortable position. I wondered if the guy flew coach class. For his sake, I hoped not. He wasn't so much fat as huge—probably six-foot-seven and nearing three hundred pounds.

"What about Strauss?" Maggie said. "Didn't he write a famous horn concerto?"

He blinked even more rapidly and gazed at Maggie, bedazzled. "Yeah," he said. "Yeah." After a few more blinks, he said, "I'm sorry, what do you do?"

Maggie gestured at the two of us. "We're lawyers."

"She's a lawyer," I said. "A very good criminal-defense lawyer. I'm not doing much of anything myself."

Maggie patted me on the knee. "She's got a lot going on right now. We're here to do some research on her family." She leaned a little across the aisle toward Bernard, asking a question about Beethoven that seemed to absolutely flatten him. After a moment's stunned pause he shifted his massive torso in the chair so he was turned more toward her and began to talk excitedly.

The train pulled out of the station, and I looked out the window as those two gabbed.

The outskirts of Rome weren't much to look at, populated as they were with garbage dumps and tired apartment buildings crisscrossed with lines of hanging laundry. But soon, the lackluster urban scene gave way to a majestic portrait of rolling green hills and ancient stone houses.

Maggie and Bernard talked the entire trip. He told her that he was Filipino, midthirties, and had been raised in different towns in California. He went to Juilliard, got a couple of master's degrees and was now with the Seattle Symphony Orchestra, although he was on sabbatical to teach in Europe for the summer. He and Maggie traded stories and info, talking louder when the train dipped occasionally into blackened tunnels, laughing when the train burst forth, back into the sunshine.

They tried gamely to include me, but it was nearly impossible because they seemed to have so much to say to each other—one of those conversations where one topic led to another to another to another, so that they kept saying things like, "Oh, don't let me forget to tell you about the time I played in Boston," or "You'd love my mom. Remind me to tell you about her."

When Bernard lugged his hulking self to his feet to go in search of the restrooms, Maggie turned to me, her big eyes round. "Oh my gosh, don't you think he's cute?"

"Uh…" A loaded question if I'd ever heard one. I settled for, "You know we never have the same taste in men." I had thought Maggie's last boyfriend, Wyatt, entirely too slick (and if I do say so myself, I was right). At the same time, though, Maggie had found Sam too All-American.

"I think Bernard is adorable," she said. "And he must be so talented." She sighed.

"You realize, of course, that he's more than twice your size?"

She shrugged, as if she hadn't thought about it, as if it didn't matter a whit.

"How do you even know all that symphony stuff? I know you go with your grandfather occasionally."

"More than occasionally. And he's had me listening to it all my life. It's like this bond that he and I have."

"Really? Interesting. I thought you guys were close just because of the criminal law stuff." Strange that there was this one thing I didn't know about Maggie. But then she hadn't known a rather big thing about me—my moonlighting with Mayburn—until the last hour or so.

She leaned toward me, lowering her voice to a whisper.

"Look, we have to spend the night in Naples, okay? I mean, I know you're set on chasing your aunt to Ischia, but he's been telling me about this pizza place in Naples. He says it's the best pizza in the world."

"We live in Chicago. We have amazing pizza."

"It's not about the pizza," she whispered, more fiercely now. "He wants to take us to this place, and I want us to go. Please, Iz."

"Well, of course."

"And I'm really jet-lagged," she threw in, although she looked as perky as I'd ever seen her. I didn't remind her that she'd told me she had gotten a great six hours of Ambien-induced sleep on the plane.

Bernard lumbered back down the aisle, smiling bashfully at Maggie as he sandwiched himself into his seat again. And then the two of them were off, veering conversationally all over the map.

I took out my cell phone and scrolled through my e-mails. Nothing exciting. Certainly no job offers or anything like that. I was, it seemed, missing absolutely nothing in Chicago.

Except maybe one person.

I looked at my texts.

There was another one from Theo. *Are you okay?* he wrote. *I have this weird feeling that something's wrong.*

I glanced at Maggie but she and Bernard were deep into a discussion about a sheep's-milk cheese from France they both loved. Another thing I didn't know about Maggie.

I excused myself and went to an empty seat a few rows away. I gazed out the window at fields of yellow wheat, the train's rocking motion making them seem as if they were undulating.

I wrote Theo back, *I'm in Italy.*

He texted back almost immediately. *Italy?? What are you doing there?*

It's a long story.

The phone rang almost right after I hit *Send.* "I'd better hear this long story," Theo said.

"It's too long. I swear."

"Who are you with?" Did he sound a little jealous?

I looked down the aisle at Maggie. She and Bernard were laughing, both of their heads thrown back. They almost looked as if they were in an odd sort of play, with their matching clothes, their different sizes, their drastically different looks. "My friend Maggie," I said. "Except…"

"Except what?"

"Well, now she's met a friend."

He laughed. "Ah, so she's just like you. Meets a guy within ten seconds."

I laughed now, too. We were both thinking about the night I met Theo. I'd walked into a club with a friend of mine and within five minutes I was enthralled with him and our conversation.

"I'm not usually like that," I said, "and neither is Maggie."

"So, where in Italy are you guys?"

"On a train. Almost to Naples. Tomorrow we're going to Ischia."

"Where's that?"

"Off the coast."

A pause. I tried to envision him, somewhere in the apartment he lived, the apartment I'd never seen. In fact, we'd rarely been anywhere together outside my apartment. Theo and I existed inside a bubble, almost. A very sexual one.

"You know," he said slowly. "I have my own plane."

"I remember that." Theo wasn't a pilot like my father,

but he and his business partner had a corporate share of a plane, a Falcon, or something like that. I'd discovered this the first time we'd dated when Theo and his partner had taken off to a remote site in Mexico, an annual surfing trip.

"It takes a couple of hours to get international clearance…" He sounded excited. "But I could be there before midnight."

I didn't know what to say. "Are you seriously talking about coming here?"

"Yeah."

"Don't you have to work?"

"Since you blew me off this weekend I worked most of the time. If I came I couldn't stay long. Just a day or two but…" He gave a nervous laugh, which made him seem fallible and human. "Would you even want me there? I guess you didn't really invite me."

I looked up the aisle at Maggie and Bernard. He was showing her what looked to be sheet music, his black hair almost touching her gold curls as their heads met in the middle of the aisle. "Consider yourself officially invited."

26

Dez Romano sat in his office, thinking about Isabel McNeil. He'd learned she was heading for Naples.

His mole inside the antimafia office talked to the idiot notary she'd had coffee with, and the guy had been only too eager to brag about his "date." Yes, she had talked about the Camorra, the notary said, and he had told her that if she wanted to know about the Camorra she should go to *Napoli.*

Once he knew about the Naples potential, Dez had put out a watch for her name. Because she'd given her passport to a travel agent to buy train tickets, his people had been able to find her reservation.

What was she doing? he wondered now. Was she after *him?* Was she really a federal agent, one who was trying to bring down the Camorra?

He lifted the phone and called a familiar number. Speaking in *italiano,* he described the situation in vague terms to the man who answered.

"Her name is *McNeil?*" the man said.

"Yes."

"And she is looking for her father? Is that Christopher McNeil?" The guy's voice was rough now.

Dez had never heard of Christopher McNeil, but he wasn't sure if he should admit that. Luckily, the man kept talking. "*Il duca* will want to talk to you about this. Stay by your phone."

The man hung up, leaving Dez surprised. *Il duca* was "the duke," the nickname for Flavio La Duca, the head of Dez's clan in Naples. It was La Duca who'd known Dez's distant family members in Italy and had reached out to him in the U.S. and brought Dez on board. Flavio La Duca was his boss.

Dez's phone soon rang and the gruff tones of the duke filled his ear. La Duca told him that Christopher McNeil was a *traditore,* a traitor of the worst kind. He told Dez how they had killed him two decades ago, put an explosive in his helicopter.

"So when this girl was telling the antimafia office that she was looking for him," Dez said, "you don't know what she meant by that?"

"No. But this is a man who was against the System, always had been. If there is any chance he is alive, any chance for us to bring him in and kill him, that would mean the world to the top."

The top was the person at the head of the Camorra. The clans warred against each other, and yet the person at the top knew all of them, could get the clans to do just about anything, except to stop fighting each other.

Dez thought he could do better. He wanted to be *the top,* the head of the Camorra, but he first needed to know who the person was. Once in control of that knowledge, he would be able to formulate his message to that person and eventually grow his own power not just in the U.S., but in Naples, as well. Then he would not only unite the clans and bring more power into the United States, he would take the Camorra around the world. He would operate the System worldwide.

This goal Dez had, it wasn't just for ambition's sake.

He was doing it because there was so much *potential* for this business—for money, for power, yes, but ultimately because it would allow him to craft his life the way he wanted it. Dez thought that everyone should be able to do that. He simply had grander tastes than most.

He and La Duca discussed the possibilities. La Duca said that Isabel McNeil was probably just a woman having issues getting over her dead daddy. Dez disagreed as kindly as possible, told him that Isabel McNeil was a keen woman, someone who learned quickly, acted quickly. He'd asked around about her since that night at Gibsons, since she had eluded him at the nature museum, and he'd learned that she had been involved with a string of bizarre events over the last year—a fiancé disappearing with a bunch of her client's money, a friend who ended up dead, causing McNeil to be considered a suspect in her murder. And yet when he'd met her, in that fucking purple silk dress that clung to her and with a gaze that said, *Yeah, I see you looking, go ahead,* she seemed as if she'd never been challenged, as if she wasn't bothered with any bad emotions from those situations.

La Duca paused when he heard Dez's assessment of Ms. McNeil, then said, "And you think that you are reading this correctly, *il diavolo?*" The devil. It was Dez's clan nickname.

Over the years Dez had gotten the feeling that the duke was presenting him with unique situations, one after another, testing him and yet also telling him that the Camorra didn't entirely trust any of their *americano* contingents.

So, as he always did, Dez now reassured La Duca of his commitment to him, to the Camorra and to establishing their place in the United States. He told him that the McNeil he knew, the girl, was a threat to them here, that she was the one who had brought down their launderer, Michael DeSanto.

"What should we do with her?" La Duca said, and Dez flushed with pride. For the duke to ask his opinion meant only one thing—he was finally being trusted. But Dez was smart enough to know that such trust was only for now, and he'd better prove himself by handling this situation with precision.

"Have someone waiting at *Centrale* in *Napoli,*" he told Flavio. "She's easy enough to spot." He described her with three words—*la testa rossa,* the redhead. "You'll see what I mean."

"Sí," La Duca said. "And then what do you want with her?"

"I want to know who she's with. I want to know where she goes. Any information your men can give me." Then he told La Duca what he eventually wanted from *la testa rossa,* and the duke agreed completely.

27

The station in Naples was nowhere near as nice as the one in Rome, and the line outside for taxis was at least a block long. When we finally reached the front of the line, Maggie and Bernard started to say their goodbyes, if only for a few hours. He was taking a taxi directly to the school where he would teach later in the week, but we'd all promised to meet up for dinner.

"So I definitely have your number, right?" Maggie asked, peering at her phone, then peering up at him, her head cocked back so far that her gold curls hung over her shoulders.

"You've got it," he said, a calm voice, a calm smile. He looked at his own phone, rattled off Maggie's number.

"But I don't know how to make a call over here." Maggie's voice was worried.

"I know how, Mags," I said.

"Here." Bernard raised his phone aloft. "I'll text you right now so you have it. You text me when you find a hotel."

"Okay, that'll work." Maggie kept gazing up, giving him a sunbeam of a smile.

"And I'm going to call you in one hour," Bernard reminded her.

He put his suitcase on the ground, bent down and gave her the most gentle of hugs.

When he turned and got in his cab, Maggie turned to me. "He's so amazing."

"He seems like a sweetheart," I told her.

"No, he is *amazing.*" She shook her head in wonder.

When we got into our own cab, our driver spoke perfect English and Maggie began chatting with him. "So what's the name of a really nice hotel here in Naples?"

"Grand Hotel Vesuvio," he said immediately. "On the waterfront. Looks at the bay."

"Perfect," Maggie said. "Take us there, please."

"Mags…" I said.

She held up a hand. "Stop. Please. I've got the money right now so let me spend it. When I'm flat broke in the future, you can take care of me."

"I will take you on a tour of the city on the way there," the driver said.

"No, no," I answered. "That will be too expensive."

"I do not charge for that."

I looked at Maggie.

"Let's do it," she said.

The driver took off, but then right away Maggie's office called. She spent most of the cab ride on the phone, while the driver pointed out the streets and sights. Naples was different from Rome—dirtier and certainly more dangerous-looking. The driver showed us the massive port where miles of boxy container ships spread out into the sea, Mount Vesuvius hulking over them all. The streets that surround the port were wide and flat, but the real Naples—the bubbling, chaotic inside—consisted of rocky, steeply angled streets, where children played along piles of street-side trash and under canopies of washed clothes strung from *appartamento* to *appartamento.* There were cafés on these streets, too, their doors open, their tables with pristine linens pushed against the soot-covered walls.

But when we turned onto the broad street that ran along the bay, Naples got pretty. The sea was a crisp teal-blue. About halfway down, a medieval castle made of brown stone seemed to rise out of the sea.

"*Castel dell'Ovo,*" the driver said, pointing to it. "Built in the sixth century."

Like so many buildings in Italy, the ancient edifice was flanked by a contemporary setting, in this case a gaggle of bars and cafés that stretched along piers where boats were tied.

Halfway down the block, the cab pulled in front of Grand Hotel Vesuvio, and Maggie finally hung up.

The bellman began to pull the luggage from the trunk.

"Wait," I said to him, hopping out of the cab. "Do you know if they have vacancies?"

"*Sí,* the hotel has rooms."

I bent down to talk to Maggie, still in the cab. "Let me go see how much it is."

She shook her head and scooted out. "Whatever it is, I'll bargain them down, and I'm in desperate need of a nap, so we're staying here." She gestured at the bellman to go ahead with the bags and paid the driver.

"Thank you," I said, stopping Maggie with a hand on her shoulder. "You are a good friend."

"Of course I am." She hoisted her bag higher on her shoulder. "Now, let's go check in."

Inside, the lobby was indeed grand and decorated with oriental rugs, potted palms and crystal chandeliers that hung from high, sparkling white ceilings. The front desk was made of carved dark wood topped with marble. As the clerk checked us in, Maggie pulled her phone from her bag. "I have to text Bernard." She smiled as her little fingers flew over the keys.

When she was done, I said, “Okay, can I get your attention for one second without Bernard or your office?”

She put her phone away. “Yes. Shoot.”

“Theo is on his way.”

She slid her credit card across the counter to the clerk. “On his way where?”

“Here.”

“Here, as in *Naples?*”

I nodded.

“When in the hell did that happen?”

“When you were falling in love with Bernard.”

“I’m not in love.” She made a little face that seemed to say, *At least not yet.*

I told her the story of how I’d called Theo, how he had a corporate share on a plane and said he’d be in Naples by midnight.

“And then what?” Maggie asked.

I shrugged. “I guess I didn’t think much after that. He said he couldn’t stay more than a day or two.”

The clerk handed the credit card back, and Maggie tucked it into her wallet. “Do you really like this guy, or is this a reaction to finding Alyssa in Sam’s apartment?”

I winced at the memory. “If anything it’s a reaction to Sam and me saying goodbye. It was just so…so final.”

“If it’s a reaction to that, why not just pick up an Italian guy? Why have the kid fly all the way over to Italy?”

“It was his suggestion, not mine.” I thought about it some more. “And there’s just something about him.”

“I can’t believe I haven’t met him.”

“Well, you will tonight.”

The rooms at the hotel weren’t large but they were beautiful. The floors were tiled in blue and yellow. A tall window overlooking the street and bay was covered with tasseled robin’s-egg-blue drapery.

While Maggie took a nap, I went back downstairs to the concierge desk. I was here in Naples to talk about the Camorra, but I had no idea where to do that. Once again, all roads pointed to Elena.

The concierge was an older gentleman who looked as if he took his profession very seriously.

When I asked for information about traveling to Ischia, he nodded somberly and gestured to a seating area to the left. "Please," he said, "sit down and I will bring you information."

A minute later, he had spread maps, ferry schedules and hotel pamphlets over the table. He sat down across from me. "Okay," he said, "you tell me what you want to do in Ischia."

"Is there a place called Poseidon?"

"Poseidon, yes." Now he sounded pleased. He riffled through the materials and pulled out a white brochure with blue-and-green lettering.

"I was told that this is a place for healing waters."

"Sí, sí," he said. "The island is…how you say…volcano? And so the water on the island is like medicine. Full of minerals. You may go different places on Ischia to sample the waters. Poseidon is one of the best." He made a gesture, his fingers and thumb together, and brought it to his lips as if he tasted something delicious.

"How do the waters heal exactly?" I asked.

"Well," he said, "how do I explain?" He looked upward, lifted his shoulders high and dropped them slowly, showing me that they did the Italian shrug as well in Naples as they did in Rome. "You sit in the waters. There are different temperatures with different minerals. You move from one pool to another. You relax, you are quiet, you eat well, you do not drink alcohol." Another shrug. "When you leave, you feel wonderful."

"Sign me up."

He opened the Poseidon brochure, and explained that Poseidon Gardens was essentially a park that charged daily admission. You spent the day in the different pools or on its beach and then you went home at the end of the day. We'd have to find somewhere to stay, he said, and showed me different brochures with hotels of varying costs.

"Thank you," I said. "Now, if I may ask you something different about Ischia?" *What the hell,* I thought. *Give it a shot.*

"Of course." He nodded gravely. "This is my job."

"I have heard that Ischia is a place where some Camorra people are from. Is that true?"

The concierge drew his head back and looked around swiftly. He looked back at me, his eyebrows pushed together, a stern expression on his face. "Why do you ask about the Camorra?"

I shrugged, giving my best impression of the Italian version. "I just wondered."

He shook his head. "No, no. Please. You don't ask about the Camorra."

"Why not?"

He sighed deeply. "The Camorra has done nothing but bring ruin to this city. Did you see the garbage outside?" He gestured with an arm toward the front door.

"Yes. I saw it." I thought of the children kicking balls and playing next to that garbage.

"That is all because of the Camorra. They take over the garbage, the recycling, so they say, but they cannot handle it. It was so bad, the Italian military had to step in." He made a disgusted face. "And did you see down at the docks? Did you see all the big ships?"

I nodded.

"The Camorra, they ship goods from China." He shook

his head, made a sad expression. "But they dump the waste into the waters. Everyone becomes sick." He shook his head again. "My mother, my family, ah! So many of my family have died because of the terrible waste that the Camorra puts into our water. Miss, you do not want to ask about the Camorra. No one around here wants to talk about them. This is not something for *turistas*."

I sat back and nodded. "I'm sorry," I said simply. Then, "I know it's not a matter for tourists, but my father died, and I think it was because of the Camorra."

The concierge swallowed, his mouth twisted a bit. He looked over his shoulder at the front desk. The few people behind it were on the phone, talking to guests. "What do you mean when you say this?"

"I believe my father was working on a case having to do with the Camorra. He died many years ago. I am trying to find out what happened."

The man's face softened. "What is your name?"

I held out my hand. "Isabel."

He shook it. "And I am Carlo." He gathered the brochures and pamphlets in his hands. "Come. Let's go somewhere where we can discuss this."

He led me past the side of the front desk and up a double staircase trimmed in silver and gold. Upstairs was a set of meeting rooms. But it was as if we were inside a grand *palazzo,* the walls decorated with art from all different periods—sketches, paintings, sculptures. Carlo took me into a meeting room where staff was cleaning up from a previous event. Coffee, tea and other refreshments still sat on a buffet table.

Carlo pointed at the table. "Please have something to drink."

I helped myself to a sparkling water with lemon. He said something in Italian to the cleaning staff, who left the room. Carlo poured himself a cup of coffee and we sat at one side of a table designed to seat ten people.

"Now," Carlo said. "This is unpleasant, but...okay. What do you want to know about the Camorra?"

I told him I just wanted the basics. What did the Camorra do or specialize in? Were they also in the United States? I really didn't understand much of anything about the group.

He took a sip of his coffee, then crossed his hands in front of him, lacing his fingers tight. He nodded. "The Camorra is not a group. Here in Naples, we do not even call it Camorra. We call it the System, and the System is not a group, either. It is made up of many clans. But for our discussion, let us call it the Camorra, okay?"

I nodded.

"The Camorra does many things. One is drug running. They take the drugs in at the port, then they take them around the country. They go to *Roma, Milano*. They have teenagers who take them to these big cities, and they reward the teenagers with a motorcycle when they are done. They do not tell these teenagers that if the *carabinieri* stop them, they will be arrested and they will spend ten years in prison. So that is one thing, the drugs. But really that is something little. They also try to do the garbage, which I tell you about already. The big thing for the Camorra right now is in fashion."

"Fashion?" I was definitely confused now.

"Yes, the Camorra deals in fashion. You see—" he spread his hands across the table "—this is how it works. The designers, the *italiano* designers will come to *Camorristi* brokers here in *Napoli*. They will say to these brokers, 'Okay, here is this fabric and from this fabric we want to make these dresses.' He gestured again at my dress. "They will tell the brokers, 'Please, find us the cheapest but best seamstresses.' The *Camorristi* then take the fabric, they go to different teams of seamstresses around *Napoli,* around the country, sometimes even in China, and they pick the groups they like. Those seamstresses then work all day, all night, around the clock, Saturdays, Sundays, every day.

"They work around the clock until they finish. Whoever finishes first, and also has the best product, the *Camorristi* broker will award them the contract. The designer then pays the broker, who pays that seamstress."

"What about the other seamstresses? The ones who have been making the dresses and still have the fabric?"

"A very good question. They get to keep that fabric, and the dresses they have made. The fabric is cheap. The designers do not care about it. So the *Camorristi* brokers pay those seamstresses, but less, for the dresses, and they sell them on…what do you call it? The black market?"

"Yes, the black market. Underground."

"*Sí,* but it is not always so underground. Sometimes they sell right to stores, and you *americani* will never know the difference. Very few people can tell the difference. Sometimes they sell to discount stores. Sometimes to *africani* who sell on the streets."

"Like in New York?"

"*Esattamente.* Exactly." He gestured at my yellow sundress. "For example, what designer has made your dress?"

"It's Parker Casey, an American designer." I twisted around and tried to see the tag on the dress.

"If that had been an Italian designer," Carlo said, "it could have been a Camorra dress. The problem with the Camorra is that they don't care about people. They use these people who work for nothing. The people don't stand up for themselves, because they live in an area where there's no other industry. There is nothing else for them to do to make money to feed their families. So they work for the Camorra. Many times, they give their earnings back to the Camorra, hoping that the Camorra, like a bank, might be able to provide interest. But often it doesn't. Many people lose everything. My mother was one of those people. My grandfather also gets sick from the garbage and the water. My whole family…" He waved his hand, disgusted. For a second, he looked on the verge of tears.

"I'm so sorry."

"Be glad you don't know about the Camorra."

"Do they have a presence in the United States?"

"As to the clothing, *sí*. As to everything else?" A shrug. "For your sake, I hope they are not there. I hope that you will never, never have to deal with the Camorra in your life." He gazed at me miserably. "Miss," he said. "If you do not have to ask about the Camorra any further, if you do not have to deal with them, then please, *per favore,* do not."

28

She was with a girlfriend, Dez learned, a short woman with blondish brown hair

"And where is she staying?" he asked the man whom La Duca had asked to call him from Naples.

"Grand Hotel Vesuvio."

"Good work."

Since his mole first called him, Dez had done more homework on *la testa rossa.* He'd called some of the old guard Camorra in *Napoli* and asked who was this father she was talking about? He learned that her father was indeed a *traditore.* And one who paid the ultimate price. Pathetic the *rossa* even cared enough to ask about him.

The man in Naples spoke. "The duke wants to know. What do you want to do with the redhead now?"

He beamed internally that the duke still trusted him, was letting him help run this game. And yet the question he'd just been asked was at once the easiest and toughest. He knew what he *wanted* to do to her. In fact, it would be *facile,* easy. But while the authorities wouldn't blink at the killing of a Camorra drug pusher or even a higher-up, they wouldn't turn away from the killing of an American woman. They couldn't. Such an event would get too many headlines, bring too many eyes. And that was exactly what Dez was looking to avoid.

So Dez came up with a slightly different plan. He would scare her back to the United States. And when she was here in the red, white and blue, he would make sure she was red, white and dead.

29

We followed Bernard out of the Grand Hotel lobby and onto the twilit streets of Naples. A sultry feeling hung in the air—heavy and salty. People strolled along sidewalks that wrapped around the sea. Across the street, the cafés near the sailboats were bright and hopping.

"The best pizza in Naples," Bernard said as we walked, "is a subject of massive debate. When I told people I was coming here, I started getting recommendations, and people *really* have opinions. They take this stuff seriously."

Maggie gazed up at him and grinned, looking as if she was ready to hear more, to hear whatever Bernard had to say.

He'd changed from the baggy jeans and orange polo shirt to darker, still-baggy jeans and a navy blue polo shirt. I thought I spied a uniform of sorts.

"So, I've heard about this one restaurant from ten different people," Bernard said. "Are you guys willing to try it?"

"Sure," I said. "It's good to know someone with the inside scoop."

Bernard led us through the streets of Naples to Antica Pizzeria Brandi della Regina on a street called Anna di Palazzo. Like many other Naples streets, it was chaotic, but Pizzeria Brandi della Regina was a refuge, its ivory awnings shading it protectively from the craziness of the rest of the street.

I took a peek inside and saw a huge wood-burning oven, tiled in mosaic, the name of the restaurant spelled proudly on its flank.

As we took our seat outside, a waiter came over and boasted about the restaurant. "We are the inventors of the pizza Margherita."

"The pizza Margherita?" Maggie said, and even in English, you couldn't mistake her disbelief.

The waiter puffed up his chest. "Yes. In 1889. Other pizzerias, they will tell you that they invented it. They will tell you they have the real pizza of *Napoli,* but it is here. We invented it. We make it."

He and Maggie had a standoff with their eyes. She caved and gave him a little shrug. Bernard laughed.

When the waiter walked away, Bernard leaned in. "They passed a law here. In order to be official pizzerias, your pizza has to be a certain width and height, and there are all these rules, like the dough has to be kneaded by hand and certain olive oil and mozzarella have to be used."

"Seems like a lot of trouble," Maggie said. "If a pizza is good, who cares if it's official?"

A passing waiter apparently heard Maggie's words and understood English. He stopped and gave her a grave look, his hand still holding aloft a tray of glasses, before he moved on.

"Sheesh," Maggie said.

But when the pizza came, we could see what all the fuss was about. We had ordered the traditional Margherita, which sounded boring, but it was divine—the crust spongy and buttery, the buffalo mozzarella soft and bubbling, the tomatoes tasting as if they'd been picked today.

We also took the recommendation of the waiter and ordered a broccoli and sausage pizza, which was enough to make all of us swoon.

In two minutes, both pizzas were gone.

Bernard looked at the empty pans, a forlorn expression passing over his features.

"We should order more," Maggie said.

Bernard's face lit up, and the two of them bent toward each other to consult the menu.

"What do you want, Izzy?" Bernard asked.

He seemed like the kindest of men, and since we'd left the hotel, he'd been trying hard to include me in their conversation, but it was impossible to ignore the feeling that I was on a date—*their* date—and yet I couldn't have been more pleased about it. Other than Wyatt, the much-older two-timing slick boyfriend that Maggie had tried twice, she hadn't dated much in the last few years. She'd been the third person on many an outing with Sam and me, and I was happy to return the favor.

"Whatever you guys want," I said. "I'm game."

As I sat across the table from the two of them, my thoughts crept to Theo. Why in the hell had I asked him to come to Italy? Aside from the night we met, I had spent very little time with him outside my condo. So what was I doing agreeing to have him come to Europe?

I looked at my watch. From what he told me, he would be landing at ten Naples time. Which was only three hours away. And what would I do with him then? Well, I mean, aside from what I usually did with him?

It was tough enough to travel internationally with a good friend. Could Theo and I handle being in another country together? Could *he* handle it? The kid was only twenty-two after all. Would I even like the guy outside the sex-charged confines of my condo?

After the second round of pizzas, we left the restaurant and wandered down the street until we came to a coffee bar across from a beautiful cathedral. The waiter in his white shirt and black vest frowned when I asked for something *decaffeinato.*

"*Decaffeinato* espresso?" he asked, clearly put off by the thought but willing, grudgingly, to put in the order.

"Actually, do you have *decaffeinato* tea?" The concept of decaf tea only made the waiter frown more.

Bernard stood, towering over the waiter as he did everyone else, although I noticed that he always stayed a step away from people, as if not wanting, intentionally, to intimidate them. But it was hard not to be intimidated when looking straight up at a huge Filipino guy, as the waiter was now doing.

Bernard said something in Italian to the man, gesturing at his watch.

"Sí, sí!" the waiter said excitedly, before pulling Bernard away.

"Be right back," he called over his shoulder.

"What is that about?" I asked Maggie.

"I have no idea." Her voice was tinged with awe as she watched Bernard's retreating back. "So when is Theo getting here?"

I put my phone on the table so I'd hear it when he called or texted. "Soon."

"I can't wait to meet him."

"I'm just realizing that none of my friends has *ever* met him."

"No time like the present. And hey, you look great tonight."

That afternoon, when I'd gotten back to our room after talking to the concierge, I changed out of the dress I'd worn all day. I told Maggie now what I'd learned from the concierge. "Bizarre," she said, and she was right. Whenever I thought of the Mafia, I imagined the Mob being involved in gambling, drugs, prostitution. But fashion?

I'd had a slightly more pressing fashion dilemma that afternoon. What to wear now that Theo was coming? Maggie and I had spent some time selecting my outfit—a navy-blue sundress that showed a little cleavage.

The waiter came back and placed white cups of espresso in front of Bernard and Maggie's seats. Then he placed a blue cup on a saucer in front of me. A silver tea strainer drifted in the steaming water.

"Decaffeinato," the waiter said with pride. He pointed to the flecks of white on the saucer. "Sugar, if you like." He placed a tin with a spoon in it on the table. "More sugar, if you like." He followed that with a tiny white pitcher full of milk. "And *latte.*"

"Thank you," I said, not feeling marginalized anymore.

A few minutes later, Bernard returned to the table.

"What did you do?" Maggie said. "Suddenly, Izzy got the tea she wanted."

"Good, good." He lowered himself into his chair. "My first French horn teacher was Italian. From Naples. He made me an Italian football fan."

"Soccer, right?" Maggie asked.

"Football. Always call it football."

"We're Bears fans," Maggie said, giving him a frown. "That's the only kind of *football* we recognize."

Bernard paused, looked about to argue, then he smiled and nodded. "Well, the Naples soccer team has an interesting history. They dropped to Serie B. It's like if the Cubs got demoted to a farm team. But they keep working their way back to Serie A, the top level. I asked the waiter if the game was on. He took me back in the kitchen and we watched for a while. We talked about the glory days of Diego Maradona, and—" he nodded at my cup "—you got your tea."

"Thanks to you."

"Well, if you're a fan and you root for the same team, it almost doesn't matter what you say. You have a bond. So I just had to give them a few words of encouragement."

Maggie squeezed his massive upper arm. "You are so smart."

He grinned bashfully in her direction, then looked at me. "It didn't hurt that a couple of the waiters in the back were asking about the *rossa.*" He gestured at my head. "They must have a crush on you."

"Any man who loves redheads loves Izzy," Maggie said. "This is a constant thing."

"No, it's not," I said. "God, I wish men were always having crushes on me."

"Well, you're always getting noticed for your hair."

Bernard took a sip of his espresso. "I kind of understand that. I feel like I'm always noticed with this." He gestured down at himself, at his *big* self.

Maggie looked over her shoulder. "Are those the *rossa* fans?"

Two men stood at the entrance to the kitchen, and they were staring at our table.

"That's them," Bernard said.

I smiled in their direction, but neither smiled in return.

"Sheesh," Maggie said. "The Italian guys really are different than they used to be."

My phone beeped from the table. A text message. *I just landed,* Theo wrote, *and I can't wait to see you. Where are you?*

"Theo?" Maggie said.

I nodded.

Maggie turned to Bernard. "Theo is the guy Izzy has been dating that I told you about. A very *young* guy."

Bernard raised his espresso cup to clink with mine. "Good for you," he said. "From what you guys were telling me about your last year, you need that."

I laughed. "I do actually."

I texted Theo back. *Grand Hotel Vesuvio,* along with the address.

"Come with me?" I asked Maggie and Bernard. "We can have a nightcap in the lobby bar."

Bernard downed his espresso, nodded. "Let's go."

30

It was almost eleven at night, and Theo hadn't shown up at the hotel, hadn't texted or called.

At first I didn't care. *The Maggie and Bernard Show* was entirely entrancing.

A woman of Maggie's size should never ingest more than two alcoholic beverages. She certainly shouldn't try to match a huge three-hundred-pound Filipino drink-for-drink. But that's exactly what she did. Within forty minutes of being at the lobby bar—a luxurious, rather sedate place with plush couches, oil paintings and a musician playing a grand piano in the corner—Maggie was on a roll.

"Hey, do you think you should maybe have a water?" Bernard said when she ordered another Moretti beer, right when he did.

"I'm in Italy!" she bellowed, as if that explained it all.

The waiters, who were exceptionally friendly and had to handle only a few other patrons in the bar, happily brought her a cold one and put more snacks in front of us with a look that said, *This will soak it up for her.*

When Bernard got up to compliment and tip the piano player, I told her, "Mags, slow it down, sister."

"But I'm happy!" She seemed shocked to find this sentiment true. She raised her glass, the foaming beer almost dripping over the side.

Bernard returned and sat down.

Maggie looked between the two of us with a huge smile. "I really am happy, because I'm with my *best* friend and…" She seemed to catch herself and realize that it was probably a tad too early to categorize anything with Bernard. She let the sentence trail off, returning her beer to the table in front of us, then cocked her head and stared at me. "I do love you soooo much, Iz."

"I love you, too." I laughed and gestured at the waiter for another wine for myself. When Maggie got liquored, which wasn't often, the emotional outpouring started. And really, who doesn't like being told how much they're adored?

Maggie turned to Bernard and described how we met in law school. "I walked into the student lounge, and she was sitting there with this guy. I'd seen her around—she's hard to miss—but we were in different sections and we'd never talked. After the guy left, Izzy and I ended up at the vending machine at the same time. I introduced myself and told her that she and the guy made a cute couple."

"It was Blake," I said, picking up the story. "And I was standing there trying to figure out how to break up with him. It just wasn't right between us. Never had been."

"So she told me about this," Maggie said, "and I helped her figure out how to lose Blake, although it took a few tries before their breakup would stick."

"Yeah, Mags helped me, and in the process of losing Blake, I got Maggie." It was what we always said when we told this story.

"And ever since we've been best friends." Maggie slugged back more beer. She told me she loved me again—about twenty-three times—and then we continued on with some of our favorite stories. Like the time Maggie and I went skinny-dipping in Lake Michigan and got out to discover that our purses and clothes had been stolen. And the time we were in a department store, Christmas shopping, and Maggie dared me to sit on Santa's lap.

"She did it!" Maggie said. "She was like this..." She put her beer down and climbed onto Bernard's lap. He seemed more than happy to play Santa in the reenactment.

Watching tiny little Maggie perched atop this large Asian man, watching them giggle happily, that I realized I would like to climb in someone's lap myself. A very specific someone. I glanced at the clock on my cell phone.

"Theo landed a while ago," I said. "I wonder where he is."

"Could be dealing with customs," Bernard said, dodging his head under Maggie's arm to look at me.

"But he flew private. It shouldn't take that long, should it?"

"Don't forget this is Italy."

I called Theo. No answer. I texted. Also nothing.

I was just starting to get worried when I felt him.

I mean just that—before I had moved an inch, before I had turned around, I could feel him.

"Yowza," Maggie said, looking over my shoulder.

I turned, and there he was, standing at the entrance of the bar, taller than I remember, his hair longer, and his face even more beautiful. He wore jeans and his army jacket. When he saw me, he dropped his bag on the ground. And he grinned.

I got up and walked to him. "You made it."

"I made it."

"Wow."

"Yeah." He nodded across the room at Maggie and Bernard. "Your friends?"

"Yep."

"Can I kiss you in front of your friends?"

"Yep."

That's exactly what he did. The bartenders started clapping. Maggie hooted and shouted. And yet it all receded when he wrapped his arms around me, as if everything had been pulled away into a swirl, and we were the only things left standing.

When he finally let me go, it all rushed back in—the tinkling piano music, the lobby's marbled floors, the laughter of Maggie and Bernard.

We picked up Theo's bag and walked back to join them. I introduced everyone. But then suddenly a voice in my head began hollering. I tuned in and heard that voice say, *It's time to leave, Iz. It's time to leave NOW.*

I froze my body. I listened harder. *Get out, you idiot,* the voice screamed.

The thing is, I'd heard this voice before. And it had always been right. The fact that I didn't hear that voice last autumn, when Sam disappeared and my world fell apart, had bothered me. Had I lost my intuition?

But no, here it was—intuition that was screaming bansheelike, *Get out!*

"What's wrong?" Theo said, a chuckle in his voice.

I peered around him. Two men walked into the hotel and approached the front desk. They were both wearing black pants and black jackets, their dark hair making them look almost indistinguishable. For a second, I thought they might be the waiters from the coffee bar, the ones who had a crush on the *rossa*, but no, not the same guys.

One of the front desk clerks was shaking her head at them, gesturing as if to say, *Leave, leave.*

Carlo, the concierge I'd spoken to earlier, was still there, and after listening to the men talk, he glanced up at me, and his expression seemed to be saying the same thing as my hollering intuitive voice. *Go! Leave!*

The men must have caught his look. They jerked their heads over their shoulders and looked right at me. Then one of them raised his arm and pointed through the lobby, right to me.

31

I grabbed Theo, pulling him by the hand. "Get up," I said to Maggie and Bernard. "We're getting out of here."

"What's wrong?" Maggie hissed as I half pushed them toward the back of the bar, where a white-banistered staircase went up and away. To where I didn't know, except that it was away from those two guys.

I had no idea who they were. I had no idea what made me run from them, other than the yelling in my head and Carlo's fearful expression.

Theo clearly thought I was losing it. "Uh…" he said. "What are we doing?"

"Just take your bag and go upstairs, please. There's something wrong with those guys, the ones who just came into the hotel. I don't know why, but I feel like we've got to get away from them."

I looked back and saw them. They looked directly at us, walked directly toward us. They glanced around like animals sizing up territory, then looked back, at me.

Bernard, climbing the stairs, saw them, too. "Izzy, if you're scared of those guys, Theo and I can handle them."

Theo stopped and glanced over my shoulder. "Hell, yeah, we can." Why did he sound sort of gleeful about it, as if he'd like to get in a fight with them? Such a twenty-two-year-old.

"Just get up the stairs. Please!"

They did as I asked—Maggie, then Bernard, then me and Theo. When Bernard and Maggie were about to the top, I heard Theo say, "Whoa."

I looked back at the guys. They were moving toward us. And I saw then that they were both reaching into their jackets and holding guns.

"Move," Theo said. Apparently, his gleeful thoughts of a fun-filled rumble had ended at the site of weaponry.

But if that moment was scary, it was even worse when we saw one guy extract the gun from his jacket and aim it at us.

"Keep moving!" I yelled at Maggie and Bernard.

Maggie stopped at the top of the stairs, her hand on her hip. "*What* is going on?"

"Go, go, go!" Theo bellowed. When he added, "They've got guns," Maggie spun and took off running, Bernard right behind her. I'd never seen a big man move as fast as he did.

At the top of the stairs, there was another restaurant/bar. But it was closed. I remembered the meeting rooms where Carlo had taken me on the other side of the same floor.

"Come on, you guys." I pushed the doors and hurried into the empty restaurant, headed for the other side of the hotel. I gestured for the group to follow me.

"What's going on?" Maggie said again.

"Don't ask, just run." Bernard said. I liked the guy more and more all the time.

We ran around tables and through a door.

"Damn," Theo said.

We were in a kitchen.

"We're *trapped,*" Maggie said.

From the restaurant, we heard footsteps and the sound of tables being shoved aside.

"There." Theo pointed to a door next to shelving that held bowls, mixers, pots and plates.

He tried it. The door swung open into the other side of the hotel where the meeting rooms were. We went through it.

"Elevators," I said, pointing, hoping the guys following us didn't know the hotel, that maybe it would take them a moment to find that back door from the kitchen.

Bernard banged on the elevator button. "What floor?"

"Six," Maggie said. She turned to me. "*What* is happening, Iz?"

"I think we should get our stuff from the room, and I think we should get out of here."

"Who are those guys?" Theo said.

I looked at him and all I could say was, "I'm so sorry I got you into this. I'll explain."

He shrugged a little. The kid could roll with anything.

But why wasn't the elevator coming? Bernard punched a meaty finger at the button again.

We heard the sound of footsteps. "It's them," Bernard said.

The elevator opened then and Bernard shoved us all in. I hit the button for the fourth floor.

"Six!" Maggie said.

"We'll go to four and take the stairs, so they don't know what floor we're going to."

"Good idea."

"Let's just get out of here fast."

"Are you sure?" Maggie said. "I mean, did they really have…"

"They really had guns," Theo said, "and we're really getting the heck out of here."

Maggie frowned and looked at Bernard, who nodded at her.

Once in our room, Maggie and I grabbed our suitcases and shoved everything in them.

When we opened the door, Bernard and Theo were standing in the hallway, looking up and down.

"We haven't seen anyone." Theo took my arm. "Are you okay?"

"I'm not entirely sure."

We ran to the elevator, once again pounding on the button. Finally one came. And then we heard a dinging sound. Another elevator had arrived at our floor. Bernard corralled the group to the back of our elevator, and as the doors closed, we watched, horrified, as the men burst out of the other elevator and sprinted toward our room.

And then we saw, right before the elevator closed, a door in the hallway being thrown open with force, cracking the first guy hard in the face. He gave a strangled, surprised cry and his hand flew to his face. The guy behind him knocked into him, and they both crumpled to the floor.

32

We went to Bernard's hotel, a small villa near the school where he was teaching.

Bernard led us into his room, minimally decorated with white walls and simple furniture. "Ladies," he said. "I think you owe an explanation to two men."

"Dude," Theo said in return, nodding like *hell yeah.*

Bernard bent over a small refrigerator and took out four Peroni beers. He opened them, handing one to Maggie, then me, then Theo.

Theo and I sat on one of the twin beds. Maggie and Bernard on the other.

"So?" Bernard said.

Maggie and I exchanged frightened looks. "Here's the deal," Maggie said. "Izzy thinks that her dad, who died when she was eight, might not be dead. And so she came here to Italy to look for him."

Both Bernard and Theo stared at me, their mouths open in surprise.

"Thanks, Mags," I said. "Thanks for making me sound like a freak."

"I was trying to be succinct."

"Okay, well, here's the long version..."

We talked and talked, the four of us an odd and bizarre quartet. An hour later, I had told Theo and Bernard everything about my father and how I'd been looking for him. I skipped over the part about working for Mayburn. Maggie didn't disclose that part, either. Maggie was always a vault. The information you told her went in and never came out unless you wanted it to.

I told them about my aunt Elena, how we were heading to Ischia to find her, how the Brothers Rizzato—the guys whose case my father was working on when he died—had been from Ischia, too. I told them what I'd learned about the Camorra so far.

I kept looking at Theo, anxious for his reaction. If I had been afraid it might be a little much to have him come to Italy, then certainly dumping this boatload of information on him, was way too much, wasn't it? And yet he didn't look freaked—or maybe I just didn't know him well enough to tell. He simply kept nodding when I talked, his face tense with concentration, as if he had discussions about reincarnated fathers often.

"So, let's go back for a second," Theo said now. "Some Camorra guys killed your grandfather?"

"Right. His wife, Oriana, who was my grandmother, was from a Camorra family originally."

Theo brushed his hair out of his eyes and nodded thoughtfully again. "Oriana was originally from Naples?"

"Right."

"What was her maiden name?"

"Lombardi." I'd found that information among my dad's papers—the ones that my mom had saved for me—but it hadn't led to anything more significant. "It's a common name around here."

"And after your grandfather died, your aunt Elena moved to Italy," Theo said. "I don't get why."

"She said that her mom, Oriana, was having a hard time after her husband was killed. Oriana moved to

Arizona to try and put the whole thing behind her. Apparently, her family must have thought Oriana was a bit unstable. They thought it would be good if Elena went away from anything that reminded her of her father. So she moved in with a cousin who lived outside of Rome."

"What about your dad?" Bernard asked.

"He was a senior in high school when his father died. So he just went off to college."

"And got a psychology degree," Maggie said. "He met Izzy's mom in college."

"Then he got his master's degree," I said, "and he landed with the Detroit police."

"And they had two kids," Maggie said.

"And then he died."

"So, who were those dudes in the hotel?" Theo asked.

"I have no idea."

"Do they have anything to do with your dad or your grandfather?"

"Again, no clue. All I know is that I asked my aunt questions about my grandfather and my dad and the Camorra, and I asked questions at that antimafia office, and then I decided to come here and now this happened. Maybe it's a coincidence?"

"That's a hell of a lot of coincidences," Bernard said.

"It's just hard to know…"

There was quiet in the room except for the faint *tick, tick, tick* of a round, black clock on the nightstand between the beds. And a quiet *tap, tap, tap* on the window.

"It's raining," Bernard said.

More quiet.

My phone rang and we all jumped.

I looked at the screen on the phone, then I looked at Maggie. "Sam."

She pursed her mouth, gave a slight shrug.

"Excuse me, you guys, I should take this."

I felt Theo watching me, wondering. He didn't even know who Sam was, but it was probably pretty easy to figure out that he was someone important to me. And that was still the case, no matter what had happened at his apartment, no matter what our status. Sam would always be important to me.

I gave Theo a smile, then I took the phone in the hallway and answered it. "Hey," I said.

"Hey," Sam said back.

We were silent. I walked down the hallway of the villa and into the breakfast room. It was a lonely room at that moment, only one weak lamp lighting the yellow wood tables and the blue plates stacked on a side table.

"So," Sam said. "How are you?"

"Well..." I sat down at one of the tables, put my elbows on its painted yellow top. What should I say? *I'm freaking out right now, because I just got chased by some guys with guns, but other than that I'm peachy.* "It's been a little tumultuous."

"Yeah, I know what you mean." Sam exhaled. "I've been so damned sad since I saw you. I mean, I feel like... I don't know... We broke up a while ago, but for some reason I feel like the other night... I guess I felt like that was..."

"Yeah, I know. For some reason it felt like that was *it*." I swallowed hard, fought back a rush of tears.

Sam sighed again. "I love you, Iz."

"I love you, too."

More quiet. The rain *tapped, tapped, tapped* on the windows.

"So what have you been up to?" Sam asked.

I paused, then ignored his question and instead spoke what was on my mind. "We would have been married right now," I said. "And now we're down to this. Down to small talk."

He said nothing. I said nothing. I think we both knew what the other was thinking. I was thinking that the reason we weren't married right now was Sam's fault, and he was thinking that although he'd done some things that were tough to get over, I *should* have gotten over them, and therefore, it was my fault.

But we'd had that conversation ninety-seven times before, so I just said, "I'm in Italy."

"You're kidding? That's great. What made you decide to go there?"

"I wanted to ask my aunt Elena some questions about my dad. And after seeing you at your apartment, I decided I needed a vacation."

"Jesus, Red Hot, I'm so sorry about that."

Red Hot was what Sam had always called me when we were dating. Now the nickname, coming from his lips, sounded wrong, awkward. "I'm sorry," he continued, "that you had to see Alyssa."

The image of her flashed across my brain, then returned to stab me a million times. "Yeah, me, too."

"I don't know how in the hell that happened."

I laughed. It sounded bitter. "You don't know how that happened? You're dating your ex. You let her sleep in *my* T-shirt. That's how that happened."

"Izzy, you're the one who stopped by without calling."

"Yeah, Sam, because that's what we always used to do. I know we're broken up, but I didn't know I had to be careful of *that*." I said *that* as if I were saying the worst word possible. And Sam knew that in my world, Alyssa was the worst thing I could have seen in his apartment.

Sam started to say something then stopped, then tried again. "Look, I'm really sorry. But I'm not going to apologize for dating her. You and I *are* broken up. But it killed me that you had to see that."

There was a pause. Neither of us knew what to say.

Finally Sam spoke. "So who are you with in Italy?"

"Maggie's here."

"And who else?"

Sam knew me so well. He knew when I was leaving something out.

"Well..." How to say this?

At that moment Theo appeared in the hallway outside the breakfast room. He looked at me with raised eyebrows, as if wondering if I was all right. He held up a thumb and gave a questioning expression. I nodded and returned the thumbs-up. *I'm okay,* I mouthed.

As Theo turned away, Sam spoke again. "So who else are you with? Charlie?"

"No. I asked Charlie to come. But he's got a job."

Sam coughed as if he was choking, then laughed. "*Charlie* has a job?"

"I know, I know. I couldn't believe it, either. It's at WGN, the radio station."

"Incredible."

"I know."

"So who are you with then?" He never was able to leave any detail unresolved behind when we were dating, and apparently he wasn't going to break that habit now.

"He's a friend of mine."

Through the silence, I could almost hear Sam stewing.

"Who is he?"

In our life together I'd never wished that Sam and I had known each other *less,* had understood each other less, but now that's exactly what I wished for. I really didn't want this conversation. "It's just someone I'm dating."

"Huh. I guess I don't have to feel so bad about Alyssa."

"I don't know about that. I wouldn't have had this person come to Italy if I hadn't seen what I'd seen in your apartment."

"So it's my fault?"

"There is no fault here. He's a friend and he's visiting me. That's all."

"What's his name?"

"Theo."

"How did you meet?"

"I don't think we've been broken up long enough to have this conversation."

"We're going to stay friends, right?"

"Yes."

"Friends have these conversations."

I bit my lip. It sounded logical, but wrong. And yet, having this conversation, this awkward and yet normal conversation, appealed to me, felt like a balm in contrast to being hunted by scary men in a city I didn't know.

"Tell me, Iz," Sam said softly.

"Okay, well, I met him when I was out with a friend one night."

"How long ago?"

"It was back in April, but we haven't been dating the whole time."

A silence. "Do you like this guy?" He sounded hurt, and I almost felt bad about it.

"Yeah, I do like him."

"You must. You invited him to Europe with you."

"It's a long story, Sam. I didn't exactly invite him. He has his own plane and so…"

"Whoa. You're dating a dude with his own plane?"

"It's a corporate share."

"How old is he? Sixty?" Sam asked with faint scorn.

"If you must know, he's in his early twenties." I said

this with some pride in my voice, then immediately felt embarrassed.

"Well, well, well," Sam said. "Someone in their early twenties."

"Hey." I sounded defensive now. "*I'm* in my twenties."

"Not for long."

"I'm surprised you remembered." I immediately regretted saying it. "I'm sorry I said that." I stood from the breakfast table and walked to the window, which overlooked a tiny Naples alleyway, dim now but for a few soccer flags flying under a streetlamp. The rain tapped away on the glass, sounding like a soft but distinct drum.

"Iz," Sam said with weight in his voice, "this whole thing makes me so sad."

"Me, too. But that doesn't mean it shouldn't be happening."

"No. It has to go down this way. This has to be more than a break. This has to be it for now. I mean—"

I interrupted him. "You don't have to say it. I know it as well as you do." I stared down at the cobblestoned alley, watching the rain run in rivulets through the cracks. "We're over."

He said nothing, but I heard, very clearly, his silent *yes.*

33

When I got back to the room, Bernard and Maggie were on one twin bed, Maggie flat on her back, snoring with her mouth wide-open, while Bernard hung over the side, huddled into a tight ball, apparently trying not to disturb her, and snoring softly himself.

Theo sat on the other bed, and he looked up when I came in. He patted the space next to him. I sat down.

"This is all so crazy," I whispered. "Are you freaking?"

"I guess I should be, but..." He shook his head. "You gotta tell me, though, are you always like this?"

"Like what?"

"Drama."

"I'm not drama!"

"Shh." He pointed at Maggie and Bernard, neither of whom stirred a bit.

"I am *not* drama."

"Dude, when I met you—"

"When you met me there was no drama. Not even a little!"

"Okay, I guess that's true, but within a week or so it was Drama Central."

"I'm not like this all the time. I *swear.*" I paused and then thought about it. "You know what? It's true that I'm not usually Drama Central. Honestly." I looked at my left hand where my engagement ring used to be. "But it has been a bizarre year. I've never told you about my fiancé. My *ex*-fiancé. There was a lot of stuff that went on there." I waved a hand. "But you know what? Now that I think about it, that craziness has brought me a lot of good, too. It's almost like it pulled a scab off of me, something I didn't know was there, and it opened me up to everything. *Everything.* I mean, I've been tested in so many different ways, and generally, I'm pretty proud of the way I've responded. But I'm still the same Izzy I always was." I turned to face Theo, crossed my legs. "So it's been crazy, but the crazy keeps bringing interesting stuff into my life."

"And that's a good thing?"

I reached out and tucked a lock of his silky hair behind one of his ears, looked at the pillow puff of his bottom lip. "Yeah. A really good thing. I met you. And I've met some other amazing people, too. And my friends and family have shown me that they're there for me no matter what. I guess I always knew that, but it's nice to see." I held out my hand and grabbed his. I squeezed it. "But, anyway, you're right. It has been drama. I guess. And I'm seriously sorry if it's put drama in your life."

He leaned toward me, kissed my forehead. Then he looked down at my new necklace and lifted the stone. "I've been meaning to ask you about this."

"I got it from my aunt. She got it from her mom, my grandmother."

He tugged gently on my necklace, tugging me with it until we were close, our faces just an inch from each other. He kissed me again, this time on my lips. Slow. "I think we need to find another room."

"Why?"

He grinned.

"Are you serious?" I whispered. "You still want to fool around with me with all this going on?"

He nodded.

I laughed, then stood up. "Let's go."

We went in search of an innkeeper to ask for our own room, but everything was shut down for the night, and no one was around. I led him into the breakfast room, closed the door behind us and turned off the lamp. It was dark now, only the alley lights barely seeping through the windows. The rain began to pound harder against them, blocking out all other sounds.

Theo picked me up and wrapped my legs around his waist.

"This is getting to be a favorite position of ours," I said.

"Mmm-hmm." His mouth was on my neck, just below my ear.

He walked, my legs still around him, until he reached the table at the far side of the room, where everything was covered in darkness. He sat me down on the table and drew me closer. I thought I knew what he would do. I thought he would do exactly what we'd been doing in my condo stairwell the few nights before I left town. But instead, he put his arms around me and embraced me gently. For minutes. I don't know how many exactly, but they were long, soothing minutes.

And then he started kissing me. He kissed me as though there was nothing else he wanted to do, not at that moment, not ever. He seemed to be drawing something out of me, something from a very small pit deep inside me that the eye couldn't see, a place that held calm and clarity. With every kiss, I felt myself loosening, felt that calm rising to the surface.

We never did have sex that night. We kissed on the table for an hour.

Finally, he said, "Let's go to bed."

That night, in a twin bed, tucked in Theo's arms, I slept better than I had since all the craziness began.

"She doesn't scare easily," said the voice on the phone from *Napoli,* telling Dez exactly what he didn't want to hear.

But then again, that's what he prized about Neapolitans, about his "coworkers" in the System. They told it the way it was, not how you wanted it to look.

"Well, then handle it," he said. "Try harder."

34

The ferry port was a chaotic place, full of garbage and concrete that smelled of urine. Behind the port, the city slept while the sun crept up, its shimmering backdrop outlining Naples, making it appear, for the moment, a simple, straightforward city. On the other side of the harbor, Mount Vesuvius loomed in the distance, looking more like a huge, grassy mound than an active volcano.

Few people at the port seemed to speak English, or maybe it was simply too early for them to be accommodating. As a result, the four of us scuttled from ticket counter to ticket counter, asking for a ferry to Ischia, only to have surly clerks shout, *No, no, no!* followed by a lot of pointing and unintelligible strings of words.

Theo, it turned out, was unflappable in these situations. “Let’s try there,” he’d say, pointing at yet another counter, not seeming tired or annoyed, just matter-of-fact.

Bernard, an unexpected companion on this part of the trip, didn’t seem to be the type to get ruffled, either. He made it his job to pacify Maggie, who grew crankier by the minute, muttering, *Jesus Christ* and *Oh, that’s helpful.*

When Bernard’s alarm had buzzed earlier that morning, he had sat up, his black hair standing at odd angles on his head, making him look even taller than he was. “We’ve got to get to the ferry, right?”

We had all grumbled and hauled ourselves up into seated positions. I looked at the clock—5:30 a.m. The first ferry to Ischia was to leave in fifty-five minutes, and I wanted to be on it. I wanted to be away from Naples and those guys, whoever they were.

"You're coming with us?" Maggie asked Bernard. She put a hand on his shoulder and rubbed a little, a gesture that made it look as if they'd been together for years. "Don't you have to teach?"

"Not yet. Not for two more days. So, if you'll have me…" He and Maggie looked deeply into each other's eyes, then Bernard seemed embarrassed. He looked around the room. "I mean, if you'll all have me, I'd like to go to Ischia."

"Hell, yeah," Theo said. I nodded sleepily. It seemed that all that Maggie could do was smile.

Then Maggie gasped. She stood and clapped. "It's Izzy's birthday! Happy birthday!"

"Damn," Theo said. "I forgot."

"So did I," I said.

"Happy birthday," Theo said. And then right in front of Maggie and Bernard he gave me a birthday kiss. A really, really, really good one.

"Okay, enough," Maggie said, pulling me to my feet and into a hug. "Wait, I have your present." She went to her bag on the floor and rooted around inside it. She pulled out a small package wrapped in green paper and handed it to me.

"Mags, you're not supposed to get me anything. You've been paying for everything on this trip already."

"It's nothing big, trust me."

I pulled off the paper. Inside was a small wooden box, and inside that, a small bag of seeds.

"They're wildflower seeds."

I looked at her with a question on my face. I've never been a gardener.

"I was thinking," Maggie said, "that you're starting your life over right now, you know? So in a way, you're repotting yourself. And I know you're going to flourish. But I just thought that you should put some other flowers in with you. Remind you to look around and see how amazing life is and how different it can be. So when we get back home, I have another present for you. It's a flower box for your roof deck, and we're going to plant these wildflowers, and whenever you see them, you're going to remember that you're growing, too."

"Mags, you're a sweetheart!" I stood and hugged her.

Bernard went and found an innkeeper to get a pastry with a candle in it, and I blew it out, surrounded by Bernard and Theo and Maggie and thinking that, so far, it wasn't a bad birthday at all.

At the dock now, we finally managed to score tickets and boarded the ferry to Ischia. The outside deck was painted white, no seats in sight. Once on the ship, all the passengers trudged inside to a big room carpeted in blue and rows of what looked like airplane seats. At the front of the room, a large TV blared an annoying Italian cartoon. No one seemed to notice. Most of the passengers grabbed seats, threw their bags down and promptly went to sleep.

The ferry pulled out of the harbor slowly, but when it hit open water, the captain must have pulled back on the throttle because the boat picked up speed. Meanwhile, I paced around the ferry ten times, staggering a little when we hit a wave, pulling Theo along with me until he finally declared that the guys who'd run after us last night were definitely not passengers, at least not ones we could see.

Once we got that out of the way, the ferry was rather

calming. Theo and I tucked ourselves onto blue upholstered chairs and watched as we sliced through the cobalt sea. Outside our window, Maggie and Bernard stood at the railing, talking fast, not even noticing their surroundings. Bernard had to bend down and lean on the railing in order to hear Maggie.

As I watched them, I smiled at first. Maggie was clearly head over heels, and although it was hysterical to see her with a big bear of a guy like Bernard, it was somehow fitting, too.

Theo took my hand in his and followed my gaze out the window. "So she just met him yesterday?"

"Yeah, he came up right as we got on the train and helped Maggie with her bag. It was so cute because they were wearing the same…" I let my words die away as my mind got stuck on a phrase I'd just uttered—*he came up right as we got on the train.*

I thought back to yesterday. We'd gotten on the train and Bernard was there immediately. *Immediately.* Where had he come from? And the train car wasn't full, so what were the odds that his seat was right across from ours?

"What are you thinking about?" Theo said to me.

I stared out the window at Maggie and Bernard. Suddenly, he seemed not so much a gentle giant, but possibly a sinister one.

"I'll be right back."

I went out on the deck. The air smelled sharply of salt and fish. In the distance, we saw little villages perched on rocky outcroppings.

"Mags," I said, stepping up to them. "Can I talk to you for a sec?"

"You two hang out," Bernard said in what seemed a friendly tone, but who knew? "Izzy, I don't mean to monopolize your friend."

"You're not monopolizing me," Maggie said.

I stayed quiet.

"I want to say hi to Theo," Bernard said. "We really didn't get to talk or meet properly."

He went inside, and I watched his back, waiting until the doors closed behind him.

I turned back to Maggie. "You know, he's right. He is monopolizing you."

She raised her eyebrows. "Are you jealous, Iz? That's so cute."

"I'm not jealous. I'm just concerned."

I told her what I'd been thinking—how Bernard had gotten on the train so quickly after us, that he was the one person we'd told where we were staying, how those guys had come in the hotel and run after us last night, right after we got back to the hotel with Bernard.

"I don't get it," Maggie said. "What are you accusing him of?"

"I'm not sure, but I went to the antimafia office in the morning, and told them I was looking for someone with knowledge about the Camorra. It would have been easy for someone to follow me when I left there. I got you, and we got on the train, and there he was."

She shook her head. "Still don't get it. Are you saying he's Camorra?"

"Who knows? Maybe."

"He's *Filipino,* for Christ's sake."

I looked over Maggie's shoulder, trying to get a glimpse of Bernard inside. He was sitting with Theo, and it looked like a typical guy-bonding kind of conversation—lots of nodding, laughing.

"Iz," Maggie said, "I think you need to be taking a vacation on this trip instead of…"

"Instead of what?"

"Oh, baby girl."

I snapped my head back to look at her. Maggie only called me "baby girl" when she was *really* worried about me. It was what she called her nieces, like the niece I had once babysat. Her name was Kaitlyn, and she was a handful. But even kids like Kaitlyn had bad days, and so if she fell down on a playground and busted a lip, and *then* had been bullied by a pack of older kids, Maggie would sit her down and say, "Oh, baby girl." And now she was saying it to me.

"Are you seriously that worried about me?" I asked.

"Well…" She drew out the last word. "You have been… I don't know how to put it… You've been a little off lately, and who wouldn't be? I mean, this thing about your dad, the thing with the police a few months ago, Sam disappearing a few months before that. You've been going through a really hard time. It would be nuts if someone wasn't, you know…going *nuts* from all that. I just think you need to take a breath."

"Are you saying I'm being paranoid?" I wasn't even insulted. I was in such a tailspin with all this, who knew what was cooking inside my head? And I trusted Maggie to be an objective observer.

"No," she said. "Not paranoid. I just don't think Bernard has anything to do with…anything." She looked over her shoulder and stared at him inside the window. "Except me." Bernard saw Maggie looking at him. He smiled, waved. She did the same.

"Wow, you are *into* this guy."

She nodded.

"I don't think I've ever seen you like this."

"I don't want to jinx anything. Let's not talk about it. Let's talk about Theo."

"What do you think of him?"

"I think he's the most gorgeous guy I've ever seen in person."

"Hey! We finally agree on a guy."

"I agree about his looks, but I could never date him."

"Why?"

"I can't date a guy who's better-looking than me. I don't have enough self-esteem."

The ferry hit a few waves and the boat lurched. Maggie and I gripped the railing. Inside, Theo mouthed, *You okay?*

I gave him a thumbs-up and looked back at Maggie. "Do you think he's prettier than me?"

"I think you guys are sizzling together."

"Really?"

"Really."

"Ischia!" a voice called over a loudspeaker. *"Ischia!"*

Inside the ship, passengers began to gather their stuff. Bernard and Theo got up from their seats.

"You ready?" Maggie said.

"I guess." I only wish I knew what to get ready for.

35

Ischia was a sandy, hilly island covered in wide swatches of grass and shrubs—all a vibrant green. Amongst the green were purple flowering trees and pristine white houses with arched doorways. The port was full of vendors selling coffee, snacks, trinkets and maps. We found a cab station and squashed ourselves and Maggie's huge bag into one.

The driver knew the Poseidon Gardens and squealed away from the port, heading to the right and forcing the little car upward.

We would, we decided, go to the gardens for the day and look for Elena. If we didn't find her, we'd get a hotel. The driver told us that hotels were plentiful, especially on the other side of the island where Poseidon was located.

"What are the chances we're actually going to find Elena?" I said, suddenly deflated.

Bernard turned around from the passenger seat in the front. "What does she look like?"

I described Elena, a woman in her fifties with chestnut-brown hair and brown eyes flecked with green.

"We'll try, Izzy," Maggie said.

"Yeah, we'll try," Theo said, taking my hand in his. "That's all we can do."

* * *

The cab dropped us at the Poseidon gates. We paid and were given maps of the place. When Theo asked the ticket taker exactly how the garden was laid out and what we were supposed to do here, she held up a finger. "Wait, please for *inglese.*"

Soon another woman came over. She spoke English. "You see," she said, pointing at one of the maps, which was dotted with different blue shapes. "These are all pools. The pools marked with number one are the coolest. The temperatures rise, so you go to a pool with number two, then three and so on." She looked at us. "You understand? You go inside any pool number one, then you relax, then find a pool number two, and then three, and you keep going until you get to a number six. Then you do the whole thing over. But make sure you rest in between." She pointed at the other areas of the map. "Lots of places to rest and to eat. Maybe you lie on the beach."

We thanked her and wandered through the gates and into the gardens.

The place was stunning, full of lush green bushes, magenta bougainvillea, cypress trees and orange blossomed plants, all of it riding the coast of a sandy beach and the sparkling blue sea.

The gardens were full of nooks and crannies, lots of lounge areas, each with yellow and orange canvas chairs and thatched umbrellas. And scattered throughout the property were steaming pools, waterfalls running alongside them, coursing down from the cliffs above.

When we got to the locker rooms, an attendant directed us to the one for *donne*—women—and the other for *uomini.* In halting English, she told us bathing caps were required. I had never worn a bathing cap in my life, and I must have looked perplexed because the woman pointed to a boutique, then redirected her finger to my hair, frowning.

"Wow, she's right," I said, looking over her shoulder at one of the pools. Everyone bobbing in the water wore a cap. Even the people lounging around the sides had bathing caps on. "That's going to make it even harder to find Elena."

"Let's give it a shot," Maggie said.

In the locker room, we stowed our luggage and I put on my blue bikini, while Maggie slipped into a red one-piece with black racing stripes, the kind designed for swim teams. I had never been able to convince her to wear anything other than a trusty one-piece.

I had bought a blue-and-white cap, and after changing into my bikini, I stood in front of the mirror and pulled the cap over my head. The material was thin, and I couldn't seem to stuff all my curls under the thing. Orange spirals sprang out on all sides.

A woman walked into the changing room, saw me, laughed. She dug in her bag and fished out a ponytail holder.

"*Grazie, grazie,*" I said.

The woman laughed, nodded, walked away.

Maggie and I grabbed towels and walked outside. Bernard and Theo stood there, Theo in long surfer shorts slung low on his hips, showing those distinct muscles that carved lines over every inch of his body. Bernard wore a T-shirt and baggy brown trunks that looked about twenty years old. They both held bathing caps in their hands.

"We're the only guys not wearing Speedos," Theo said.

We glanced around. It was true.

"*Lots* of banana hammocks," Maggie said.

"I'm starving," Bernard announced. He had said the same thing at least four times since we'd gotten up that morning, and he'd had something to eat each time.

"Let's find something." Maggie took him by the arm. "We'll all look for Elena, and text each other if we see her. Otherwise, we'll meet back here later?"

Theo and I nodded, then walked around the sprawling gardens, studying the pools, the beach, the *ristorante.* All the while, my eyes were searching for Elena. I seemed to draw a lot of looks from the other bathers, some of them openly staring at me as they bobbed in one of the pools or gazed at me from their supine position on lounge chairs. I knew it wasn't my hair, which was now under the cap and out of sight, so at first I thought maybe I was looking particularly good in my bikini. But when I heard an older man murmur, *bianco,* I realized that they were commenting on my Casper's-ass-white skin. Everyone else in the place was tanned to perfection. Actually past perfection and moving toward crispy.

I kept glancing at people's faces, checking for Elena's eyes, but everyone looked the same under those caps. I began to relax when I realized that aside from my Casper's-ass skin, *I* looked the same. My hair hidden, I was anonymous. There was nothing to do but move from pool to pool, consulting the map and deciding which number two pool to head to next, then which number three and four. At each pool, we eased ourselves into the soothing water, and I found something equally soothing about being with Theo, being with him in that beautiful place so far from home.

Each pool was shaped differently, one like a kidney, some perfect circles of differing sizes, a few long rectangles, a couple of squares. Some of the pools were surrounded by shrubs and plants, others lounge chairs.

Theo stopped outside one pool. He pointed. "Look at that."

I glanced across the length of the pool, this one a

number four and shaped like an oval. At the end of the pool was a stone throne built out of the smooth rock of the cliff that bordered the gardens. The throne held a woman in a green bathing suit and a yellow cap. Her head was down, eyes closed, shoulders slumped. Behind her, water poured from the side of the cliff as if it were coming from inside Ischia itself. It cascaded from the mountain and onto her shoulders, and she looked as if she were experiencing ecstasy.

We watched her for another minute as she continued to sit there, in complete silence, her eyes closed. Finally, she threw her shoulders back and yawned as if she'd just experienced the best massage of her life. Then she stood, and another person who'd been waiting outside our view sat down in the throne.

"Want to try it?" Theo said.

"Absolutely."

We walked to the other side of the pool and sat in orange lounge chairs where there was a small line of bathers waiting for the water throne.

When it was finally our turn, Theo gestured at it. "You first."

I got up and walked across the wet stone floor. I felt almost nervous as I saw that water pouring down. Finally, I slipped onto the throne and sat. Like the first woman we'd seen, I closed my eyes and hunched my shoulders and let the water beat upon me. I let it pound out the questions I had about my father. I let it pound away my desperate hope to see Elena. I let it pummel out of me any thoughts about Sam. I let it strike away the day and anything but that moment until, finally, it was just me. Me on a stone throne, the sun hitting my face through the cascade of water, without any thought of all that had happened the last year.

Theo went next, grew as blissful as I had. When he got out, he gestured with his head at the pool. "Let's get in."

Instead of looking around and studying faces for Elena, I merely let my toes, then my feet, then my shins, my knees, my thighs slip into the pool until the water was at my waist, then the depth at my chest. At last I ducked my head under and stayed beneath that water, weightless, timeless.

When I came up to the surface, Theo wasn't there. Momentarily alarmed, I swung my head around.

And there he was, at the opposite end of the pool, his arms behind him on the ledge, staring at me, grinning a little as if he were watching his favorite show on television. Somehow he managed to make his black bathing cap look adorable.

I paddled to him, not hurrying. There seemed nothing to hurry for just then.

When I reached him, I said, "Are you happy?" I never asked him those kinds of questions.

"Never more." He grabbed my arm lightly, pulled me to him and wrapped my legs around his waist, our favorite position. But this time, in the water, he didn't have to hold me so tight. Loosely, my ankles met behind his back. I let myself float backward in the pool until I was lying there, my back supported by the water, legs around him. I looked up at a blue sky softly dotted with cotton puffs of clouds.

Theo let me lie there like that. He didn't do anything, not anything sexy…nothing at all. He simply let me be suspended, and after a few seconds I felt as if I had slipped into a deep sleep. When I sat up, the sun had shifted, angling now onto the beach a hundred or so feet below us. I put my hands on Theo's arms. He was always muscled. But now, his body was slick and wet. I could feel every tendon, every sinew, every vein, every part and portion of his muscles. And it was as if I could feel, for the first time, every part of Theo. He looked in my eyes, and I knew he was thinking something similar, that he was feeling me, seeing me, in a new way, as well.

Slowly, his hand traced its way onto my lower back, pulling me gently toward him until I was closer, my arms around him, my legs wrapped tighter.

Around us, the water moved from the soft jets of the pool, hypnotically lulling us. It shimmied us back and forth, like a mother coddling a child. I bowed my head and leaned on Theo's shoulder. He squeezed me tighter until there was no space between us physically. And I felt that there was no other kind of space between us, either. I felt one with Theo. The feeling was not only soothing, not only profound, it was sexy as hell.

I reached my hand down, below his waist, and through his bathing suit took a hold of him. But the feel of him shocked me.

I sat up straight. "Jeez," I whispered. "What am I doing?"

Theo shook his head lazily, then he nodded across the pool. I could see another couple embracing. Because the water was high, you couldn't tell what, if anything, they were doing underneath the water. A third couple was sitting on the steps at the entrance to the pool. A few individual swimmers dotted the water. Those on the lounge chairs surrounding the pool were all sleeping or reading. But no one seemed to be observing anyone. People kept to themselves, soaking in the healing waters, the healing atmosphere.

I looked back at Theo. I reached down again, slowly, careful not to show what I was doing, and I took him in my hand.

He inhaled sharply, his head hanging back a little. "God," he whispered. "God, God…God."

I kept touching him like that. He was completely at my mercy.

Finally he raised his head. "We have to find somewhere to go."

A few minutes later, wrapped in towels, we climbed the steps of the cliff to the highest point of the gardens. There were a few lounge chairs up there, no one around. Theo pointed at a corner, where the rock curved slightly. We tucked our heads around it and saw that there was another throne there, a seat carved into the rock, this one without water and hidden from view.

Theo sat on it. He started to pull me toward him. Then he stopped, shook his head. With his eyes locked on mine, he reached behind my back and untied my bikini top. I tossed it off. He tugged at the bottoms and pulled them down. Now I was standing naked before him.

He stood and pulled off my bathing cap. "There," he said. "I have to see that hair."

He slipped off his own bathing suit and cap, his long, soaked hair settling around his face.

Soon I was on top of him, my head smashed into his wet hair, and then I threw my face back, stretched my neck long so that all I could see was the slick ceiling of the throne, and at that moment it felt as if the two of us were one being and we were somewhere else, in a distant but distinct world that was so delicious, so wonderful, I hoped we would never leave.

Later, satiated beyond description, we made our way down a stone path.

"Don't forget to put your cap back on," Theo said behind me when we had almost reached the populated area of the gardens.

I stopped and looked up at him. "Thanks." I pulled my cap over my head. I could feel the smile on my face.

When I'd wrestled my hair back into place, we headed

down the path. I glanced at the pools below. "Which should we go to now?" I called over my shoulder to Theo. "Or maybe we should sit there." I pointed to my right, where a small deck overlooked a square pool, a bubbling number six.

"Sounds good."

We began to make our way to the deck, but halfway there, I stopped as something flashed in my eyes. It happened again. Squinting, I realized that it was the sun glinting from the metallic arms of a woman's sunglasses. I moved a few feet closer, stared harder at the woman. The sunglasses were black, with silver braided arms. The woman took them off then and settled back in her chair, her face to the sun.

"Elena," I whispered.

36

"Isabel," she said when I was standing in front of her. *Ee-sabel.*

I hadn't pulled off my cap, and for some reason I felt pleased that she had recognized me.

Elena wore a rose-colored bikini with geometric shapes on it. She had a toned body and a light tan. Next to her, a lounge chair held a few wet towels as if someone had just been there.

She stood and I introduced her to Theo. They shook hands, and then Theo pointed at a chair across the deck, about twenty feet away. "I'll be over there."

Elena sat on her lounge chair, her feet on the stone floor, and patted the space next to her. I sat.

She slipped her sunglasses back on. "What are you doing here, Isabel? Isn't it your birthday?"

I nodded.

"Happy birthday," she said, smiling fondly.

"Thanks. So, I spoke to your assistant. She mentioned you might be here. And we were looking to get out of Rome."

"We?" She looked at Theo, then back at me. "A beautiful man. Who is he to you?"

I explained that we'd dated a short time. I told her about Maggie coming over to visit me and meeting Bernard, how I'd then invited Theo. It sounded like a real vacation, and I liked that. I didn't want to make Elena cautious, not just yet.

"Isabel," she said. "Why are you here, really?" She shook her head a little. She sounded faintly annoyed.

"I just want to ask you a few questions."

Something niggled at my mind.

I just want to ask you a few questions. It was exactly what I used to say when I was a trial lawyer, in a courtroom, in front of a witness I was about to cross-examine.

And right then, although I was sitting on a canvas chair on a Mediterranean island, I decided to interrogate my aunt.

I remembered in a rush the training in law school and all the times I'd stood in front of witnesses. Some of them were expert witnesses, some lay—most of them reluctant witnesses who didn't want to talk to me. My trial teacher had always said, *Use a witness before you abuse a witness.* In other words, get all the concessions you can, be as friendly as you can, before you attack. I realized that was *exactly* what I needed to do here.

"Is that okay?" I said. "If I just ask you a few questions?"

She gave a brief nod.

I felt the calm that comes over a trial lawyer when they know exactly what they're going to ask and how they're going to ask it—a series of questions, general at first, then more specific. Never asking the ultimate question (which in this case was, "Is my father alive?") but hopefully drawing so close to the issue that the witness has to admit it because there seems no other conclusion at which to arrive.

I turned so that I was facing her, but I backed up a little on the chair to give her some room—*Never physically intimidate a witness too fast*—and I put a congenial expression on my face. "I just want to understand our family. Where I come from."

Elena nodded.

"Okay, so let me start at the beginning. Your mother, Oriana, was from a Camorra family, right?"

"Yes." But she glanced around. "Please. Keep your voice down."

I glanced around with her. The deck we were on was raised, and there was no one else on it except Theo, who was out of earshot. Still, I lowered my tone. "And Kelvin, your father, was ultimately killed by two men who were in the Camorra, is that right?"

She nodded.

"And the men who were in the Camorra, who killed Kelvin, they were never brought to justice, correct?"

"They were not," she said stiffly.

Time to switch to a different topic. "My father was a psychologist."

Silence.

"Is that correct?" I said.

"Yes."

"And he worked as a police profiler."

"That's right."

"He worked for the Detroit police."

"That's correct."

"He worked on Mob cases, right?"

"Yes, Isabel." She was growing a little weary now. Any witness being cross-examined gets to that point—where they are simply tired of it. That was fine. I knew exactly where to go from there.

"And at the time my father died, he was working on the case of the Rizzato Brothers, is that right?"

A pause. Then, "That's right."

"The Rizzato Brothers were Camorra."

She glanced over my shoulder as if she were looking for someone. "That is what I've heard."

I followed her gaze. We were still alone on the deck. "You're not sure?"

"No, I suppose that is correct."

I heard my trial professor—*Always get an exact answer to your question.*

Elena shifted slightly on the chair and adjusted her silver sunglasses.

"Elena," I said, "would you mind removing your sunglasses?"

Though I'd said it kindly, it was a rather forceful request from a niece to an aunt, but my aunt complied. Her eyes, brown and flecked with green, were sad, and a little confused. I hated that confusion, and yet it was exactly what I needed to see.

"So, I'll ask again. The Rizzato Brothers were known to be members of the Camorra, right?"

"Yes, Isabel. Why all these questions?" Another glance over my shoulder.

"Just give me a few more minutes. I'm trying to figure out something."

She bowed her head a little as if to say, *Continue.*

"Thank you. Now, the Brothers Rizzato, who were Camorra—they were from Ischia, correct?"

"I suppose I have heard that."

"You've heard that?"

"Yes."

"Okay. And Ischia is outside of Naples, isn't it?"

"Yes.

"And Naples is the home of the Camorra, right?"

Elena nodded, and in that instant, I felt as if I *were* back in the courtroom. I could see myself standing at a distance from the witness, then moving closer.

"And last night in Naples," I said as I scooted forward on the lounge chair, leaning a little toward Elena. "I was chased by two men with guns."

She shook her head quickly, her eyes blinking. "Is that true? Did that happen?"

"It happened. In Naples. And do you know, Elena, that the day before I was at the antimafia office in Rome, asking about the Camorra?"

"I did not know." Her eyes were alarmed.

"And at the antimafia office, I asked about my father. I also mentioned the fact that he was working on a Camorra case when he was killed."

Elena dropped her head in her hands. When she looked back up at me, her eyes were in agony. "Is that true?"

"It's true. What is also true is that your family, this family—" I pointed to my chest "—has believed their father to be dead for all these years. It is true that I—" once again I pointed to myself "—will not stop asking about him. I will not stop asking questions. I will never, never stop. So let me ask you a simple question now—Isn't it, true, Elena, that you do *not* want your family to be in torment?"

"No," she said. "Of course, I do not."

"And you do not want your family to be in danger, do you?"

"No. I do not."

"And you do not want your family to live like this anymore, do you?"

Elena began to cry, or rather, a single tear slipped from her right eye. She acted as if it hadn't happened. She didn't move to brush it away.

"I was thinking about something this morning," I said. "You didn't go to his funeral."

She didn't reply. And right then I decided to deviate

from cross-examination rules and go for it. "You didn't attend the funeral, because you knew it wasn't true. You knew he wasn't dead. Isn't that right?"

She didn't reply right away. But she did respond—she nodded.

37

Americani. You could tell even from this distance.

He stopped for a moment and watched them. No matter what their looks, their personalities, their age, they all had a certain coltish quality that was easy to spot. Particularly for an Italian, someone forever jaded, whose ancestors had seen so much more than any *americano* could even imagine.

He wondered who they were. Strange that she seemed to know them, and yet he had no knowledge of these people. He moved closer, staying low behind a surrounding circle of shrubs, until he could hear their conversation but was still hidden from view.

One of them, a woman with pale skin, was questioning her, asking about family members, it sounded like.

But then she began asking about the System, talking as if she knew something about it, which was strange since most *americani* knew nothing of the Camorra. That used to bother the System. Now they realized that this lack of knowledge could actually help them. They could operate covertly, until the *americani* would look around one day and realize not only who the Camorra were, but that they were a strong force, part of the American fabric.

So, this was strange, this *americana* speaking to her, her words coming forth quicker.

He listened, and then he listened some more. When the questions began to get more precise, and the answers continued to stay in the affirmative, he started to frown. Possibilities formed in his mind and were discarded until it began to dawn on him exactly of whom they were speaking.

He got a feeling he didn't like at all, a feeling that he had been duped, and by one of his own. Someone he'd thought of as part of himself. He clenched his fists as he listened to the rest.

Then he heard the *americana* say, *You didn't attend the funeral because you knew it wasn't true. You knew he wasn't dead.* He strained in anticipation to hear the response. At first there wasn't one, but eventually they began to talk and he heard the words, *I will take you to him.*

His mind seethed, a fire lit up every portion of his brain and at the same time ignited and destroyed what was left in his heart for her. Unbelievable that he had fallen for this. Unbelievable that she had known all this time. That she had lied to him. *To him.* He had spared her. He had pleaded her cause when others in the System wanted to destroy her. *He* was the reason she was living right now, that she was who she was.

Not for long....

But no. He caught himself. Retribution and brute force was the old way of the System. It had worked for a long, long while, but now it was backfiring, causing uproar and strengthening the government forces that wanted to eliminate them.

He took a step toward a stone wall and put his back against it, thinking. If this came out, it could fall on his own head because he should have seen it, he should have known. Somehow he would have to handle this before anyone in the System heard about it or understood it.

And *then* there would be retribution for her. Then he would take care of her. Then it would finally end.

When he heard her making plans to go back to the hotel, to pack her things and take the young woman to *Roma,* he knew he would be on that trip, only they wouldn't be aware of it.

38

I said goodbye to Theo at the train station. His hair fell forward as he looked down at me. He tucked a lock behind his ears. I remembered when I had done that to him last night. It seemed aeons ago.

"Are you going to be okay?" he asked.

I looked up at him. "I have no idea."

"Is she really taking you to meet him?"

"That's what she says."

"This is surreal," Theo said.

"Tell me about it." My mind skittered about, unable to stop on one thought.

Theo said once more, "Are you sure you're going to be okay?"

I turned back to him. "I honestly don't know. Because here's the thing. I don't know who I am now."

"What do you mean?"

"I feel like...I don't know how to put it..." I thought about it, but my thoughts kept jumping one to another, different voices attached to them, all talking. One voice, who clearly didn't care about my no-swearing campaign, was screaming, *Are you fucking kidding me? He's ALIVE?* Another, who sounded as if she was softly weeping, said, *I don't understand. I don't understand. I don't understand.*

"I feel like I'm not who I thought I was," I said to Theo. "I'm not half-orphaned. If you really think about it, I'm someone who was, well, abandoned. I mean, my father is alive. He left us."

"But you don't know why."

I looked over my shoulder at Elena. "She says she's going to tell me everything on the train back to Rome. She says he's there. In *Rome*."

I turned back again. I stared across the station. Passengers were hurrying to the track area. Everyone looked so *normal*.

I gazed up at Theo. "Thanks so much for being here."

"Are you sure I can't go with you? I don't need to fly back. And I could have the pilot meet me in Rome."

I shook my head. "You have to get to work. You told me you could only be gone a day or two."

He stared at me for a moment, which gave me a second to stare back. His upper lip, perfectly shaped with two pink peaks, disappeared as his bottom teeth bit it, and he looked as if he was thinking hard.

"I've never seen you make that expression," I said.

He stopped biting his lip. "What expression?"

I shook my head. "Never mind." There was still so much about Theo that I didn't know, but whether it mattered now, I couldn't tell. It seemed as if my life had been split in two big books—*Before I Knew My Father Was Alive; After I Knew My Father Was Alive.* I felt as if I was on a freaking soap opera. The shrill voice in my head piped up again. *Who has a dead parent who's not really dead, for fuck's sake?*

"Look, I don't care about work," Theo said.

"Of course you do. You have a company to run…" I trailed off, stumbling over another thing I didn't know about Theo. I knew generally about his company, knew it was legit, but we didn't talk about things like work. We didn't talk that much at all, I suppose. And yet despite the absence of all the technical information about him, I felt I knew him. And that I adored him.

"I'll throw work to the curb right now if you need me to," he said.

"I don't know what I need. All I know is she's going to take me to him." I said this as if by repeating it, it would sink in.

Suddenly, I felt as if I had taken some kind of drug. I remembered in law school when Maggie and I thought it would be fun to take mushrooms. It wasn't. The whole experience seemed enjoyable at the start, and then it had all gone bad, bizarre; it felt broken. And that was exactly what the search for my father had been like—almost exciting at first, fantastical, but then it had spun away from me and now seemed ugly, sinister, wrong.

"Izzy!" Maggie called across the station. She held Bernard's hand with one of hers and with the other pointed at the board, where lit-up track numbers and departure times were quickly changing and flashing. It was hard to know which one to concentrate on. "Our train is about to leave."

I looked at Theo and smiled. "You're the best for coming. For putting up with all this."

"I didn't put up with anything but some fun."

"Oh, you think getting chased by guys with guns is fun?"

"Hell, yeah. It'll make a good story for my boys back home."

"I've never met any of those boys."

Suddenly, I wanted to ask him, Who is your mom? Who is your dad? Where were you raised? What high school did you go to? Why did you leave college? Did you always know you would be a success? Who are your friends? I knew nothing about him. Nothing. And yet that realization didn't leave me empty. Rather, it made me feel kind of hopeful, kind of excited about something to learn in the future.

Meanwhile, the questions about my father? Those didn't excite me. They left me cold with fear.

"I know," Theo said. "You need to meet my boys. And hey, I liked meeting Maggie and Bernard." He nodded across the station in Maggie's direction. She was standing on her tiptoes, clutching Bernard around the neck in a goodbye hug. "So when you get back," Theo said, "we'll set up something with my buddies, okay?"

It sounded like such a normal request, one that I would have said "yes, of course" to yesterday or earlier this morning or even two hours ago. Now, I had no idea how to answer that question. What would it feel like *after* I met my father, *after* I heard the explanation of why he had done what he did? I had so many questions. The situation had too many potentials, too many avenues to crawl down. It could go too many ways and none of those ways seemed good.

But I couldn't—*wouldn't*—live my life just for my father or whatever I would soon learn about him, so I looked at Theo and said, "Yes. I want to meet them when I get home."

He smiled. He bent down and with those perfect lips kissed mine. He was such a beautiful kisser. At that moment, it was hard to remember kissing anyone but him.

He tugged my bottom lip with both of his. And then he folded me into a hug.

"You are fine," he said. And, as if he knew I didn't believe it, he said it again and again as he embraced me. "You are fine. You're fine. You're fine."

When he finally let me go, I had tears in my eyes.

"Don't," he said, "or you'll make me do that, too."

That made me laugh, the thought of him crying—for some reason I couldn't envision it. He seemed like someone who always brought the sun with him, who brought the happy life.

"I'll see you when I get back," I said.

"Let me watch you walk away."

"You got it." And with those words, for one moment, I felt some levity. I felt the way I always felt with him—sexy, amusing.

I kept that feeling in my mind as I sashayed away from him, for a second almost believing I was one of those normal people walking through the *Centrale* station. I swung my hips a little in an exaggerated way, then I stopped and I tossed him what I hoped was a sensual look over my shoulder.

Theo was beaming.

He gave me a thumbs-up, and then he turned away.

39

My aunt and I sat on the train hurtling back to Rome. I was jumpy, moving around in my seat, almost rocking with anticipation, but Elena was as still as night. She looked out the window, her eyes obscured by her sunglasses, the silver braid on the arm of those glasses glinting occasionally with the disappearing sun outside. Once or twice, I attempted to make conversation, first a stab at small talk, then a direct question about my father.

She didn't respond.

I waited for ten more minutes, then said, "Please, Elena, please just tell me."

She didn't react to my plea. She continued to stare out the window. We fell into silence, the train making a soothing, rocking motion. A few times, Maggie walked halfway down the aisle from her seat and gave me a questioning look as if to say, *Need any help? Need anything?*

Each time, I only shook my head sadly. The sun slipped away, night fell. And yet Elena's sunglasses remained on her face.

When we were about twenty minutes outside Rome, Elena spoke. "I guess I cannot wait any longer." She turned to me. "I was the one who caused this."

I sat and looked at her, wondering what she meant. I was

about to ask, but she opened her mouth, and, finally, my aunt removed her sunglasses. Only then did she tell her story.

She clasped her hands tight in her lap, gazing down at them. "When we were in high school, they killed my father because of your dad, Christopher."

"What do you mean?"

"The Camorra wanted Christopher."

"In what way?"

"Here, in *Italia,* they call the Camorra the System." She shrugged as if this didn't matter or she didn't care. "The System wanted your father, because the Camorra was trying to establish a presence in the United States. The Rizzato Brothers were already in the States and they were doing well. But they needed more members. The right members. The System thought it would be perfect if someone like your father, who was Camorra but not Italian-looking at all, who had a name like Christopher McNeil, could be an active part of the Camorra. They wanted him to infiltrate businesses, to learn everything and then give everything back to the Rizzato Brothers and the Camorra. They had big plans for him. He would eventually help the Rizzato Brothers run the System's operations in the United States. Eventually, he would be a boss, one that no one would suspect of being in the Mob. They thought it was perfect. But my father wouldn't hear of it."

The train raced around a corner and everything in the car lurched to one side. For a second, I fell against my aunt.

"Sorry," I said.

She smiled a little. "Do not be sorry, Isabel."

"You were saying that your father wouldn't go along with the Camorra's plan?"

"No. Christopher heard a conversation about it one night when he came home earlier than expected. He was a senior in high school then. Our parents didn't know he was in the house, but he heard one of the Camorra bosses who'd come from Italy telling our parents of the plan to use Christopher. Our father told this man, in no uncertain terms, that his son would not be a pawn for the System." She shook her head. "This is not my part of the story to tell, but you already know the facts. My father, Kelvin, was killed."

I felt a sick knowledge dawning. "They killed him because he refused to let his son work for the Camorra."

"Yes. It was a message. To my father certainly. The last message he would ever get. It was also a message to your father, Christopher. To our mother. The message was, *We will ask and you will say yes, or there will be punishment.*"

"But there was no further punishing. My dad went off to college after your father died, right?"

She dipped her head slowly in acknowledgment and seemed to be drawing in breath for strength. "Yes, Christopher went to college." She looked at me, eyes unblinking. "He also joined the System."

I don't know why I suffered such shock, but I felt it like a long, steady electrical charge through my whole body. "My father joined the Camorra?"

"*Sí.* After what they had done to our father, he saw how strong they were, how unflinching. He knew they would stop at nothing to get what they wanted. And therefore he agreed to their wishes."

"He said he would work for them." I had to say it to believe it. The electrical charge fizzled, and all I felt was disappointment.

"But he also joined the FBI, Isabel."

"I don't understand."

"Christopher contacted the FBI as a freshman in college. He told them he wanted to work for them, but he said that he would be working for the Camorra, too."

"He would be a double agent?"

"Yes. It was the FBI who put him through college and then paid for his master's degree in psychology. It was the FBI who moved him and your mother to Detroit and placed him in a government job with the Detroit police, although the Camorra took credit for it. They thought they had an inside man. But what your father was doing was reporting on them and consulting on any cases having to do with the Mob, particularly with the Camorra. As I said, the Camorra wanted desperately to establish a foothold in the United States in the seventies. Because of your father's work, because of what he knew, the FBI was always able to find the men who were in the U.S., and those who were coming to the U.S. They were able to shut them down. The Rizzato Brothers were killed, we believe, by some men whom they had stolen from. And many Camorra members eventually gave up and returned to *Italia*."

Until now, I thought, thinking of Dez Romano and Michael DeSanto. But I didn't want to stop Elena from talking.

But she did anyway. Her words died away and she dropped her head into her hands. My aunt began to weep softly. For a moment or two, I didn't move, didn't do anything. I stared at the empty seat in front of us. Then I looked back at Elena. I didn't know how to comfort her, didn't understand exactly what she needed comforting about. Her tears grew more powerful then, her back began to tremble.

I saw Maggie stand in the aisle, a number of seats in front of us, a sad, concerned look on her face. She held up her hands. *Do you need anything?*

I shrugged then shook my head no.

It was killing me to see my aunt in that state, so I put my arm around her shoulder. I tried to pull her close, but aside from the sobs that shook her body, she was as stiff as a block of wood. I kept squeezing her a little, kept drawing her ever so slightly nearer. Finally, she seemed to succumb. She crumpled a little, her shoulders sagging farther. She turned her head and placed her forehead on my shoulder. And then, even though I didn't know why, tears began to stream down my cheeks, as well.

Maggie was kneeling in her seat now, turned around and watching us. She looked agonized.

Eventually, Elena's sobs were reduced to gulping tears, and eventually those diminished into sniffles. But finally, she'd had enough. My aunt sat up.

"*Grazie,*" she said to me.

"*Prego.*"

She took a tissue from her bag and dabbed at her eyes, rimmed in red now. "*Allora,*" she said. "Now I will tell you more."

40

According to my aunt, my father was careful while he worked for the FBI, so careful, she said, that the System did not seem to realize it was Christopher McNeil, the Camorra's star whose cover was being a police psychologist, who was the cause of their undoing. And so it was all going fine, Elena said, until Christopher brought down the wrong person—the brother of her husband, Maurizio.

Elena knew the whole time what Christopher was doing. She was the only one, aside from his FBI handlers. He'd told her so she would understand that he was not truly in the System, that he was trying to right the grave wrong of their father's death.

"But when he told me that he had targeted Paulo, Maurizio's brother, and that they were about to bring him down, I begged him not to do it," she said. "I told him, you cannot do this. This is my *husband's* brother. Paulo is like you are to me. Maurizio loves him as I love you. If you do this, the entire family will collapse. Paulo is the patriarch of this family. He is the reason we all have money. Paulo takes care of everyone."

"Is Maurizio part of the System?"

"Yes." Elena dabbed her eyes again. "I didn't know it when I met him. I didn't know that nearly everyone I met when I moved to Italy was Camorra."

"Did you ever live in Naples? I thought the Camorra was only in Naples?"

She smiled grimly. "The Camorra's stronghold is in *Napoli.* Their home is *Napoli,* but they are everywhere. They are in Rome. In fact, it is easier for them to operate from Rome, where they are still not expected to be strong."

"So you and Maurizio stayed in Rome after you were married?"

"Yes, but the family had a house in *Napoli,* too, and so we went back and forth. It was a very good life." She sighed. "You must understand that I have known Maurizio since I was seventeen. When my family had all deserted me—or at least that's how I felt when I was moved to Rome—it was Maurizio's distant family who took me into their fold, introducing me to him."

"Your father was killed by the Camorra and yet you moved to Italy and moved in with them? I don't understand."

"Isabel, please don't try to understand this in a simple frame. There is nothing simple about the Camorra. As I told you before, my mother's family was traditionally Camorra, but many members of the family did not want to be defined by that. Many chose not to participate, others did, but even if someone did work with the Camorra, it didn't mean that the entire family was a part of it. I believe my mother thought I was safe, because I went to her family in Rome, not *Napoli,* and all the Camorra members that she knew were from *Napoli.*"

A pause. Then I decided to say what I was thinking. "It sounds like you were a sacrificial lamb."

The muscles in her face tensed, then she laughed. "That is what your father once said, too. But by then it was too late. I was part of Maurizio's family—my only family, it felt like—and they were part of me. And it was okay for a long while, because although your father knew

Maurizio's family was Camorra, his clan wasn't trying to work in the United States, so he wasn't part of any operation that your father was focusing on. But then Paulo began to move into America, and it came under your father's jurisdiction, and then there was this operation to bring him down. As I said, I begged him not to."

"And how did my father respond?" How strange it was to speak those words—*my father*—and be referring to someone alive, someone I was about to meet. Again.

"Your father was torn. On one hand, it was his job to stop people in the System. And I had always understood what he was doing. But now there he was, bringing down one of *my* family members. We were going to have no money left if Paulo went down. And we all loved him. Despite what he does with the System, for work, he is a good man in many ways. I finally decided I had to let them know, the people who were my family now. I told Maurizio and his brother what was going to happen and that it was going to occur very soon. When they didn't believe me, I finally had to tell them why I knew this—because my brother was an undercover agent for the FBI. And he was spying on the System." She shook her head now and looked up.

I stayed silent.

"Can you understand how torn I was?" Her eyes beseeched mine.

"Yes, of course."

She slipped her sunglasses back on. "It was horrid. I wanted so desperately to protect my brother, but I also wanted to protect my husband and his family, my *life*. I had already lost one life, you know. I couldn't bear the thought of the death of yet another."

"What happened?"

She dropped her head and began to sob again.

"What?" I said. "What happened?"

A few more shuddering cries, then she restrained herself. "They couldn't get to Christopher. Not right away. Being with the police force and having protection from the FBI meant he was not an easy person to reach." She looked out the window then back at me. She took off her sunglasses, and her eyes were dead. "So they killed my mother."

"Grandma O died in a car crash in Phoenix."

"Is that what you were told?"

I thought back to that time. I'd been eight years old, and although I hadn't spent much time with her, I was fond of Grandma O. I liked her musical voice, the way she broke into songs in Italian whenever there was a tense moment. She was funny like that—she could defuse almost any situation.

And then one day, my father sat me down and said that Grandma O had died.

"Yes, I think so," I said to Elena. "My father told me…" I drifted off for a second, thinking. "He told me that she had problems with her car and she died. I assumed it was an accident. I felt like that's what he was saying."

Elena squeezed her eyes shut, then opened them. "I'm sure that is the impression he was trying to give you, but the truth was that her car exploded. The official story from the police was she had put a propane tank in the trunk and the propane tank leaked and ignited when she started the car. But I know that wasn't true." She grimaced. "Or rather, it was true, but she had not placed it there. One of the System's men did and he turned the tank on so that it was leaking."

"They *killed* your mother."

Why hadn't I found it suspicious that my grandmother died such a short time before her son? I suppose because my parents had done a good job of dialing down the violent nature of her death. And soon her death was overshadowed by my father's.

Elena nodded, her lips pressed together, making the skin around her mouth bleached white.

"They did it as a way to get a message to Christopher, to my father?"

Another nod. She relaxed her lips and blew out a large breath. "They were trying to say, *we've killed your mother and we will kill you, Christopher, and your family, too. It is only a matter of time.*"

"Oh my God," I said.

She shook her head again and again, as if she was trying to shake away the memories and all that had been done.

"How awful," I said.

"You have no idea. I had killed my mother. And now they were trying to kill my brother and his children." She stopped and looked at me, and then she spoke very, very softly. "And so he…"

But now I could pick up the story. "And so he faked his own death."

She nodded, she stopped, she nodded again. She turned to me. "Yes, Isabel. That is what he did." She gave me a grim look. "It nearly destroyed me, the thought that they might kill you. And trust me, Isabel, they *would* have killed you."

"Weren't you worried that they would kill *you?* I mean, after what they did to Grandma O. Weren't you afraid they would do the same to you to send a message to him?"

She sighed and shook her head. "The System is very difficult for an outsider to understand. They are ruthless, yes, but there is still a circle of loyalty, and I fell within that circle. Your father knew that, too. He knew that they were coming for him next and for his family, and they wouldn't stop, and so he went to the FBI. He told them what was going on. The FBI said that they would immediately put the family in the witness protection program. But your father said the witness protection program was no way to live, no way to move on. He didn't want you all to have to change your identities and your lives. It would have been awful. And so instead of doing that to you…" Her words trailed off.

"But when there was no body, didn't the Camorra suspect something?"

She laughed but it was without mirth. "Your father was very smart. He played on their egos. He landed the helicopter on the water and rigged it to explode after he'd gotten out. To this day, I know different clans, different members of the Camorra who pride themselves on having killed my brother."

"So, like I said before—that's why you weren't at his funeral. Because you knew he wasn't dead."

She nodded. "I couldn't bring myself to act like he had died. It was enough that I had killed my mother."

"You didn't kill her, the Camorra did."

"Because of me. Because I told them about Christopher." She clutched her stomach and rocked forward, her head bent.

I put a hand on her shoulder, leaning closer. "Are you all right?"

She nodded.

I had to ask. "Where has he been in Italy this whole time?"

She shrugged. "That is your father's story. I will let him tell you."

She seemed depleted by what she'd told me so far. I decided not to push her.

We sat for a while in silence, the train gently rocking. Elena made a huge exhale of breath, then turned to me. "Those men who chased you in Naples," she said. "They weren't trying to kill you."

"What do you mean? They came in the hotel, they seemed to be looking for me and they ran after us with guns!"

She shook her head dismissively. "Trust me. When the Camorra wants to kill you, they kill you. They don't look, and they don't chase. They just *do.*"

"Then what *were* they doing exactly?"

A small shrug. "My guess is they were trying to scare you."

"They did a great job. But why?"

Another shrug. "It would be difficult to kill you. To kill *italiani? Sí.* That happens all the time. But if the Camorra kills a young, attractive American woman, it could cause problems for them."

"And when I go back to the United States?"

She examined my face. She glanced from my mouth to my hair and back to my eyes. "I would be very careful."

41

We went to the hotel on *via Giulia* where we'd had the reservation for yesterday and checked in. The lobby there was cool and quiet, just like a former convent should be. While Elena went to the lobby restroom, Maggie got a bellman to take our bags upstairs. Then she drew me over to the small library in the lobby. "Sit," she said, pointing at a low white couch.

I did, and looked up at her.

Maggie stood in front of me. "Look, I'm just going to tell you what you tell me when I'm about to go on trial."

"Okay. Good. Hit me."

She glanced over her shoulder. There was no one near us. "Here's the thing. You can't let your mind go crazy and think about all that could happen. You just have to go through it, minute to minute, and make smart choices along the way. Like right now, you can't let your mind run over the possibilities of why your dad did what he did." Maggie started pacing. "You can't be angry about it, do you understand?"

I nodded. God, it was great to have a friend doing your mental prep for you.

"You can't think about anything other than right now," Maggie continued. "You can't let your head run around and around in fifteen different circles. Essentially, don't be a conspiracy theorist. Just be you in this situation." She stopped, nodded like, *Got it?*

"The thing is, I can't believe it's *me* in this situation. I can't believe this is happening to me."

She pointed at my face. "You're doing it. You're letting your head run around in circles." She sat on the couch next to me. "Okay, let's think. What would help you to get your mind around this? To really feel like it's happening. Right now."

"Well, I can't stop thinking about my mom. Did she know?"

Maggie shrugged, then looked at her watch. "She's up. Call her."

I nodded. It felt good to have some course of action to take, rather than simply waiting for Elena, reacting to her.

I called my mother's cell phone. "Izzy!" she said. "I was just going to call you. Happy birthday!"

I'd almost forgotten. "Thanks, Mom."

"Do you know that I can remember exactly what happened on the day you were born?"

"Really?" I said with a laugh. She told me this story every year.

"It was a beautiful Friday. It had been cold that summer in Michigan, but this was the first real summer day, and so your dad had taken the day off, and he and I were working in the garden. Do you remember the garden we had in Michigan?"

I said I did. My parents both loved gardening, something they'd shared together but never really taught Charlie and me. I told my mom about the wildflowers Maggie gave me and the flower box she was going to put on my roof deck.

"Wonderful!" my mom said. "I'll help you with it." She sighed. "Well, I remember that day you were born.

I was kneeling next to the tomato plants and staking them. They were just starting to bloom, and I couldn't wait until they grew and ripened."

My mother went on, saying how, kneeling there in the Michigan soil, she'd realized that her water had broken, that she was about to have her first child. She'd spent a moment by herself appreciating that, before she called for my father.

She was so happy recounting this story that for the moment I decided not to mention my father. We chatted about Italy, about Maggie being there. My mom told me that she and Spence were supposed to go to a barbecue later at their friend's house on Astor Street.

After a few more pleasantries and questions about Italy, I asked her, "Do you know how Grandma O died?"

"Oriana? Awful. She died in a car explosion."

"Why wasn't I told that when I was younger?"

"Weren't you?"

"Dad told me she had car problems and that she died."

"Well, that's true, isn't it? And you were seven or eight, Isabel. It's not the kind of thing you tell a young child—that her grandmother has been blown to bits."

"What caused the explosion?"

"They said that your grandmother had put a propane tank from her barbecue in her trunk the night before, because she was going to have it filled. This was before there were laws about refilling. They said the tank leaked, and when she started the car the next day, it ignited."

"Grandma O had a barbecue? That doesn't sound like her. I just remember pastas and bread and those big mushrooms."

"She was a wonderful cook. I thought it strange about the barbecue, too. I remember asking your father about it at the time. Even the fact that she had carried the tank to the car surprised me. Those tanks are heavy and she was a small woman and getting up there in age."

"What did Dad say to you?"

"Not much. He was so traumatized. It was a horrible time."

"And then a month later, he was dead." Supposedly. *Allegedly.*

"Yes, and your grandmother's death took a backseat. Losing your father was just so all consuming."

Did you know? Did you know he faked his death? This was what I wanted to scream into the phone, but I wasn't sure I quite believed it, even now, even having spoken to Elena. And I couldn't upset my mom unnecessarily.

In the background, I heard Spence calling to her. I could see him rushing into the kitchen. "Say hi to Spence for me," I said. I would ask her later, when I knew for sure, when I understood the whole story.

"Will do, honey. Have a fun birthday, and we'll celebrate when you get home."

I hung up the phone and looked at Maggie.

"You didn't ask her," she said.

I shook my head. "I couldn't. Not until I know myself for sure."

"Okay. I get that. So look at me. Where are you right now?"

"In Rome. About to meet my father. For the first time in almost twenty-two years." I sat and stared at her. We were both silent.

A family filed into the hotel lobby. They looked jubilant and tired after a day of sightseeing. One of the kids was saying, "Let's go to the Vatican again tomorrow." The dad laughed, ruffled his hair.

"I never had that," I said. "Sightseeing with my father."

"This is exactly what I'm telling you not to do,"

Maggie said. "Do not think about things like that. Do not think about anything except the fact that you are about to meet him. Nothing before this meeting, nothing after. Now, let me ask you again, where are you right now?"

"I'm in a hotel and my best friend is pretending to be Eckhart Tolle."

Maggie laughed. Then she lost her smile. "Seriously, just be here. Just be sitting here right now." She looked over my shoulder. "And right now, your aunt is about to come up to us. So just be someone who's about to walk out onto the streets of Rome."

I opened my mouth to say something.

She shook her head, "Iz, there's nothing else you can do right now except walk onto the streets of Rome." She put her hand on my shoulder. "I'm not going to ask you if you're okay. You are. I'll be here when you get back." She took her phone out of her pocket and pointed to it. "Call me if you need anything."

"What are you going to do?" I looked at my watch. It was 4:00 p.m. "A lot of museums are open until six. Or you could walk along the Tiber or go see the Coliseum."

Maggie put her hand on my shoulder once more. "Iz, I know I'm in Rome. And we both know I love this city. But you know what I like best of all."

"Sleep."

"Yep. But if you need anything, I'm up in a minute."

Maggie looked past me and smiled. "Hi, Elena." She hugged me. "See you guys later," she said, as if this were any other day.

I turned to Elena.

"Ready?" Elena said.

My head screamed, *No,* but a different answer came from somewhere deep within me. I think it was my heart.

And my heart said, *"Yes."*

42

Like any Roman, Elena was quick on the cobbled streets, dodging down one alley, one street, rushing through another section of town, then another, striding in front of taxis with her hand held out, assuming (correctly) that they would all stop for her. The afternoon had turned humid, the air thick with exhaust and heat. The tourists were easy to spot—all scrutinizing maps, their faces confused and sweating—while the Romans breezed by, seeming not to notice them and not perspiring a drop.

We passed through the Piazza Navona, where street vendors ran after tourists, trying to sell belts and bags. I wondered if they were fakes made by the Camorra. We skirted the Pantheon next, the circular temple still and solid amid the chaos of the city. I glanced across the piazza and saw the ivory-colored awnings of Fortunato, the *ristorante* where Elena had taken Maggie and me when we were here years ago. Had my father been here, too? How had Elena sat across from me then, knowing my father was—what?—maybe a mile away?

Meanwhile, where we were going now, I had no idea. Elena had told me to follow her. That was all. Elena walked faster as I struggled over the cobblestones, always a step behind. She dodged around more tourists, she darted into deserted alleys and then would turn again onto the bigger streets like the Corso. I kept following her, past *gelaterie,* past piazzas with center obelisks and columns decorated with enough symbolism to study for years.

All the while, Elena was quiet. I kept sending glances at her, murmuring my appreciation for taking me to him, for being honest with me. When these comments were met with nothing more than a scared look in my direction, I decided to ignore the topic of my father, and instead started commenting on a church or a facade of a shop as if we were out sightseeing. Elena responded to the overtures with a terse nod, a quick smile, her face always returning to one of deep thought. I decided not to say anything more. I was afraid she would change her mind.

We turned another corner, and I gasped at the sight of the Trevi Fountain. Tucked in an otherwise average and rather small piazza, the fountain was a massive white marble wall, carved with a commanding figure of Neptune in the center. Streams and arcs of glistening water shot into a huge oval pool that glittered silver and gold from the coins coating the bottom.

Tourists were packed in front of the fountain, snapping pictures and throwing coins over their left shoulder, a superstitious way to ensure your return to Rome.

Elena stopped, too, as if giving me a short break. She followed my gaze to the pool. "Do you know," she said, pointing at the coins, "how much we collect every night from the *Fontana di Trevi?* Three thousand euros."

"Every day?"

Elena nodded. "They say they give the money to a supermarket for food for poor families." She shrugged as if to say that might happen and it might not. She touched my arm. "*Andiamo.*" Let's go.

Elena started moving fast again, skirting the fountain,

not giving it another thought. I got my legs moving and scurried after her, but I kept slowing inadvertently, darting glances at the fountain. I felt envious of the tourists, and I wondered if I didn't throw a coin, would I get back to this city? I shook the thought away. It didn't matter. How could it possibly when I was about to meet my father, to see him resurrected from the land of the dead?

Elena threw a glance over her shoulder at me. Her expression seemed to say, *Hurry or I'll change my mind.*

At a corner of the Trevi's piazza, I followed Elena to the right, into a narrow, jaggedly shaped street. A bookstore was on a corner. Elena turned left in front of it, then right, then left, weaving away from the fountain, the sounds of its crowds and splashing water receding quickly.

Suddenly, Elena stopped at a wood door. Many of the doors in Rome are works of art—some are tiny, others three stories tall and arched at the top. They might be made of hammered metal or studded with iron posts or boasting handles the size of a globe and shaped like a lion's head. Some were painted faded red, others a vibrant green. They might be trimmed with marble or decorated with brass finishings. But this door was boring in contrast to the usual lot. It was the same size as the doors at home, rectangular, nondescript—made of wood that was clearly thick and solid, with fist-sized circles carved at the four corners.

Elena reached up and pressed the top right circle. The seemingly solid wood depressed, then just as quickly regained its shape, so that nothing about the door appeared different.

There was a clicking sound. Elena looked over her shoulder, past me, her eyes darting up and down the street, then she pressed the door with the flat of her hand and it swung inward.

She gestured at me to follow her. We stepped into a foyer, cold and dark, made of white marble with streaks of gray. The only light in the small space came from two iron sconces high on either side wall. There was nothing else in the foyer—not a piece of art on the walls, not a chair or a hall table. Elena took a few steps toward the other end. I did the same and stood behind her. It was so quiet that I began to notice the pulse in my ears, the beat of my heart. Both sounded like drums, thudding slowly, then faster and louder, faster and louder.

I watched as Elena reached out and touched the marble wall, sliding aside what was apparently a small panel. A keypad was behind it. She punched in a few numbers and then letters with an elegant finger, not bothering to hide them from me. The letters I recognized—*V-I-C-T-O-R-I-A.*

"My mother's name," I said.

Elena nodded.

"And what were the numbers?"

"0618."

I thought about it for a second. "June 18. The day they got married."

Elena nodded. "It changes frequently, but yes, that's correct." She slid the panel shut.

I noticed, right then, that I was trembling a little. I tried to calm myself, tried not to think any thoughts at all, because, if I did, they would only be a battalion of warring questions—*What am I doing? Where are we going? Where is my father?*

But the questions broke through anyway, muddling my mind, the whole experience reeling with the surreal.

I looked at Elena. Her mouth was grim, her eyes worried. She seemed to see me studying her, and she gave me a smile that broke the tension in her face. But then just as quick it was gone.

A whirring sound, and suddenly the back wall of the foyer began to move. It was a pocket door of sorts, I realized. I stared in awe at the space behind it. Would my father be standing there? What would he look like? Would I want to hug him? Or would I want to slug him for disappearing on us? Or would it be something else altogether—would I feel nothing upon seeing a man who was, after all, just a stranger now?

43

But there was no one there. Beyond the marble foyer was a metal gangplank that spanned a vast subterranean space of light brown crumbling brick. A few sconces illuminated the place, casting circles of golden light around them and eerie shadows below.

Elena gestured. "These are archeological ruins of the ancient aqueducts. We find them whenever we dig in this city."

Who, I wondered, was the "we" she was referring to? The government? She and my father?

Before I could ask, Elena made her way across the gangplank, then down a set of metal stairs. When we reached the bottom, there was another gangplank, which Elena crossed immediately. I followed her but she was moving fast again, and I couldn't keep up with her. The anticipation and the uneven gangway made me feel off-kilter and shaky.

I began to feel paranoid. "Elena, where are we going?" I was following my aunt to…where? She'd said she would take me to my father, but what did that mean?

"He keeps an office here," she said. "When he first left the United States, he needed to hide himself, but he still wanted to continue his mission, to work to shut down the Camorra."

After a few more gangplanks and stairs we came to a thick iron door with a simple round knocker. Elena looked at me, that worried expression taking over her face. I sensed a change in her energy, an anticipation that was suddenly greater than mine. She gave me a little smile and a raise of her eyebrows that seemed to say, *Here we go.*

The blood pounded in my ears, taking over my head, so that I felt a sudden intense headache. I was, I realized, holding my breath. I made myself breathe.

Elena raised her hand toward the knocker on the door.

And then suddenly, I was overtaken by a force of emotion—dread. A terrifying dread that was so strong, I literally felt as if it would kill me. My throat began to close, a feeling I'd never had before. And then I felt something cool on my forehead. I raised my hand and touched it. Sweat. My face was coated with it. My body temperature had soared. I felt my face flush deeply. *God bless it,* I thought, then *Goddamn it.* I knew what was happening—I was suffering a flop sweat attack.

Occasionally, when I got supernervous, like at the beginning of a trial, I experienced what can only be described as extreme perspiration. This little problem of mine was mortifying. It felt as if someone dropped burning charcoals into my stomach and then threw some gasoline on them. And then a truck full of lumber. The waterworks in my body would kick into gear, and my face would get as red as the fire inside me. The last time it had happened was months before when I was about to go on air as an anchor for Trial TV. The only thing that had stopped it was some emergency Benadryl. I had no Benadryl on me now.

"I can't," I choked out to Aunt Elena before she could knock. "I can't do this right now. I need some air. Just for a minute." If I didn't try and stop it, it would get worse and I didn't want to meet my father in this state, sweating like a bull and glowing like a lit Christmas tree.

"Maybe this is too much," Elena said, a frown on her face.

"No, no. It's just that it's too much for the moment. I just need a few minutes. Can we go up, please? Please?"

Elena paused, inhaled sharply.

I didn't want to lose her, to lose this opportunity. "Just a few minutes," I said again.

She gave a terse nod.

We retraced our steps. When we arrived back at the foyer, the place seemed too tiny, the walls felt as if they were shrinking into themselves. Elena said nothing but led me outside. We walked a few blocks away, and finally I stopped and leaned against a mustard stucco wall, sucking in air, fanning my face with my hand.

"I'm sorry," I said to her. "I have this little problem that happens sometimes. But I'm fine. Really. I'm having a hard time making my brain process this. Do you understand?"

"Certo," she said. Certainly.

"Does he know we're coming?"

She studied me for a second, then said simply, *"Sí."*

For some reason, that stopped the sweating. "Is he okay with that?"

A small smile. "Yes, *cara.* He is more than okay with that."

I closed my eyes and leaned my head back against the stucco wall, my breath coming easier, the color draining from my face. My father knew I was here.

I took a breath and looked down the street at an ancient stone archway leading to a garden. It could have been thousands of years old. That archway had likely been standing there during wars and strife and the marching past of a hundred generations. Likely it had seen much more overwhelming and even gruesome and troubling sights than a redhead American who was recovering from a flop sweat attack and about to meet her father for the first time in over twenty years.

Get your act together, Izzy.

He knew I was coming to meet him. He was okay with that. And right then, I was, too.

I raised my head and looked at Elena. I bent down and dabbed my forehead with the skirt of my dress, then I threw my shoulders back.

"You are ready now?" she asked.

"I am." And I meant it.

44

We retraced our steps until we were down inside the aqueducts, across the gangplanks and outside the door. Elena knocked. Nothing happened. She knocked again. Her eyebrows knitted together. She looked down at her watch, then took hold of the knocker and rapped once more. Still nothing.

"Should we call someone?" I asked. *Like my father?*

She shook her head. "There is no service down here."

"Of course. I should have thought of that."

Finally, Elena shrugged. "I usually don't just go in..." she said, her voice trailing off.

Elena grasped the knocker and turned it to the right. The door clicked and popped open just a little—not enough to see what lay behind it.

Elena gestured at the door, then nodded at me. "Go ahead," she said.

"Go ahead," I repeated inanely. This was the moment I'd been fantasizing about since that night in Chicago when the man in the garage saved me, when I'd heard those words, *You're okay now, Boo.*

"Okay," I said, remembering.

My aunt stepped aside, and I pushed the door. It was made of heavy iron but it glided smoothly.

Behind the door was an office, a dark, wooden desk

in the center, bookshelves along the wall to my left. I scanned them quickly, seeing a hodgepodge collection—psychology texts, books on the Mafia, current thrillers, tall leather tomes that looked like ledgers.

But there was no one in the room. I was about to turn to Elena when a book caught my eye. I took a few steps and touched the spine. *Poems & Prayers for the Very Young,* a copy of the book my father used to read to me.

I closed my eyes, and I could hear his voice: *I wake in the morning early; And always, the very first thing; I poke up my head and I sit up in bed; and I sing and I sing and I sing.*

When my father read that book to me in bed—*Close your eyes, Boo, and just listen*—I understood it. And yet when he was gone, the poem seemed to be about some other girl. I couldn't imagine that I would want to wake up and sing ever again. For a long time, I didn't even want to wake up.

I opened my eyes now. I was about to say something to Elena, but something beyond her caught my attention.

That's when I saw the blood.

45

On the other side of the room, a red couch was pushed against the wall. Except that one side of the couch had been pulled away, and behind it… I peered closer, took a step closer…

Elena swung around and gasped.

He was lying on the floor beside the couch, one arm draped over his face as if he'd raised it to wipe sweat from his brow, just like I had, and had been stopped midgesture. His face was splotched with blood. He wore a brown linen blazer, cream slacks that were spattered red, and a blue shirt. And in the center of that shirt was a hole, black on the sides, crimson from where blood had recently coursed from another wound.

I took another step. "Oh my God, someone shot him."

"Wait!" Elena moved toward me. Her steps were slow, cautious. When she reached him, she took a hold of the hand that rested near his body. She grasped the wrist, obviously looking for a pulse.

She stood and a strangled sound came from her. I stared at her, my brain reeling. Her mouth was open, her eyes horrified. A cry escaped her mouth, sounding like a distant note, a long "O" that didn't stop.

"Elena!" I said.

She snapped her head to mine, seemed to realize I was

there. She looked at the body again, then her head swiveled around; her eyes careened about the place.

"*Andiamo!*" she said. "We must go!"

She grabbed my arm and propelled me through the office and into the hallway.

"No, wait," I said. "We can't leave him." I tried to push around her and back into the office, but she gripped my arms and tugged at them.

"Isabel," she said, her voice like a slap. "We are going."

"What if he's alive? We have to help him."

"He is *not* alive." Another strangled sound came from her throat. "We must go. Now. We must run, Isabel."

We raced through the aqueducts and over the gangplank, then up the stairs, away from the sight of my father cloaked in blood.

"This way!" Elena yelled, grabbing my arm again when I tried to run down a gangplank. "That's the wrong way."

I tried to catch my breath. I made sure to stay close behind her.

Finally we reached the front door, and Elena threw it open, the fading sunlight of Rome sneaking inside the marble foyer.

She drew me outside and down a block before she turned to me. "You've got to leave me."

"What happened down there? Who did that to him?"

Elena shook her head fast, so fast that her perfect chestnut hair ruffled, and she squeezed her bown eyes closed. "You must get away from me. I bring nothing but tragedy. You must leave before something happens to you."

And with that, Elena turned and ran.

I tried to follow her, but my mind couldn't catch up with my feet. My mind kept seeing that blood pooling, running in rivulets across the ancient floor. I shook my head to try and dispel the images, but they wouldn't go away. I stumbled over the cobblestones, falling on one knee. I stood, couldn't get myself to run. I took a few halting steps in one direction, then another. I had no idea what to do. I had no idea what just happened. In the distance, I heard the splashing of the Trevi.

Run, Iz. Let's go!

Finally, I got my head to connect with my body and I ran in the direction of the noise. At least there would be people there.

Once I reached the piazza, I stopped at the sight of the huge white fountain, of the water, clean and light blue, splashing almost gaily. It all seemed an insult to my father. I turned and dodged up a small alley, not knowing where I was running. Rome, if you don't pay attention, will lead you in nothing but circles, and soon I was lost. And yet it seemed fitting, since my search for my father had led me in nothing but a circle. He'd been dead when I started, and he was dead now.

46

"Call her again," Maggie said.

We sat across from each other on the hotel beds, both of us wide-eyed, our skin white with fear.

I hit Redial again for Aunt Elena's number, let it ring, then hung up. I shook my head. "She's still not answering."

I'd finally found *via Giulia.* By that time, it was night. When I'd gotten to the room, Maggie was curled up against the headboard, talking to Bernard on the phone.

She was laughing at something, her tiny giggle filling the room. When she saw me, she said, "Oh my gosh, she's back." She threw back the covers and knelt on the bed. She was wearing a pale green nightie that made her look like a little girl. "How did it go, Iz?"

When I didn't answer, her eyes swept my face. "Call you back," she said to Bernard.

Maggie had gotten dressed by now in a pair of cuffed jeans and a T-shirt that read *Chicago Fire Department.* "This is scary," she said. "This is awful. Who killed him?"

"Maybe he shot himself? Is that possible?" I wanted to cry. I felt so bad for the father I didn't know. "Maybe the Camorra killed him. Maybe they found out he was still alive. Or maybe he had done something so awful he couldn't live with himself. Maybe he was still with the Camorra, like really with them."

"But if he was still Camorra, he would have to be a ruthless guy, so why kill himself?" Maggie stared up at the ceiling, as if willing answers from the heavens. "Unless maybe he knew you were here…"

"Why would that matter?"

She looked back at me and seemed to hesitate, as if considering whether to speak. "Well, if he knew you were here, and he knew you learned that he had been in the Camorra, and he was still in it, still a bad guy, and he thought you were going to find out, maybe it gave him an attack of conscience."

"So it would be my fault?"

"I'm not saying that. I'm just throwing out a possibility."

I nodded. I couldn't be irritated at Maggie. I needed the truth now, and only that. "Well, here's another question—shouldn't we tell the police?"

She shook her head. "I don't know. Because, Iz, it seems like anytime you've told someone something, scary stuff happens. I mean, you asked questions at the antimafia office, and next thing you know we're in Naples getting chased by those guys with guns. You asked Elena questions, and she told you your father was alive, and now he's…he's dead."

I winced.

"Sorry. I'm sorry to just say it like that, but I have to be your lawyer here, too, and I just don't know who you should trust. I don't know who we should talk to."

I looked down at my hands, crossed on my lap. "I have to tell someone. Or I have to do *something.*" I raised my head again and looked at Maggie.

Her face was creased in concentration. "Here's the thing. But what if the cops think you were involved somehow? In Italy, if they suspect you of a crime, they can hold you for up to a year without charging you."

"If he killed himself, there's no crime. So why would they charge me?"

"What if he didn't kill himself? What if someone else did, or if they think it wasn't self-inflicted for some reason? You're the one who found him. If they suspect you for a second, it's your word against...I don't know whose, but it won't look good." She shrugged. "Think about that college student who was arrested in Italy. Her roommate was killed, she found the body, and then they charged her with murder. There's also the issue of this legal system. Aside from stories like that, I don't know the Italian system. I couldn't represent you. I wouldn't even know who to call to do that."

"Mags, I've been suspected of murder once this year. I don't think that's going to happen again."

"I don't know, you've got some crazy energy going on lately. You've had a *lot* of weird stuff happen to you."

We both went silent. There was no arguing with that point. Another brutal truth.

"I can't just leave him there," I said. "I have to go back."

Maggie slumped down onto her bed, her elbows propped up behind her, and looked at me. "You realize that will only multiply the crazy-weird energy."

"What would you do if you were me?"

She studied me. "If I were you, I'd go back. And if I were me, I'd go with you."

47

Maggie and I left the hotel. Relative quiet reigned in the city since there was a soccer match in play, and everyone in the restaurants and bars was glued to TVs. I led Maggie through the streets, consulting a map over and over. Every time a goal was scored, a collective shout would ring through the city—*Roma!*—and each time it startled me, made my breath stop.

But I made my feet continue to move. "I can't believe this. I can't believe this." I kept saying that mantra over and over.

"Stop, Iz," Maggie said gently.

I stopped the mantra, but different words rolled out of my mouth. "I had him. Or I *almost* had him, and now he's dead. Just like that."

Maggie eyed me.

"In some ways I think it's worse than losing him when I was a kid."

She reached out and touched my arm.

I stopped in front of a brightly lit but empty clothing store. I waited for Maggie to say something profound, one of those things that only a best friend can say to put things straight.

She nodded, said nothing.

A tick, two, then three went by.

A roar leapt out of the doorways and into the street as another goal was scored or maybe one blocked.

Maggie still said nothing.

I nodded back.

We both knew there was nothing she could say.

When we got there, the Trevi Fountain was still crowded, although less so. I guided Maggie past it, down the tiny side streets until we reached that plain doorway, the one that looked as if there was nothing behind it, certainly nothing exciting. Nothing dead.

I turned to Maggie. “Are you ready?”

She shrugged.

I studied her. Eyebrows drawn together, forehead creasing, she looked more stressed than she usually did at work. And Maggie was always stressed at work.

I touched her shoulder. “Mags, you don’t have to do this. *I* have to do this, but you don’t.”

She shook her head. “I’m with you.”

“Some vacation, huh? Getting chased through a hotel by those guys and now this?”

In an exaggerated way, she lifted her shoulders and let them drop. “Girl, you forget that I usually represent guys who own TAR 21s, so a couple of handguns don’t freak me.”

“What’s a TAR 21?”

“An Israeli assault rifle. So, really, all this stuff…” She pointed, made a circle with her finger as if including all of Rome, all of Italy and everything that had happened so far. “Nah, this doesn’t faze me.”

She was lying. We both knew it. It was one thing to represent the bad guys from the safety of a designer suit, your grandfather’s office or the heavily guarded confines of Twenty-sixth and Cal. This—*this*—was something different. But I was afraid to say that, to speak the truth, because I might lose her. And I didn’t know if I had enough balls to go down there, into the depths of that place, by myself. But my father—*my father*—was there.

I turned, and as I'd seen Elena do, I reached up and pressed the fist-size knob at the top right of the door. Nothing happened. I tried it again. Nada.

"She did it just like this," I muttered.

But maybe she'd done something else, too, or triggered the opening mechanism some other way?

I tried again, pushing the side of my fist down with all my might.

A soft *whoosh* came from the door, and then *click.* Just as Elena had done, I pushed opened the door with the flat of my hand, and we entered the white marble foyer. The coolness inside was a bitter contrast to the still muggy night. It felt like a tomb. Sconces flickered but barely.

I went to the keypad and pushed the numbers and letters Elena had used. *V-I-C-T-O-R-I-A* 0618, and the door clicked open.

"What was that combination?" Maggie asked.

"My mom's name, and the day they got married."

"Wow. He still loves her."

"Yeah." For the first time since I'd seen the body, a crop of tears grew up from my belly, breaking through my heart, and shoved themselves into my throat. A few made their way to my eyes.

I pushed the tears away with my fingers. They felt hot, alive. "Let's go."

"What is this place?" Maggie asked as I led her through the aqueducts, sinking farther and farther into the earth.

I told her what I'd learned from Elena.

When I found the last gangplank, I led Maggie across it. I felt an intense sense of vertigo but ignored it completely. At the iron door at the end of the gangway, I halted. I didn't want to see that sight again. And yet I couldn't just stand there. I grabbed the round knocker in the middle of the door and pushed it open.

48

"We found her again," La Duca announced.

"Great." Dez said, as if it were par for the course, as if he wasn't completely relieved. "Where is she?"

"*Roma,* but that's all we know. Our contact who was following them seems to have dropped off, hasn't checked in."

The duke kept talking. He said it didn't appear that the McNeil girl had any plans to leave Italy anytime soon. And then he dropped a bomb. "We have information," La Duca said, "that her father is alive."

"You're kidding—" Dez started to say, but he halted, then corrected himself so that his words were one of an associate of the duke's, not an employee. "When were you apprised of this?" he asked calmly.

"A few days ago. And from what we can tell, he has been trying to sideline the System the whole time. He has been working for the antimafia office against us for all these years."

Dez felt remorse for a second, then embarrassment. They hadn't even told him. "Why didn't you mention this to me?"

"We didn't need to involve you."

Dez sat down at his desk. *We didn't need to involve you.* That wasn't good. Even though he was in Chicago, an ocean away from them, he needed to be an integral part of the business. He was the United States *boss* after all. He needed to be updated on all this, so he could properly wield his power. But he couldn't tell the duke that.

He was just starting to formulate his response when the duke spoke. And his words changed everything.

"But we need your help now, my friend," La Duca said, although the word *friend* didn't sound particularly friendly. "But you will only be able to help us if you can do so *fast.*"

49

Immediately, we smelled the blood. A gagging sound came from Maggie's throat. She put her hand over her mouth and stepped into the room.

I followed her inside, unable to look at the right side of the room. Instead, I just raised my arm and pointed at the couch. "There."

But as I said the word, my body turned against my will, needing to see. Then I turned more fully, my eyes opening wide, blinking, because…because…

There was no one there.

"He was…" I said. "He was right…"

A moment passed—a moment that seemed so long, contained the power of so much sensory information. That smell, a soft ticking of a clock on the desk, the low rumble of something—subways?—somewhere in the city, the sound of my breath coursing, jagged, in and out of my lungs, the sight of the red couch still pushed aside, of the pool of red liquid next to it.

"Are you sure?" Maggie asked.

"*Look.*" I pointed to the blood. "Obviously, something happened. He was lying right there."

Maggie shook her head. "But where is he now?"

I paced the room, my eyes wildly scanning the place,

my brain scanning every memory I had, every sight I'd seen, looking for something that made sense.

"There are drag marks over here. Elena must have had the body removed. After we saw him, when we got upstairs, she took off running."

"Where would she take the body?"

"I have no idea."

"We have to figure out where she could be."

I was about to make the same response—*I have no idea*—but then I stopped. "I think I know." I grabbed Maggie's hand. "Let's go."

50

"Charlie!" the producer yelled. "That author is at the front desk. Get her and take her to the green room."

Charlie removed his headset and shot off his chair. He left the booth where the producers ran the radio show and made his way through the studio. Two walls of glass overlooked Michigan Avenue, right where the street met the river. The desk in the studio, in front of those windows, was massive and triangular, each side having two or three headphones and mikes, except for the host's side, which had only one headset and a soundboard in front of it.

The host glanced up at him, gave a half smile and kept reading a newspaper. A commercial was playing, but you couldn't hear it in the studio, and although the guy would have to be back on air, live, going out to millions of listeners in twenty seconds, he was unfazed.

Which never failed to amaze Charlie. The skill this guy had—hell, the skill that nearly everyone at the station had—was impressive and inspiring. Charlie had been sitting on his ass for so long in his apartment that he hadn't seen this kind of expertise up close and personal for a long while. Sure, his mom and stepdad and Izzy were successful, but Izzy had been flaking lately, which made Charlie feel rather simpatico with her. Yet it was

Izzy's meandering in and out of jobs that made him realize he needed to get one. A real one, which he'd never had before.

Charlie had worked during high school and college, and he'd had the dump truck gig, but since he was an adult he'd never had a truly professional job. Of course, this thing with WGN was just an internship, something a college student could probably do, but it was perfect for Charlie. He got to watch the way people worked, the way they thought, the way they prepared. He knew the host was always up early in the morning—Charlie sometimes got e-mails from the guy sent at 6 a.m.—watching the news, boiling it down into witty, passing quips that sounded like off-the-cuff opinions. Charlie observed the head producer, too, who was a master of scheduling and glad-handing. The guy had to stack the book every day with interesting people—authors, comedians, politicians, celebs, sports guys—and then make the show feel as if it had exactly the right balance. When one guest called to cancel, or when the publicist for a better guest jumped in, the producer had to juggle the whole thing, moving this guest here, rescheduling another there.

The host dropped the corner of his newspaper. "Who do we have next?"

"The author." Charlie gestured in the direction of the front desk. "The one who traveled with that band, The Decker Brothers, for a year."

"It's a kid's band," the host said, "right? They're like six and eight years old?"

"Eight and ten." Charlie had been up last night reading all the press releases.

"And this grown woman traveled with these…" The host shook his head, his voice trailing off, ending with a short sigh. Then something seemed to catch his eye, and he stared out the window onto the street.

Charlie followed his gaze. Outside was the usual collection of tourists, some trying to take pictures of the studio through the glass, others cupping their faces around it to see inside. Sometimes people stood and waved until the hosts would wave back, even though they were live. Sometimes the people outside brought signs and jumped around with them until the host read them out loud, and hearing their signs read through the speakers on the street, the people would jump higher and cheer.

But today, there was something else going on. Two guys dressed in Cubs jerseys and baseball caps were staggering around outside, sort of tussling with each other.

"Drunk," the host said fondly. Charlie heard he was a recovering alcoholic.

One of them, a big guy with tattoos up and down both sides of his neck, threw the little one against the glass, and it made a huge *bam* sound. It looked like a fight, but then both of the guys just laughed. They turned to the glass and pressed themselves against it, pounding with their fists as if someone could open the glass and let them in.

The producer stuck his head out of the booth. "Charlie! Go control those idiots!"

Charlie hustled to the door. He was about to leave the studio when the host spoke up again. "Get the guest first. Make sure she knows we're a little delayed."

"But what about those guys…" Charlie pointed out the window where the two men were now doing some kind of cheer. The one with the tattoos on his neck threw his head back and looked as if he was howling. The other one cupped his hand and peered inside the glass then started banging on it again.

The host just rolled his eyes. "Guest first, then bozos. Hurry."

Charlie rushed from the studio and ran down the hallway, past the executive offices to the front desk. He greeted the author and hurried her to the green room, which wasn't green at all but brown, and strongly resembled someone's rec room basement from a few decades ago. The author looked around with big eyes and pronounced it "Great!" Charlie's producer said she was a first-timer and would be a little nervous.

"We're just about ready for you," Charlie said, "but we're running a little late."

"Sure, sure!" she chirped.

He turned and took off down the hall, past the reception desk and outside. It was a crisp, almost cool June day. The heat didn't really blast Chicago until July. Charlie jogged through the plaza toward the street and the men.

When he reached them, they didn't look at him. They were too busy banging on the glass.

"Hey, guys," Charlie said in a loud voice, raising his hand in a sort of surrender gesture so they wouldn't think he was being aggressive. The truth was, Charlie didn't even know how to be aggressive. "Hey, guys," he said, "we've got to stop that." He thought the "we" was a nice touch.

The one with the tattoos on his neck turned to him. "What do you mean?" Now here was a guy who knew how to be aggressive.

Charlie looked at the tattoos. He never could understand what counted as art—or body art—to some people. The tattoos were all gruesome little images surrounding one big red tattoo—a large *A* with a circle around it.

"Guys," Charlie said, "I have to ask you guys to stop." He thought of how the producer was always talking about appreciation of listeners, so he went on. "We're really glad you're our fans, and we're glad you're here, but we just need to…"

They still weren't listening. The little guy looked as if

he was about to drop his pants and moon the studio. Charlie took a step closer. He'd have to control this situation or he'd lose his job. And even though this job didn't pay a dime, he liked it. Really liked it.

So he took another step closer to the men, raising his hands higher in surrender. "Dudes, seriously, you got to stop knocking on the window. Why don't I get you some T-shirts? Some hats maybe…" His words trailed off. The guy with the tattoos looked at him, and he didn't seem drunk or even aggressive anymore. He was calm and focused, and he looked as if he recognized Charlie.

Both guys darted toward him, grabbing Charlie around the neck and dragging him to a stairway that led down onto Lower Wacker. Charlie fought against them, but they were powerfully strong, and so was the scent. What was that he smelled? Charlie realized then that they were pushing a cloth over his mouth and nose, and it smelled intense. But just as quick the smell went away. And so did the rest of Charlie's world.

51

The Trevi piazza still held a bunch of tourists who didn't care about the soccer match. Maggie pushed through them, and then I took the lead, dodging past one beautiful church after another and eventually heading down the Corso.

"Where are we going?" Maggie asked.

"I remembered something Elena said. I know where she might be."

"Where?"

"Palazzo Colonna."

"The gallery where she works? It's closed."

"She keeps a private office there that she said she uses when she needs to escape or to think. I don't know why it didn't occur to me earlier."

When we reached the gallery, the tiny side street was mostly dark except for a café up the street, its outside tables empty.

I buzzed at the door of the Palazzo Colonna. No one answered. I looked up at the windows. There were three windows that I figured would have been in the anteroom just before the *galleria,* then a few high windows in the *galleria* itself, and finally two others at the tail end. All were dark.

"Doesn't look like she's here," Maggie said.

"Maybe not, but there's a chance. If I could just figure

out…" In my mind, I followed Elena through the *galleria*, into Princess Isabelle's apartment, to the far side of the room—twisting and then pushing the pink dress—and into Elena's office, a hidden one, just like my father's. I heard Elena saying, *This is where I come to escape, to think.*

I led Maggie down the tiny street, explaining about the location of the office. "I think once you get through the *galleria* and the apartment, the office is on this side…" I pointed up at the stretch of building. "There were two windows. They were high up in the room and small."

"Like those?"

I followed the direction Maggie was pointing. There, two stories above, were rectangular windows lit up orange.

"That's them."

"Try to call her again."

I did. No answer. "Elena, we're outside," I said to her voice mail. "Please let us in." I thought about my first few days in Rome, when I called her over and over. She hadn't called me back until I texted her.

I picked up my phone and wrote her a text. *I'm outside the* galleria. *Please let me help, whatever is going on. I will stay out here until you are ready to see me.*

I showed it to Maggie and hit Send. We stood on the street, waiting. Soon, another ring of shouts burst into the city. Apparently, the soccer match had been won. People streamed into the street, singing soccer songs, chanting and cheering. A crowd of young boys rushed up to Maggie and me, trying to make us dance with them. It made me feel ancient. I could remember a time when I would have found fun in such a scene. I would have linked arms with one of the young boys and let him twirl me around the street. Now, though, it only made me anxious. I wanted to shove them away and yell *Basta!* the single Italian word that meant, essentially, *Enough!*

Stop it. Get the hell away from me. But I stopped myself. It would have been rude, I knew. I had no right to rain on the parade of these young boys. Finally, they left us. Other people pushed through the streets, clapping and cheering. Still, the two lights upstairs in the *galleria* remained on.

"Maybe she's not there," Maggie said.

"Maybe. I guess I don't know her well enough to know what she'd be doing right now. It's the only thing I can think of. It's the only thing I know to do. It's the only thing…" My voice rose, taking on a note of panic. I closed my mouth, then looked at Maggie. "Mags, what should I do?"

Maggie furrowed her brow. "Okay, you're right. We have to do something. Something else." She stared back up at the two rectangular windows shining into the night. "There's got to be a fire escape, don't you think?"

I shrugged. "This is Italy. There's no rhyme or reason to these buildings, and they don't have codes like we do. Or, at least, they don't always pay attention to them."

"What about that?" Maggie pointed to a small garden terrace one floor up from the street and below the lit windows of Elena's office. "If we climb over that—" she pointed at a stone wall to the right "—we could get to the stairway that leads up to that garden."

"They must have a security system."

Maggie raised her eyebrows. "Which would bring anyone inside the *palazzo* outside."

"And which would also bring the police."

"Not if we do it fast enough to trigger the alarm, but just be standing here like we have no idea what happened."

"Don't be crazy, you—"

But before I could finish, she was lifting her self onto the fence like a gymnast onto a beam and swinging her legs over it. She landed on the other side. "So far so good."

"Mags, don't be deranged. This is my mess. My family. You don't need to get yourself in trouble."

She stared up at the terrace and at Elena's windows, then she turned to me. "Iz, we're best friends. I know Sam took that spot for a while, and he should have. He was your fiancé. But following you around for the last hour, seeing you go through this hell, it reminds me that the best friend spot is my job again. And so your mess is my mess." She turned away.

"Wasn't it my mess when I wanted to call the police a few hours ago? Now you're going to try and get arrested?"

"I'm not going to get arrested. I just want to trip an alarm. Let me just look around."

She walked up to a French door on the ground floor and cupped her hands around her eyes, peering inside. The moment her hands touched the glass, a shriek screamed through the night, louder than any cheering shouts from the soccer fans.

"Maggie!" I yelled.

She leapt back over the wall and trotted down the street to me, an *Oh, shit, did I just do that?* look on her face.

I peered up and down the street as the alarm screeched. "Should we go?" I yelled at Maggie, who looked as if she might have changed her mind.

But she only shook her head. "What thieves would stand here and wait for the cops?" she shouted back at me. "And we're not going to tell them about your dad."

An image of him lying in that blood hit me, made not just my stomach but my whole internal body constrict with pain.

A police car zipped up the street and parked outside the *palazzo.* Two *carabinieri* got out. They didn't look particularly alarmed by the alarm. Maybe they were used to false ones.

Maggie and I tried speaking to them in the little Italian we knew, but it was useless. One of them said something into his radio, squinting at me above it, and something in his look made me nervous. I'd had more than enough experience lately with suspicious cops, and the reminder sent a shot of terror to my brain.

But just then the front door of the *palazzo* opened. Elena stood there. One of the *carabinieri* approached her. They had a quick conversation in *italiano.* From what I could make out, she was saying, "They are fine. They are with the *galleria.*"

She gave me a long look and spoke a few more words to the police. The one who seemed to be in charge finally shrugged, nodded and gestured for the other officer to leave with him.

Elena waited until they got in the car. She waited until they pulled away. She gave me a stern, sad look. Her eyes were red, and there were swaths of dark skin below them.

She glanced at Maggie, then back to me. "Come," she said. "Come in."

52

Inside, the *galleria* was mostly dark, lit eerily with red security lights dotting the exits. We followed Elena through the grand hall. Maggie swiveled her head as we walked, squinting at the artwork, at the gold, at the frescoed ceiling three stories up, murmuring, "Jesus, this is unbelievable."

Elena said nothing. She was wearing the same outfit she'd had on this afternoon on the train—taupe linen slacks and a matching jacket. But the linen was sagging and creased. She kept clenching her hands into tight fists.

When we got to Princess Isabelle's apartments, Maggie made more murmurs of appreciation. The door to Elena's office was already open, sending a block of light into the apartment. She stopped and gestured for Maggie and me to step inside. Once there, she slid the door closed and waved her hand at the light blue chairs under the windows. Silently, Maggie and I sat there, while Elena took a seat behind her marble table-desk.

Maggie looked at me as if to say, *You want me to try and talk to her or do you have it?*

I shook my head and looked at Elena. She had clearly been crying. She pursed her mouth together now, as if stopping more cries from erupting.

"What happened to him?" I said gently.

"He was killed. Apparently. I cannot believe it."

"By who?"

Elena swallowed hard. Her eyes looked too wide. The whites surrounding her irises were too thick, frozen in shock.

"Elena, are you okay?" I asked.

"Of course." Her voice was automated, her eyes alarmed yet vacant.

I was on the edge, near crying for the dad I'd almost had. But seeing Elena, I was reminded that *she* was the one who'd grown up with him. She was the one who'd known him so long, for her whole life, even when the rest of us didn't know he had a life. For her this had to be so, so, so much worse. I couldn't fathom it.

My phone rang as we sat there but I just stared at Elena, not knowing what to say or do. I'd thought, somehow, that once I found her, she would be the one to fill in the blanks, the one to make the next action happen.

But nothing was happening except the faint sounds of horns and occasional sirens from outside.

My phone rang again. Then again. I opened my purse and glanced at it.

The call log read *Mom* three times.

My mother was not a call-three-times-in-a-row kind of girl, especially when I'd just spoken to her. I narrowed my eyes and looked at the screen. And then she called again.

"Izzy," she said when I answered. Her voice was breathless. "It's Charlie. He's disappeared. He's...he's been kidnapped."

53

"Charlie has been *kidnapped?*" I asked.

The words hit the room like a small bomb. Elena, whose eyes had been staring blankly, suddenly came to life.

Maggie's mouth fell open, and she stared at me. Then she nodded at the phone. "Let us hear this."

I put the phone on speaker. "Mom, tell me what's happened."

"He was at work. Some men were outside. They were doing something outside. They saw the men. They told Charlie to go. He went outside..." My mother, always calm even in the most stressful and tragic situations, was running at the mouth.

I heard voices in the background, then one of them, a woman's voice, said, "Give me that. Izzy," I heard then, "it's Bunny."

Bunny Loveland was my family's housekeeper when we first moved to Chicago. Upon finding herself a suddenly single mom, my mother hired her, thinking, apparently, that since Bunny looked like a grandmother she would probably act like one. But this book would *not* be judged by its cover. Bunny was about as sour as they came, but the thing was, she was honest as hell, a trait I'd come to appreciate, even if her opinions usually felt like a punch to the throat. And eventually Bunny grew protective of us. The last time I'd seen her was a few months ago when I found her outside my condo smacking around some journalists who were hounding me.

"Bunny, what's going on?"

"I heard about Charlie on the radio. So I came right to the house. Your mother is having a rough time."

"Well, I'm glad you're there."

"Yeah, yeah. Anyway, here's all we know. There were two rowdy assholes—" Bunny did not share my goal of trying to stop swearing "—and they were fucking around outside the station. Your brother was sent out to calm 'em down."

"Who where they?"

"Apparently, they were Cubs fans. Idiots." Bunny didn't partake in the Sox versus Cubs debate that split apart the Chicago population. She thought they both "sucked tomatoes," whatever that meant. "Or they were dressed like Cubs fans," she said. "One had a tattoo on his neck that was a red letter *A* or some crap. It was that guy who grabbed Charlie around the neck and hauled him away. If I find that fucker, I'm going to—"

"A tattoo on his neck?" I thought of Ransom, chasing me through the Nature Museum. In that moment, my concerns and questions about my father disappeared. All I cared about was Charlie. "Do we know anything about where they took him?"

"Nope," Bunny said. "All we know is he was working, he was asked to go outside and then they snatched him. No sign of him since." There was a faint beeping sound. "Izzy, they're getting another call. Might be those idiot cops. We'll call you back."

She hung up.

I sat staring at my phone. I looked up at Elena. Her eyes were narrowed, confused.

I looked at Maggie, stunned. "That guy who chased me through the museum with Dez Romano—his name was Ransom, and he had a tattoo on his neck. A red letter *A* with a circle around it."

"So this thing..." she said, "this abduction isn't random?"

We heard a click, and the office door behind me slid open.

"It's not random," a man's voice said.

I turned. All I saw at first was gray hair, green eyes, copper glasses. I looked down. He was wearing boat shoes.

They were scuffed.

And then he spoke again. "Happy birthday, Boo."

Part III

54

Charlie looked around the room. He never wore a watch, and there were no windows, but he was pretty good at figuring out the passing of time, and he thought that he had been in that room for about five or six hours now. He'd been sitting or standing in the room, studying it, for all that time. There was nothing else to do. There was no furniture. The walls were made of brick, the floor concrete. He walked to a wall and looked at the ceiling, studying it again. A fluorescent strip illuminated the room, but it was too high to reach without something to step on.

He sat on the floor and thought about his mother. He hoped she hadn't learned that these guys, whoever they were, had hauled him in here. She didn't do so well in a crisis, and there certainly was nothing she could do for him now. Hell, it seemed there was nothing Charlie could do for himself. He'd tried to get out of the room for the first hour or so he was here, but with no window, no furniture and the door bolted tight, there wasn't much effort to be made.

Charlie crossed his legs, deciding to practice his meditation. Really, what else was he going to do? He pondered for a long while why these guys had grabbed him, why he was sitting here in this windowless room. No one came to visit him. No one gave him any information.

And so, he decided to just accept what was. He had been kidnapped, he guessed, and now he was in this brick room. Surely it would all work out. It always worked out for Charlie.

The door opened. A man he'd never seen before stepped inside. He was a handsome man in his midforties. He wore his dark black hair with lots of product in it and a black suit that looked, to Charlie's admittedly inexperienced eyes, to be expensive. Under the suit, he wore a mint-colored shirt along with a gray-and-ivory patterned tie. His expression was *feral.* Charlie had never before used the word *feral,* but that was exactly the word to describe it.

Charlie waited for the man to speak. He seemed to be doing the same thing—he stood with his arms crossed, staring at Charlie and leaning against the door. It occurred to him that maybe the man had been taken, also.

"Did they get you, too?" Charlie asked.

The man didn't respond. Charlie was pretty sure this guy wasn't a fellow kidnappee. (Was that even a word? Was that what they called someone who'd been kidnapped? He reminded himself to look it up in the future.)

Charlie eyed the door. If he could get around the guy…

"Don't even think about it," the guy said.

Ah, Charlie thought, a *kidnapp-ER.*

Charlie studied the guy back. Who was he? What did he want?

But Charlie didn't get much further than that in his thoughts.

Like a tiger, the man took three quick steps and was at Charlie's side. At the same time, he raised his left hand and—*whack!*—hit Charlie with the back of that hand.

Charlie heard the *crack,* felt himself bite into his lip.

"Jesus!" Charlie yelled, cupping his cheek.

He had never been hit before, had never been in a fight. Charlie always considered himself a pacifist, even when he was a kid. It was Izzy who got into fights on the playground, arguing with people who tried to bully him and then eventually smoothing things over with words. Lucky for him, Charlie grew tall and soon most people simply didn't bother him.

But this man was not scared of him. In fact, as Charlie gripped his cheek and licked the blood away from the side of his mouth, he noticed that the man was snarling, looked as though he wanted Charlie to fight so he could dish out some more.

Charlie opened his mouth to ask, *Why am I here?* but before he could form words, the man's arm shot out and—*whack*—he once again bashed Charlie's face with the back of his hand.

The man winced this time, squeezed his eyes shut and clenched his hand, but his face cleared quickly. "That's for your sister, Isabel," the man said. "And I got lots more of that."

Charlie said nothing, which made the man sneer.

"I'll be back with your phone, kid," he said, "and then you and me…" The guy pointed at Charlie, then at himself. "We're going to write some messages. Maybe a text, maybe an e-mail."

The man turned and left the room. Charlie could hear the door being bolted from the outside.

He licked the inside of his mouth again. The blood streamed in earnest now. There was nothing in the room to stop it. There was nothing he could do to stop any of this.

55

There he was. There he was.

Seeing him was like stepping into some altered universe. I was eight years old and thirty at the same time. I was in Italy and also in Michigan on the lawn behind our house when my mother told us he was dead.

It was one thing to wonder if he was alive, it was yet another to have him truly standing in front of me. My father. After all these years.

"It's… It's… It's." I stopped. People always say *I was at a loss for words.* I had never understood that so well—so very, *very* well—until now. Finally I managed, "You. It's you."

Sometimes it's tough to see your friends and family age. It's surreal, though, to have someone immortalized, eternalized, forever in a certain body, a certain form and face, and then to see them twenty-two years older. It wasn't that he looked so terrible, but it was bizarre, like watching a flower bloom or a canyon form on fast-forward at high speed.

He was a handsome man in his late fifties, his hair a salt-and-pepper gray instead of chestnut brown like Charlie's or Elena's. He was still trim and lean, but he seemed different than I remembered, more refined. His dark blue slacks were slimmer cut—Italian tailored, I realized. He wore a white shirt and an olive linen blazer that had breast pockets, as well as regular ones. He looked very much like a man who had lived in Italy for many years.

I looked down at his feet again. "You still wear boat shoes."

He followed my gaze, seemed at a loss for words himself, then we both looked up, locked eyes. His eyes were like those of someone much older. They were the kind of eyes seen in photos of people who have lived through a terrible war—they were open too wide, they'd seen too much, and they were a little dead to that world that remained in front of them.

He nodded at Grandma O's necklace around my neck. "You wear that well."

I couldn't stop staring at him, this man with the copper glasses and the boat shoes. Christopher. I couldn't call him *my father.* I'd been calling him that in my mind forever. But now, seeing this man standing in front of me, I realized I didn't know him. My *father* was the man I knew twenty-two years ago, the man I knew in my memories.

"But the body in your office…" I managed to say.

The silence in the room crackled. My skin tingled. The thoughts in my brain careened.

Christopher and Elena looked at each other. Elena started to weep. I glanced at Maggie, who was blinking madly, her mouth slightly open. Seeing Maggie, usually so bossy and full of advice, now silent made everything even more serious somehow.

I turned to Christopher and Elena. "Who was that body in your office? Was that another faked death?" My voice was loud and surprisingly angry. I hadn't seen that emotion bubbling up.

Everyone stared at me; the air bristled around us.

"Whose...body...was...in...the...office?" My voice was demanding now, the voice I used when a witness on the stand wasn't cooperating.

But Christopher was not your typical witness. He stared at me with his green eyes under those round copper glasses. His eyes were unblinking, almost in shock, and yet there was something else behind them. It looked like pride, directed at me.

He glanced at Elena again, as if in a silent question. Like Charlie and me, they didn't seem to need words.

Elena threw her shoulders back and opened her mouth. "It was Maurizio."

"Your husband, Maurizio?"

Her face sagged; she nodded.

"Did you...?" I said, looking at Christopher.

His eyes watched me. He nodded.

"You killed him," I said, to make sure I understood.

Another nod.

I glanced at Elena, whose chin was trembling, tears starting to stream.

"What in the hell is going on here?" My voice was angry again. I had no idea how to interpret this situation. Was Christopher—my father—a ruthless killer? Was Elena scared of him. Should *I* be scared of him?

Maggie spoke up. "Maurizio was in the Camorra, isn't that right?"

How great it felt to hear Maggie back in defense-lawyer mode.

Elena and Christopher both nodded.

"Did he threaten you, Mr. McNeil?"

"Yes, he tried to kill me. So I killed him."

I felt my bottom lip move away from my top. I felt my head recoil at the stark simplicity of his words, as if they were easy to say—*So I killed him.*

He saw my reaction. He nodded as if he understood, didn't expect me to think any differently.

I didn't know what to think. My mind screamed and staggered.

"How did Maurizio know about your office down there?" Maggie asked.

"No one knew until today. We believe he followed Isabel and Elena from Ischia. He was there with her on the island. As best we can gather, he must have heard her and Izzy talking. When Elena told him she was going back to Rome, he didn't give anything away."

Elena began to weep again.

Christopher moved fast to her desk and stood beside her, a gentle hand on her shoulder.

Elena looked up at Christopher, her chin still trembling.

He crouched beside her chair, and, as if begging forgiveness, held out a hand. "I am sorry. Truly sorry."

Something in me said, *Where's my apology?* but I knew Elena had suffered so much more than me.

Elena took Christopher's hand, grasped it with both of hers. They stayed like that for a long moment.

Then Elena sat up and looked at us. "What have we done to Charlie?"

Christopher shook his head back and forth, making his gray hair move slightly at the sides. "This is not your fault. This is *not* your fault. It is because of me that they have done this to my son. They are trying to get to me."

Something about the words *my son* rankled me. They were technically true, but what right did he have to use them?

Elena shook her head. "Don't give in to them, Christopher. Don't give them what they want."

"Who are you talking about?" I said. "Who is *them?* The Camorra?"

"Yes," Christopher said. "They must know I'm alive, that I have spent the last twenty years fighting them."

He looked at Elena. She shook her head slowly. "It wasn't me. I didn't tell them this time. You must fight them."

"At the cost of my son? I have already given them my life. I gave up my children. I can't now sacrifice my son's *life.* And you know that they will kill him, Elena."

Elena stared into the eyes of her brother. "I'm surprised they have not already."

"What?" My insides felt as if they were ripping apart. "Do you think they would really kill Charlie?"

"If they don't get what they want," Christopher said, "then yes."

"Then give them what they want! And what in the hell *do* they want?"

Christopher took a step away from my aunt. "Me. They want me. And I'm guessing they want something else, too, but I'm not sure what. What I am sure about, though, is that I'm going to give them what they want if it will spare Charlie."

I wasn't sure what he meant. "How?"

"They kidnapped Charlie in the United States, in Chicago, and in a very public way. They clearly were sending us a message."

"Us?" I said with trepidation. I couldn't stand the thought that I might have contributed to what was going on with Charlie, but I knew that he was right. "Dez Romano," I said.

Christopher nodded. "Between your involvement with him—"

"I wasn't *involved* with him."

Christopher held up a hand, as if to say, *It's not the time to discuss that,* and I resented that hand, the way he seemed to be telling me what to do as if he were a father who knew me, a father who'd been around.

He continued talking. "And the Camorra likely finding out about me, they turned to someone who would be a message to both of us—Charlie. I've gotten that message. I'm ready to respond."

"So, what? You're going to go to Chicago and turn yourself into them?"

"Not exactly like that, but yes."

I paused. Then, "I need to go home, too. I can't stay here while this is happening to Charlie."

"Then you are responding to their message, too."

I looked at him defiantly. "I guess I am."

He opened his mouth, about to protest, but then he nodded. "I understand. But it might complicate things if we all travel on public airlines."

"Why?"

"Because they're clearly looking for me, for us, and by flying a public airline, we'll be easier to find. The American passport system and airline system is impossible to infiltrate right now, but in Italy? The Camorra could easily find out passenger lists in and out of the cities."

"I know someone who has a private plane. Would it help if we flew private?"

My father turned to me, his eyes locking back into mine, but this time it seemed as if he were seeing me, really me, for the first time since he'd appeared. His gaze gave me a strange, almost violent sensation. My head could not catch up.

So I just repeated my question. "Would it help if we flew private?"

My father nodded.

I looked at Elena. "Is there a phone I can use that we know for sure is secure?"

Christopher took a phone from his pocket. "They do not know this number. Who do you want to call?"

I looked up Theo's number on my own phone and dialed it. "Hi," I said when he answered. "Any way I could borrow your plane?"

56

A private plane, I learned, is *the* way to travel. None of that racing to the airport, getting there hours ahead of time. Instead, you roll up by means of a taxi, right to the airplane, and calmly hand your bag to the pilot. There's none of that stripping down to your underwear in order to get through security, no shoving of products into two-ounce bottles and then shoving them farther into a freaking quart-size baggie so all the world can see your eye cream and deoderant.

Theo had had to bargain with his partner and other shareholders to get the plane so last-minute, but he must have been persuasive, because there it was, just for us. Theo had offered to personally pick us up, but I'd told him to stay put. There was no reason for him to fly to Italy and back again. But as I stepped on the plane, I wished he were there with me.

Eight single seats were on either side of the cabin. They were huge, made of ivory leather.

Maggie sat in one, bounced up and down. "These are great!"

My father and I got in next. We inadvertently sat in seats across from each other, right at the same time. It felt weird. Maggie seemed to sense the unease and said, "Izzy, come here so I can show you something."

She drew me up to the cockpit, introduced ourselves to the pilots, then pointed, rather randomly, at some of their instruments.

She dropped her voice then. "Are you sure you don't want to tell your mom about…" Maggie's gaze drifted over my shoulder to my father. *My father.*

"I can't. I can't just tell her on the phone. *Hey, Mom. I know your son was kidnapped, and that's because a Mob group wants revenge or leverage or something against me and your ex-husband—who… Oh, yeah, by the way…is alive.*"

Maggie grimaced. "Guess not."

She turned and led me back to the seats. Maggie took the one across from my father. I nodded my thanks and took the seat across from Elena.

Maurizio's body had been left in an area where they were sure to find him today. We had convinced Elena to come with us, despite the fact that she desperately wanted to be in Italy to plan funeral services for her husband. However, my father was certain that the Camorra would question Elena in detail about Maurizio's killing, and because her niece had been asking around about her father, the Camorra would soon, if they hadn't already, figure out that Christopher McNeil was not only alive but involved in Maurizio's death. My father was also certain that although an extreme loyalty existed in the System, they wouldn't be so kind to Elena as they had in the past, not when they realized that she had known the whole time that her brother was alive. And working against them.

My poor aunt was understandably distraught. She sat on her ivory leather chair, fiddling her hands in her lap as if she could not decide what to do with them. She glanced up at me a few times, seemed to be on the verge of tears.

I spoke to her softly, trying to comfort her, but all I could say was, "I'm sorry. I'm so sorry. I'm so sorry."

"It's my fault," she said. "My fault."

But even as I failed in comforting her, I began to wonder if *I* should blame myself. It was *my* curiosity, my wanting to find my father that led me to Italy, that led Elena to take me to his office, that led Maurizio to follow us, that led my father to kill him.

Determined to be of service and not the source of more agony, I tried a few more times to say something appropriately soothing to Elena, but when she shook her head, fast and for a long time, as if she could not stand any words, any thoughts, *anything,* I stopped.

My father had *killed* someone. I returned to that thought as I looked out an oval window while we slowly began to taxi the runway. My father had killed someone. In his line of work, the possibility that he had killed more than one person was a distinct one. The recognition of this fact was as bizarre and surreal as the rest of the experience. I kept looking at him, one row up, thinking that I did not know this man. Not at all.

Maggie tried to make small talk with my father. Actually, as the plane began to pick up speed, she was quite successful. Soon she had him interested in a story about a Mafia case she'd handled, where the sheriff in charge of taking the alleged mobsters to court had tracked down one of their key witnesses, and then let the mobsters know where that witness was.

"Of course the whole thing was taped," Maggie said. "So the sheriff was arrested. And when they questioned him, they asked him, why did you give them that information? He said it was because he had grown up in the same neighborhood as the mobsters and twenty years ago they had given his sister money for a dentist visit. *Twenty* years ago."

My father nodded. "There is a lot of loyalty in the Mafia." His voice was clear and smooth but he always spoke in a low register, as if not wanting it to carry.

There it was—that talk of loyalty again. Before I knew what I was saying, my voice rang out louder than anyone's, clearly ringing out over the plane's engines. "And you have that kind of loyalty, too, right? You *really* know about loyalty." Oops. There was that anger bubbling up again, speaking for me. And it was laced with sarcasm, something I'm not usually prone to.

Christopher turned and looked at me in the row behind him, no expression on his face. Maggie turned, too, eyebrows raised.

I leaned forward and squinted at him, irritated beyond control. "What?" I said. "Why are you giving me that blank look like you don't know what I'm talking about? It sounds to me like there's loyalty to 'the family'—this *Mob* family—and obviously you had a lot of loyalty to your father, because you did all this to avenge what happened to him, and I respect that, but where was your loyalty to *your* family? The one you created with my mother?"

My father said nothing. We stared at each other for a long time. I had no idea how to read him. Was he angry at me? Wounded by what I said? I couldn't tell.

Finally, he broke the stalemate. "Are you ready to have this conversation, Isabel?"

The plane launched itself into the air, and I nodded.

57

"We believe they are returning to America now," La Duca said in Italian.

Dez clenched the phone then tried to make himself unclench it. "Are they on a flight?"

"*Sí,* we assume so. They did not take Alitalia or any commercial flights. My men followed them as far as a regional airport before they lost them. Christopher McNeil is good." La Duca's voice wasn't livid as he reported that. He was the kind of boss that respected proficiency in others. Not that he wouldn't still kill the man when he got the chance. "We believe they are on a jet."

Dez fully released his grip on the phone.

"Which means," La Duca continued, "that you acted quickly, just as I asked you to do. You did something to get them to return immediately. *Complementi.*"

Complementi was the Italian way of saying *nice work, good job.* And La Duca was not the type to toss praise easily.

"*Grazie,*" Dez said simply.

"This is your show now."

"I've got it," Dez said with authority.

"You are sure?"

Dez knew La Duca was speaking as much about Dez proving himself as he was about taking out the McNeil family.

"Certo," Dez said. "All of them."

"I ask that you will be discreet."

Dez froze. "You are asking me to conduct this operation in quiet?"

"*Sí.* You and I will know. But the news will not go up. At least not until it is all done."

They both knew what La Duca meant. The act that Dez had planned was splashy, one might say explosive, so the act wasn't really going to be done in quiet. What La Duca was speaking of, though, was that the planning of the McNeils' deaths would be kept between the two of them. It wouldn't go up, which meant it wouldn't reach *the top*—the top boss of the Camorra. The top boss was the one who, it was said, let the clans duke it out so that he was the only one who saw everything clearly.

"There is something strange," La Duca continued, "very strange about the McNeils. Christopher McNeil has been a thorn in our side for entirely too long. I want us to handle this quietly. Later, we can reveal how and when it was done."

Dez liked the words *us* and *we* coming from La Duca's mouth. He had hoped that by handling this situation well he would prove himself immediately to the top. He had also put a plan into action for learning the identity of the one at the top. Although La Duca didn't know it, that second part of the plan was still in play.

"You place your trust correctly," Dez said finally.

What was about to happen would be very Camorra, and yet it would also be very *American* Camorra, putting the U.S. and Chicago on the radar of the System in the same way Spain and Madrid had done in the past. His nerves tweaked a bit in anticipation. The game had already started. The McNeil brother, little Charlie, was already installed at the place where it would go down. As

Dez had hoped, his abduction had drawn an immediate response from Isabel McNeil and her daddy. Isabel McNeil, who had seemed such a problem, was turning out to be his solution.

"Christopher McNeil is good," La Duca said again. "For him to evade the Camorra for years, to trick us like this, is incredible. And worthy of caution. We have been able to find out little about where he lived or what he did during these twenty years since we thought we killed him. But we are certain now that he has been working for the antimafia office, working against the System. You should be careful of him."

"Of course. And what is your opinion of the other family members?" Dez liked the way this conversation was proceeding, as if he and La Duca were equals, comparing professional notes.

"They are amateurs." La Duca made a dismissive noise. "Your *testa rossa* apparently has some skills, but purely amateur."

"I can handle amateurs."

Dez spoke a few more words, reassuring La Duca, then hung up the phone.

He would eradicate Christopher McNeil and his family. Even if they kept it quiet for now, as La Duca had asked, word would seep out, so that eventually those in the System would know it was the Camorra who had taken care of the deed, and Dez in particular. But the authorities would not suspect that the hit was Camorra. The rampant desire for public glory that kept showing its ugly face in *Napoli* would be placed on the back burner.

The building where he held Charles McNeil was perfect, owned as it was by a Mexican "company," one that provided drugs and runners to Dez's operation. Right now, the company was behind. Way behind. They had taken a lot of money from Dez, but then fallen back on providing what they'd promised. And now they were running scared. Rightly so.

Disposing of the McNeils would not only be an eventual signal to the System that Dez was truly in charge in the U.S. and someone to be taken very seriously, it would also act as a clear signal to the Mexicans. To the authorities it would appear that Family McNeil had tried to save their wayward, drug-troubled brother but their attempt had gone wrong, and they'd all died. There would be no warning—not for the McNeils, not for the Mexicans. Not for any of them.

58

Christopher saw his life in two different ways. The beginning of his life—the life he had led with his mother, father and Elena on the East Coast—was in color. They were a typical family. Everything they did, from the summer vacations at Jones Beach to the winters they spent tucked in their little house, was typical. Although they didn't necessarily think such normality made them happy at the time, in looking back, he could tell they were.

Later, once his father died, Christopher McNeil's world shifted from one of bright tones into…how should he put it? It wasn't that his world went straight to black and white, because that would imply sharpness in some way. No, it was more of a sepia life, where all the edges were muddied and brown.

And yet… And yet here was his daughter with her bright orange hair and her blazing green eyes against this white airplane seat. His whole life had suddenly caught up with him and shifted back into color.

She changed seats with Maggie, and then asked that they move another row of seats ahead so they would have some privacy. He followed her request without saying a word.

He watched now as she threw her shoulders back, glancing out the plane window as they climbed above the Italian night, then back at him. He watched as her face cleared.

"Okay," she said, and even that one word was commanding. "Let's go back and establish some things, just so I can understand."

He nodded. For decades, no one ran the show except for him, and it felt oddly soothing to have someone establish authority like this. He felt a swell of pride, which he knew he had no right to feel.

"Elena told me…" Izzy stopped, glanced over her shoulder at Elena two rows back. She and Maggie were in a quiet conversation, and Christopher was relieved to see that, for now, his sister appeared calm.

"Elena told me," Izzy said, her voice lower, "that this all really started when the Camorra came to your parents and told them they wanted to get you involved in the business."

He nodded. "They said I was perfect for the Camorra. I could infiltrate different groups and circles of society without anyone knowing who I really was. I had the McNeil name, a name no one would ever associate with Camorra, or even the Italians. They said they would let me go to college for a year or two and then I would come home and work for them, eventually heading up their U.S. operations."

"What about Elena? Did they want her to do the same?"

He shook his head. "You have to remember that at that time, women were looked at differently than they are today. Women were essentially prized for their ability to have children and raise the family."

"And what did your parents do when they heard this?"

He sighed. "My father told them no. They were in the living room, and I had been out with some friends. I remember I thought it was strange when I got home, because it was warm out, but all our windows were shut.

I came in the house from the garage and I heard arguing. I stood there and listened. My father protested. He insisted that I would never be brought into the Camorra. He said he would never allow it. I remember hearing my mother weeping." My father's face contorted. "I'll never forget the sound of her crying. It was like a cat mewing."

"Did they know you were there?"

"No. I listened to the conversation, then I left. When I came back inside, I made lots of noise. I just wanted to forget what I'd heard. Plus, I was sure my father would win the argument. He was such a strong man. You always felt protected by him." He dropped his head. "But two days later, he was dead."

"That must have been horrible."

"It was."

"So you decided you would get back at them another way."

"Yes. I already knew much about the Camorra from growing up. I knew about the different clans and that they were always warring, which meant they could be pitted against each other. I knew that although they continued to assert their presence in the U.S., many had melded with other American Mafia groups. They'd never really had success on their own. But after what happened to my family, I knew they were trying hard."

"What was your major in college?" The hard tone of her words had changed, softened, and his daughter had asked this last question as if she were speaking with a friend. The quietly personal nature of it broke his heart and yet made it soar.

"Originally my major was going to be Business," he said, "but I changed it to Psychology so I could officially go into profiling."

"When did you start working with the Feds?"

"In college. I had my counselor contact someone at the FBI, saying I wanted to learn about job potentials there. I got a meeting with someone, and I told him I had no money, that my father was dead and my mother was struggling, but if they put me through college, I would work for them for the rest of my life, and I would help them find and put away members of the Camorra. At that time, the FBI didn't allow its agents to work close to home or with any kind of culture they were familiar with. I'm not sure if it's the same now, but it went back to the days of J. Edgar Hoover. They thought if you were close to the subject of the investigation then you could get personally involved, and that could cloud your judgment."

"But they let you get involved."

"Yes, the Camorra was what they called an 'old dog' within the bureau, a file that had been on the books for a long time and that no one had been able to crack."

"So you went undercover? That's what Elena told me."

"Not right away. Despite what people think, not many FBI agents do undercover work. Instead they rely on informants." He shrugged. "Eventually, I became both."

Izzy turned momentarily and looked out the window. There was nothing out there, just the black night, and yet, despite that blackness, just watching her, Christopher knew he was right. Because of her, he was back in color.

59

Victoria McNeil sat at the table in the bay window of her kitchen and looked outside at the flowers she had planted a few weeks ago. They were all blooming in red and white. Her patio furniture, heavy black iron with ivory cushions, was artfully arranged. She had envisioned that this summer she, Charlie, Izzy and Spence would spend a lot of time on that patio. But now Izzy was in Italy and, more importantly, Charlie was… Who knew where Charlie was?

Charlie, Charlie, Charlie. Her little boy. The boy who skated in lazy circles through life, smiling all the while. The only time Victoria had really worried about Charlie was after he got in the accident with the construction truck. But even then, he had laughed it off. But where was Charlie now?

Charlie, Charlie, Charlie. She couldn't believe this. Why had he been kidnapped? She looked across the kitchen at Bunny Loveland, who was at the counter putting marshmallows into a bowl. She had announced that she was making Jell-O, that awful Jell-O with the marshmallows that no one liked, but Victoria appreciated the effort, appreciated Bunny's cranky optimism.

Her husband, Spence, was in the kitchen, pacing back and forth, the phone in his hand, while he jabbered at his friend George, who was the superintendent of police in Chicago. George had always been able to help them before, like when Izzy needed information last year. But now George was helpless, too. There were no leads in Charlie's case.

Spence wore a light blue Oxford shirt. He'd rolled the sleeves up, past his elbows, as if ready to chip in with heavy physical work. Spence hated to be helpless. He was happiest when of service to his friends or family. She knew the situation was killing him.

It was killing her, too. She could feel it. She was familiar with the signs of death within herself—the dying of her spirit, which she held on to tenuously anyway.

God, Charlie. What was happening? She had never felt so useless in her life. She played with her cell phone in her hands, waiting to be inspired with calls to make, something to do. Surely something would happen soon, some direction, some action to take.

Her phone lit up. She had a text message. Probably from Cassandra, her best friend. Victoria was not a huge fan of texting and only used the service with a few people like Cassandra and her kids. And Cassandra was the only one Victoria had told about Charlie. She had this idea—immature, she knew—that if she didn't tell many people, it wouldn't really be happening.

Victoria looked at the phone and scrolled to the texts. There were two—or rather it looked like one message that was long and had been split into two by the phone company. And… *Oh my God.* The text messages were from Charlie! Alarm went through her body. She sat up straight.

"Spence," she said, but he was walking out of the kitchen, talking loudly, telling George that he would get Charlie's social security number and other information right now. Bunny was muttering about not having bought enough marshmallows.

Victoria looked back down at her phone.

Charlie had written, *Mom I'm okay. Don't know how to tell u but got in trouble with drugs. These guys kidnapped me cuz I owe money. They say they'll kill me if I don't pay. But if the police get involved, they'll kill me, too. Is there any way u could get $1200 and meet me tomorrow? Please don't tell Spence or the cops.*

Victoria's back stiffened, reading the text message again. She felt a charge go through her, one of purpose. It was the opposite of the way she usually responded to a crisis. She fell apart so easily. She had always done that. She was never vocal with her emotions. And when she retreated, it was into herself. She disappeared piece by piece, alive on the outside, but dead inside.

But now, instead of feeling herself recede, she felt as if she were stepping into her skin, coming into power. *This* was something she could do for her son. But then she shook her head. Could this really be true? Could Charlie really have a problem with drugs? Certainly, he was always drinking wine. And everyone said that people with drug problems usually started with alcohol, but she'd never seen any signs that Charlie had drug problems or even any drug usage. She thought then of Cassandra, whose own daughter had a battle with drugs, and when Cassandra found out about it, she'd had no previous idea. *I never suspected for a second,* Cassandra had said.

Victoria squeezed her eyes, sick with the thought that Charlie was putting something horrible into his system. What kind of drugs? Where did he get them? Then she shook her head again. It didn't matter.

Spence came down into the kitchen, still on the phone with George. He was so involved with the conversation, so used to Victoria always waiting, never taking any action herself that he barely noticed her, just kept pacing through the kitchen, into their library and back.

Victoria looked back at her phone, read the texts again and again and again, memorizing the words. Could this be a trick of some kind? But the words sounded like Charlie, and it would explain this bizarre occurrence.

Once more she read Charlie's words, and then a decision came to her. She was going to take action. She raised the phone and texted back one word. *Yes.*

60

I closed my window shade and thought about my conversation with the reporter, the one Mayburn and I had spoken to about the witness protection program.

I turned back to my father. "Families can enter the witness protection program together." I said it as a statement and it was intended as one. I wasn't asking him a question of whether it was a possibility that we could have all entered the program together, but simply why he hadn't exercised that possibility.

My father gazed at me somberly. He nodded. "But that program is no place to grow up. I didn't want you to have to move and start over, and change your identities, and your friends, and your schools, and I didn't—"

"Are you kidding me? That's *exactly* what we did anyway. We moved to Chicago. We had to get all new friends. It was an entirely new identity. And we had to do it all without you."

Neither of us said anything. I could feel Maggie and Elena looking at us from a few rows back.

"But you were well," he said. "You didn't live your life in fear. That's what scared me the most. I didn't want my children always looking over their shoulder. You and Charlie and your mom…you have always done well. You have excelled and without fear."

I pursed my mouth to stop words from flying out. I studied him, replaying in my mind what he'd said. "Why do you sound so certain about that? That we've always done well?"

No answer.

"Have you been watching us?" The volume rose again at the end of my question.

"I have been keeping tabs on you, of course." He didn't look chagrined about it.

"Wait a minute. Have you been following us our whole lives?" My mind scrolled back to different times in my youth, times when I felt my father watching over us. Had he *really* been watching us, somewhere in the stands of the bleachers at Charlie's baseball games? Somewhere on the street as I walked to school with a house key on a pink shoelace tied around my neck?

"No. I have been in Italy. Usually. But I came to the U.S. from time to time to ensure you were all right."

"And for work, of course."

My father dipped an ear toward his shoulder, his salt-and-pepper hair hanging down a little at that side. His green eyes peered through his copper glasses, looking at me as if he didn't understand.

"Of course you were coming to the U.S. for work," I said, "because isn't that what's most important to you?"

A look of agony seared across my father's face, causing lines to cut into his forehead. "No, of course not. Work is not the most important thing. *You* were the most important thing. *Victoria* was the most important thing. *Charlie.* That's why I left." Now it was his voice that rose, his features slightly contorted in anger, irritation, and something else. I couldn't yet read him, but I could tell that he was struggling with his emotions. Almost as if it was the first time in a long while that he was experiencing any emotion at all.

His face quickly drained of all expression, though. He settled himself back into place, but as he did, something else dawned on me.

"Wait a minute," I said. "Were you one of the people following me last year after Sam disappeared?"

He said nothing. But I could tell he knew what I was talking about.

Just to make sure, I said, "You knew that I was engaged and that my fiancé disappeared, right?"

My father opened his mouth, but I could see the answer. I was correct.

"No *way.*" My voice was filled with disbelief. "So you were one of those people." Now my voice was very loud and very angry. "I got followed last year, and I was scared *shitless.*" Oops. There went my no-swearing streak. "I never knew when I walked out the door who was around, whether someone was tailing me. It was terrible. I can't believe it was you."

My father shook his head and held his hand up. "Isabel," he said with determination. In fact, he sounded very much like a father who had heard enough, and was about to set the record straight. "Isabel," he said again. "Of course I have watched over my little girl and my little boy and my wife." He cleared his throat. "My former wife. But I was never intrusive. I never followed you in the way you are talking about. Of course, I heard about Sam disappearing and your client dying, and then a few months later I heard about your friend dying and you being suspected of her murder. So, of course, I was around more at those times. That's why I was still around when I saw you meet with Dez Romano. But I never tailed you so you felt watched, never so you felt me there. I had to make sure you were okay. Certainly you can understand that. I had to ensure that you were protected. I just could not believe when I saw who you were hanging out with."

"Hanging out with? What does that mean?"

"Michael DeSanto."

"I wasn't *hanging out* with Michael DeSanto."

He held up his hand again. "I realize that. I figured out that you were doing undercover work with John Mayburn. What I couldn't figure out was if it was some kind of trap. I knew that DeSanto was working with Dez Romano. I knew Romano was in the new version of the Camorra in the United States. The thing is, Romano and these U.S. guys in the System work differently. I had no idea what was going on. It took me a while to determine that it was just a coincidence—an entirely freakish coincidence—that you were involved with them."

I stopped and thought about it. "That must have been bizarre."

He shook his head. "You have no idea."

We both chuckled, but then I stopped short.

"What?" he said.

"That's the first time I've seen your smile in twenty-two years."

That made him lose his smile. Both of us fell silent for a moment.

"I never intended to step out of the shadows, Izzy. But then that night when Romano and DeSanto were running after you..." He shook his head, as if trying to shake off a horrid memory. "I had to save you."

"Well...thank you."

He nodded.

After a minute of uncomfortable quiet, we began talking again. And we talked for an hour. It was a quiet conversation filled with short questions designed to find the most minimal amount of information without prying too much. We were like new parents dancing around a baby, not wanting to wake it up, afraid of what might happen if we did.

"Where did you live the whole time?" I asked him.

"Rome," he told me. "Mostly Rome, but also Milan and Naples."

"What did you do with yourself?"

"I joined the antimafia office. I practiced my Italian. And I went back into profiling."

"Trying to bring down the Camorra."

A solemn nod.

"You just couldn't leave it behind."

His face turned fast to mine, his eyes flashing, then he looked back at the seat in front of him. "I knew nothing else."

"So when I went to the antimafia office in Rome, did they let you know?"

"Not right away, but yes. Hardly anyone knows that I work with the office. Almost no one knows my real name or identity. But word of your visit eventually got to some people I know. And they briefed me."

"And then I was followed to Naples, and those guys came after me with guns." Something occurred to me. "Elena said that those men were just trying to scare me, because the Camorra doesn't chase, they kill."

"That's true."

I felt a little frozen with fear. "Did *you* send those guys after me? Were you trying to scare me into going home or something?"

"No." His voice was curt, distinct. "Of course not. I never want you to be scared. From what I can tell, there must be a Camorra spy in the Rome antimafia office, a mole who told someone you were in there. They must have figured out you were going to Naples and followed you."

I replayed that night when the guys were chasing me, when they were getting off the elevator near ours in the hotel and ran down the hall toward our room, only to get clocked with that door.

"That was you, wasn't it?" I said. "The door opening when those guys were running down the hallway at the hotel?"

"Yes."

"Very Laurel and Hardy of you."

He chuckled again. "Sometimes you have to go back to the basics."

I folded my hands in my lap and looked down at them. "Did you ever remarry?"

A sad smile, a definitive yet soft, "No."

"Do you have any other kids?"

A shake of his head, a flash of pain across his face, as if the thought seared him.

He seemed so strong, someone who could endure anything, even the forced loss of his family, and yet, now that the secret was out, there was something that arose from within him and was revealed in his eyes. It was… What was it? He was wounded. Yes, my father was a wounded man.

How strange to think of him alive, as someone suffering right now, instead of thinking of him as *my father, who passed away when I was young.*

"And you," he said. "I know a little more about you. And I have to say, from what I saw, I liked that Sam."

That Sam… I felt a wave of sadness. It was so powerful I closed my eyes against it. But then I realized it was just that—only a wave, one that crested and went away. When it was gone, I opened my eyes and looked into my father's—green eyes that looked like mine (minus my eyeliner and two coats of mascara).

Thinking of Sam and me, of the couple we used to be, made me think of another couple, and I had to ask. "Does Mom know?"

"That I'm alive?"

"Yes."

He shook his head no.

The internal wounds seemed to pain him now, and his eyes took on an anguished tint.

"I guess we need to figure out how to handle this," I said.

He nodded. "Yes, there's a lot to think about."

I said, "Who did you tell?"

He looked at me questioningly.

"I mean who did you tell that you faked your death? Anyone?"

"Elena."

"But no one else?"

"Of course not. That's part of the deal."

"No one. Wow. That can't be good for you."

He shot me a question with his eyes.

"You know," I said, "you must be really fucked up."

He laughed. I laughed. Then we started to laugh harder. It wasn't particularly humorous, but somehow a funny bone had been struck, one in both me and my dad. *My dad.* That was the first time I had thought of him like that since I learned he was alive.

61

Dez Romano looked at his date next to him at the bar at Fulton Lounge. She was a medical student at the University of Chicago, having returned to school after a successful career at a pharmaceutical company, and she was fucking hot.

Dez thought back to when he was growing up and how he'd believed women were either gorgeous or they were brilliant. Never both. Or at least that's what his father always told him. Thank God he eventually realized that wasn't the case. And in a way, today's breed of women, like this one, had shown him the path and made Dez want to be at a different level himself.

When Dez married his ex-wife, they were both from the South Side of Chicago. He envisioned that his marriage would be like that of his parents'—his father ran the roost, his mother did whatever his father told her to. Dez thought he wanted that kind of relationship. Dez's wife, however, ran circles around him. She got a college degree when he didn't. She went on to get her MBA. During all that time, all that education, he was the one who had the pocket change.

He was just starting to work with the Camorra and learn the business. There wasn't much money to go around, there certainly wasn't any glamour, but he was the one, not his ex, who was making whatever money they had, he funded her financial loans. After finishing MBA school, his ex skyrocketed. She worked for one big corporation after another, eventually moving up to a CFO position at a Fortune 500 company. She had an affair with another executive and left Dez. She didn't even marry that executive. It occurred to Dez years later that she might have had the affair just for an excuse to walk out. After they were done, she just moved up and up and up, and now she was one of the top execs at her company, set to take it over in the next few years.

Dez was glad for the divorce. It had kicked him in the ass, made him step up his work with the Camorra. He wasn't able to seek success the way his ex had. He wasn't going to get an education and climb his way up the ranks. But as he started dating this new breed of women, who were so feminine, so sexy, and so in charge of their intellect and their lives, he decided he wanted to be like that, too.

"So," the med student said, swiveling on her stool and facing him, "what should we do after this?" She had a guy's name, Chad or something, and she was from a little town in Tennessee. But she owned this town now, or she was about to, like so many other women like her. She had been telling him how the pharmaceutical company was paying for med school, how she would eventually go back to work for them. "Nightcap?" she said, cocking her head to her shoulder.

"Great." Dez left the topic of sex alone, although he knew she wanted him to bring it up, to make a flirty, seductive overture of some sort so it was clear exactly what they were about to do. But no, Dez liked making these women work, and then let them think he was taking a backseat, that they were subtly in charge of it all.

He had to admit, he thought he'd played that route with

Izzy McNeil, thought that he'd played her to talk to him, to hang out with him. The truth was he'd seen her glancing at him the moment he walked into Gibsons. Of course, he realized now that he was the one who'd been played. Of course she had glanced. Of course she had spoken up. She had been sitting there specifically waiting for him to come into the restaurant.

He hadn't been able to figure out what McNeil wanted at first. When they were at the nature museum, she'd tossed out the comment about working for the Feds, but he didn't believe that, not unless the Feds were doing things really, really differently. Instead, he figured she worked for the bank, the one that had brought Michael down. And now he knew she was probably working for her father, working to bring down the Camorra.

But ultimately it didn't matter who she worked for. Soon, she wouldn't be working for anyone ever again.

The med student leaned forward a little and sipped her wine. She flashed him a gorgeous smile. She had long, shiny brown hair that hung flat next to her head. She looked at her watch. "I have rounds tomorrow with the gastro service at five o'clock."

"I have to be up early myself. But we still have time for our nightcap."

He downed the last bit of red wine in the glass in front of him, then he made like he was going to signal the bartender for another round.

She caught his arm and smiled. "Let's get out of here."

He thought of what he really had to do tomorrow. He had to wait for Izzy McNeil and her father to come back to the United States, had to wait for Mommy McNeil to show up. And once he had the McNeil family together, he would kill them.

Dez had arranged something ingenious, if he did say

so himself. He had gotten the place rigged so that on his command, a natural gas leak would seep into the building. His boss, La Duca, appreciated the beauty of the irony and had told Dez that a well-placed gas leak was what had led to the death of Grandma McNeil down in Arizona. Eventually, a buildup of gas in the basement of the Mexicans' building would ignite the flame of a commercial water heater and the building would go up, and the McNeils would fry, just the way Grandma had, just the way they thought Christopher McNeil orginally had.

The cops would suspect that the Mexicans had set their own building aflame. They would have good reasons to think that. Dez had been slipping information to the authorities, through one of his other dealers, about the Mexicans. Their group was getting arrested one by one. The walls were closing in. And the motive for the four bodies discovered there, four bodies that the Mexicans sent up in flames along with their building, would be clear. Charlie McNeil had gotten into trouble with drugs. Trouble he couldn't pay for or dig himself out of, and so to send a message, the Mexicans had lured his family in and taken them all out. They were ruthless, those Mexicans. The cops wouldn't come looking for anyone else.

There was one thing Dez had to do before he killed the McNeils. And this part La Duca didn't know about. He would get Christopher McNeil to talk before he died, get him to tell Dez the identity of the top boss, the one in Naples. McNeil must know who that boss was, having studied the Camorra and worked against them in secrecy for as long as he had. Once Dez knew the identity of the boss, he wouldn't be relying solely on information trickling down through La Duca. He wouldn't be operating so much in the dark. Instead, he would know his audience, and he could create his other plans—the ones for the rest of his life, the Camorra, the city of Chicago. He intended to play the city the way it used to be played—with personal agendas served, but always giving back to the community at large. Letting the cops bust the Mexicans certainly had that theme in mind.

And then, yes. He was going to bring the Camorra, the new version of the Camorra, to the world.

The med student stood and tucked her black alligator purse under her arm, jerking her head at the door with a smile.

Sex, Dez decided, would take the edge off and kill some time. He stood, giving her the same smile back.

He trailed her to the door, looking at her ass. Too bad Izzy McNeil hadn't turned out to be Easy McNeil, like this chick. The interesting thing about these women was that most of them had finally realized that it didn't lessen their power to have sex with a guy. Totally the opposite. It empowered them. It was just that some of them waited longer than others, waiting until the time was right for them. He had the feeling McNeil wouldn't have let him close to her physically anytime soon, even if she hadn't been playing him. Which only made her more attractive.

But tonight he would close his eyes and pretend the girl he was slipping inside was *la testa rossa.*

"Let's go," he said, and gestured at the door.

62

The plane hit the runway with a startling bump. I grabbed the arms of the seat and looked at my dad. He didn't even flinch. He just continued to argue with me about whether I would go with him to find Charlie. "This is not a play thing, Isabel."

"Not a *play thing?* I'm not a kid, and I know it's not a play thing, and this is *my* brother. He hasn't seen you in twenty-two years. He doesn't even know you're alive. If you do find him, you can't just show up out of nowhere. It's bad enough he's been kidnapped…" My voice caught on some tears that flushed up out of nowhere. "How much trauma do you want him to suffer?"

My dad said nothing.

From a few rows behind us, Maggie said, "You guys okay?"

I turned around and glanced at her. Her hair was matted on one side, standing up in golden crests on the other. Maggie, being Maggie, had slept just fine on the flight. Elena didn't look as if she'd even closed her eyes.

"Aunt Elena?" I said. "Do you need anything?"

She sent me a beseeching look, shook her head. My stomach twisted with anguish for her.

Wanting something, anything, to distract me, not knowing what I should say to my dad, I turned back around and took my phone out of my bag, switching it on. A bunch of text messages flooded in. A couple were from Theo. *How are you? How is the plane? I can't wait to see you.*

I grinned at those texts, seeing his image in my mind. Theo had shown me in Naples and Ischia that he could handle more than just acrobatic sex in my apartment. But now?

Now, I decided, I wanted to feel normal for a second. I started to text Theo back, then stopped. Mayburn had said it was difficult, nearly impossible, to tap cell phones, and he'd said mine hadn't been tampered with before I left. But what if someone had done something to it when I was in Italy? I couldn't imagine that was the case, since the phone had almost never been out of my possession. And then I decided that even if it somehow was tapped, it didn't matter. I wouldn't give out any identifying info. I wanted just an everyday exchange in a world in which every day lately had been surreal.

We just landed, I wrote to Theo. *Can't thank you enough.*

What are you doing today? he wrote back.

Looking for my brother. You?

Good luck. Let me know if I can do anything else. I'm working today and then going to Old St. Pat's.

The block party?

Yeah, they're doing it early this year. But if you need me, just tell me what you want me to do.

I could think of nothing to say to respond to that. God, block parties. They were staples of Chicago summers, but the thought of attending one seemed too childlike and innocent.

I glanced across the aisle at my dad. He was real now, not just an imaginative theory, and Charlie, the most innocent and childlike person I knew, was in real trouble.

I tossed my nonswearing campaign to the Chicago winds and thought, *Jesus fucking Christ, if they hurt my brother I will...* I will what? What would I do?

Futility—one of the worst feelings in the world, and second only to the big doozy, regret—flooded into my brain, into me, until I felt as if I was swimming in it.

I looked back down at my phone, leaving the last text from Theo unanswered. I began scrolling through my e-mails, trying once again for distraction. One e-mail was from Dena Smith, a partner at a law firm where I had applied last week.

I stared at that e-mail. *We were pleased to receive your résumé, and we are, in fact, seeking lateral attorneys at this time...* But the words didn't matter. It seemed so long ago that I cared about something as mundane as a job.

I clicked to the next e-mail. It was from Charlie! Sent a few hours ago.

"Oh my God, Dad," I said. We both froze for a second. I had just called him *Dad.* Out loud. "It's an e-mail from Charlie."

The plane slowed. My father unclicked his seat belt and shot out of his seat, leaning over me to see the phone. "What does it say?"

"Nothing. But hold on, there's an attachment." I clicked to open it. An eternity passed. Then there was the image. Of Charlie. His curly brown hair was messed. And his face...bleeding and swollen on one side.

"Oh God," I said. "Charlie."

Below the photo was a caption. I read it fast, handing the phone to my dad. There, below the picture, someone had written, *Isabel McNeil. Come see your brother. Bring your daddy, too. Both of you or there's no deal. Bring cops and your bro goes bye-bye. You'll get the address later, and when you do, you'll have 25 minutes to get here, or he's gone.*

63

The plane doors opened and bright morning light filled the cabin. It made me suck in my breath. The air *smelled* like the Midwest somehow—like trees, like something scrubbed clean but with a lingering layer of smoke. I inhaled again. Chicago. I was back on my turf, in my hometown.

Following my dad, I moved to the plane door and walked down the few steps to the ground and swiveled my head around. I'd never been to that airport in the suburbs before. A small one-story building stood to the right. I looked to the left and flinched. Four men, dressed all in black, stood there.

"Isabel," my father said. He was a few steps from the plane. "They're here for us."

I noticed that the men wore black baseball hats, just like my father had that day when I'd seen him outside of Gibsons. I took a step closer to them and lowered my voice. "Who are they?"

"Old friends."

"FBI?"

"No. I have no association with the FBI anymore. They don't know I exist."

"But these guys do?" Other questions hung in the air. *And your wife didn't? I didn't?*

He gave a terse nod. "Only recently." No other explanation was forthcoming.

The men walked toward my father and he to them. They all bent their heads down as if in a huddle. A minute later they broke apart. One of them handed my father a set of keys, then two others walked to one of two black town cars and stood outside it.

"They've been here since we left Italy yesterday. They've done a complete sweep, and there's no one here at the airport. Either Romano couldn't figure out what airport we were coming into or…"

"Or he doesn't care, because he wants us to come to him."

My father nodded. "But at least we know we're on our own for now."

Maggie and Elena got out of the plane. "Maggie," my father said, gesturing to the men near the cars. "I don't want you going home. Is there somewhere these men can take you where you'll be safe?"

"Sure," Maggie said. "My grandfather has been a defense attorney for a long time. His house is a fortress."

My father nodded and pointed at the town car. Then he smiled a little at Maggie. "It was nice to meet Izzy's best friend."

He and Maggie shook hands. I gave her a hug and she got in the car.

Elena's face was pale, her eyes darting around.

"Elena, I am so sorry about this," my dad said to her, his words tender. They hugged. He whispered something in her ear.

She nodded and, still trembling, followed the two men toward the other town car.

As it pulled away I looked at my dad. "Where is she going?"

"You don't need to know."

My irritation flared. "Why not? I'm sick of your secrets."

He gave me a look of consternation. "Izzy, I'm not telling you these things for your own good. The less you know the better. Your aunt will check into a hotel suite. She is fine, for now."

I looked back down at my phone. What about Charlie? Was he fine?

My father gestured to another town car parked apart from the others.

"Shouldn't we have people with us?" I asked.

"What did that e-mail say?"

"It said, 'Bring cops and he goes bye-bye.'"

"Right." My dad looked up at the sky then back at me. "I don't know the American Camorra well, but what I know for sure is that members of the System make good on their threats. So, while we wait for their signal, we're going to ask a few questions, we're going to try and figure out what their endgame is. And if the situation appears stable…"

"Stable?" I said, unable to stop the indignant tone. "How is any of this stable?"

He glanced at me. "I'm grading on a curve here." He began walking to the car, his eyes scanning the place as he moved. "If the situation is stable, relatively, then we'll wait for the address and go on our own."

"What could the endgame be?"

"That's what I can't figure out. If we were in Italy, they would have killed Charlie already."

I closed my eyes and felt myself sway.

My father put a hand on my shoulder. It was the first time he had touched me since I'd seen him.

I looked at his hand then back at him.

He drew his hand away quickly. "Sorry," he mumbled.

I shook my head. "That's okay." And it was.

"Let's get in the car and we can talk more."

I felt safer once we were inside. We drove away from

the airport and I pointed out the highway exit to my dad.

"I can't figure out what they want," my dad said as he drove. "I know they want *me.* But there's no reason for them not to kill Charlie, and then try to find me later."

I closed my eyes and winced. "Will you please stop saying that about Charlie?"

He looked at me curiously. "It kills me, too. But I've learned that the way to deal with everything I've seen and done is to simply be up front about it. Hiding anything from myself, even my worst fears, never leads to anything good."

I stared at him. The skin around his mouth sagged as if he'd spent a lifetime frowning, but he was still an attractive man, one of those guys who used to be cute but has aged into handsome. From what he told me on the plane, he had spent most of his life on his own. That made me incredibly sad.

He must have felt me looking and glanced my way.

I turned and put my hand on the gray felt armrest. "So you think they want to draw you there and then kill you? Or us?" *Was I really having this conversation?*

My father glanced at me again, then back at the road. "It's obvious they want something from me. I know you don't like me to say it, but I have to analyze it from an intellectual capacity. From what I know, there is no reason not to—" another glance at me "—harm Charlie if they simply wanted to send me a message. We've been watching Dez Romano for a long time. He is an exceptionally smart businessman and a shrewd strategist. He wants something from me. I just wish I knew what it is."

"Why isn't he in trouble with the Feds if Michael DeSanto was arrested?"

"Excellent question. The charges against DeSanto are the closest things the Feds have been able to get on Romano, but the truth is they don't have anything lock solid on him in particular. They can't prove that he and DeSanto are tied. The evidence the Feds have on Michael DeSanto, they didn't even get themselves, or at least they didn't start the trail that led to that evidence. *You* did that." He looked at me, and if I could read his expression, it was satisfaction. He shook his head. "I couldn't believe it. My daughter." Another shake of his head. "The work you did with Mayburn and the bank brought DeSanto to his knees."

"But if they bring Michael down, won't they be able to do that to Dez, too?"

"They can't tie Dez to the corporation that Michael was laundering money for."

"Advent Corporation," I said, remembering what Mayburn had told me. "They were in the suburbs, and they did corporate consulting or something like that."

"Right. Allegedly. It was mostly just a shell corporation."

"Who were the registered agents or officers?"

"Dez was never listed. The registered agent was a lawyer who sets up corporations over the Internet. He never met anyone face-to-face. And the president was listed as Michael DeSanto. And although they're pretty sure it was Mob owned, by Dez or the Camorra, they couldn't tie it to him, but they wanted to send a message to him. And by prosecuting Michael, whether they're successful or not, the message is still clear."

"We're on your ass."

"Exactly."

"It sounds like what we need is something on Dez then. Whether it's something the Feds can use or not, it would give us more equal footing when we see him. It might stop him from..." I opened my phone, looked again at the photo of Charlie and the swollen, bleeding side of his face. I looked back up at my dad. "How are you so calm? My insides are boiling and it's all I can do to not scream or cry or pass out."

I held the phone toward him. I thought that seeing the image would make my dad crumble. But he only glanced at it, then set his mouth firm so that the folds of skin grew taut. "You just have to turn it around."

"What do you mean?"

He looked at the picture again, then narrowed his eyes. "Don't let that make you weak. Let it make you stronger. More determined."

"Right. More determined to get this mother hen in a basket," I said.

My father's steely look turned to one of confusion.

"I'm trying to stop swearing," I said. "What I meant was it should make us more determined to get this motherfucker."

My dad laughed. "Now you got it."

64

Victoria drove up and down Lake Street. Minutes before, she had found the address Charlie had sent her an hour ago, but she was still trying to get her bearings. That was something she often had problems with—getting her bearings, her footing...whatever you wanted to call it. Her whole life she had been like that. Not someone who assessed a situation and adapted immediately—like Izzy—but rather someone who was constantly surprised by life and needed to watch and wait and, yes, often retreat before she could act. But she didn't have that kind of time now. She was delivering money to her son's drug dealer. Charlie's drug dealer. She'd been saying that over and over in her head—*Charlie's drug dealer, Charlie's dealer*—as she drove from the Gold Coast into the Loop and then west. The mantra didn't work. The reality wasn't settling in, and it didn't help that the world around her appeared so normal—tourists snapping pictures and dawdling on Michigan Avenue, bike messengers zipping past them, almost hitting the tourists and yet not even seeming to notice them. And certainly no one was noticing her, a woman in her late fifties driving her car, wearing her sunglasses.

She drove up and down the block once more, having decided that it was time to park the car, that she would never get used to the situation that presented itself. She'd lain awake all night, debating and debating whether to tell Spence but finally deciding against it. She would do what her son asked. *She* would help her son.

She pulled up to a restaurant. It was called Carnivale.

The valet opened the door for her. "Here for lunch?" he said with a bored, fake smile.

"Just parking," she said.

She lifted her purse from the passenger seat and got out of the car, wondering if she was someone who looked as if she was about to make a drug deal. Except that in this case the drugs had, apparently, already been purchased, taken, ingested, whatever you called it, by her son.

She walked down Lake Street. When she approached the spot where the street hovered over the Kennedy Expressway, she felt a clenching in her stomach and she tucked her arm closer to her side, holding her purse even tighter. She had driven over this spot often, easily a hundred times, but she had never walked it. Underneath her feet, cars sped by, horns blared. Exhaust rose up and circled her, the street shaking as a semi rumbled by.

Finally, she reached the address—a three-story building, probably once a warehouse. At some point, it appeared the building had been turned into offices or residences—back in the seventies, judging from the glass blocks. The brick was now flaking, chipped away in parts.

She looked around for a doorbell. Seeing none, she raised her hand and knocked on the black metal door. No answer. She knocked again, thinking about how to handle Charlie when she saw him. With compassion? With a stern lecture of some sort? She had never been much of a disciplinarian. She'd been lucky that, until lately, neither of her children had needed much guidance.

Victoria looked with a keener eye around the door and

finally noticed a black knob on the right. A buzzer? She pushed it. She couldn't hear anything inside.

But then the door clicked open—just like that. No one said anything, no one stepped outside. She pulled the door toward her a little bit and peered around it. Inside, it was dark, and with the sun behind her, she couldn't make out much of anything.

"Hello?" she called out. "Hello?"

Nothing. But then she heard a distinct *clack...clack... clack...* Footsteps. Someone's heels hitting the floor. She wanted to draw back with anxiousness, but she didn't let herself. She pulled the door open farther and dipped her head inside.

She could make out a hallway now, bare with a gray cement floor and brick walls. A man in a suit appeared next to one of the few lights fastened to the brick. He looked like someone Victoria might see down the street from her, having a drink at the Pump Room. He had dark hair, and the suit was well-tailored. His hands clasped behind his back, he appeared, almost, as if he were a host, waiting for the first guests to arrive at a party.

"Mrs. McNeil?" he said.

She nodded.

"Do you have the money?"

She nodded again, a little tentatively, then stuck her hand in her bag and withdrew the cash.

"Who did you tell?"

"Excuse me?"

"Who did you tell that you were coming here?"

She looked at him. What answer was he looking for? She told the truth. "No one. My son asked me not to tell anyone."

She held out the cash to him. He took a few more steps forward with the *clack, clack, clack* of his heels on the floor. She moved forward a bit, stepping inside, her arm outstretched, and just then, the door behind her slammed shut.

65

"Where are we going?" I asked my dad. I'd been paying no attention to where we were driving, but now I saw that we were almost to the exits for the Loop. "I know you said you wanted to ask some questions, but where?"

"WGN. The radio station. If someone saw Charlie get snatched by those guys, we might be able to figure out more about the whole situation."

I looked once more at Charlie's picture on my phone, then stowed it in my bag.

"So, you…" my dad said. But just those two words.

I looked at him. He was simply driving, as if he hadn't said anything. "So, I…what?" I asked.

He shifted a bit in the seat. He'd taken off his jacket. The white cotton shirt he wore was wilted, and there were perspiration stains under his arms. I looked away. It was too human a thing to see.

"So, you…" he continued. "You went to the University of Iowa for college, is that right?"

I glanced at him. "Sounds like you know all about it."

He swallowed hard, kept looking at the road. "I know the facts. I don't know if you liked it."

I stared at the dashboard, then I leaned forward and drew my finger over it. I don't know why. I guess I just wanted something to do, wanted to think for a second. But there didn't seem to be any reason not to respond. "I liked it a lot. I loved it. Iowa gets a bad rap outside the state. People think pigs or corn, but it's idyllic actually. The perfect place to go to college. Great little town, nice people, good football program."

My dad coughed. It sounded like a fake cough.

"What?" I said.

"Well, my family was never into football growing up, but during my masters program and later when we lived in Detroit, I followed Michigan football."

"Oh, for Christ's sake. You mean, I not only have to deal with you being alive, but you being a Michigan fan?"

My father blinked for a second, then we both started laughing.

After a minute, we fell into silence. Then, staring out the front window, not even seeing Chicago, I started telling my dad about how I'd floated through a few majors at Iowa like Pharmacy (too much science) and Leisure Studies (it sounded more leisurely than it actually was), and eventually ended with a Communications Studies degree.

My dad nodded the whole time I was speaking, as if he was gulping up the information. "You do communicate well," he said.

I chuckled. "Thanks."

"And law school? What was that like?"

"Fairly brutal. I mean, during the first year you can barely see, there's so much work, and then it gets a tad easier the second year, and then by the third year when you've just got the hang of it, you realize that you have to find a job and get your butt out of there."

"Did you have a hard time finding the job at Baltimore & Brown?"

I looked down at my hands, tapping my fingers together. "You know about that, too, huh?"

He cleared his throat. "Like I said, just the basics, that you worked there."

It felt weird that someone I didn't know, not really, had known all about my life all along. Yet it felt familiar, too, like a recognition inside that I'd always known but never called to the forefront.

"I lucked out by getting a summer associate position at Baltimore & Brown," I said. "And after seven months of nail biting they finally made up their minds and gave me a permanent offer."

We kept talking. And it got easier. Even enjoyable.

I was about to ask him some questions when I realized we were on Wacker Drive, not far from WGN, and then all I could think of was Charlie, and I veered the conversation back to today, to what we were facing.

"Okay," I said, "so let's figure out what Dez Romano wants from you. Because if he's not going to be prosecuted by the Feds, then why isn't he just keeping his head down at this point?"

My dad nodded thoughtfully. "He must know that I know more about the Camorra than he does."

"So he wants information?"

"That makes the most sense."

"What kind of information?"

My father shook his head. "I'm not sure."

"We need some dirt on Dez Romano to counter with, something we can use as leverage."

My father nodded again.

The WGN producer, a young guy with prematurely gray hair and frameless glasses, had a horrified look on his face. He'd agreed to talk to us immediately, and now he walked us outside onto Michigan Avenue to show us where they'd grabbed Charlie.

"We were on the air." He pointed at a glass wall that looked into a radio studio.

Two guys were broadcasting now. They were talking into their big microphones but looking out at us with curious, somewhat fearful expressions on their faces.

"Everyone is freaking out," the producer said.

"What's the purpose of this glass around the studio?" my dad asked.

"People watch us while we're live. They walk by all day and they wave, and do silly stuff. Sometimes they hold up signs or something. But this time, these two guys started pounding on the glass and yelling. They wouldn't stop and you could hear it on air. So I told Charlie to get out there fast and get them to stop."

"Don't you have security for that?" my dad asked.

"Yeah. In the Tribune Building. But by the time I called them and explained the whole thing, I thought it would take too long. I thought these guys were just drunk out-of-towners here for a Cubs game, and I figured it would take two seconds for Charlie to get them to stop."

"But they didn't?" I asked.

The producer threw his hands up into the air. "They grabbed him. It happened so fast, I'm not even sure how it went down. I looked up and saw them hauling him that way." The producer pointed to stairs.

"Where does that lead?" I asked.

"Lower Wacker. There's a parking lot down there, and access to the river." He ran a hand over his anguished face. "I called security and the cops. I couldn't get out here myself because we were on air, and by the time security got out there, there was no sign of him. He was gone." The producer shook his head, looking as agonized as we felt. "He was just gone."

* * *

We got back in the car, and the air somehow felt bleak. We hadn't learned anything. We were no closer to figuring out this situation. I looked at my father. His eyes were narrowed as he stared out the front window, looking as if his mind were working hard but failing to find any solutions, anything that would help.

I thought back to when I hacked into Michael DeSanto's computer last year, downloading information from his hard drive. Mayburn and I knew such information wouldn't be usable in a lawsuit or federal investigation, since it was an illegal search and seizure, but Mayburn used the information to get the ball rolling, used it to direct the bank in the right direction to get enough information for a warrant. Once they did, the authorities found the same information under their warrant, information that was then used to charge DeSanto. The thing was, I was sure Mayburn still had that information from Michael's hard drive.

I looked at my dad. "Does your cell phone work here in the States?"

He nodded.

"Can I make a phone call without it being traced?" I was still a little nervous about my phone being tapped, and I didn't want anything to interfere with getting another e-mail from Charlie via Dez Romano.

My father took his phone out of his jacket pocket and handed it to me.

I called Mayburn. "Where are you?"

"Hi, to you, too."

"Where are you?" I repeated.

"Working from home. Paperwork. You still in Italy?"

"Nope. See you in fifteen minutes."

66

Christopher McNeil didn't keep journals. He never wrote his thoughts down. He never left any trace of himself. And that was, in some ways, reflective of what had happened to his soul over the last twenty years.

He pulled up to a single family home a few blocks south of Lincoln Square. He watched his daughter exit the car, make a 360-degree turn, looking every which way, and then head inside to meet John Mayburn.

When she was inside, Christopher scanned the area himself, noting the other shingled houses on the street, the nicely manicured lawns. He didn't close his eyes—he never did unless he knew he was safe and nearly asleep—and entered the relaxed state of mind where he could write in his mental journal:

I am as flat as a penny. Although I see things outside me in color again, there is little left of me. My child recognized me physically, but no one truly knows me or sees me, because I have all but disappeared. If I give myself up to save my children it will be no sacrifice. There is nothing left to sacrifice.

He exhaled hard, then put away his mental journal.

He and Izzy had decided he would stay outside to make sure they hadn't been followed. So he spent the next thirty minutes in silence, glancing continually in the car mirrors, scanning the streets with his eyes, but it was rote work. For decades now, he had searched for someone that might be following him. It wasn't second nature. It was first.

The front door of John Mayburn's house opened, and Izzy stepped out. She was wearing a black skirt and a teal T-shirt that she had changed into on the plane. She took the stairs fast, and was in the car a second later.

"I think I might have something," she said, talking quickly. "Last year, after I got into Michael DeSanto's computer, Mayburn turned over the original copy of the hard drive to his client, the bank where Michael used to work. Mayburn told the bank and the Feds he didn't keep a copy." He glanced at her and saw her roll her eyes to the roof of the car. "But of course he did. That's so Mayburn. Anyway, most of the stuff is financial, encrypted records of transactions Michael put through for Advent Corporation. I asked Mayburn if he remembered anything in there having to do with Dez Romano, but like you said, there was nothing solid that could tie Dez to Michael or Advent Corporation. So, Mayburn and I started opening all the documents on the hard drive and scanning them, trying to see if we noticed anything. But we didn't find anything that the Feds hadn't, but then…"

"Then?"

"Well, I started thinking. If Dez and Michael had formed Advent Corporation so they could run financial transactions through it, maybe they formed other corporations. We got on the Secretary of State Web site and searched for Michael's name and Dez's, just to check, but of course nothing came up. We thought of the name of the lawyer you mentioned, the one who was the registered agent for Advent, so we searched for his name, but you can't search by the names of the agents on the site, only the names of the corporations. So I tried to think like

Michael. I kept thinking that now that I know Lucy pretty well and have heard her talk so much about Michael that maybe something would jump out. So we did all the searches I could think of, using Michael's street name or number, stuff like that. And then I remembered from the day I got on his computer that he's a huge Notre Dame fan. Huge. So we started running searches with Notre Dame words."

"Like what?"

"*Irish, Fighting Irish, ND, Domer.* When we found corporations that used those words we'd look at the information on file and check out the registered agents or the officers. We couldn't find anything at first. It was such a long shot."

"But then you found something?"

"Yep. When we clicked on the name of one corporation called UND, LLC, it showed a registered agent named Paul Crane. We used Google to search for him and he's like the other one you mentioned—a lawyer who incorporates for people over the Internet. But guess who the principal officer was?"

"It couldn't have been Michael DeSanto or Dez Romano or the Feds would have found that."

"Nope. It was Belle Joseph."

"Who's that?"

"Belle is the name of Lucy and Michael's daughter. Josephine is her middle name. I heard Lucy call her by her full name when we were at the museum."

"And by using her name, no one would be able to search for it. They wouldn't *know* to search for it."

"Exactly."

"Wow." He was filled with awe at his daughter's ingenuity. What would it have been like if he had been with her for her whole life, getting to witness triumphs like this?

"And get this—Mayburn did some digging and found that UND, LLC previously listed Advent Corporation as one of their subcontractors."

"You're kidding?"

"I suppose UND could be a legit business, something Michael is working on outside of Dez, but..."

"But with a tie like that to Advent, there's a damn good chance UND is *just* like Advent Corporation. There are so many similarities."

She nodded. "I think so, too. And maybe it won't even help when we see Dez, but—"

"Good work!" he said, interrupting her, surprised at the enthusiasm in his voice. He wanted to pat her shoulder, to hug her.

She smiled.

But just then his eyes narrowed as he saw something over her shoulder, through the car window.

"What?" Izzy said, catching his look and swiveling around. "Oh, it's just Mayburn."

A guy in his forties, wearing jeans and a T-shirt, was leaning toward the car, holding up one hand.

Izzy rolled down the window. "Mayburn, this is my father, Christopher McNeil."

His own name, being spoken from the lips of his daughter, made something tremble inside him. But when he reached out his hand to shake John Mayburn's, he frowned. "Nice to meet you," he said coldly to the guy who had put his daughter in the line of fire more than once.

Mayburn seemed to understand his look. He nodded. "I appreciate your daughter. I won't let her get hurt."

He said nothing. Wasn't sure this Mayburn guy could protect Izzy even if he wanted to.

Mayburn looked at Izzy. "I called Lucy."

"You told her about Michael's company, UND?"

Mayburn nodded. "He swore to her that Advent Corporation was it. He swore they'd never had any other affiliation."

"Did you tell her about the name of Belle Joseph as the principal officer?"

He nodded. "I told her she couldn't say anything to Michael for a few days, but the 'Belle Joseph' thing, that's what pushed her over the edge—using the kids in any way."

"So you think it will make a difference? With the two of you?"

He nodded again. "Yeah," he said. "I think everything is going to be good. Real good." He glanced at Christopher, then back at Izzy. "I know you have more important things to worry about, and if there's anything at all I can do, tell me. But in the meantime, thanks, Iz. Thanks a lot."

"You're welcome," Izzy said.

John Mayburn gave a small wave, then turned and walked back into his house.

Christopher had just pulled away from the curb when Izzy's phone, which lay on the console between the seats, came to life—the phone trilling, the screen lighting up.

Izzy grabbed it. "An e-mail." She scrolled with her thumb. Her face lost the excitement that had just been there. "It's from Charlie."

Despite his earlier lecture to Izzy about "turning around" negative emotions, Christopher was walloped by fear.

He pulled over, and Izzy leaned toward him, holding the phone so they could both see.

You don't need the exact address, the e-mail read. *Just come to Lake Street, just past Kennedy. Look for the building with the black door. You'll figure it out. You'd better, or this kid is dead. Your 25 minutes start now.*

67

My dad floored the car down Lincoln Avenue, blaring the horn several times to get people to move out of the way.

When we were almost at a light at Sheffield Avenue, I pointed. "Turn there!" I looked at my watch. "Fifteen minutes." Then I looked back at the phone, despair and panic warring within. "We were supposed to get the address," I said, still staring at my phone. "And you said when we got the address, you'd have one of your buddies run a search on the address to see if we could find anything out about the building."

He shot through the light, turning. "And now we can't do that."

"So we just go in there cold?" My voice started rising. *Keep your cool,* I thought.

I watched as my dad reached down toward his ankle with his left hand. When he sat up, there was something in that hand, something black and gleaming. I drew back against the car door. "Where did you get that?"

I had never seen a gun up close before. The men in Naples had guns, and they were pointing them at me, but the proximity of this gun was different. Menacing. And I didn't particularly like it.

I looked up at my father and into his eyes, and for some reason I was nervous.

"I carried it on the plane," he said.

"They just let you do that?" I thought back to the security we'd gone through before boarding Theo's private plane. There was little. We'd been required to show our passports and that was about it. Now that I thought about it, we could've packed hand grenades in our bags, which were placed by the pilots into the luggage compartment.

My father tucked the gun into his waistband. I stared at his profile. How quickly I'd sided with him, assumed that because he was my father he must be a good man. But he'd killed Maurizio, even admitted it. And Elena had been a mess around him. That was expected, of course, since she'd lost her husband, but was it something more than that? She was the only one who had known Christopher McNeil all these years. Was she afraid of him?

The air in the car seemed stale. I opened the window a little. My father's eyes darted to my window, then went back to the road. I pushed myself farther into the side of the passenger door, felt for the handle, just in case.

He saw it. "What are you doing?"

"I don't know, I'm just…"

"Are you afraid of me?" This almost seemed to amuse him, which was bizarre. *I don't know this man at all.*

"I don't know what I'm afraid of anymore."

He blinked as if surprised, then his face cleared and he nodded. "I understand that." His voice had been full of life when I was telling him about finding Michael's UND corporation, but now it was flat again.

"Is there any reason I need to be nervous of you?"

He stopped the car at a light at Armitage and looked at me. He didn't look amused now, but rather wounded. He shook his head. "But I understand if you don't believe me. I have given you no reason for trust." He looked back at the road. "Let's just focus on what we have to do, and then I'll be out of your way again. In one way or another."

"What's that supposed to mean?"

He shook his head, not answering. "Let's concentrate on Charlie."

The reminder of Charlie made my heart skip. I looked at my watch. "We have eight minutes."

Just then the light turned green and my dad pressed on the gas.

I glanced toward his waist. "I don't want you to use that gun. Not even on Dez."

"I won't use it unless I have to."

"You did with Maurizio."

A single nod.

"You had to?" I said.

"I did." His tone was grave and regretful, but resigned.

I looked out the front window, pointed at Clybourn Avenue. "Turn left here," I told my father. "Then right on Halsted. We can take that to Lake."

He did as I told him, flooring the car down Halsted, dodging around slower cars, edging up to the front at lights and shooting ahead of the others.

"Go faster if you can," I said, looking at my watch. "Six minutes."

He ran a light that had just turned red.

"What's going to happen?" I asked, scared and overwhelmed.

He shook his head. "I don't know. I want to tell you not to worry, but I haven't dealt with a hostage situation since my training at the academy."

I exhaled loudly and looked at my father. I realized that I'd allowed myself a tiny false sense of security. It was a sense that assumed that my father, who'd been able to survive for the last few decades, would not only allow us to survive today, but to succeed. I saw now that he was fallible, that I was going to have to continue to be part of our survival.

"All right," I said, "so let's think. We know Dez wants something from you."

My dad nodded. "Right. Hopefully, I possess whatever that information is, whatever he wants. If so, I'm hoping to keep stringing Romano along, maybe using the UND corporation. I'm hoping to do that long enough to determine the setup of the place and to get Charlie and you out of there."

"But earlier you said he wants you, too. Like he wanted you as a person, not just information you have."

My dad nodded. "If Dez Romano were able to kill me today, it would be huge for him. He's a somewhat small fish in the System, but if he took me out, it would catapult him to Camorra stardom."

I studied his profile. "Why don't you sound upset by that?"

He glanced at me, then back at the road, veering around a car that was parallel parking. "I've fought the Camorra long enough. I'm done. And I'm willing to give Dez Romano what he needs just as long as it means the two of you are safe."

I stared at him. "You can't go away again."

We came to a stoplight. My dad looked at me. "You don't know if you trust me. Why would you want me to stick around?"

"So you can give me time to figure it out."

He laughed. And it made me feel good.

Another glance at my watch. "Three minutes."

He looked back at the road and shot through another yellow light. "How am I going to accomplish anything if you don't want me to use my gun. Why would you care whether Dez is hurt or not?"

I stared past my father at the side of a building where a fat, smiling Buddha was painted in bright colors—an advertisement for a bar called Funky Buddha Lounge. "Two months ago, I found my friend a few minutes after she was killed. And I saw Maurizio yesterday. I don't want to be a witness to any more death."

He said nothing.

"Plus, I don't believe in an eye for an eye. If we hurt Dez, or someone else, when we don't need to, it just hurts us in the long run."

My father stayed silent.

"You don't agree with that?" I asked.

"No."

I held up my wrist to my face. "Two minutes. Thank God we're almost at Lake Street. When you get there, take a left."

My father nodded and leaned forward a bit as if he could make the car move faster. His mouth moved back and forth, his eyebrows pulled together under his copper-rimmed glasses. He opened his cell phone and started to dial.

"Who are you calling?" I asked.

"One of the men you saw outside the airport. I've changed my mind. I'm calling them in as backup."

"But we were told *not* to bring backup. He said if we do that, he'll kill Charlie."

My father's jaw worked more intensively. He breathed out a loud puff of air through his nostrils and threw down the phone. "No one should ever have to be in this situation. No one should ever have to do this on behalf of their son."

"You brought it on yourself," I said, then immediately regretted it. "I'm sorry." My words shot out fast. "I shouldn't have said that. I know you did the best you could do but..."

My father pulled to a stop at the light at Lake and looked at me. "You're right. I brought this on myself, and I will handle it."

68

We found the building easily. We got out of the car and looked at it. My heart thumped as we walked to the door. I looked at my dad. What were we supposed to do here? I had left my purse in the car, putting my cell phone and my ID in my pocket—*in case they need to identify me*—and now I felt naked, unarmed.

But my dad wasn't.

His head swiveled, his eyes searched the neighboring buildings. What was he looking for? Snipers? I had no idea.

I let my eyes do the same, trying to learn from him, even though I wasn't sure what we were studying.

At the door, my dad found a buzzer and pushed it. He looked at his watch.

"Are we here in time?" I said.

He gave me a terse nod.

The door popped open but only a crack. Nothing else happened. I stared at that sliver of black in between the door and the frame. It seemed vast, as if an entire galaxy might be contained within it.

My dad pulled it open. We stepped inside. We had to blink until our eyes adjusted to the faint light.

But then I saw him clearly. Dez Romano. He wore a dark suit, black shoes and a blue tie with tangerine and white dots. He looked dressed for a wedding or some other fashionable social event.

"Isabel," he said with a big grin. "Or I hear you prefer Izzy." He waved his left hand, as if to say, *It doesn't matter.* "You ran away from me that night at Gibsons. You won't be running away from me tonight."

I heard a gurgle behind me, sort of a half laugh, half clearing of the throat. I spun around, flinched. That Ransom guy. The guy with the fucked-up tattoos on his neck. He was smiling big at me as if he was really happy to see me. His lips were thick and moist and one of them had a couple sores on it. I tried not to make a disgusted face. But he must have seen it, and it only made him smile more.

He took a step toward us. I noticed he wore a walking boot on his foot, probably because of Mayburn running over it outside the nature museum.

"Spread your legs," Ransom said. His words were the most sadistic I had ever heard—garbled and rough, as if he had stones in his mouth, but with a leer, as though he loved to say them.

When neither my father nor I complied, Dez Romano shouted, "Spread your legs. Both of you. Or I'll kill little Charlie. In front of you. Do it. Right. Now."

I snapped into action. My father was slower to do the same. I saw him shaking his head. Ransom went to him first, easily found his gun and tossed it to Dez, who looked at it, then back at my father. "I suppose I can let you get away with this. I didn't tell you not to bring any weapons. But I did tell you not to bring any backup. If you did, the deal is beyond dead. And so are you two."

Ransom stepped in front of me then and grinned, his mouth wide and wet.

He ran his hands over my arms first, then my waist. He took my ID and cell phone and tossed those at Dez, too. Then he dropped to his knees, the walking boot not seeming to affect his movements at all. He looked up at me, and I wanted to kick him in the face. I wanted to smash his nose and crush his windpipe with the heel of my shoe, but instead I let him grin, let him look up at me as if he was about to perform some sort of sexual act. He drew his hands up one of my legs, then the other. When he got near the middle of the left leg, he paused, then his hand kept moving up. It was horrible. I stopped my body from trembling, stopped myself from showing terror, and the monumental effort caused something to bubble up inside me, caused movement of the one thing I've never been able to control. My mouth.

"Just so you know," I said, "I'm easy, but I'm not cheap."

Ransom's hand jerked away, and when I looked down, his face went blank. He looked over his shoulder at Dez, who started to laugh.

And then I couldn't control it—I kneed him. Not hard. I knew I couldn't get away from him, and I knew kicking him too hard would only bring more of his sick wrath upon me, but I couldn't help but give him a firm knee into his shoulder when he looked at Dez, just so he knew I could do it.

The action didn't make Ransom fall from his crouch, but it did make him pissed. He glared up at me with a snarl, his wet lips open in surprise, then stood and leaned over me.

"Oh, Isabel," Dez said. "You really, really don't want to make him mad. You wouldn't believe what he wants to do to you already. Don't make him want it more."

His words made my stomach churn with sickness and fear. But I wouldn't show it.

"Get away from her, Ransom," Dez said.

Ransom licked his lips, but then finally moved behind me. I could feel his breath on the side of my neck.

Dez pointed to my father, using the gun. I flinched instinctively. Dez saw it and shot me a small smile, the way you would a little kid who'd done something adorable.

"You and I," Dez said to my father. "We need to talk privately. In case that talk doesn't go well, I'm going to let you say goodbye to your son first."

"That's not necessary," my father said.

"Sure, it's necessary," Dez said. "I think goodbyes and that kind of thing are important."

"Really, that's not—" my father started to say.

But Dez interrupted. "Plus your wife is in there, too. I'm sure you'll want to have a chat with her."

We both froze, looked at each other.

Did he just say "your wife"?

Dez cracked a big smile now. "Ransom, let's show these folks where the rest of the little family is."

Ransom put a hand on my biceps and squeezed hard. Instinctually, I flinched and tried to yank my arm away, but then I heard a soft, distinct *click.*

I turned to look at Ransom. And found myself looking at the barrel—*was that even the right word?*—of a handgun. I forced myself to look away, to look at Dez. He was pocketing my dad's gun, holding one of his own and pointing it at my dad. "Mr. McNeil, if you'll walk down this hallway, we'll just follow you."

My dad did nothing for a second. Then he looked at me, and his mouth was open a little, his face flushing red.

Randomly, idiotically, I thought, *I must get that blushing thing from him.*

"Now," Dez said, dropping his smile.

My father followed orders. We walked the dimly lit hall, our shoes silent on the concrete floor. We passed a few rooms with open doors. Entirely empty.

Ransom held tight to my arm, kept his big solid body

right behind me, breathing wet sighs into my ear. I could hear saliva gurgling at the back of his throat. An alarm rang in my brain. Loud. And louder. I wanted to whimper every time I felt that breath, but I steeled myself.

Finally we came to a closed door. Dez shoved my dad against the wall next to it, putting the gun to his head. Then he opened the door and shoved him inside. Ransom heaved a wet sigh into my ear, his lips almost touching my skin. Then he pushed me inside, too, and I heard the lock click behind me.

69

My mother stared—with a deeply confused look on her face—at her former husband. The frown deepened the faint vertical crease between her eyes. Her expression was so bewildered she looked as if she had been thrust into a parallel universe where she recognized nothing.

Charlie, meanwhile, cocked his head and just stared at my dad. "Huh," he said.

"Victoria. Charlie." My dad said these words as if he was trying them out for the first time.

Neither Charlie nor my mom said anything.

"This kind of thing is very hard to process," my father said, gesturing a little with his hands. "Technically, the mind will take anywhere from five to seven minutes to catch up with any traumatic or shocking experience."

He continued on, but I shook my head and held out my hands. "Dad, shut up."

My mother's glance snapped to mine, then back to her former husband. "What is going on here?" she said. Then again, louder, "What is going on here!"

Charlie and I both stared at her, surprised. My mother never raised her voice. Never. I had literally never heard her yell at us, never scream at anyone, never even laugh loudly. Victoria McNeil had a certain elegant, almost monotone voice that always remained at the same level and never shifted.

She moved back until she was near one of the walls. "I do not understand." She enunciated each of her syllables distinctly as if by controlling her voice she could gain some control in this situation. But she looked around at all of us wildly, on the brink of losing it. And that was hard to see.

I stepped forward slowly until I was near her. She looked at me, fear in her face, but didn't make any movements. I reached out and touched her arm, then made a smoothing motion over her skin in the way she always did to Charlie and me when she wanted to calm us.

She looked down at my hand on her arm, then jerked her arm away, moved away from me.

"Mom," I said. I glanced at my brother. "Charlie." I took a breath. "I just figured out that dad was alive. Yesterday."

Charlie's eyes opened wide—or at least the one that wasn't swollen shut. "Huh," Charlie said again.

My mom shook her head. Laughed. Then she repeated the sequence over and over, staring now at my father, until the shake of her head turned into a nod, and she was just bobbing her head and laughing and laughing, a hysterical laugh with a horrible edge.

I didn't know what to do.

But then just as quickly as she had started, she stopped. "What is all of this?" She drew a circle around the room with her hand. "I don't understand." She looked at her son. "Are you really a drug addict?"

Charlie shook his head. "Mom, I told you I was kidnapped."

"I know," she said, irritation in her voice. "And I believed it. Until this..." She pointed at my father, her expression shifting into one of horror, hurt.

My father crossed the room quickly to her, dropped to

one knee and put his hands over his heart. "Victoria," he said. "Victoria."

A choking sound came from my mother's throat, and she began to cry. Hard. Charlie and I stared at her in wonder. We'd both seen my mother cry on a few occasions, and when she did, it was always an oddly beautiful sight—a woman who rarely allowed herself to show emotion, letting tears fall like crystals from her blue eyes, letting them glide down the milky smoothness of her face.

But this was different. The choking sounds continued. She grasped at her throat as sobs wrenched her body. Her chest was heaving; her face turned deep red.

I wanted so badly to help her, to calm her in some way, but I recognized there was nothing I could do. Charlie seemed to realize the same thing. He sat down on the floor, crossed his arms, and looked down, as if to give them as much privacy as possible. I sat next to him.

My father stayed there on his knee, his hands one on top of the other over his heart, tears streaming down his cheeks.

"You used to do that," my mother said, her words mere rasps between the sobs. "That's how you proposed to me." She pointed at my father, still holding the same position. "That's what you did when you wanted to thank me for having your children."

My father nodded.

"And then you left me. You died. But I never really believed you were dead. It never made sense to me. It didn't seem real. I even took a job as a traffic reporter, flying in a helicopter every day so I would think of you, and I would know you were really dead. But I still didn't believe it. And so I had to live my whole life knowing one thing was true but believing another." She began to sob again.

My father stood. "I am so sorry, Victoria. I didn't see any other way."

He began to talk then. He explained about the Camorra, about trying to bring them down. He told her the Camorra had found him out when they lived in Michigan, had wanted to kill the whole family.

"Remember when all the police officers were around?" he asked my mom.

"Yes, but you said they were friends."

"They were. They were also protecting us."

But then his mother was killed in a car explosion, he said. It was a message, and my father knew he had to take action.

"It was either move all of us…" He gestured at the four of us. "Or I had to go."

"You chose to go," my mother said, squeezing her eyes shut, as if she couldn't process her own words. "You chose to go?" she repeated, but in a question now. Then she moved away from him, and then my mother opened her mouth, and then she shouted, "You *chose* to go!"

My father could say nothing. He only nodded.

70

Dez Romano felt his body buzzing with excitement. God, he loved this moment. Manipulating it as he had.

He was in a room that had been used as an office in this building years ago. The only thing left in the room was an old metal desk. It was bulky and heavy. It would work.

A second later, Ransom opened the door and shoved Christopher McNeil into the room, handcuffed. McNeil looked distraught, Dez was happy to see. The family must not have known he was alive. That must have been a hell of a thing to explain.

Dez pulled out his handgun, a Sig Sauer P250. He rarely got to use it or even flash it around. He'd decided years ago to run his business the gentleman's way. But even gentlemen needed a piece sometimes. And he had no idea what McNeil was capable of.

He pointed with the gun at the desk. "Cuff him to the leg."

Ransom shoved McNeil again, who fought against the momentum, but with his hands cuffed, he fell to his knees. Had to hurt like hell, but McNeil's expression never changed.

Ransom pushed McNeil into a seated position on the floor, undid the cuff of one arm and secured it to the leg of the desk. Dez nodded, then jerked his head at the door, indicating to Ransom that he could leave. He didn't want anyone else to hear this conversation. If it went right, he would be one of the few people in the Camorra to have this information.

Ransom didn't look happy at first, then a thought seemed to go through his head, and with a slight smile he moved toward the door.

Dez knew exactly what that smile meant. "Don't touch the redhead," he said.

Ransom stopped, looked at him.

Dez shook his head. "Not just yet."

Ransom smashed his lips together, looking like a starving dog being held away from food. But he nodded and left.

Dez stood taller. He liked looking down at someone like McNeil, who seemed sickened and defeated by the talk of his daughter. "Who's at the top of the System?" Dez asked him.

McNeil's glasses slid a little down his nose and they cocked slightly to one side, making him look like a once-brilliant professor gone senile. "The top?" McNeil asked.

"You know what I mean."

Earlier, McNeil had looked like a pretty fit older guy, but now his chest sagged toward his bound hand, which wouldn't allow him to sit up much. "Jesus, is that what you want to know from me?"

Dez gave him a single nod.

"No one knows who's at the top."

"You've been fucking with the System for twenty years, pretending you're a part of it but working for the government the whole time, right?" That was what his boss, La Duca, had suspected.

McNeil nodded, and Dez felt his first wave of triumph. He couldn't wait to call the duke.

"So all those years," Dez said, "and you don't know who's at the top? Why don't I believe that?"

McNeil shook his head. He looked fatigued and ancient. "*No one* knows. If I did, I wouldn't have to keep fucking with the System, as you said. If I had that bit of information, we could have shut the whole thing down. You know it as well as I do. The top likes the clans to war. I'm sure the top likes that *you're* one of the clans now and that you're fighting against the others, too. Maybe you're not fighting in the same way they do in *Napoli,* but you're still trying to scratch your way up."

He was right. Every word of it. Dez said nothing, gave nothing away with his face. He tucked his gun in his waistband and withdrew an automatic switchblade from his pocket. "This is called a Bradley Mayhem, and—"

"I know what it is."

He glanced at McNeil, then back at the blade, touching his finger to the tip. He kept talking, as if he hadn't been interrupted. "I used to use a different blade when I was growing up. This one's sharper. Much. I don't like to use it anymore, but it does a good job—"

"Look, save me the tough-guy speech about how you're going to cut me until I tell you who's at the top. I've been tortured by better than you, and if I knew I'd tell you. I planned on telling you whatever you wanted. I'm done fighting you guys."

Dez took a breath and steeled his eyes at McNeil. He ignored the comment about others being better than him.

"If you like," McNeil said, "I'll tell you who I've considered. Who I think it might be, especially given recent events."

"Keep talking."

"The second in command to the top is the one who gets the face time with the clans."

"And who is that?"

"The brother to my sister's husband. Paulo Traviata."

Dez nodded. He'd heard of the guy.

"I've known of his position for…well, for a long time," McNeil continued. "He's kept his power ever since, but you could never tell exactly who he was answering to. For a long time, we thought it was Antonio Crispino. You know him?"

Dez nodded.

"Then we thought maybe it was Crispino's cousin, the guy they call the Hammer. He got his nickname because—"

"I know how he got the name," Dez said, and he felt thrilled that it was true. "But it wasn't him?"

"No. We had a couple of other guys on the line, too, but truth is we've never been able to know for sure."

"What happened recently?"

McNeil closed his eyes, swallowed hard. "My brother-in-law, Maurizio." He blinked his eyes against something only he could see. "I won't bore you with the details, but his body is about to be discovered. If it hasn't been already."

Dez felt his eyebrows rising. This was interesting news. He might be the first to know it, and to know it from the U.S. would be an accomplishment. "Did you do it?" he asked. "You killed him?"

McNeil glanced up at him with a pitiful expression, then looked back at the floor. Nodded. "Had to. He came after me. Knew where I was."

"And you think that makes Maurizio the one at the top?"

McNeil nodded. "It makes sense with his brother, Paulo, being the number two."

"If he was, why would Maurizio try to take you out on his own? Why not tell Paulo to have one of their guys do it?"

McNeil breathed out a long breath. "Because it was personal. Because it was me."

"Maurizio Traviata," Dez said to make sure he had it right.

McNeil nodded. "There. You got what you wanted." He looked up at Dez, directly in his eyes. "Now keep up your end of the bargain."

"By letting you go? Along with the family you ran away from?"

McNeil said nothing.

"Are you sure it's Maurizio?" Dez said.

A pause, then, "No."

Dez studied him. Believed him. McNeil didn't know for sure. Fuck, that was disappointing. The whole story about Maurizio Traviata was good, sure, but it wasn't solid. He couldn't use it to his advantage if he didn't know for sure. He felt disappointment flood his body. And yet, he reminded himself, this was still a coup. And now, Dez would walk out and get Ransom; they would go into the basement and activate the gas leak, and they would leave. The duke and whoever was at the top—unless it was the recently deceased Maurizio Traviata—would sit up and take note of Dez's feat. He would kill McNeil, the traitor of all traitors, symbolically taking out his family at the same time *and* making an example of the Mexicans, who hadn't been living up to what they'd promised him.

"It's too bad you didn't have the right answer." Dez closed the blade, put it in his pocket and looked down at Christopher McNeil. Sad how the guy had slipped. He would die here, alone in this room, which was what he deserved.

71

I explained quickly to my mom and Charlie what had happened, my eyes veering to the door every few seconds. Where was my dad? Where were Dez and Ransom? What in the hell was happening?

My mom and Charlie both looked shell-shocked, not surprisingly, and so when I came to the end of my tale, I ran through it again, as much for them as for me. My skin and my body were jumpy. I told them how I'd been doing some moonlighting for a private detective after Sam disappeared, that I still worked with him occasionally and he'd asked me to chat up Dez Romano at Gibsons in order to get some dirt on someone he wanted to put back in jail. Dad saw me with him, and when the situation spun out of control, he stepped in and saved me.

I told them about Italy and Elena and Maurizio. I just kept talking until it looked as if the information was settling in. My mom was leaning with one side of her body against a wall, her arms crossed. Her face was composed now.

"It's so bizarre we're having this conversation," I said. I looked around the room—so plain, so simple compared to what was going on inside.

"It's bizarre and cool," Charlie said, leaning against a wall.

My mother sent him a look I recognized, one she gave Charlie a lot, which said, *I love my son, profoundly, but where did he come from?*

My mother stepped forward and knelt to look at Charlie's face, turning it this way and that and examining him. It was really just a split lip and some general swelling on the right side more than anything. Some blood dropped from Charlie's lip onto my mother's white shirt, but she didn't seem to notice or care.

"Nothing seems broken," she said.

"What's he like?" Charlie asked, looking over her shoulder at me.

I thought about that. "He seems like someone who's been through a lot. Too much, probably. Seems like a lot of his life has been bled out of him, so he's hard to really get a read on. But he still knows how to laugh."

At that, my mother nodded slowly, as if she understood what I meant.

Just then the door banged open, and we jumped.

Ransom. He grinned like, *How do you like that entrance?* He waved a gun at my mother and Charlie. "Over there," he gargled through his thick lips. After they'd complied, he looked at me, smiled sickeningly and walked toward me.

72

Christopher stared up at Dez Romano, blinking rapidly under his glasses. He'd intentionally let his head fall toward his shoulder, letting the glasses slide farther down his face. He made himself shrink even more, into an almost fetal position. Romano was buying the cowering routine and liked it, Christopher could tell, which was good. The guy would have his defenses down. But Christopher needed to bring them down further.

Dez Romano took a few steps toward him, looking down over his nose with arrogant sympathy, as if he were coming upon a beggar on the street. "It's too bad you didn't have the right answer. I really wanted this to work out for all of us." He shook his head back and forth in a grand show of discontent.

Dez didn't deliver any cliché parting words, even though Christopher could tell he was thinking about it. He simply gave an audible exhale, then started to turn toward the door.

"I know about UND, LLC."

Romano froze and cocked his head toward him.

"Paul Crane is the lawyer who set it up and is your registered agent."

Romano turned now.

"And I know Belle Joseph is the principal officer," Christopher said. "I know everything."

Romano sniffed deeply. "What else do you think you know?"

Which meant there was something else to know. Which meant Dez Romano must be running some of his money through UND, LLC, just as they'd thought. *Good work, Izzy.*

"Why should I tell you?" he scoffed at Romano. "You're going to leave me here anyway, right? You're going to kill my daughter, my son, my wife. And then come back and kill me." He acted as if saying those words didn't cause succinct blows of pain to his stomach.

"Yeah, that's right. That's exactly what's going to happen. And if you don't tell me what else you know, I'll bring your family in here and make you watch it. I'll bring your daughter in here, and—"

Christopher forced himself to interrupt Romano. He couldn't bear to hear what the man was about to say. "Do it," he said loudly. "If anything happens to me today, my associates will take that information and have it to the Feds within hours. DeSanto won't take the fall this time."

Dez Romano did nothing, but Christopher could tell he'd hit a chord. Dez had thought no one knew about UND, LLC. He believed that he and Michael had covered their tracks.

"I know how you're working it with DeSanto," Christopher said. "You're going to act all sympathetic, right? Tell DeSanto to do his time and you'll have a place for him when he gets out, yeah? And then you'll fuck him. He gets out and he's persona non grata. He'll have a record, which will make it tough to get a job, and so he'll be forced to take whatever dregs you leave him. He'll—"

"Shut up!" It was Romano who interrupted him now, taking a step forward as he did.

Which was exactly what Christopher was waiting for.

In one second, Christopher filled himself up with the power of his breath and let his body unfurl out of the cower. His leg shot out. His right foot hooked Romano's, and not expecting it, he went down fast. Christopher summoned up every bit of strength in his body, and with a roar, he heaved himself toward Romano, pulling the desk with him. He managed to get to a crouch and and then launched himself right toward Romano, falling atop him. As he'd anticipated, Romano reacted quickly, using his strength to throw Christopher off him, tearing Christopher's shirt in the process. And Christopher used the extra momentum to lift the desk off the ground, just for a second, to slip the cuff out from under the leg.

His hands free now, he wrapped one around Romano's neck and yanked his head to the side. He raised the hand still cuffed and brought it down with a blasting punch against Romano's temple. Romano crumpled, temporarily knocked out. Christopher knelt over him, felt under him until he found the gun and the blade and shoved them away. He wanted to blow Romano's skull to pieces, knew that legally, he was in the right to do so—self-defense. But he didn't want to explain himself, or his Italian passport, to the Chicago police or anyone else. And he thought then of what Izzy had said about not hurting people even if they'd hurt you. Just as he'd told her, he didn't agree. Not at all. But he wanted his daughter to respect him. If that was possible.

He rolled Romano onto his back. In his dark suit and dotted tie, Dez looked like a well-dressed corpse waiting for his casket. Christopher wished that were so.

He crouched at his head. He didn't have much time until Romano came to. Five minutes, maybe. But that was all he needed.

Counting off the seconds, he manipulated Romano's

head, neck and body in a series of maneuvers, holding certain positions. He cocked Romano's head forward at the neck, tugging back at the base of the skull; he pushed Romano into a seated position then cocked the head slightly left; he twisted Romano's head one way, then another, moved his torso to the left, then slightly right, counting out the seconds.

When he was done, he laid Romano's head back. When he regained consciousness, he would sit, and the room would tilt and spin. With the swirling of his surroundings he would have a very hard time getting to his feet or executing even simple bodily tasks, all due to BPPV—Benign Paroxysmal Positional Vertigo. BPPV was usually brought on by natural calcium debris in the inner ear that sent false signals to the brain, severely affecting balance, but it could be induced manually, as well. Christopher had utilized it before, often using weak electrical currents to excite neurons in the brain, but if he had to he could also do it positionally, the old-fashioned way.

He raised his hands off Romano and took a step back. Romano was still out. Perfect. When he came to, the BPPV wouldn't last forever, but it would buy them a fair amount of time.

Christopher spun and opened the door. He shut it behind him, then took off in a sprint down the hallway, barely noticing the handcuffs on one hand banging into his thigh.

73

Ransom leered, one side of his mouth curling up, then he licked his lips, making a loud smacking sound.

Even though he was across the room, I instinctively took a step back. He laughed a gurgling laugh and moved slowly toward me.

"Get away from her," Charlie said. "Or I will fucking kill you."

He sounded fairly tough, and I appreciated the effort. But Charlie didn't know how to fight. *Oh, God, what should I do?*

Ransom took another step, a low growl emanating from his throat.

I glanced at my mom. She wore an expression of terror. That expression, coupled with the trauma I knew she'd suffered over the last twenty-four hours, made me violently angry. In that instant, I thought of what she'd been through—hearing that her son was abducted, getting lured and being abducted herself, finding out that her first husband and the father of her kids had been alive all this time.

Thinking of all that, seeing her, made me put my hand on my hip and look at Ransom with a resigned expression. "Let's do this somewhere else."

That stopped Ransom in his tracks. He frowned a little with confusion.

"Let's go in another room." I made my voice sound like someone defeated.

Ransom's face brightened, but the dude wasn't stupid. He shook his head and kept moving toward me.

"I'm not kidding," I said, my face growing more stern. "You want at me, I'll let you, but only if we go in another room. So let's go." I took a step toward him. "Let's just go."

His eyes dodged to Charlie and then my mom to see if he could read their expressions, and I took that moment to do something, thinking, *Please don't let this be the most stupid thing I've ever done.* Instead of walking slowly toward Ransom, I shot forward and dove at him. He must have been caught off guard, because he stumbled and fell backward, the two of us crumpling to the ground.

But then he was on top of me, easily pinning my arms. I could smell him—a stale, sweet sort of smell, as if something had rotted deep inside him. I struggled against him, but it was impossible. He raised his fist, and I knew he was going to hit me. Hard. I glued my eyes shut, but before I felt the punch I heard a *crack* of a gunshot.

Ransom jumped off me and spun around. He hadn't been hit.

But my mother—my mother!—was holding his gun. And then Charlie, maybe motivated by his female family members, charged at Ransom, and the two of them dropped to the ground.

The door banged open and my father rushed inside. His gray hair pushed every which way, his shirt was untucked and ripped, his eyes wild.

He paused for a minute, as if struck dumb by the sight of his son and Ransom tussling on the floor. Ransom was on his knees first, and he drew his fist back, ready to pound my brother, but before I knew it, my dad was at Ransom's side, throwing him off. Ransom managed to jump to his feet. He spun around, launching his arm in a swift arc toward my father, who dodged the punch so that it landed on his shoulder.

I grabbed Charlie's arm and pulled him away as my dad stepped back toward Ransom, hitting the big guy with the base of his hand, ramming that hand up into Ransom's nose. Ransom reacted momentarily with one hand to his face, and my father took the moment to hit him in the eye with a left, then into his ribs with a right. Something snapped. It sounded like a tree splitting. Ransom grabbed at his ribs. My father jacked him in the side of the head and Ransom went limp, crumpling to the floor, his head lolling.

My father leaned over him, panting like an animal and snarling for more.

"Christopher," my mother said, her voice sharp.

He turned and saw my mother standing there with a gun. And with that the fight drained out of him, as if another presence had inhabited him for a moment and was now quickly leaving.

He looked down at Ransom. "Charlie," he said. "Hold him down."

Charlie tentatively walked toward my father and Ransom's bulky, unmoving form.

"It's okay," my dad said in a voice you might use when coaxing a child to pet a horse. "Here you go." He took Charlie's hands and guided him into a kneel. "Put your forearm here." He positioned Charlie's forearm over Ransom's throat. "Now kneel on his chest in case he starts to move."

Charlie followed his instructions.

"Good, good." My father slowly reached into Ransom's front jeans pocket and withdrew a pair of tiny keys, using them to unlock the cuff on his one hand.

"Okay," he said, letting the cuff fall to the floor, as if he'd barely noticed.

"Victoria," he said, standing. "Do you want me to take that?" He pointed toward the gun.

She looked down at it, unsure. Then she looked at me as if to say, *Can we trust him?* It was so sad, that look.

I nodded. "It's okay, Mom. But here, let me take it."

She glanced again at the gun in her hands and held it out to me, but before I could reach it, I heard the sound of the door opening behind me and a voice saying my name.

Ee-sabel, it sounded like.

I turned. Had I heard that right?

"Elena?" my mom said.

74

She looked so different than she had on the plane. My aunt Elena now wore dark blue jeans, a black T-shirt and a fitted black jacket, her dark hair pulled into a tight ponytail. She held herself differently, too—like a snake coiled but ready. The only familiar thing was those sunglasses with the silver braided arms, pushed onto the top of her head.

Elena held a small gun that was silver on the top, black on the bottom. That gun looked as if it belonged in her hands, as if she had carried it all her life.

She pointed the gun at Ransom. "Is he out?"

"Elena, what are you…?"

"Is he out?" she demanded.

"For now," my father said, "but what…?" He peered at her.

"Christopher," Elena said simply. "Nothing else."

My father inhaled sharply. "My God, you're the top," my dad said, looking at Elena. "*You* are the top of the System, not Maurizio."

"Really?" I said, and I couldn't help the surprise in my voice.

My aunt glanced at me with no expression, then looked back at my father.

His mouth opened, as if he were about to say something, but he paused and I could see him working through something in his head. "You're the reason why we could never take down the Camorra."

My aunt gave him a chagrined smile. "No, Christopher, *you're* the reason. Everything you've told me allowed me to keep my clans just in front of your men for years."

"Unbelievable."

Aunt Elena gave the grand Italian shrug. "You chose to fight them. I chose another way."

"To join them?" my father said incredulously.

She nodded. "And to rule them, to feed off them, to have the life I wanted because of them."

"Was it worth it?"

"Was your choice worth it?" Her gun still out, now pointed at my dad, she took in all of us with her eyes. "Was it worth it to give them up?"

Neither my father nor aunt said anything for a moment. Then my father dropped his head. "No," he said a moment later. "No."

Another moment of silence before my dad raised his head. He appeared weary from his admission. "And now?" he said, gesturing at us. "Now you're going to kill your niece, your nephew, your brother, his only love?"

I glanced at my mom when he said that and saw her eyes open wider, staring at my dad.

"No," Elena said. "I'm going to save you."

She raised her gun then, pointed it at Ransom and fired a shot into his head.

"Aunt Elena!" I said.

She fired another shot, this time into his groin, and blood spurted into the air, a few drops splashing onto my shirt.

"Jesus!" Charlie yelled.

"Oh, Lord," my mother whispered.

Elena lowered her gun. Her eyes darted to me. "He would have killed you. And worse." There was little emotion in her voice, just someone delivering the facts.

My hand over my mouth, I glanced down at Ransom. A different smell rose from him now—that blood smell. The blood pooled, dark and thick.

"Now you know who is at the top of the System," Elena said to my dad. "But you will not turn in your sister. I know that. I know you well, Christopher, and now that Izzy has found you, you are done living this life of secrecy."

My father looked at Ransom, then back at her. "And you aren't?" His voice was incredulous again.

She shook her head. "I enjoy my life. Most of it. And the parts I don't enjoy?" A glance at Ransom. "Well..." Another shrug. "Like most people I manage those parts. I do what needs to be done."

"What about Maurizio? Did he know of your position?"

A wave of pain seemed to ripple through her features. She gave a single nod. "*Sí.* Of course. He and Paulo. But they didn't know about you being alive. No one did. Twenty-two years ago, I used the secret of you being an FBI agent to rise to the top of the System. But then I helped you plan your demise—your fake demise—and I kept your existence secret all these years. But Maurizio must have heard me talking to Isabel in Ischia about you."

"I thought I'd convinced you to talk," I said. "I actually thought I'd cross-examined you into telling me."

She looked at me, her eyes keen and clear. They were the same eyes, I suppose, that I had seen before, but they appeared different coming from this body, this version of Elena. "You did convince me, Isabel." Her eyes slid from me to my dad. "And Maurizio died thinking I had betrayed him because I hadn't told him that my brother was living. I *would* have told him about you as soon as Isabel found you, because I knew once that happened you would be leaving this life."

My dad's face grew sad. "You wanted that for me."

A solitary nod from Elena. "Of course."

"I'm sorry," I said. I had pulled a string a few weeks ago when I started looking for my father, after that night in the parking garage, and now so much had unraveled.

My father held out his hand, as if to stop me from falling. "No, *I'm* sorry. I wanted to get caught, to be found. Otherwise I wouldn't have spoken to you that night in the stairwell. Elena is right. I was done with that life."

My mother barked a disbelieving sound. We all looked at her. She rubbed her forehead as if too many realizations were flooding in.

My mother took a step. "Enough," she said forcefully. "I am taking my son—" she gestured for Charlie to stand "—and my daughter out of here. Away from the two of you."

Elena nodded. "You should. Immediately. Dez Romano has rigged this building with a gas leak. It hasn't been activated, but if he—"

A distant clanging sounded in the building, and then thudding, as if someone were climbing stairs. And then Dez Romano staggered past the room, clutching his head.

"Romano!" my aunt said, her voice like a drill sergeant. "Stop."

He kept moving, his feet shuffling down the hallway.

Elena spun and sprinted out of the room, her feet and her body moving like those of a woman years younger.

In the hallway, she kicked Dez Romano behind the knees, causing him to pitch forward, his face slamming the concrete hallway. An animalistic moan arose from his throat and he clutched his head again.

"What's wrong with him?" I said. "Is it exposure to the gas?"

"No," my father said, "he's suffering from vertigo."

"Your father's trademark move," my aunt said. "But Romano might still have been able to activate the gas." She kicked him in the stomach, pointing the gun at his head. "Romano," she yelled. "Did you start the leak?"

Still lying on his back, he clutched his head, his eyes swinging wildly at the five of us standing over him, his gaze landing on Elena. "Who the fuck are you, bitch? How do you know..."

Another well-placed kick to Romano's gut caused him to yelp and move his hands from his head to his stomach and roll onto it.

"I own you," Elena said. There was no mistaking the pride in her voice, and something else. Pleasure. She clearly enjoyed this role, being this Elena, much more than she did the weak, sad wife role I'd seen in Italy.

She looked over her shoulder at us before returning her gaze to Dez. "Go," she said. A direct order. "I want to have a little chat with my friend here, and there is time. If he did activate the leak, it will take at least fifteen to twenty minutes before it ignites the flame. Isn't that right? That is what you told the duke, right, *il diavolo?*" She scoffed. "He gave himself that nickname. Pathetic."

With the heel of her foot, my aunt kicked Dez in the side, forcing him to roll over onto his back. She pointed the gun at him, releasing the safety. "Isn't that right, *diavolo?*" she yelled.

He tried to sit up, failed, nodded.

"Now, go," Elena said to us.

"Come with us," my father said.

"No. I will handle this. You all must leave. Go somewhere where there are many people. You must be seen by many people. All of you together."

"That sounds like an alibi," I said.

My aunt nodded, although she was still staring down the barrel of her gun at Dez Romano.

"What do we need an alibi for?" my mother said. "We haven't done anything wrong. We need the police."

My aunt shot her a glance. "There will be questions after this. Many, many questions, and it could mean trouble for all of you." She pointed her head in the direction of my father. "Christopher faked his own death and hasn't paid taxes for twenty-two years. And you—" she nodded at my mother "—collected life insurance benefits because of it. That is fraud, a felony."

"I didn't *know* he was alive."

I spoke up. "And the statute of limitations would have run on some of that."

My aunt scoffed. "That's the least of your problems," my aunt said dismissively. She stared at my dad. "You have killed, Christopher. You killed my husband. And your daughter, knowing that, helped you to escape to the United States. You could both go down. Hard." She nodded in the direction of the room we'd been in. "And don't forget the body in there." She shook her head. "Get out. Now. Be seen together by many people."

"But what are we supposed to tell the police?" my mother said. "The superintendent has officers everywhere looking for Charlie."

"Does anyone know you are here? At this address?"

My mother shook her head no.

"And you, Isabel and Christopher," she said. "Does anyone know you are here?"

"No," I said.

"No," my father said.

"Then it was a prank," my aunt said. "Charlie has no drug problems. No one will say he did. A friend, someone, was playing a prank. You can think of something. It will be easier than trying to explain the rest of it."

"What about his face?" my father said.

"Make something up," she said fiercely. "You've always been good at that, Christopher."

"What are you going to do?" my father said.

His sister gave him a small smile but it faded fast. "This is where we part ways, brother."

Dez tried to sit up. "Gotta get out of here," he said, raising his hands to his head again.

My aunt looked at her watch, a large white circular face with a black band. "Now. Go."

"Goodbye, Elena," I said.

She smiled a sweet smile that made me remember the woman I'd spent time with in Italy. "Goodbye, *cara.*"

75

We pushed the door open, all of us shooting outside. We hurried up the street, running over the bridge suspended above the Kennedy Expressway. When we got to the other side, my father stopped us. We tried to catch our breaths, tried to focus our minds on what was happening.

"Where can we go?" my dad said.

I thought of Theo and his text from that morning. "Saint Pat's Block Party."

My father looked completely confused.

"It's lots of people," Charlie said. "About ten blocks long."

"Let's go."

We turned and took off jogging down Lake Street, cutting over to Madison and then continuing west.

We got to the entrance of the block party.

Behind the gates, people were packed on the street, the crowd stretching back block after block after block. Beer and food tents lined the sides of the streets. A huge music stage stood on the right, and a band was going through sound check. Everyone was in a giddy mood, laughing and drinking and milling around in the sun.

I reached in my skirt pockets and found them empty. "I don't have any money."

My mother whipped out her purse and paid for all of

us to get in. I wondered why Dez hadn't taken it. He'd underestimated her and that had been a mistake.

The ticket taker frowned at us before she let us through the gate. "Do you need security?" she asked.

For a second, we all stopped and looked at each other. Charlie's face was swollen, his blood was on my mother's shirt, and my father's shirt was torn so that a flap hung down from the shoulder, exposing his chest. I looked down at my own shirt and recoiled. A few drops of Ransom's blood were clearly visible.

Make something up, Izzy.

"We're fine," I said. "We drove four hours just for this street fair. We got into a little car accident, but we've been treated and we just want to go in and enjoy ourselves."

The ticket taker didn't move, frowned more. A badge on the chest of her green T-shirt read *Volunteer.*

I looked around, pointed at a T-shirt stand. "We're going to get T-shirts." I gestured at the volunteer. "Just like that one."

From the corner of my eye, I saw my mother raise an eyebrow. She was never one for uniforms or group dressing.

At last, the ticket taker shrugged and stood back for us to enter.

Once inside, we pushed past people to the stand and purchased four green T-shirts that screamed *World's Largest Block Party!*

My father accepted the T-shirt silently, his head swiveling around, appearing like a lost fish dumped into a big foreign pond. An intoxicated couple, walking while making out and sloshing beer at the same time, bumped into him and he glared at them.

Meanwhile, my mother was glaring at her T-shirt with a look of distaste. But gamely she said, "Now, where should we change?"

"The Porta-Johns." Charlie pointed.

My mother frowned.

"Mom," I said, "have you ever been in a Porta Potti?"

She looked at me blandly. "What do you think?" She turned to the bathrooms. "There's a first time for everything." My mother marched toward the Porta Potti, her T-shirt in hand.

The lines for the women's bathrooms were at least ten feet deep with women holding beers or talking to their friends behind them.

"Hurry if you can," my dad said to us. "And when we're done, we need to pick a spot to meet."

"How about the back entrance to the stage?" Charlie pointed to the area where the band was still sound-checking.

"Great," my dad said. "Let's go."

I turned and followed my mother to the ladies' lines, but instead of getting in one, my mother marched toward the front.

"Mom," I said, "no one is going to let you in. People get downright territorial with these lines."

"They'll let me in." She walked up to the very first person. "Hello. Is there any possible way I could utilize the restroom ahead of you?"

The woman was already wearing an irritated look that said she'd been in that line for a while. She opened her mouth, clearly about to reject my mother's suggestion.

But my mother opened her mouth faster. "I'm having a terrible hot flash. Menopause, you know. I need to give myself an anti-hormone shot." She gestured at me. "And I need my daughter to help me."

The woman blinked and held up her hand in front of her face as if to say, *That was more information than I needed,* and then she pointed at the door, which opened right at that minute.

My mother and I went inside.

"My God," she said. "It's truly horrible in here. This is why I've never been in one of these." She smashed her back against the locked door to give me room. "You change first."

I took off my shirt and pulled the green T-shirt over my head. "How did you know that woman would let us in? Are you really having a hot flash?"

My mother *tsked* and unbuttoned her blouse. "Of course not. And if I was, I certainly wouldn't tell anyone. But the thing is, you young women are so afraid of menopause. You don't even want to be around someone having a hot flash."

My mother pulled the green T-shirt over her head.

I started to laugh.

"What?" she said.

"I've never seen you wearing anything like that."

"Well, like I said, there's a first time for everything." She tucked the ends into her slacks. "Izzy, I have to tell you something, but let's get out of here first."

A few seconds later, we spilled from the Porta Potti, gasping in the relatively fresh air of the block party.

My mother pulled me over to the side of a beer tent. "Izzy," she said, looking me in the eyes, her hand on my shoulder. "Before we find them, I just want to tell you that I'm proud of you."

"Really? Thanks."

"Today, I feared losing both you and Charlie, and I realized that I never tell you enough how much you mean to me."

"Sure you do." I got jostled from behind by a pack of guys walking by. But then I thought about it. My mother was right. She rarely said anything about us or her attachment to us. "Thanks, Mom." I gave her a hug. She hugged me back tighter than I ever remember her doing before.

I pulled back. "How are you about this…this whole thing?"

She shook her head. "I'll think about it later." Now, this was the mom I knew.

I glanced at the stage. No sign of Charlie or my dad yet. Then I glanced around some more. The place was packed. "There are almost too many people here to help us with an alibi," I said to my mom. "We need to make sure we talk to people who will remember later if we need them to."

I thought about it for a second. Theo was here. I pulled out my phone and sent him a text. Then I thought, *Who else might be here?*

"I got it!" I said. Grady, my friend, always went to Old St. Pat's. I texted him, too, telling him where we were standing.

Not even a minute went by before I heard, "Iz!"

I turned around.

"Grady!"

Grady Fisher and I had been raised as a brother and sister at the law firm of Baltimore & Brown. After Sam disappeared, we dated for a while, and I'd been the one to end it. Since I didn't have the job any longer, I rarely saw Grady. And I missed him.

A happy smile spread across his face now. "I'm so glad you texted. I haven't seen you forever."

"I know." I gestured toward my mother. "You know my mom, Victoria."

"Sure, sure." Grady gave my mom a happy shake of his hand.

"How are you, Grady?" She had always liked him.

"Great!" Grady went on to talk about the law firm, how things were going well for him. He was getting clients on his own now, he said. He was finally getting the hang of work. He seemed happy and lighthearted and at ease in his professional life, which made me realize it was something I sorely lacked.

He seemed to sense my unease. He looked at me. "How are *you* doing, Iz?"

I raised my hands, and in the grand tradition of Italy and my aunt Elena, I gave an exaggerated shrug. "I don't even know."

Grady gave me a glance, then he looked at my mom and I wearing the same T-shirts and his expression grew confused. He knew my mother and I weren't the type to wear matching clothes.

"I'll explain some other time," I said, but then I realized I would never explain. Not entirely. I wouldn't tell him that my father had killed someone, that my aunt had, too. It made me feel heavy, as if I'd literally added weights to my body along with the secrets.

One of Grady's buddies called from behind him, raising a beer. "You want one?" the buddy yelled.

"Yeah, yeah," Grady said, raising his almost-empty beer in response. He looked back at me. "I guess we're going to see a band on the other side."

I felt envious of Grady then, of his happy afternoon filled with decisions like what bands to see, whether to have another beer. He stepped forward and gave me a quick hug, patting me on the back. It was a buddies' pat. We were back to that. I patted him back exactly the same way.

"See you," he said.

"See you," I answered.

I glanced at my phone. Nothing from Theo yet.

My mom and I made our way through the crowd to the side of the stage. Charlie was there, talking to a friend, gesturing at his swollen face. "Yeah, dude, I just got jacked. Came out of nowhere." He made it sound as if the punch had just happened, inside the street fair.

"Dude, you gotta get that looked at," his friend said.

"Yeah, I will," Charlie said. He glanced at my father, who stood next to him, uncomfortably shifting back and forth, his eyes scanning the crowds.

Charlie looked back at his friend, a weak smile on his face, and I saw in that instant that Charlie had been weighted, too. Carefree Charlie would walk around with secrets now, too, and I didn't know how he would handle them.

My mother and I exchanged concerned glances, then I saw someone familiar out of the corner of my eye. I turned my head and saw him behind the stage, staring at me. Theo.

I broke into a smile. So did he. He gestured me toward him.

I met him where the bouncers were taking backstage passes.

"Can you let her in?" Theo pointed to me and the rest of my green T-shirt crew. "And her friends."

The bouncer looked annoyed, but after a second, he did as Theo asked.

"Who's the band?" Charlie said when we were in, gesturing toward the stage.

"Poi Dog Pondering," Theo answered.

"That's the name of a band?" my mother said.

"Sweet," Charlie said. "I love these guys." He started telling my mom about the band, leaving me standing with Theo and my father.

Theo glanced at me as if to say, *Is this who I think it is?*

I nodded. "Theo, this is—"

Before I could finish, Theo reached out his hand and shook my father's. "Good to meet you," he said. He put his hands in his back pocket and kept looking at my dad. "I have to tell you your daughter is one of the most incredible people I've ever met."

My dad seemed not to know what to do or say. Finally, he said, "I had nothing to do with what a wonderful person Izzy is. But thank you."

Just then my mother stepped up to us, too. "Theo, this is my mom and my brother, Charlie."

They all shook hands with him. I saw my mom send a little questioning glance at his long hair and the tattoo. Definitely not her type. But soon, as they chatted, the two of them somehow stumbled into talking about the Robie House, a Frank Lloyd Wright landmark home where my mother happened to be a docent. I had no idea Theo even knew who Frank Lloyd Wright was. And then Theo and my brother were discussing the band that was about to take the stage—Theo knew them and sometimes helped them out—and another band they both liked.

When my mother asked, "How do you know him?" I found myself answering immediately. "He's the guy I'm dating."

The band started a bouncy, happy summer song, causing the crowd in front of them to cheer and dance. *Get out of your head, and into your heart,* they sang.

A guy came running up to Theo. "We blew an amp. There's another one in the van." He held out a set of keys. "Can you grab it?"

Theo took them. "Sure, no problem." He turned to me. "I'm going to help these guys out, if it's okay with you."

"Of course, go."

"You're sure."

"I'm sure."

"This might take a bit, and if we lose each other, I'll see you soon, right?"

"Definitely," I said. "But I'm not going to lose you."

He leaned down, his long soft hair brushing my face, and he kissed me.

When he'd walked away, I turned back to the group and saw them watching me.

"Is he someone important to you?" my dad asked.

My mother raised her eyebrows as if waiting, interested, for my answer. Charlie smiled a little.

Finally I spoke. "Yeah. He is important to me."

I looked at the three of them. My mother was shooting glances at my dad, but she seemed to have adjusted at least momentarily to him being there. To him being alive. Charlie, despite his dinged-up face and a split lip, looked at the two of them in wonder.

I stepped forward and took Charlie's hand, then my mother's, and moved them so that we stood in a little circle with my dad. "I'm not trying to be all kumbaya or anything," I said, "but I think we need to have a moment for Aunt Elena. She's a different person than we thought we knew, but she saved us today."

"What's going to happen to her?" Charlie said.

"I'm sure she'll go back to Italy," my father said. "Back to her life."

Just then the sound of a huge explosion came from behind us.

Someone in the crowd screamed. My mother gasped.

We turned toward the Loop and saw a red orb of fire rising into the sky.

"Oh my God," my mother said.

My father closed his eyes shut, then opened them and looked at us again. None of us seemed to know what to do.

Charlie squeezed my hand tighter. "Is she okay?" he asked.

My father stared at the red sky. He nodded, whether to reassure himself or answer Charlie's question I didn't know. "For Elena," my dad said, squeezing our hands.

"For Elena," I echoed, squeezing back.

Another explosion sounded and people started to scream "Fire!" "It's a bomb!" "Call the police!" There were murmurs of terrorism, word spreading fast. Soon people were running in every direction, the world's largest block party thinning out quickly.

I saw Charlie reach out his other hand and take my mom's. And then the oddest thing happened. My mother lifted her free hand and took hold of my father's.

As the four of us stood there, I thought back to my conversation with Q and Maggie a few weeks ago. I'd said that all I wanted for my thirtieth birthday was to be around family and friends.

I looked around at the four of us, at my…

Finally, I allowed myself to say it in my head…*at my family.*

That was true, whether or not my father stuck around. That was true whether or not the four of us would ever be together again. They were my family. And, yes, my friends. I squeezed their hands. I smiled at them all. And they smiled back.

LAURA CALDWELL

32183	LOOK CLOSELY	___$6.99 U.S.	___$8.50 CAN.
32309	THE ROME AFFAIR	___$6.99 U.S.	___$8.50 CAN.

(limited quantities available)

TOTAL AMOUNT $________
POSTAGE & HANDLING $________
($1.00 for 1 book, 50¢ for each additional)
APPLICABLE TAXES* $________
TOTAL PAYABLE $________

(check or money order—please do not send cash)

To order, complete this form and send it, along with a check or money order for the total above, payable to MIRA Books, to: **In the U.S.:** 3010 Walden Avenue, P.O. Box 9077, Buffalo, NY 14269-9077; **In Canada:** P.O. Box 636, Fort Erie, Ontario, L2A 5X3.

Name: ________________________________
Address: ____________________ City: ____________
State/Prov.: ________________ Zip/Postal Code: ____________
Account Number (if applicable): ____________________

075 CSAS

*New York residents remit applicable sales taxes.
*Canadian residents remit applicable GST and provincial taxes.

www.MIRABooks.com

MLC0609BL